THE
Fatal Choice

The *Fatal Choice*

An Epic Love Story From War-Time

KNUT HORVEI ESPESETH

Copyright © 2023 Knut Horvei Espeseth.

All rights reserved. No part of this book may be reproduced in any form or by any electronic or mechanical means, including information storage and retrieval systems, without permission in writing from the author and publisher, except by reviewers, who may quote brief passages in a review.

ISBN: Hardcover   978-1-962313-78-0
       Softcover   978-1-962313-77-3
       eBook   978-1-962313-76-6

Some characters and events in this book are fictitious and products of the author's imagination. Any similarity to real persons, living or dead, is coincidental and not intended by the author.

Book Ordering Information

Executive Book Agency
https://www.executivebookagency.com/
admin@executivebookagency.com
+1 (949) 415-3402

Printed in the United States of America

CONTENTS

Acknowledgements ix
Preface xi
Summary xiii

THE FIRST BOOK

Odesa Ukraine, the back carpet 3
The Rabbi brothers, Armageddon, The families are to be saved 7
The generations, The Elvegårds 26
The special high summer 1939' 29
Christmas 1939 35
Eva 40
The Germans are coming 43
Fathers' homecoming 45
Ragnhild his frail sister 47
Karelen, Finland, Forever Love 49

THE SECOND BOOK
HIS ROAD TO GERMANY AND GROSS DEUTSCHLAND

The Hippodrome 55
Loke, and who is he 65
Lars comes of age 70
The winter wars 72
The Good-byes 74
Farewell Norway, meeting up with the new recruits 77
The departure and Bad Tölz 84
Berlin 91
Division Gross Deutschland 95
The letter from Eva 105

The letter from his dad 107
Loke and Lviv 110
The Great March South 118
Huckleberry Finn 124

THE THIRD BOOK
THE WOMEN, DRAMA, TRIANGLE

Armageddon 133
The escape through Odesa 141
The death march 144
Joseph's farm 150
To Ari and the Carpathians 152
Living the partisans' life 159
Odesa and the hospital 169
Karelen and the family's farm 175
Chief surgeon Johansson 184
Birgitta 188
Svetlana 197
Denounced and on the run 205
Back at Ari 's and Inna's 217
A child is born 222
Lars is back in Odesa 226
Farewell to Eugenia 230
The Russians are coming 233
Rebecka, back in the camp 238
The end of the Partisan Group 241
Farewell Loke, and farewell to his father's land 243
He is to live 246

THE 4TH BOOK. THE OLD DOCTOR AARON

The new doctor 253
Doctor Leo Volgov 258
Farewell Chaim 261
Germany and Nazi-Norway capitulate 263
The total collapse 265
Lars, the fugitive 270
Back to Ari and Inna 274

Home again in Odesa 280
The old Doctor Aaron 284
Eugenia 287
Another Good-bye 291
The grandchild Theresa 295
Moscow 299
The diary 303

THE 5ᵀᴴ BOOK, THE GREAT REUNION

The last voyage of Lars 309
The 9ᵗʰ of August 311
The old Judge 315
The Judge's farmhouse 318
The night at the Judge's 322
Breakfast and admissions 325
Farewell to Karstein 329
Crying and more crying 332
To Eva or home? 346
Eva Lars' fiancée 348
The first night with Eva 351
The journey with Lars 353
The SS-Hauptsturmführer Lars 355
Junior's world 360
On with the diary 368
Bitterness or forgiveness 373
The day with Junior 376
12 months later 383

Epilogue 385
Sources 387
Key-notes, references 389
SS-degrees 393
Sketch East front 394
Sketch Odesa center 395

ACKNOWLEDGEMENTS

This novel, in part fiction, in part scenes from reality; the latter with reference not least to the genocide in Odesa, Ukraine, during World War II. My thanks go to Jews in Odessa, the few survivors I had the chance to interview. They have all passed now.

The very first time a published this novel, then in Norwegian, was back in 2010/11. When there later was an interest to it from the English-speaking world, then I took it upon me to have it translated. This was done in cooperation with my cousin, Joan Hammerquist, maiden name Joan Horvei, resident in Vancouver, Washington state. I am utterly grateful for her help with getting it published in English.

PREFACE

There are numerous books about young Norwegians that joined the German armed forces during the Second World War. Books telling about those who fell on the East front, or even in Berlin itself and there are books about those coming home to punishment and derision.

Not so much attention has been given to those that decided to stay in a foreign country, wherever, be it in Europe itself. Those having chosen the wrong side in 1940 or later, not having the courage to come home and meet with the defeat for the second time, forever labeled Nazis.

In this novel I have written about a young Norwegian, a med-student and sent him on a journey through Europe, now as a field-medic, but even as a soldier, although with a lieutenant title, blown-up friendship, witness to extermination of Jews and not least deeply involved, yes in love with women he met on his way. Finally, to find his grave in Odesa by the Black Sea. Deprived for going home to his one-time fiancée

For sure there must have been many others just like him. And the overruling question in this novel is why young kids like him landed on one or the other side, England or Germany? Just by chance, ideology, close relations through centuries between the countries, foremost England and Norway.

All the persons that are listed in this novel are fiction, exceptions are 3 top brass German officers.

The widely, gruesome exterminations of the Jews, I have tried to relate to actual happenings, but sources are scarce for obvious reasons and in most cases, there was no account on women- and children's casualties.

I have paid many visits to most of the sites mentioned in the novel, in particular to Odesa where much of the plot is taking part.

This novel was published in Norwegian in 2014, now being introduced to a greater market in English in 2023.

Juan les Pins, November 2023
Knut Horvei Espeseth

SUMMARY

This novel picture two families and the two grandchildren of the lead character Lars, and who were to meet long after World War II.

The grandchild on the Ukrainian side is Theresa, coming from the Opera house in Odesa, the city of Culture by the Black Sea, up to the start of World War II also known as the "Jew city" of East Europe. More than 1/3 of the inhabitants in Odesa were said to be Jews.

Close to 100 thousand of them where either hanged, shot to death, or burn to death losing their lives, many being buried alive, all these atrocities in Odesa were said to have been carried out by Rumanians, partisans and of course various divisions and commandos on the German side, particularly by the "Einsatzkommandoes".

The other grandchild, Trygve, nickname Junior, leading farmer and doctor to his own surgery there in Hedemark, rural Norway. Unknown to his grandfather Lars the front fighter and SS field-medic. Lars getting his medical degree in Germany, was first sent to the East front and later he got the chance to fulfill his dream, fighting for his mother's land, Karelen, Finland, against the Bolsheviks. His one and only reason for choosing Germany, and by that choice: Adolf Hitler.

He was after the war to be a doctor in Odesa, primarily to Jewish patients, those having gone undercover or having returned to Odesa after the war.

We follow Lars all through his participation in the war. We also follow his fiancée, Eva at the upper of the two farms, Junior's grandmother. She had grown old now Eva, meeting with her once fiancée's other grandchild, the opera star Theresa, there at the end of her life. Theresa who had come to Norway to see her grandfather's native country and not least to meet with his Eva.

The novel is a description of the fate of young Norwegians that took the wrong side in 1940. Young Norwegians from 15 and upwards and who barely knew what they were enlisting to, when signing up with the Germans. The novel is picturing their experiences of the war, not least the one of Lars's. Could he go home to Norway once the war was over? Home to his father's farm, his place at the surgery as a doctor and not least meet with his fiancée Eva?

Lars for sure had picked the wrong side and if he was to come home, then he would cause enormous pain to his closest and what about his heritage, his father's big farm? Would it be lost not only to him, but to his offspring as well?

The law and not how it was to be interpreted did make no room for exceptions. You were either a hero or a betrayer to your country.

But our Lars never felt it in him that he was at all fighting for Hitler, he was merely a part of his troops on his way to fight for his mother's land in Karelen. But once having signed up there was no way out. So better to be registered as fallen in battle and then start a new life on foreign soil. Thus, the kinfolks at home would not have to live with the shame of a homecoming Nazi.

And now he would be forgotten from all and everyone, but not by his love from youth, Eva. She was to know about his life in exile through Lars's Ukrainian born grandchild, Theresa, looking for her roots there in Hedemark, rural Norway.

THE FIRST BOOK

SETTING THE TABLE

THE BACK CARPET – ODESA UKRAINE

It is cramped here, and I feel my dad's heart beating terribly fast. If I shall live from this day on, October 23rd – 1941, then I and those dear to me shall have this day as our Memorial Day. Not only because of the unthinkable that 20.000 of our Odesa Jews-community have been murdered only since yesterday morning; not because my uncle and my auntie together with my two first cousins Levi and Japhet have been stringed up, burned or shot to death. I do not know how they met their maker; I only know that they suddenly were gone, together with all the others. I only heard Japhet's cries towards the sky to Jahve, he together with all the others when the heat from the pyre was at its most intense. I could see it all through an opening in my dad's big coat, see the smoke from the pyre where all the Jews were burned to death, all from my family. Soon the Parade square was darkened by the smoke and the ashes of the death-burned Jews.

I shall of course remember them all and not least my mother; they came for her this morning, and she was sent on the long march from west Odesa onto the North, sadly she ended her life by being shot in a ditch in the snowstorm raging. If she had not been shot to death right there, she certainly had not made it much further before she froze to death. Maybe she had just tumbled on the slippery cobblestones, and even the Schäfer dogs had been onto her before the merciful neck-shot put an end to it all. They were no doubt hungry, the dogs, as well. Maybe she had just tried to help a thinly dressed mother having a baby on her arms, already blue with cold, 25C below and a beating storm in the gusts. If she had managed to help this woman and her baby, they would certainly have been shot all three of them!

But this day, in memory of all these Jews burnt or frozen to death, this day will above all be in memory of my dad. I am hanging on to his chest in a kind of harness shown to me only last night. It was in this hour, when dad started to tell me about life and death and our family and we were to take our goodbyes with his wife, my mom. She was to stay with her sister so she would not disturb my father in the preparations for tomorrow, let alone give us some hours sleep. "You are going to need all the sleep you can muster", these were her last words. My dearest mother, clearly, she did not have to her that it was the final rest that waited for us all, even me if I did not get lucky.

Nonsense, we never got to sleep, the three of us just sat there weeping, me as well as my father and we talked about my first cousin, little Chaim and love and the fact that I had sinned, he as well, and got to take the brunt to that. But neither of us wanted to die without having experienced life's ultimate pleasure. But my dad said that an even greater pleasure it would be to have one's own child and that the greatest grief was not tomorrows certain death, no, the greatest grief was never to meet with one's grandchildren.

Then suddenly it was morning and I crept on to his heart and he covered me with his old, far too big winter coat and we were off to the rally at the Parade square. It was here we were told to meet all with the yellow star of David on our chests, except those selected for the long march North. My dad was tall and big, his normal weight would be close to one hundred kgs and now, with me under his coat probably no less.

All the people we met there, most of them knowing us quite well were puzzled by my father's poise, seemingly not have lost any weight, on the contrary, although his meagre face told a different story. When questioned, he just shrugged it off; "you know with the biting cold these days I have dressed well, double shirts and sweaters".

I am not able to see anything now, but for sure I can hear the Schäfer dogs and then the voices of the Rumanian soldiers enjoying themselves by each Jew they are stringing up. "They are all hanged by their feet", my father whispers to me. "The one close to us is my elder brother, the Rabbi Chaim. But now it is my turn my child and I cannot tell you anymore; farewell my dearest". His chest was all wet from my tears, and then, just then the Rumanian soldiers were on to us; "let's get this fat Jew stringed up, but make sure to give him an extra lash, so he won't slip down!"

"Hang me by the neck and I shall pay you in pure gold!" "Yes, but do give us the gold first. Or maybe we shall wait and take your gold when you are all dead, you fat Jewish swine". They tore his coat now looking for the gold and I was terrified that the buttons could not take it. But my mother had sewn some extra seizings the night before she left for the Death march North.

"So, this Jew has gold then!" Two more soldiers had joined looking for their share and my dad handed them one gold piece each. Where had dad got all this gold? He was not at all a rich man?

"What about me?" Someone new with an authoritative voice came close now, had to be some sort of higher command, maybe an officer. My fear was creeping onto me now; if they were to hang my dad by his feet, then I should fall out of the harness and on to the ground and the Schäfer dogs would have been attacking me in seconds.

I felt the beating from my father's heart, more and more agitated and not least the fear in his voice: "A word is a word, is it not? Even to someone facing death. Look, I have two more gold pieces, so get going now, hang me by the neck!" This had to be gold he had stolen, not so? But my dad wasn't that kind of a man; Even for the purpose of saving me, would he have stolen this gold? Would he have done just that, to save his only child alive now?

No more discussions, the Rumanians were in a hurry now and my father got an extra rope round his neck. The soldiers could almost touch my head when they made fast. But the seizings done by my mother saved me this time as well, his big coat covering me.

We were swinged up to the wires connecting the light poles and then they let go so it was just the neck rope that held us up. I heard my father's sigh, we started to swing up there and I sensed a crack from his back or maybe it was his neck, and the soldiers were shouting, and more vodka was floating and then it was over. No more heartbeats from my dearest dad.

What now, should I take the chance of lowering myself, get out of the harness, or better wait until they were busy with the next to be stringed up? Suddenly there was a strong, very superior voice: "The gold belongs to the Führer!" We were joined by a German officer now. Four pistol shots in a row and then one more and the attention was no longer at my dead father. The Rumanian solders no doubt were shot by this officer craving the gold for his Führer.

I could hear children crying now and there was a strong sense of burned flesh. Yes, it had to be human bodies burning. My own family's burning bodies and then there were hundreds of voices, like a huge choir towards the sky. Those still being able to breath cried out loud for Jahve; I felt the heat of the burning of bodies closer now. Then there was a big explosion from like a bomb and I felt now was the time to run for it. Next second, I was down on the ground following the escape route my father had drawn up. I heard shots from a Schmeisser machine gun. Something hit me in my upper left arm, but the bullet must have gone right through, no harm to muscles nor ligaments. I hardly felt the wound, could only see the blood pulsing. But then I was at the first post, the top of the sewer and thanks to heavens, someone had lifted the heavy concrete lid off, but there was no revolver, no knife that we have agreed upon, but luckily the torch was there.

I just dumped myself down away from the shots and got lucky; my feet were on to the third stairs down in the dark in no time. I managed to get the lid in place and then only seven stairs down to the stanch and the rats. But no matter, I just ran and ran through this sewage tunnel. Sometimes with sewage above my knees. I even fell at times, and I probably swallowed a lot of this horrible liquid. I did not dare use the torch, not yet, just kept running further on in this dark, foul-smelling night, knowing that my lover, little Chaim would be waiting there at the end.

THE RABBI BROTHERS, ARMAGEDDON, THE FAMILIES ARE TO BE SAVED

In the far East corner of Europe, by the Black Sea there was a fight for survival, a fight to live or to die. Death was close here for the many, not least for those of Rebecka's family already hunted down by the soldiers and now waiting at Parade square. But death would wait in vain for her, she was determined not to die, not now when all in her family, maybe the whole tribe was butchered or frozen to death, let alone those to be hanged and burned. Someone had to survive this Armageddon, yes live and give an account of the murder of Abrahams' children.

She had seen them sitting there together one last time the two siblings, her father, and his brother, both quite mature, her uncle close to sixty now, both with grey-white beards, both Rabbis for a congregation there in the beautiful Jew-city by the Black Sea, Odesa.

They both knew what was coming to them and they had known it for some time. Did it affect them? Well, yes and one of them more than the other. Chaim had been the leader for his congregation just like his father was before him until he passed away. His father had always wished for the office to be inherited by his son. But now it was to be the end of it all. Once the Rumanian soldiers had come and joined up with the Germans, he had realized that he would be the last Rabbi. This was much talked about in the congregation, and some had even thought about escaping to the USA. Money would not have been an issue. But the mere thought of leaving to save his own and his closest family's hides, leaving the congregation and the responsibility his office was trusted? No, that would have been a too easy way out of the coming inferno. He had touched upon the subject with his wife, but she had immediately gone into hysteria and when he finally managed to calm her down sort of, then she had come up with all possible objections.

"But my dear wife, I have not made any decisions on leaving Odesa as yet". "And how could we possibly do that, think about your sons and their fiancées and what about the elderlies? Just leave them behind? If we were to go, then we all had to go. This big family, you think we could manage to leave Odesa without attention from the rest of the congregation. Leaving them to a very certain death, no one to console them, their Rabbi just left them? And my dear husband, you should know it is already too late. The Germans have already pushed all Jews into this corner and have blocked all possible exits. And you know well that the big liners, they all leave from Hamburg in Germany".

"But Maria, then we are bound to stay here in Odesa and take what comes to us". "Yes of course we are, and so is probably your brother Melchior as well". "Admittedly Maria".

From this day forth, the Rabbi Chaim seemed growing older by the day and his pace becoming more and more heavy, although he seemed maigrer one day to the next with the lack of food.

One of the oldest in the synagogue held on to his arm one day, it was Elias. "Are you sick dear Rabbi, I mean have you got a serious illness? I beg you excuse me, coming onto you with such a question, but we are many in our congregation worrying for you". "No Elias, not sick to my body, but to my soul. What is going to happen to us, with these Rumanians and the Germans, not to forget all the so-called Partisans who wants to rob us and then have us killed?"

Into his sixties now and he had already become lye, no slow process this, on the contrary. And his concern and his worries were difficult to hide when having the small-rationed breakfast with his family. Their only topic for everyone at this meal was the war and what was there to follow for the large Jewish community.

Chaim, the older one of the two Rabbis had three sons, the two older ones still lived at home with their parents, having chosen their father's path: Be open to talks, negotiations, turn the other cheek and foremost not being provoked by the Germans and even more so by the Rumanians' daily abuses. The Rumanians, they were the worst, right so? No, the worst by far were the so-called partisans, many of them behaving like devils saturated by Stalin's ideology. Before the war they had been good neighbors to the Jews, these Ukrainians that now exposed their hatred to the Jews and their communities. But this hatred, where did it stem from and was it there all of a sudden? No, they must have hated the Jews all the time, no? Or was it just because this war had given them the opportunity to take over their homes, their businesses and finally denounce them to the new rulers deciding over life and death? This war of Stalin was it just a welcome apology to overrun the Jews? Daughters of Jews had played with the now partisans' children, even passed the night with the non-Jewish neighboring friends. Having their teenage love amongst those now looting the Jews' homes and, in the aftermath, killing her family?

But the younger son, Chaim, or little Chaim he did not follow to his father's reconciling strategy. He had eloped to Rivne to his half-uncle Ezra. And there he found the fellowship he had longed for in contrast to his lenient father. A fellowship standing up against the abusers and murderers. But his father came for him, to take him back to Odesa and the talks between the two, Ezra and Chaim had become violent and little Chaim had to leave the room.

Ezra had already started to build a resistance group with the foremost aim to take care of women and children, sending the men on to the forest for military training instead of being ordered to labor camps organized by the Germans.

"No doubt the Germans have good use for all of us Ezra, we Jews are known to be super clever craftsmen. The tales you are telling Ezra about labor camps synonyms with death camps, our men to die from hard work and starvation is not correct. Hitler craves his Autobahn from Berlin to Baku, and he needs one and each of us Ezra".

"With the rations set dear brother, the average survival time could be 3 months, maybe only 2, comes winter and cold weather". Ezra would not yield, nodding to his nephew quietly back in the room. "It is all a question of survival or freeze to death in the camps".

But his brother was just as adamant. He looked at his youngest son. "And you, my younger one, honored with my name, are you to join the resistance, get arms and stand up against the Germans and the partisans, thus defying your father?"

"Yes Dad, I have made my choice. I shall not be treated like cattle, but I shall not be with you in Odesa every day either, opposing the strategy you have chosen for your family and the congregation, so I choose to stay here with your half-brother Ezra".

Admittedly he was proud of his youngest, proud seeing him now as himself at the same age, although he the Rabbi to be would never have been allowed to mark his opinion, his inner feelings. His stern father, also a Rabbi would for sure have denied him that, merely by a glance. And now way could he now show his inner admiration to his son nor for Ezra to see. What was to happen to this proud young man, standing there, tall, raven black hair to his neck and obviously ready for a mission, camouflage outfit, hand grenades in his belt and a Schmeisser laying there for him on the table? So, this was his fierce son, now soon to be gone together with his uncle to hunt down, kill Rumanians, taking their food supplies. All this against the laws as written in the Torah and for every Jew to know by heart.

The lot was thrown. "Alea jacta est", and Chaim the Rabbi was to return home, knowing that this would be the last he was to see of his youngest son.

It was already evening now in Odesa and the two Rabbis were facing each other in the loft above the temple. They both knew that it was only a matter of hours now. Admittedly the younger had made the right decision, fled Odesa and the "death machine" that was to ensure that there would be no survivors. The two elder sons and their close would end up on the big fire tomorrow or possibly freeze to death on the march North.

"And what about you Melchior, I on my part have my younger one in safety up with our half-brother Ezra". "You know Chaim, it took some time till at long last my woman could bear me a child and now I have my Rebecka". "But do you want for her to die together with us? Why haven't you sent her up north to Ezra she as well so she could be saved?" "You know dear brother, you and I as Rabbis we have agreed to talk and try to reconcile with the new authorities". "Yes, but it is the Rumanians that now grasps one and every opportunity to pester us. They are in control and no way they want talks about our living conditions". "I find your words strange dear brother, no doubt it is the Germans that are in control is it not and has not Hitler declared that he wants us all exterminated, removed from the earth so to speak?" "Maybe so, but it is for the Rumanians to do the dirty work for him now". Melchior was as always more on the offensive than his elder brother, had always been even from childhood. Was it perhaps the age difference that made Melchior more on the offensive, was it not? Chaim wondered. No, he consoled himself, it was his responsibility as the older one, his duty to the family that made it all different. Maybe so even now?

He wondered if Melchior had been thinking of evacuating to USA, or the States as his relatives called it over there. Only a month back, right before the arrival of the Rumanian troops there was a letter on the kitchen table and his wife ever so curious: "What's new from your cousin over there Chaim?" But Chaim wanted to read the letter all by himself, not to share before he knew the content. But this time there was only a tiny piece of paper, no problem sharing with the rest of the family. The text was a really short one: "Southampton 05.11 and 05.12, Aron".

"Tell us Father, what is it all about". "Nothing, just playing with letters and numbers". But his oldest wanted to see for himself. "This must be dates for sailings". "Yes, we were once to send a big package via England". "Right so", his wife supported him, "but now it is way too late, a big package it should have been".

"Please stay with me my brother, I sensed that your thoughts were flying, but where to?" Chaim did not respond, but said to himself, you should only have known dear brother. But Melchior did not seem to notice, he just continued: "I have a plan to save my daughter Rebecka. It is a bold one, it does however have an impact on our faith". "You think you can save her? No way better send her east in the city to my house, much easier to hide there than in a flat in the city center". "No use Chaim, the Germans have this idea that the Jews smell different from all others, and they have trained their Schäfer dogs to search for this special Jewish smell". "Do you believe this chit-chat Melchior?" "Well, yes, the Germans are known for being methodical and in their search for hidden Jews they have gotten ever so fanatic. It has been announced that within 48 hours all women and children plus the elderlies, quite much older than us are to meet at the Plaza north and from there on start what has been already called the long march North, towards Dalkin. Some has already called this march the death march. With the cold we are having now, there will be few survivors, if any". "But the two of us Melchior, we are not old enough to qualify for this march. No doubt they will consider us ready for their workforce and send us to labor camps in the East to build Hitler's autobahn". "I can hear dogs Chaim, maybe we should continue our talk tomorrow?" "But Melchior I did not get to hear about your plan to save your daughter, your only child". "No but I shall tell you about it all tomorrow. Curfew is imposed in half an hour, and I best get home in time".

"Melchior, my dear brother, and friend; you know I think we shall be exterminated all. Admittedly some will be sent on the long march, as the Rumanians do not have the capacity to kill us all in a couple of days. We are after all tens of thousands of Jews here in Odesa". "Right so Chaim, and that is the reason why some are sent to labor camps, some on the long march North, just an illusion, marching for freedom, and finally the Rumanians get the dirty work exterminating the rest of us here on the Parade square. The Germans sort us in able bodies for their workforce, the others as garbage or rats as Hitler expresses it". This was the first time he had heard his brother using such foul language. "The Rumanians have adapted the German expression, the one overriding whatever: 'Odesa is to be Juden rein', away with all Jews!"

"But Chaim, it is about tens of thousands of people, and do you think the Germans will be up to it?" "Women and children, they are to be exterminated, same fate to the elderlies. All the rest of us, the strong ones, we shall have a grace time as forced laborers". "From what source does this come Chaim?" "From my son now living up with Ezra, close to Rivne. You remember our half-brother, don't you?" "Sharpen up Chaim, I went to visit him only 3 weeks ago".

"So, this is reliable information direct from the German commander, Colonel Falkenberg". "It is true then what the women are gossiping about; we shall all be removed from Odesa the one way or the other. We all will have to go; families be split up". His face was now whiter than his beard. "I must get home to my daughter. I shall tell you more about my plan tomorrow Chaim". They hugged one another and Melchior was ready to go. He feared that the patrols, especially the Rumanians would be more than keen to round up one or more Jews ignoring the curfew.

Maybe this would be the one and only evening together with his family and then it would all be over, the one way or the other.

Now, what about his Rebecka, soon to be seventeen and only one year to go to be a fully certified nurse? But now she might not have this year to fulfill her education and start her career as nurse. If the info about the death march was reliable, then no future to her at all.

She worked long hours his little Rebecka, looking more like a thirteen-year-old, doing her studies and even finding time for an internship. She was extremely keen to get her career going, lending hands to people in need for her services. She had set her goals already as a ten-year-old, no question about it, she was to be a nurse.

Her parents worried for her spending too much time on the studies although they wished for her to get the best preparations for her later job. Still, they wanted for her to spend more time with the family. All difficult, she being the only child. "Just look to your cousins Rebecka, they spend much time with the family and learn where we all come from. They study old family books and attend the synagogue every day. And Rebecka, what about the Torah, our guide in all doings?"

And yes, she could site the Torah any time. "But the recess Rebecka, not only learn mechanically, but really understand the chapters, the true meaning and guidance. Anyone can learn the characters, but what's behind the characters is a different story. What about the concept, 'The second temple', just as an example Rebecka?"

Melchior suddenly realized he had not heard his brothers voice for some time, but there it was: "You were far away for some time brother Melchior?" "Melchior", who was Chaim speaking to, oh yes it was to him standing there in his great winter coat, ready to leave for home. Chaim looked at him. "If you do not feel at ease, maybe you should join me here for a cup of coffee. Perhaps you should spend the night here as well?" His face slowly picked up his normal color, no more pale grey, he fingered with his beard, sort of adjusting his jacket under the great coat, checked everything was ok. "You asked for what my brother?" "I asked you if you wanted to join me for a cup of coffee".

"Chaim my brother, my thoughts were with Rebecka; finally ready nurse in some 12 months. Will she ever come to use this education she has put her life to, to be a nurse; to serve others in pain?"

"You mean brother that she had rather think about making family and give you a grandson? It is ok to be egotistic Melchior. But she is almost done with the courses and the training and now she may well meet with one of our handsome, young doctors and then you will see all good".

"No, my thoughts were not there Chaim, not at all. My thoughts were with the reality we are facing, yes, the reality, we have to deal with that, but please come with your coffee". He sniffed eagerly. This coffee was undoubtedly made from real coffee beans; probably, no certainly imported illegally. But did it really matter now where the coffee beans came from, now here in his Odesa?

"I was thinking about our city, what's there to say about our city now that the Rumanians have transformed it into a death machine". "But listen up Melchior, the Rumanians are mere marionettes running wherever the Schäfer dogs are barking and one hears the steel heels clattering from the Germans. The Rumanians are the butchers, but it is all managed by the rulers, the Germans". "You wanted for me to share something with you Chaim, not only the coffee, but first, why were you that keen on Rebecka to hide with you east in the city? Are you keeping secrets to me my brother?" Chaim fell silent, now standing close to the little top window and sneak-looked through a tiny hole in the blackout curtain. All windows were to have blackout curtains from 17.00hrs. Standing order.

"You don't need to hide brother Chaim; I see clearly that you are holding back on something you should have let me know of". "Well maybe brother. But I have kept silent about it hoping for it all to pass". "It is about Rebecka is it not?" His voice had sharpened now. "Has she violated any of our commandments, something you know about, and that you should have let me in on?"

Melchior had raised from his chair, hat and cane ready to leave. His voice was both threatening and trembling, now he looked at his elder brother. "Something sinful has happened, has it not Chaim?" "No, no Melchior nothing I know of on my part". "But speak out then brother Chaim. Which one of your sons has she been whoring with?" "Don't you use such vulgar words here in the temple of God Melchior". "We are not in the temple now Chaim". "No quite so, but even this room on top of the temple belongs to our God. Many of the preparations for the Sukkot are done in this room. You have yourself been part of it have you not?" No reason waiting for an answer, so he continued. "I am totally convinced that neither of them has done anything indecent".

"But Chaim, I as her father, I have known nothing but her striving all the time for her exams, she getting maigrer by the week". "You are a stern dad Melchior, but if you had been blessed with more children, then Rebecka would no doubt have been raised in a milder way".

He was already getting enraged Melchior and Chaim could see that he was close to an explosion. "Turn off the candle and keep quiet", he only whispered now. "Is it time already now?" "Be silent!" Chaim was on to him again. "Maybe they have found what they came for". Cries from downstairs and the sound of doors being banged and then it was all totally silent.

"It was no doubt Isaac the concierge they took with them this time. They get closer by the day now. So far, these Rumanians have no idea about these rooms above the temple, but maybe they will be able to squeeze some information out of Isaac".

But Melchior was not to be distracted. "It is your younger, yes? Your own Chaim? Your son that you have little or rather no control over? Your son living up in the mountains in strong opposition to his own father?" "Well yes, he lives with our half-brother Ezra up at Rivne, and I have already told you about that Melchior". "But how do you know if your younger son and my Rebecka has not breached our laws, but lived in adultery or have they not?"

"Dear Melchior, the two of them would never have sinned under my roof. You had some sort of idea about saving Rebecka, did you not?" "Yes Chaim, but reality came sooner than expected. I was on the verge to dedicate you to my plan; how to save our tribe. But since my only daughter has come to live with your rebellious son, I then realize that I am way too late".

"Take off your great coat, you cannot leave from here tonight. You better think positive about the fact that the two young ones have found each other, so let us have your plan brother".

Melchior realized that now it would not be safe to go home this night, the curfew was long on.

Apparently, it was all good now between the two brothers. But Chaim knew that he best thread carefully as his brother would tip over at the slightest notion. It was this about Rebecka having been subject to a very stern uprising that had hit Melchior really hard, because there was truth to it. She had been their only child all the way during her childhood and now into her teens.

But Melchior had composed himself now, apparently. "Chaim, if we are to be killed, murdered, then there will still be new flocks of Jews coming here to Odesa". "Not if, brother Melchior, but when we are killed".

His brother chose to neglect the remarks. "Just think about this scenario: In a few days, maybe already tomorrow, or a week from now, we will be separated from our families, from our wives and I from my dearest Rebecka, whom they may send onto the much talked about Death march towards the North. You and your sons Chaim, you will have to meet on the Parade square from where you will be transported in cow wagons or maybe open wagons, East to the nearest labor camp. How many do you think will survive this transport, 20C below, strong wind and no food, except a small ration brought from home; and please bear in mind that we shall have to take with us the sick and the wounded, and they not having boots neither proper clothes for the winter. We cannot just leave the elderly behind to die, and what more, those of us that don't qualify for hard labor, maybe they will just string us up there at the Parade square to save on the food". But neither of them knew what was in the offing.

"Now Hitler has his wish fulfilled, all big cities and especially our Odesa will be declared Judenrein". "What a horrible expression Chaim. So, you are adamant that none of ours will ever be coming back to our Odesa? But what about the future of our children then?" "You mean those that by chance happen to live?" "Your Little Chaim up in Rivne will survive together with Ezra and his group. But now it would not be possible to send my daughter up there, even though she would have appreciated to go to your son Chaim".

"But let's rather talk about Rebecka, Melchior and this plan of yours. Now that you know about the two, would you not reconsider sending her north to the partisans?" "Not all partisans like us Jews and some are even worse than the Rumanians. There are reasons for their zeal to get rid of us. The first one being that we are far more intelligent, intellectually superior and third, because they want our houses, our homes, our money". Chaim looked at his brother, curious as to what would come next. "My Rebecka learns every day about saving lives, not killing. But if she gets caught and sent on this long march that may come anytime, then there is no hiding to her in that train of people".

"Melchior that isn't all". Chaim looked at him, something untold, was there more to come? "Had they in fact sinned against the commandments the two? Has your son made her pregnant Chaim?" He could not let go, simply had to know.

It was Chaim's face that now reddened under his white beard. "Skip these lowly thoughts. It is you who have sinned by expressing such thoughts Melchior. But still, maybe you are on to something brother".

"Meaning what?" "Well, your Rebecka is beautiful, even now with her maigre body she has curves, her mother's wonderful eyes, not to forget her hair, copper colored sort of. The Germans are used to blondes, but not so the Rumanians". "Speak clearly then brother". "Don't you understand Melchior, with her looks she will be singled out, abused, and possibly set to work in an officers' brothel. German officers, no way they can permit themselves to sleep with a Jewish girl, no problem so to the Rumanians. So come with your plan for saving her my brother".

"Chaim, in a week or so hell will break loose. The two of us will no doubt be considered too old to build this motorway. Then the choice is simple, on to the long march or getting stringed up on the Parade square like all the others too old to march. No doubt there will be some prestige, hanging two Rabbis at the same time, even brothers now hanged by their feet on the light poles at the Parade square." "Hanged by the feet?" Chaim was already shivering by the mere thought of it. "Why hanged by the feet?"

"More fun to them, we will have a slow death and they may kick our heads like footballs and then the dogs will be over us. They have probably not been fed over the two last days, just to mount their hunger".

"Now Melchior, from where does it come all this knowledge about what is going to happen?" "Isaac, your concierge, had been invited to a meeting where he and his family was offered to be smuggled out of this iron ring round Odesa, taken to an abandoned village, halfway to Mykolaiv". "And how much was he to pay to this Rumanian officer?" "100gr in pure gold". Chaim had himself a laugh. "Yes, I know that I should not laugh in such a situation, when we know that poor Isaac was taken only minutes ago, downstairs. But how stupid could he possibly be and from where would Isaac be able to come up with pure gold?"

Melchior looked at his brother. "Come on then Chaim!" "Do I need to speak it straight to you then Melchior? Is it not quite obvious that Isaac planned to rob us of our holy treasures?

I caught him red handed while he was wrapping something up by the alter. When he saw me coming, he just pretended he was brushing some candle". "And you, what was your reaction? Did you take him to the elders' council? You did, did you not?" "No, I just changed the lock to the temple, not for me to be the axman, given the times we are enduring". "And you heard the sound of the iron-clad booths downstairs, when they took him as well as his family? You had heard about all this, and it might have been in your power to save them?" "Rumors brother, only rumors". "But then it all proved to be true brother?" He looked into his eyes. "But Melchior would I be to save a few by having them rob our precious treasures?"

Melchior fell silent for a while. Finally, he opened up. "I on my part have also heard some rumors. Rumors saying that the Rumanian Commandant is no way popular amongst the Germans. There have been talks about him to perish in an explosion and then blame it all on the Jews. Killing two birds with one stone". "When is this to happen? I am impressed by your flow of information and after all thanks to that".

"Tonight, it is, and the so-called revenge is well planned apparently. The Germans have demanded the Parade square cleared and light poles of extra height and force installed, same with blockades, probably barbed wire have been mounted. The official statement is to have the ground secured for training of their dogs. But so far, no dogs, but numerous gypsies have been caught and many of them will be hanged there by the light poles, just to see that it works according to plan. And Chaim, if it is true that the Commandant would soon be killed and we will get the blame, well then, we will be stringed up there as well and in no time dear brother".

"Well, many of the gypsies have been exterminated already. They were stringed up and then taken to a ravine and burned. Soon it is our turn Melchior". It was no question on his part, but more to acknowledge the fact. "But why are we to be hanged by the feet?" "But I did tell you Chaim. The soldiers will enjoy doing just that".

"Quite ineffective Melchior. This must be something cooked up by the Rumanians. Even with this freezing temperature, this method no way is an effective one, the victims may be alive for hours. Not very German this

Melchior, no efficiency at all. Maybe we should send a formal complaint to der Führer!"

Did he fancy himself as the victim or just someone picked at random? But Melchior did not want to take this any further. He was somewhere else in his mind, somewhere with his masterplan and it was now he had to convince his brother about the need for the gold, all the gold.

"This first part of my plan Chaim is to avoid being hanged by the feet. Being hanged by the neck is by far more effective, less painful and it is the only way making the rest of my so-called plan feasible." "Have you been sneaking around reading the Germans' manuals brother? It seems like you have studied all this in detail, but I am anxious for you to present your plan in total, so?"

But Chaim had no idea of the elements in this plan and his brother was cunning in hiding the conclusion right to the end, until it became unbearable to wait for it. This had been Melchior's style under all the childhood, much to Chaim's and others despair and irritation.

"Patience my dear Chaim, that's the gift that is given to the first born and never to the second born and you are the elder one as you know well". "Old news this Melchior, but how long will you keep me waiting?" But Melchior took his time, tasted every word somehow. "Well, yes I do have a plan". "Yes, you have always had plans you Melchior. I on my part I was never allowed to have plans on my own, I just had to follow my father's strict orders, always like that".

Melchior looked at his brother, weighed every word carefully now. "My Rebecka weighs barely 25 kgs now, ok maybe 30 with boots and overclothes. We are all quite skinny now, she not least. I am to make like a skeleton, a kind of a carrier, as lightweight as possible, but still strong enough for her to hang on to i". "You mean on your back Melchior?" "Of course not. Up front Chaim, sort of pasted to my chest. And most important, she is not to be seen under my great overcoat, you know the old one I used to wear when we had enough food to keep us in good shape". "Yeah, at the time you were good and fat brother". But Melchior just ignored his comments. "Fair enough Melchior, your Rebecka is hanging there to your chest and when they throw you on the fire or whatever she will be burned alive, your beautiful Rebecka. Is this the way it is going to be? Come now with your plan brother".

"Listen good now Chaim, when I am stringed up, she shall lower herself and run to the corner of the Parade square. Then down to the suage and start running, possibly with the dogs on her tail. But having run for some hundred meters down the in the shit, then hopefully she will reach the ladder where she is to climb up by the riverside. There will be one person waiting for her right there. And now they just follow the river, dogs onto their tails will be shot and they have free road up to the Carpathians".

Chaim looked closely at him. "So, she is still to join a partisan group? Why could she not have left yesterday with my son?"

"Too late brother, the Rumanians were at our house yesterday and made their count, checked their books. If someone had been missing, then it would have meant blind tortures to all of us. Thereafter they first had shot her mother and then me, so this is her only chance".

"But Melchior, there are three vital points out of your control, not so?" "Ok come on then". "First it is about this skeleton as you call it, will it work as planned? Second, that she makes it to the suage without getting shot. And most problematic, what if you are to be stringed up by your feet. No doubt they would like to see us Rabbis, especially you, looking that fat, seeing you lick the ground and being left to the dogs literally. Their dogs are especially hungry for tongues brother, tongues reaching out for humidity".

"Don't you bother about the first two points. What is of importance is the hanging itself and it is here that you are to play a decisive role Chaim".

His brother looked questionable at him. "I?" "Well, yes we, I need gold". "Gold to what purpose brother?" "To bribe the soldiers". "To have them string you up by the neck?" "Exactly dear brother, exactly that Chaim!"

"How much gold do you have then Melchior and for sure there will be some commotion, with their Schäfers and shouting and commandos etc. And even if she makes it, gets safe to the riverbed, how can you be sure there is someone really waiting for her to get her safe to the mountains?"

"I don't have all the answers, but the most important now is to save her from the flames or freeze to death with the others going North, not to speak about the brothels".

"You seem to have forgotten that because we are Rabbis, then we for certain will swing, right? No labor camp for us. The two of us, we are the symbol itself on the humiliation and the extinction of the rats as we are called by Hitler".

"Just skip that Chaim, the only thing that counts is that she can make it to the suage. She is the one to live and have our tribe grow. If she makes it to the suage, then she stands a chance, not so in the brothel".

"Your cynicism is overwhelming now brother". "And yours then Chaim, you who let them have our concierge Isaac and all his family, sending them straight to their mass graves, just to save one of our candles. Maybe they didn't even get to the grave, but were taken to the ravine, shot and put fire to, together with gypsies and other so-called untermenchen".

"Have you told her about this adventure Melchior?" "No, she is hardly at home these days. Whenever she has some time off, she runs to your house, isn't it just like that brother?" Chaim got red-faced, tapped his brother on his shoulder. "Come on now, how do you know this plan of yours will really do the trick, a plan to be trusted? And how do you know that the way out of the suage is that simple and above all that there really is someone waiting for her? By the way who is this someone? Do I know him?" It was for Melchior to flash now under his white beard. "Well, no doubt, you know him". The childhood Melchior again. "Who is it, come on now!"

"It is your son, brother". "Which one of the two?" "Neither of them". "Do you mean to tell me that little Chaim has been back in Odesa, in your house, not visiting his father?"

"Yes, that is how it is Chaim and no doubt you would have denied him to play a part in this if you were to know. But maybe no longer now. It is after all you who have bedded for them in your house, brother. And since this supposedly was totally unknown to you, I had to reckon that you would have been totally negative to my plan. Would you not? Just admit it!"

"Well, you may be right about this my brother, but now it is all different, is it not?" Chaim looked ever so thoughtful now, no longer his tough attitude. The business with Isaac the concierge and his brothers' accusations had no doubt got to him. Finally, he mustered: "Both of us have kept secrets to one another. Let us stop doing that and work together, but Melchior I don't quite see my role in this scheme of yours?"

"No, maybe you don't". Melchior had gotten himself a thinker as well. Maybe it would not be too smart to expose him to more stress. On the other hand, he knew that there was no way looking back. The plan was totally dependent on having his brother do his part of it. They gave each other the handshake and the following embrace.

"Melchior do you really think that tiny Rebecka will be capable of lifting the heavy lid at the sewage? And what about the rats now in the cold, they are big, aggressive, and hungry?" Chaim was clearly on the go now. Soon he was to be trapped. Melchior shivered, feeling the cold down his spine; my God, please understand my doings, it is absolutely necessary to lure my brother into this snare.

"Chaim, the lid is loose, we have checked just that, and it is even to be controlled the night before the escape as well. And she will have leggings almost to her knees to protect herself against the rats.

Under the lid she will find a torch, a knife to defend herself and even a little Browning". "You mean a revolver? Is she to take lives brother? I wonder how little Chaim has gotten all this organized and how do you know she will not get lost in the tunnel? And more so, there will be soldiers and dogs all over the place".

"Yes, I have seen they have started to prepare for their feast at the Parade square. They have even spanned steel wires between the light poles, so they can have greater capacity in the hanging. But to your question about getting lost, this tunnel goes straight forward towards the port, some one hundred meters and there is the ladder, quite visible. Up there is your son so she does not have to worry about lifting the heavy lid. From there on it is just a short run to the river and they are safe".

The first part of the plan was ok and brother Chaim, thank God he was in for it so far...

"Who knows about this plan Melchior?" "Ezra, our half-brother and of course your son, little Chaim". "And Rebecka?" "She may have her suspicions, although I doubt just that and for sure you son has revealed nothing. But I shall talk with her in the morning and of course we have to try out the skeleton she is to hang fast at, just to make sure it works according to plan". "You seem to take all this about the hanging very light Melchior?" "Chaim, we are all to die at some given time and in a few days, we are to face it Chaim, that is the way it is".

"Where have you planned to meet with her and let her know about your plan then and do you really believe you can convince her to shoot at possible followers in the tunnel?" "If she is fired at, then she will have no choice. No doubt she may have to kill some dogs as well".

"I wonder how you can be this sure about everything brother and tell me, where are you and my son to meet?" "Sorry I cannot tell you more than I know, the meeting point is to be agreed upon only tomorrow". It was obvious that his brother did not believe him, but denial and the white lie was better than to reveal the meeting point.

"My daughter will sacrifice all for the family, for our tribe. This comes above all". Melchior realized that he had to speed up now. "Even being my brother Chaim, you have to swear that even under torture you shall not reveal this plan to anyone. Rather you have your tongue cut off than telling anyone." "Don't you trust me, you my own brother?" "In these dire times I am to trust nobody, hardly myself. And this is some of the worst impacts from our enemies: harassments, destroying the confidentiality within families.

Now you look here brother. The Torah is ready for you. Put your hand on to it and repeat your promise and say the final words: To this I swear". "I never thought I was to swear to any living creature. Swearing belongs to God only Melchior". But his brother showed no sign of relentless. Did they shiver the leaves in the Torah or was it just the early morning wind? But Chaim could not reach his brother. He just had to get through with it, the demand from his brother. "Do you forgive me my God?" The words were not even audible.

Then it was over, and Melchior put the Torah aside and Chaim composed himself. "What about Rebecka and my son then?" "In the morning they shall have to take the same oath as you just did brother".

"And now to the gold Melchior. Is this all that you have in your sack?" "Yes, but it is only my wife's gold jewels, and it is far from being enough". "But does she know that you have taken her jewels?" "Well, yes, but I had to tell her that I should put them some place safe, but of course she does not know that they will be melted together with my own gold pieces. Still, this is far from being enough".

Chaim sensed that there was some demand in the air. "And now you want my modest collection as well?" "Yes, but I guess you don't have that much and by no means I want your wife involved in all this". "So, what do you have in mind Melchior as I can only help out with this little?" "My dear brother, you are our chief treasurer, our guardian of our gold so to speak". But Chaim still looked inquiring at him. "My brother what is it that you don't tell me straight?"

"You are our guardian of our holy shrines and as you know well, they are all of solid gold. I need two, maybe better three so I am certain there will be enough gold pieces. I even need some gold candles. All that thereafter remains of our wholy shrines as well as our holy scriptures I want for you to hide in a secret place if that is still to be found. Then you must notify our relatives in New York about the hiding place. I do not know how you will solve this, nor do I want to know, but I must have all the gold I need when I leave from here in the morning". He could see now that Chaim was deeply shaken by his brother's demand.

"Melchior, what do you think would be the reaction from the congregation if they were to know that we are plundering our holy shrines?" Clearly Chaim was on the go now, no protests, only how could he defend the action. Have our backs covered. Was it the love between his youngest son and his niece that tipped his decision in Melchior's favor? That the two young ones were to live and guarantee for the succession of the tribe, while everyone else was to die? The Adam and Eve of our times? Melchior did not know and really, it did not matter. This was the decisive moment to get the plan in the box, not least to save his Rebecka. Without the gold, she would for sure end up in an officer's brothel. His little kitten, his only descendent.

"I think we will be forgiven Chaim, for sure it would have been a nobler cause than leaving it all to the vandals from Rumania. It is after all a matter of preserving our people". "But Melchior, isn't precisely what you are planning to do, leave the gold pieces to the Rumanian soldiers to make sure you are hanged by the neck?" "Chaim, my brother, excuse me for expressing my thoughts this way, but aren't you naïve almost to the unbelievable if you really mean what you say? Do you for once think that the Germans would allow for the Rumanians to keep the gold. Please say that you do not believe that. You are not that naïve my dear brother".

Chaim chose to disregard the outburst from his brother. This was typical of Melchior, just the way he had always been from childhood and up, light on foot and light on mouth. He turned to his brother. "With what authority do you make these dispositions Melchior? Do you and I have any right to what we discuss now? Don't we have an obligation to bring this matter to the council of the elders?" He wanted to cover his back now Chaim, even if he had already crossed the Rubicon.

"Soon brother, very soon, there will be no one left with authority to make such decisions. It has leaked that we all shall be gone, labor camps or death marches. Death will come to us all, but the road towards death will differ, some of our strongest will survive, two maybe three months in the cold of the winter building roads and then it will be over".

"But Melchior, I have learned that there will be exceptions. Our best musicians will survive much longer than the rest of us if they volunteer to play for the Nazis in the concentration camps, at their parties. And brother wont this new Ukraine be in need for our craftsmen?" "Well, yes, to teach the craft to Ukrainians. But once we have taught them the ropes, it will be death and mass graves for our craftsmen as well". But Chaim was still holding back.

"My dear brother, have you addressed all this that is overwhelming me to our God, Melchior?" "Yes brother". Chaim looked at him; he was in his position as Rabbi now. "And did you get an answer from our God brother?"

Chaim knew what was coming, but he needed to hear it straight from Melchior. Had to know that their God was on their side in this matter. "Well speak out then brother, what was God's answer?" "Save our people Melchior, save our tribe!"

Chaim's pale face slowly got his color back and the embrace was as in their childhood. They were once again brothers and nothing but that, the two of them. "God be praised Melchior, my brother"

It was still dark there in the night and they could feel the even stronger cold from the new day. A faint morning blush signaled clear weather which would allow for the occupants to speed up their misdeeds. "I shall have to go now Chaim. This has been a blessed night for the both of us, may God help us in our endeavor". "What about your wife then Melchior? Have you prepared her for what is to come?" "She doesn't seem to care much, except for the fate of Rebecka. But what about your Maria, Chaim

and your two elder sons? Are they to wait here for the axman or will they follow their younger brother and fight?"

"My wife is not preoccupied with her fate; she takes what comes she says. But not so with my two sons, both being engaged to be married and thus part of a greater community. To leave their family or their fiancées would be a betrayal they never could live with". "So, then they will rather meet death by hanging on the Parade square, or die in a slave camp, slowly tormented by lack of food and medicines, illnesses and not least the killing cold?" "Well, yes that's the way it is, the way it should be". "But following that path Chaim, they still could be separated from their closest?" Melchior looked at his brother. "Yes, but then it is destiny, not an active separation by themselves. They do not leave their closest, voluntarily".

Melchior felt he could understand the reasoning. "But I have no sons to sacryfie Chaim, so I am not the one to have a say in this matter. But my Rebecka is to be saved, come what may".

"Go with God my brother!" There was deep sorrow in his voice, still with a solemn rabbi- tone; And Melchior knew then that Chaim gladly would have saved his sons.

It was still night when he got down the ladder and on to the street. It was all quiet, not a soldier in sight. But he walked with care, took a shortcut between some old stables and finally he was on to his own street.

In the meantime, the first rayons from the sun had made the sky purple-red, frightening him sort of. Was this a kind of an omen telling him that soon there would be blood flowing in the streets? His own people's blood? The signs had been there for quite a while now, and this talk about the attentat on the Rumanian Commandant? Had this been done now in this night that was almost gone? And would the Jews be the ones to be blamed as he and his brother had talked about it? Well then it would be a free run for the Rumanians. He could almost hear the dogs or was it just a faint sound of warning? He pressed on round the corner and finally he was indoors, safe so far. He felt the coziness of his home, his wife waiting for him with the breakfast. She should have been with her sister up north in the city. Did not care much for being alone so she had decided to wait for her husband. Maybe this would be their last breakfast together? But she was still content, his Rachel. The two of them had lived a happy marriage, although no sons. But every day she thanked her God, having blessed them with their little Rebecka.

"Will you manage to save Rebecka?" She was excited now. But all through the night she had this feeling that Melchior would succeed and that their child would be spared. "Yes, by the help of God," and Chaim, but he didn't add the latter.

THE GENERATIONS, THE ELVEGÅRDS

The landscape was rural Norway at its most beautiful. There had been talks, yes and even some film shootings to see if it was suitable for shooting of the great "Family saga". But then the director had said no, lack of a small lake was his argument. And when Trygve, farmer and local GP had learned about it all, that there were plans for an artificial lake there on his property, he had firmly said no, all should, be handed over to the next generation unchanged. There hardly was one week that he did not speak to his son Lars about the necessity of safeguarding untouched nature.

There were two farms, Upper Elvegård and Lower Elvegård, referred to as Øvre and Nedre. The buildings at Øvre were the oldest ones, possibly late medieval. "Luckily Tore up at Øvre isn't that tall as I am", he smiled to his wife Sarah. But she knew ever so well that her husband would have preferred to walk bowed rather than make the smallest changes on the buildings if they had lived up at Øvre.

Admittedly there was not too much room under the ceiling up at Øvre and a couple of times there had been discussions about lifting the roof, thus making a larger room. But then the discussion was ardent, changing something built by once ancestors? No way! This was of course all about feelings, not about practicalities and with stubbornness of the county's farmers, things were to remain unchanged. The farm was of course a post-card beauty, summer as well as winter, with the battered old timber on the main house and the barn painted ochreous. Houses and barns were painted exactly the same, even the store houses with their bell towers, were identical.

It was not a real river dividing the two farms, only a stream sort of with small trout ponds. Maybe there once was a real river? This was an ever-recurring theme. Maybe there once had been like a landslide changing it all? So, nothing conclusive until Svanhild up at Øvre, wife of Tore, she had a simple solution to it. One night when the moon was full, she had woken up early in the night, and when she looked out of the window, she had seen the moon shining in the stream, thus making it look much bigger, no longer a stream but a real river.

Maybe it had been like this also in old times and such a looming, or whatever, this came to give the names Øvre- and Nedre Elvegård. Trygve at Nedre had given it a lough, but his wife Sarah had applauded this looming from Svanhild. And Trygve, he never opposed to his wife.

River or just a stream. No question it was a big brook. Lars went for a swim there ever so often in the summer or to try for the trout year-round. Even in winter, there was seldom ice. And they often were lucky getting trout merely with homemade fishing tackles. "Real gear this" said Lars, just a rod from a birch tree and angles with a hook and maggot. "No way we go to the shop to buy fancy tackles". And Lars enjoyed teasing the girls with the maggots whenever he found some really big ones. But when the poliomyelitis severely hit his little sister Ragnhild, teasing stopped, no longer any fun go fishing. Ragnhild got weaker by the day and finally she had to be carried or taken in a cart on to the river, something she despised.

Once upon a time there was only the one farm and with a farmer having two sons, both in high esteem by their father. So, in 1633 the farm was split between the two. The elder son, Rasmus had the document from his father stating that Nedre, run by his brother, never could be sold out of the family. Whenever the question of selling might come up, Nedre should then be sold to Rasmus up at Øvre or his descendants for a prize of 1 Riksdaler (Old Dollar like). And he was in his right being the older one. But with the alternative of losing his brother he accepted that Nedre should forever be his brothers as laid out by his father. The bailiff had approved the arrangement provided that the two farms were listed under the same number in the county register.

Up to now it had never come right that the heirs on both sides had been suited for marriage, thus enabling the farms to be joined together like in the very old days. Once the dream of Rasmus it was. Live to see his grandchild being married to his brother's grandchild and the two farms being one again. But his dream was never to come through in his time.

Years went by, with new generations on the farms, and the hope for a marriage making old dreams come through never seemed to be fulfilled. But maybe now at long last it could be time?

Trygve at Nedre, teased Tore up at Øvre that maybe now is the time, his son Lars and Tore's daughter Eva may well come to like each other. Yes, they were related, but only distant, maybe 100 years back or more, so

neither the vicar nor the sheriff would have legal ways to stop them, if…
"But this is not like in the very old days, Trygve. At that time then you and I were to decide on marriages and such".

Trygve had himself a good laugh. "And maybe that is for the better Tore. Lars shall as you know pick up my trade and become a doctor and we have no guarantee for him to take over the farm like I did". "But you still have your daughter Ragnhild Trygve". His face darkened. "She would never be any farmers wife Tore, so please leave it be". Tore was sorry having brought up this theme, so he quickly changed to a political issue.

"Trygve, as our GP you meet with most people in our county, have you any news about the Nazis and their progress? You are not bound by ethics in this question, are you?"

"Tore I don't know where the limit is in this question, but overall, when people confide in you, then you must understand that I have to respect their confidence". "Damn it Trygve, we are friends and neighbors, have always been. And it cannot be a secret to you that this Nazi boss down by Mjøsa, he is keen on my daughter Eva". "Tore are you trying to speed up the engagement between your Eva and my son Lars?" Slightly embarrassed now Trygve. "I thought you and I were totally in agreement that this is a question we should leave to the young ones, not for the two of us to involve ourselves in". "But just think Trygve, think about it at least theoretically, yes think about my situation if this Nazi Jens and my Eva got together".

Trygve had stood up from the bench red in his face. "Tore this is a conversation that we never had and do promise me that you never will bring up this theme no more, ever". But Tore only looked down. Finally, he looked at Trygve: "I pray that should I ever be taken out by a bullet or be gone for other reasons, then promise me that you will do all in you might to prevent that such a misfortune should come upon my daughter and her mother".

THE SPECIAL HIGH SUMMER OF 1939

"A penny for your thoughts Eva" "Am I on sale now?" A teasing laughter followed. "I guess your thoughts are merely dwelling with you becoming the wife of a doctor now and that our little heir shall have two big farms in some birth gift".

"I do not care much for this wishy wassy of yours, me becoming a doctor's wife. Maybe you should concentrate on finishing your med-studies my Lars". Oj, what did she say? My hearings are they ok? But Lars pretended hearing nothing, he just continued: "I have a farm to run and possibly 2 farms quite soon if you behave Eva".

But she was on the go now, not letting him get away with this farm-talk. "Just you wait till you have your own patients my Lars". She straightened her skirt and buttoned the top of her blouse. "Think about my father finding the two of us here in the middle of the haystack". But Lars was excited now and it was summer, and he wanted to have her right there and then, the bulge on his shorts was for her to see now, and he felt he had no choice.

"I don't care if anyone should be finding us here in the haystack!" Then he was over her body. "If you wonna play with me, then it is ok by me". And they kept on rolling there in the hay.

"You do not look decent at all Eva!" And she did not, not at all decent she looked. She had decided that today she would risk it all, so no pantsy, nor bra, just a knee-longue ultra-thin linen helping to hold the skirt in shape. But it was not in her plan to do it in the haystack at high noon. The idea was for Lars to get excited by her looks throughout the day and come evening, then she would be ready for him. That is the way the game should be played according to Marte, her best friend. "Men are easily tricked", she had added.

But it was not all about sex. Whatever happened would be to Lars' advantage. Finally calmed down, certain to know that the prettiest girl in the county was his. Prettiest by far according to the boys. Her long, almost silky, blond hair dropped all the way to her round bottom, whenever she had it hanging loose, not in braids as was customary on the farms. She had gotten curves already at the age of 16, time for her Confirmation. And her mother worried a bit, sometimes quite a lot she worried especially for her full breasts, showed too openly in summers. Not strange that the boys at the Confirmation flocked around her. Lars not so. Not then and not know.

Yes, for sure Eva was a beauty, and she knew it well herself. But was it in despair she had dressed this way? But she had to do something, not risking living as an old spinster there on the farm. And what about this Nazi guy Jens, not easy to keep him away.

She consoled herself that it was not at all her idea to skip the pantsy as well as the bra. No, it was her friend Marte who had put her on to this idea. Marte had come to visit late Sunday night, whispering: "Don't tell it to anyone". "Tell what?" "Hush, do promise Eva, cross your heart and swear on the bible and all forefathers!" "Yes of course, now tell me Marte".

"He took me!" "Who did that?" "My Ola, you know well I have been driving after him all this early summer, but he has neglected me for this other girl to inherit a big farm, been chasing her all the time. But he would have stood no chance to that, never got the consent of her father". "But Marte what then, how did you manage?" "I dressed naked!" "What?" "Well yes to the dance. Silly you Eva", she looked at the disbelief expression on her friends face and had herself a big laugh. "Under the dress, silly you". "And what about the mosquitos then?" They both laughed exuberantly.

"Well, he had no choice then, Ola, simply had to have you Marte". She flashed. "Well yes, after some drinking". "And was this as wonderful as you have dreamt of Marte?" She flashed even more now. "Are you referring to the stories in the monthlies, how the woman melts by his touch and feel him slowly entering her and she overflows with happiness?" "Enough now Marte, spare me to further details, however exciting and thrilling". She was not to hear more about all this from Marte, as she time and again had been rejected to experience all this sweetness by Lars. That was how she had felt it, all the way, rejection.

But she need not have to worry. "Eva to me it was only one thing that mattered. Romance will be for later. I should have him and get pregnant with him, carry his baby. This should be the grand finale to it all". And then she laughed out wildly, and Eva had to join as well. Talk about a purposeful lady!

"But how do you know that he really will marry you?" "This episode goes 5 weeks back Eva and my monthly period is yet to come, so clearly,

I am to have a baby." She was overexcited now. "But what about the boy, Ola. Have you told him about it?" "No, that's for my brothers to do, they shall bring him home to me on the farm". "But Marte what if he denies and refuses to come to you?" Eva could not hide that she was worried for her best friend. "Did I not say that my brothers shall go fetch him!" She was triumphant now Marte. "So, then I am to be the first Eva as I guess there is no progress with you and Lars?" A faint sorrow in the eyes of Eva and Marte was quick with her excuse. "Dear you I didn't mean to hurt you; I am only that excited you know".

No doubt Marte had gotten her prey, Eva was more and more thoughtful and absent. "Aren't you happy for me Eva?" "Yes of course, sorry, congrat, of course I am happy for you". It was obvious to Marte that her friend was still absentminded, and she stood to leave. "But Eva, you have to promise me that this our little big secret, no one is to know until it is all official". "Yes of course Marte". "And Eva don't you forget about the trick with nudity!" Then she was gone.

But Eva was in her own bubble now. Could she at all consider playing such a trick on Lars? And what would eventually be Lars' reaction? Would he call her a whore and then goodbye? On the other hand, he being that slow and this talk about enlisting and join for war somewhere in Europe? Would he ever propose, while she would just stay at home being taken for granted once it suited him? She the neighbor girl that comes with the farm, or was it the other way round?

Lars never ever spoke about their relation. She started to get desperate now having learned about Marte's adventure. She felt tempted she as well, did she not? She looked at herself in the big mirror, beautiful summer tan and her long hair hanging loose almost to her bottom. What about her lips? Yes, she had to fix that. Not to speak about her legs, any girls fear, have they become thicker? Well, when working the farm, naturally there would be muscles. They could not be done with just like that and Lars never said a word about them, but he rarely commented on anything did he? But it rests to be seen when she now decided to follow her friend's advice.

Her thought was not far from taking action. She felt confident to herself and certainly about Lars when she felt her hard, naked nipples pointing through the thin dress.

Halfway down the road to where they should meet, she got second thoughts, ran back to her room and put on her silk linen, dropping all the way to her knees. But her nipples were still pointed and no way they were hidden. But she was already late, so she stood to test.

It was her mother who had called on her there in the haystack and she had been quick straightening her skirt and blouse. Mother had left, no words spoken, but for certain she would come back on it all later.

And what about Lars, did he ever react to her naked body? No, he was his unfathomable as always, except for the bulge in his shorts. No way, he most certainly had his mind on the war and that was it. So, this friendly advice from Marte gave no results. She consoled herself with the fact that Ola had been ever so intoxicated by alcohol and that helped to the trick. But Lars, he was never drunk, and she was happy to that.

But something got to happen soon. Maybe the simple problem was that they knew each other to well. All from childhood they had looked upon each other as brother and sister in a way. Maybe it was all good that Lars left for this war of his, he could never let go. But what if she got to lose him, he getting killed? She got real pale, but then his arm was on to her as they walked down the small road. It was Lars who picked up the thread; "What was it with you Eva, yes, a while ago you suddenly fell silent? Tell me!" Clearly, he had noticed something, maybe he had come aware of her being half naked? No way, Lars was in his own world in spite of holding on to her.

"No, it was nothing, except I was suddenly pondering about you quoting Hitler and that soon all Europe will be at war and maybe one day this will inflict on our country as well". "No danger for us Eva, we are backed by England". "But England Lars, what can little England muster against Hitlers well-trained war machine?"

The feeling of nearness was gone, and she was free of his arm. Were they never to get any further, always something on the outside taking the attention, Hitler or whatever? Why not talk about love and romance, their future together and what about having children together, if it was to be the two of them then.

The summer was at its peak with warm nights making sleep difficult, always turning around there in her bed. While her friend from childhood Marte now being well into her second month and she, she was just alone here in her lonely night, full of emotions and an aching body, flowing over by longings.

She simply could not stand it any longer, had to get up. But the night was still young only 2 AM. What about Lars, was he in bed dreaming about his war? No doubt to it. She strolled down to the little spring that separated the two farms, Øvre Elvegård and the one on the lower side,

Nedre Elvegård. Then she saw him, yes sort of a miracle it was. There he was, her boy, soon to be a man of 21 years and of age now.

He was a handsome guy and together they would make a beautiful couple, she almost 1.75 cm and he close to 1.90 cm, blonde and slim although with plenty muscles and the most wonderful grey-blue eyes. But she had never come to tell him, about his eyes. He was the one always interrupting, either by kissing or he wanted to talk about the war. Admittedly he was the talker, although at times he could touch her bottom or at best stroke her breasts, always on the bra, never beyond. It should not be easy to get any further, she willingly and he? She had never seen him naked, although she had sneak- peeked when they bathed in the little stream. She on the other hand, she always bathed with her clothes on, and he teased her for that, but what if one of the hire hands suddenly stood there? No way. She kept her clothes on.

Lars had not gotten to sleep, maybe it was the moonlight that made the night as bright as the day or maybe he had recognized she being naked under there in the haystack and now he could not get peace to himself? Marte had told her about boys relieving themselves, especially when the body would not comply, then relieving themselves was appeasing, according to her friend.

But Lars had never touched upon this subject. Likely to be embarrassing and no doubt consider as his private sphere. And what about herself? Marte had shown her how to do it, but no way she would even try it in her presence.

They were both silent now. He took her in his arms and carried her behind some hay stand out of sight from the houses. She had not been prepared to this; Lars no doubt saw her nipples standing stiff under her nighty. And what about him, the bulge on his shorts, they hardly covered his groin. Not at all decent, would have been her mommy's remark. But mommy wasn't there, nor was Eva's head, or was it? She tried to take the bulge in the shorts in her hands, but Lars stopped her. What now, did he not want her after all?

"You want me, Eva?" "You mean sleep with you here and now, having you inside me?" Her voice was as hoarse as his now. "Is this a proposal Lars?" "Yes". "Then you have to go down on your knee". He got solemn now. "If that is what it takes, so be it. Will you be mine and then marry me, Eva?"

"So, you no longer take me for granted then Lars, coming with the farm sort of, just like the herds?" He flashed now, downed on his knees. "No Eva, no more, but I had thought about waiting till I could see myself coming home from the war alive; If the war comes here then and for sure I think it will and I am off to it".

She come to shiver, standing there, her eyes on his. "So that was the reason to your holding back? Are you sure about this Lars?" "I have always meant for it to be us my Eva, and how about you?"

Suddenly they were totally naked the two of them. Her bottom did not take it too kindly with the stiff hay, but what the heck. "I do love you Lars". "And I love you". And then she felt him coming to her down there, him pressing on. But she did not want something like with Marte's. A quick fuck and then done with it. "Careful Lars, you know I have been waiting for you only, so for sure it is narrow in there, I am your virgin, my dearest".

Did she want to know if he was a virgin as well? "Let us try Lars, but real slow. Yes, just the tip, yes, but no longer in and now you lay still if you can". They kept lying there, feeling how their sexes found each other and slowly his penis came longer in and it slided in her wet, sweet juices, then almost out again. "We don't need doing something my Lars, just let mine and your limb do the job". She really wanted to say the word penis but was not up to it. "But please be patient with me my dearest".

It was nothing like Lars had wanted, but slowly he felt the sensation when Eva's sex was massaging his penis, although his body did not move. He felt the pulsation down there and had to hold back to avoid him coming

It seemed like an eternity, when Eva suddenly made the final jerk, he was totally into her now and there was no holding back for him while she had to slow down to avoid the screams pressing on and the risk of waking her mother. But no way, she gave in. Heaven and Earth and it was all wild and just the way she had dreamt about it, already from her first teens. "Are we engaged now Lars?" "Yes, my love, we are just that".

"I didn't manage to sleep at all mother, I had to get up and out to calm down". Her mother looked at here in disbelief, like she knew about it all. "What Eva, what was it all about?" "Well yes Mother I was that excited". "About what then my girl? About Lars, no doubt. And what now then Eva?" She could see a small smile in her mother's eyes. "He has proposed now mother, and isn't that just wonderful?" "And what was your answer to that?" "Mother!" It was a happy smile. "I think I shall have a good sleep now and just think about it if there will be peace as well".

Whatever she meant by that, her mother wondered as she let go of her daughter and the hugging and followed her indoors.

But come September 1st, 1939, the German assault on Poland was soon to take place.

CHRISTMAS 1939

It had been an autumn with many political rallies, not least by the Nazis even up here at the county of Hedmark. Lars and his father looked at the changes in attitudes with an exceeding anxiety. Not so much Sarah, mother and wife, but she was the one that should be really worried.

The small, local Nazi party, being the only opposition to the mighty communist party, had spread fear of the increasing influence from the Bolsheviks, referring to Finland, for sure to lose Karelen. And what will come next, Norway to lose Finnmark, bordered to the Soviet far up North. How to save this part of Norway from the likely Russian aggressor? We Norwegians, most of us without arms to defend ourselves? It was the time of the "broken rifle". So, Germany would be our only savior from the threat from the East. This was the mantra!

Following the Soviet invasion to Finland, most Norwegians feared that soon, very soon they would be next to see Russians in their land. And what about England, this coward, having promised to save Poland together with France? This France that soon was to be humiliated by the superb German war machine, and then lying flat with broken back. To everyone it should be clear that the Germans would be the only ones capable of saving Norway from the Bolsheviks, saving us to be a free, independent nation. Vidkun Quisling, the Norwegian Nazi head, he was a master in proclaiming this message, a fabulous orator he was.

One day the local Nazi leader suddenly turned up at the farm, driving a splendid Mercedes, albeit a used one, but ever so shiny. This Jens presented himself as a cordial visitor there at Øvre and according to customs they could not deny him an invite to coffee. And what was the purpose to his visit? First and foremost, to get to know one another, useful to have contacts to save the motherland. Being a widower, he was in need for a new wife as well. His eyes followed Eva's every move when she joined to serve coffee, no question to his goal. Her engagement to Lars was so far not made official.

"And how about you then Tore, you the lead man in the local Rifle association, how about your people joining up as a supportive unit to the local Nazi party? Maybe I even could get lucky and have Mr. Quisling himself come to our first official meeting once you have joined up. This could have an enormous impact on other Rifles' association throughout the country, joining up for the defense against the Bolsheviks if they were to invade us. Did I say IF? Yes, what I meant was when they come. Look to Finland. Our brother- land. We could have helped them there in their fight. But what about our government, they just sit back and let Finland do its best on their own, no helping hand".

These were dangerous thoughts, spread by this Nazi Jens and Tore felt strongly for discussing this with his good neighbor down at Nedre. So, the day before Christmas they met the two of them, axes in hand to cut Christmas threes.

"I hear what you are saying Tore, make sure you make no false steps, but in my opinion this Nazi is foremost after your daughter".

"You may count on me Trygve, I would never fancy joining up with the Nazis, on the contrary, I think it is vital that we get to organize a small unit of real partisans that could stand up against an eventual German invasion, peaceful so-called".

"Quite some new thoughts this Tore and do you for one think our Finnish brethren looked upon the attack from the Russians a so-called peaceful invasion? A merry Christmas to you all. You will know my thoughts about all this come New year's.

It turned out to be the strangest Christmas this year, a Christmas on notice so to speak. The two farmhands and the maids learned about the news on Christmas eve. There was no division between the farmers and the hire hands, so they were all gathered round the Christmas table, and the walk round the Christmas tree and there were gifts for everyone. Little Ragnhild was excited as she was the one reading the cards on the gifts, but sometimes she forgot herself when there was a special gift to her. Then she would sit under the tall 3-meter-high Christmas tree, daydreaming. Or perhaps it was her brain that just shut off more and more for every day, much to Trygve's anxiety, knowing that one day, maybe soon, she would be gone forever.

Little Ragnhild had gotten the most special gift earlier on Christmas eve, a superb Hedemark-bunad (folklore) and Trygve said there would be no difference to all when he and his wife Sarah unveiled their bunads. She left to change into her new outfit, when there was time for the special rice cream and coffee and a small glass of cognac.

Trygve, the husband was not much for bunad to himself, but he had put on his best suit though. And with no bunad he was more like the hired hands he felt, enough with the two, Ragnhild his daughter and Sarah his wife. As for Lars, he did not care much, but his mother had been on to him to dress up, not least if he was to call on Eva up at Øvre later in the night.

Trygve read from the bible about Christmas, Josef and Mary and the little child as he did every Christmas, but during the reading, his wife Sarah busted out into tears and the secret had to come out:

"As you know, my wife comes from Karelen, Finland now invaded by the Soviets, there in our beautiful brother land. But here in Hedemark County many supports the communists, albeit not the invasion of Finland. But it is not for me to examine hearts or kidneys of my fellow farmers, especially not on Christmas Eve when I have time off from my medical practice". He tried to loosen up on the sad atmosphere from Sarah's outcry. "But to those of you" and he addressed himself to the hire hands, to those of you that have sympathy with the great neighbor in the East, it may well be difficult to continue working on my land, as in a weeks' time, I shall bid you farewell to go East, enlist for service and fight against the communist invaders in Sarah's homeland.

No one needs take their decision tonight, but if there are amongst you someone that have problems with my decision, then he or she best leave us tonight, once our Christmas dinner is over".

No one raised to speak, all looking down on the table. But slowly they all looked up again, except for Jonas, one of the hired hands. They all knew about his sympathy to communism.

"Jonas no one thinks of squeezing you out from here. You just have to follow your own conscience". Then Jonas stood up, obviously quite embarrassed.

"I cannot deceive my comrades in the East, nor can I let you down Sarah, now that your husband is leaving for Finland. So, I shall stay on if you will let me". And that was how it should be.

"You will let me have one of your hire hands Tore to help with the spring works. Thus, I shall have two and should I fail to get back from this war, then you and Lars my son will have even more to talk about. And for your own sake Tore, keep this Nazi Jens away from your daughter".

"What they have between them, the young ones, is that solid that you do not need to worry. Best you get home soon, so we do not have to call upon another doctor in our county when in need". Tore gave him an inscrutable look. "Something special on your mind my neighbor?" Well maybe so!" He pictured his Eva, had a laugh and that was it. "Have a safe trip to Finland then Trygve, you will be on our mind".

The moment to say good-byes had come, Trygve was all ready. "May I go with you Dad?" "I am leaving now Lars, then the responsibility for the farm, yes and everything is yours.". "But why do you have to go Dad, this is not your fight is it?" "Is it not my son? Is your mother not from Karelen, the heart itself of Finland, now under strong attack from the Bolsheviks, in part already conquered? We have to through them out and free your mothers native land, don't you get that?"

Lars looked down, disgraced. "But you are not just a young stud no more Dad. Is it not we the young ones that should go fight the Bolsheviks?" "Your time will come son, for sure! The Russians will not content themselves only with Karelen. Maybe it will be Finnmark next". "But our government and the parliament have they no say in the matter?" "The broken rifle my son. They had rather see us fall flat on our faces than take up arms against our enemies. That is how our officials think, not least this yellow government. Keep quiet and do not mingle with the games played by the super forces. Thus, we might be able to stay out of conflicts. But the few of us, believing in justice and just cause also for the small nations, we have to be vigilant and guard our independency".

"Still could I not go with you Dad?" "But Lars, what about your mother! And what if she were to lose the two of us. And Lars you have no training in being a soldier, weaponry etc. I on my part have done my training in the Service, even if it is years back. But foremost I can help my comrades by my medical profession and as always in wars, there is shortage of doctors.

This is for you". He handed him an envelope. "This one you shall burn the minute I get home – alive. If I should not make it, then you have to open it, read the content and then burn it immediately!" "What have you written there my dad?" "You do not need to know about that right now son. Just hide this envelope so that no one may find it. Take care of your mother and guard her with your life if it comes to that. No one knows what is laying ahead for our country. But for sure we will be in alliance with England or Hitler, whether we like it or not, however unwillingly." "What do you mean Dad? Will there be war here in our country as well?" "For sure, I can guarantee you that much, only I cannot say when. But for now, it is all about Finland. Just join the local Rifle association and learn weaponry and hurry on finishing your medical degree. I have talked with Eva's father. He knows I am leaving. He has promised to let you have one of his hired hands to help out with the spring chores in the fields. So, it is for you to concentrate on your studies and safeguard your mother. And again, please do not forget the Rifle association!"

EVA

"Have you gotten any news from your father Lars? And darling what about our wedding, now the Germans will come and invade our country?" Was this the only thought on her mind his Eva? Get married, have a baby, an heir to both farms? Well, yes, her father would be overjoyed. Old dreams come through. But maybe he just wronged her. She had been talking about the wedding for months now and he should have been overjoyed he as well, should he not?

The most beautiful girl in all the county. The lass that all farmer sons were crazy after, not least the old Nazi down at Nes, a widower of forty something, rich in goods and gold.

Maybe he should have given Eva his ok to announce the engagement? But what about this inevitable war, yes it would soon come, and he knew he had to be part of it. That was the way he saw it and what if he should get killed or come home crippled, would it then be right to have Eva committed to him for life?

This Nazi Jens down at Nes, this fat Jens, he had been quite pushy according to Eva. But even if she should have fallen for him, somewhat unthinkable, she never ever would have gotten her father's consent. The old one, Jens so nicknamed by the young, he had joined up with the Nazi party long time ago and as a forerunner he would have received appraisal and position once this Quisling was in power. Lars was as confident as his father that the Nygårdsvold government, this broken rifle government, it could never endure. Soon it would be time for Quisling to take over and Nazi Jens to gain power locally. But Eva's father, no way he would accept any son in law except for Lars, that was written in stone. And Lars, he loved her as she loved him.

Like most girls she was to dream about her wedding. She had laid detailed plans long time ago although she had not dared discussed them with Lars. She felt that maybe she would scare Lars away, all the time talking about the wedding and stuff. But Eva and her mother had long time laid every single detail for the event.

While her mother was most preoccupied with the food and the arrangements in the church, Eva herself was all into the questions of her wedding robe. There was not an evening that she did not leaf through the monthlies looking for bridal pictures and possible new ideas. She had made clippings so that she was well aware of how the final result should be, veil as well as the bouquet.

Her mom had said roses. But no way, it was to be a June wedding and roses? No way, it had to be wildflowers, no question about it.

One day she had written to the publishers and had them send her a booklet picturing a large selection of lingerie. She has made sure to hide this booklet to Lars. If he by chance had come across it, he would probably have slipped downhill, the poor one. She had to laugh a little, still wondering if he had slept with someone south in Oslo. No doubt there were many pretty, young nurses at the hospital where the med student regularly hospited for practice. She had to console herself: Probably nothing but flirting and that would be it. For sure he would content himself with relieving himself when he got it too hard.

But the lingerie was ever so tempting. Maybe she should order the items she found the most seductive. But no, should she not wait for his proposal? But Eva he has proposed! Of course, he had, and she had said yes. Still, she would not risk getting some of this lingerie in house as at now because then she knew she could not hold back. She simply would have to try it on, and that would be wrong. No way she should try it on till the wedding date had been set, announcement made in the church. Still, she could allow herself to fantasize.

Lars, he was mostly preoccupied with the war his father was fighting and even more, when could they expect him home safe, no injuries. Not to forget his poor mother Sarah, getting thinner and maigrer by the day as the bad news of the war kept coming. And after the invasion of the Germans April 9th, she had almost collapsed. Even more so when the biggis of the county, Nazi Jens had presented himself at the farm while Lars was at the Uni in Oslo. So, Sarah was alone when Nazi Jens came visiting in his shiny Mercedes. He gave her the happy message, so-called: "Next week Sarah, then you shall have top brass visitors. A German colonel and his staff have chosen your farm to set up the divisions headquarter. So, it shall get ever so lively here. You best prepare yourself and start moving into the annex. But leave the house as it is with furniture and all. The staff will need all rooms. Our new government will of course pay a suitable rent. Make sure the farm will be managed as usual, if not I shall have to find a caretaker. By the way, any news about your husband?"

She was to dumfound to answer. Jens thanked her for the coffee, whisking off with "see you soon. "Then it will be the Germans serving the coffee".

If only Trygve soon would be home and what would Lars say once home from Oslo?

She had to get through to him, letting him know before coming home. But why had the colonel chosen Nedre Elvegård for his HQ? No way that the Germans had the foggiest about the farms up here in Hedmark. This must entirely be Nazi Jens's doing. No doubt about it and that it should be the trick to keep Lars away from Eva, leaving the road open to old man Nazi Jens.

THE ARRIVAL OF THE GERMANS

The 20th April was a beautiful spring day. Sarah had gotten words that her husband, Trygve, was on his way home from Finland. Lars had been warned about the "invasion", her word on the German intruders. He was due back for the weekend.

Sarah had given the house a good shining, everything should be clean and tops as the Germans were shortly to arrive and take possession. The hired hands were already busy with the spring chores. So, all was as normal, except for Sarah. She had a constant heartache every time she was moving her dearest things over from the house to her new home, the annex. But she tried to comfort herself recognizing that there was lesser importance in the things she was moving, and yes, her Trygve was due for the weekend that was her comfort.

She heard the sound of the motor trail from long distance. Up front there were two motorbikes, then a car with the staff, two soldiers in the front seat and a high-ranking officer in the back. Several lorries followed and finally Nazi Jens in his shining Mercedes. Sarah stood at the landing, bidding welcome and Jens rushed to the front to do the introduction.

Colonel Klepka turned out to be a very courteous man making his earnest excuses having to invade a private home. He said that all would be good once the uprising in Norway was over and done with and Norway then had been incorporated as a free, independent nation in the greater German Reich. Nazi Jens was doing the translation.

Sarah nodded a welcome and left for the new home, the annex, while Jens held a speech to the hire hands and asked them to behave correctly and welcoming to their new masters.

Some 15 minutes later the Swastika was flagging on the pole.

Then came Lars. Did he at all believe the sight that met him? The poster "Lege kontor" (Surgery) had been moved to the annex corner. Nothing he could do about that, but what about his little, frail mother?

Had she managed to move all the personal belongings over from the house to the annex and what about her feelings, every day raise to watch intruders in her dear home. Intruders having their way with everything and then the Swastika on the pole, no longer the pure Norwegian flag. And what would his daddy say when he came home, the surgery and his library all now in the crummy annex.

But his concern was above all with his mother. It was she that in her daily routines had to face the intruders. What about her thoughts, how could she bear it? No one to talk with, she had a very small circle of acquaintances.

As the wife of a doctor, she was not quite on the level with women from smaller farms, farm-old ladies were Lars' name to them. When first coming here she had problems with the language and of course the dialects, but that was twenty years back. But maybe she should have made an effort long time ago, inviting the county Justice, the dentist and even the local solicitor, all with their wives for a dinner or something. And now, what now? Expelled from her own home. Start over again for the second time, would she have the strength to that?

FATHER'S HOMECOMING

The war in Finland had come to an end, at least for now. Trygve was due with the train from Stockholm and Lars had made certain that the car was waiting for him there at the Central station, assuming that Trygve would like to drive himself.

There he was his father, standing straight. His great coat over his shoulders and his medicine bag, quite lanky it seemed onto his right hand. But there was something strange about him. For sure he had become quite elderly during these 6 months, but what was he hiding under his great coat? Lars sneak-peeked and saw that there was no right arm from the elbow down, just a lump with heavy bandages.

"I have been very fortunate my boy, fortunate to be back in one piece. Yes, I shall have a prothesis in due time, but no way I shall drive today, I leave it to you my son".

They embraced and then the question: "How are they faring back at the farm? Have you started the spring chores as yet?" He had to tell him, or should he wait? But Trygve instantly knew that Lars was holding back. At last, he had to come out with it: "We have visit from Jens Nazi Jens and his guests". Puzzled now; "what is it all about Lars?" "Our home is now HQ for the German division, so we live in the annex. Colonel Klepka has moved in with his staff. Yes, Nazi Jens had all by himself found out that with only mother and my sister living in that big house, then it would be very suitable to the head of the division". "And Mammy then, my dearest Sarah, she has not written one single word about all this. How does she cope? Does she cry a lot?" "I do not know Dad, at least not during the day, I think. At daytime she is eager to have things work out like in previous times, but when I am home from university and stay the night, then I can hear her walking the stairway, as a rule in the middle of the night. Yes, I have seen her face tear-wet many times. But no way will she talk about it, she just wants a comforting hug.

But she has lost a lot of weight now, at least five kilos less she is than when you left. Seems to me she eats very little and no doubt she often skips dinner. Now that you are back Dad, I think you should treat her as a regular patient". "Meaning what son?" "Well maybe you should treat her like any maigre woman from a farm in the county?" "Stop it Lars, she is your mother and my wife, please don't talk about her like that!" "Sorry Dad, I only wanted the best for her, and she needs care, your care Dad".

Trygve deliberately changed subject. He was not up to all this. Maybe he should not have left for Finland at all? "Now Lars, this should be the revenge from Nazi Jens all this?" "Because he couldn't have Eva?" Lars looked at him. "You think it is that simple Dad, just telling the Germans that he knew of a grand farm, almost inhibited, waiting for them up at Hedmark, far off the high roads?"

"Lars to the Germans this is not far off the high roads. No way, it is no more than half an hour's drive to Hamar. The Germans are used to vast distances, thinking miles(10kms) where we talk kms. And I am not talking about Northern Norway, where distances are like one day travel from one community to the other. So, I am sure they were happy for the offer from Nazi Jens". "But Dad, by what right did they have to seize our farm, not to forget you have your surgery there as well?" "This is the right of the strongest Lars. Just like they have seized a lot of buildings in Oslo, now they take my farm and my house. But let there be no doubt, it is obvious that it is Nazi Jens that is behind it all. But as for now it is of vital importance that we refrain from provocations, at least openly".

RAGNHILD, HIS FRAIL SISTER

«Und Wir fahren, gegen Engeland. Und Wir fahren……» «Ragnhild, stop it!" But she just went on little Ragnhild, her birthday April 9th, the very day that the Germans invaded Norway. Her dad, Trygve stood up, had problems holding on to the table with only one hand, the other just an iron hook. "Dearest Ragnhild I command you. Stop!" "Yes, Dad I shall just get the accord right", she then laid down her guitar and looked questionably at her father.

Had she done something wrong? They had gathered round the table in the annex the family together with their hired hands. The way things were done there at the farm. There should be no division between the owners and the hired hands, even now when they no longer had access to the main house, now occupied by the Germans.

There was someone knocking on the door. It was Colonel Von Klepka coming over from the main house. He had heard the young girl, stricken by poliomyelitis playing and singing. "I beg you excuse me Mr. Trygve, excuse for disturbing you all in your nice afternoon gathering. Maybe you will invite me over tomorrow if there still will be entertainment. Maybe you will have another song to us young lady?" Ragnhild that excited when on her way from the shop had met with singing German soldiers, she now sang "Mein Erika".

"I must say that she is a fast learner your daughter Trygve". The colonel saluted and left once the refrain was done. They all fell quiet now. "Go to your room dearest Ragnhild. The two of us need to talk".

15 minutes later she met with her father. Braids and one shoulder lower than the other due to the poliomyelitis so that her dress dragged the floor on one side. She had put away her guitar and was now holding tight to her breasts a worn-out old doll. Had to seek comfort from someone now that she should be scolded by her dad, and she knew well what was coming. Tears already visible at her right eye. Why always her right eye?

"Have I done something wrong my Dad? I was just down at the shop when a group of German soldiers came marching and singing". "Yes, Ragnhild I know how easy you catch things, we all know that. I have now asked the hire hands to forget about your little performance. My dearest Ragnhild, if people were to know that my only daughter is singing German soldiers' songs, then it would not be long before we all would be looked upon as Nazis".

"My dearest Dad, how was I to know?" She limped up to him. Clinched herself to his thighs. Despaired she was, standing there with her clubfoot. "Silly me, I thought you all would applaud to my little performance".

What a beautiful woman she would have been. Ragnhild had her mother's long, straight neck and carried her hair the same way her mother used to have it over there in Karelen, Finland, more than 20 years back. But Ragnhild was never to be a woman, nor should her closest ever see her blossom. Trygve was already deep in sorrow for his only daughter.

His tears were pressing on now, and he had to pull her strongly to his chest so she would not see his face, but she was soon to feel the tears streaming down on her, first to her cheeks, then to her hair.

Maybe the end was near now, maybe the poliomyelitis had spread to her brain? Was he soon to lose his godsent child? The little angel that had been given to them, years after they had given up hope for a second child, he and his Sarah?

KARELEN. LOVE FOR EVER

His dad, the doctor and big farmer one night took him aside. "You and I Lars we need to have a long talk". His mother had given them some looks as they disappeared into the surgery, no doubt she was curious of what the talk was to be about, but no, she did not know it all. She knew that it would be about Karelen, and Finland and memories popped up about that special summer some 20 years back.

It was the summer he had come, her Trygve, come like a storm onto her life, come into her land, the very heart of Karelen.

She, Sarah was engaged to be married to the merchant's son Isaac there in the village. He was one of her own people, both Jews. The wedding was set for two months, as soon as the harvest was over.

But then he has showed himself, Trygve and his fellow students being on an excursion from the university of Leningrad, med-students preparing for going home to Oslo and have their final medical degree, a mere formality according to Trygve. He considered himself already a doctor as good as anyone now.

They had a hired car and were to do Finland. But the car was an old one and they had only made it to Karelen and that was it. It was mere coincidence that Sarah was the one greeting them welcome in the yard, the others in her family were out in the fields. So was also her snobbish baby sister, always caring for her nails not to be harmed working the fields. But today she had no choice, her father had been ever so determined. "And what about your eye stone Sarah, she will be exempted today?"

No answer from her dad and they were off. The deal was clear, Sarah was to do housework today. But her baby sister yawned and stuck out her tongue when they left. Sarah only waved them goodbye. She was soon to grow up, her sister as well.

The old Ford was giving all types of bad sounds as it slowly advanced on to the yard and when the driver opened the hood, smoke and damp was off to the skye. The two others came out of the wreck, tapped a thank you to the one driver and then they had a big laugh all the three of them.

But one of the guys soon stopped laughing, turned towards Sarah and got really close to her. In fact, if he got closer, she would have had to back into the rosebud behind her. But then he stopped, off with the caps and he looked somewhat embarrassed there in his white linen pants, light blue sweater, scarf to the neck, blonde hair and those eyes! My God what a beautiful boy! "But Sarah, do remember you are engaged to be married!" It was her baby sister coming back from the fields, some lofty excuse to avoid the work in the fields.

But neither of the two heard her outcry. Was not apt to listen. "I shall tell dad about it all!" But none of them took notice. "I am Trygve", he introduced himself. But she did not get it, no knowledge in English. But no matter, she was like in trance, when he gave her his hand and once again said: "I am Trygve." Only one word came from her lips: "Sarah". Her voice like suddenly she had gotten a bad cold.

The fellow students clapped their hands wildly, but the baby sister kept saying: "I shall tell my dad", and off she ran to the fields.

Did Sarah know anything at all about this boy? Did she know that he was an experienced farmer, heir to one of the largest farms in Norway. And he, what about him? A face drowned in sorrow the third night when she told him that she was spoken for and to be married within the next two months. "But can you not let your baby sister take over so to speak, I mean let her marry this rich merchant's son?" He had said this half laughing, half crying, his head way down into her linnet. This was what she had fallen for, his ability to laugh it off even when dire questions like this. But this time she felt it was not a joke. "Trygve get rid of your hands, and don't you forget I am a Jew and you a protestant".

Then suddenly Trygve got serious as well. "Your people have throughout the ages been denied entry to Norway, not at all welcomed. So, Sarah do never ever tell anyone, least my friends here that you are a Jew!"

But he could not avoid the question a few nights later when they were fleeing across the Russian border, Sarah with them. "All others on the farm are Jewish, she not, as she was once adapted". His two comrades looked questionably at him, and they looked at Sarah. "Is this true Sarah? It has to be, has it not? Or you could not have joined up with Trygve and get married to him back in Leningrad?" A silent nod from her. The two and Trygve looked at each other. Well, yes, they had to trust Trygve and his bride to be. Trygve would never have deceived his friends. "Welcome then, welcome to your new home country". She smiled bravely to them, and they embraced. "I love you my new brothers".

"My poor dad and mommy", she had eloped without saying goodbye to them. Her baby sister no doubt was super happy to take Sarah's place and marry Isaac the rich son of the village merchant.

The wedding was a simple one. Sarah had gotten money from Trygve to buy her bridal dress and the ceremony was executed by a commissar having the necessary authority. Document just as plain, only confirming that they were married, in Russian. But it was as good a wedding certificate as any. It was a mere three years after the revolution, so everything was simple there in Russia.

"We will do it over and again in our proper church at Stange", Trygve consoled her. And the night of the wedding and the train ride home to Norway, now to be her new home? She did not remember much of it, but she cried whenever she stroked the three sheets from her father's Torah. Would she be forgiven by her father when he found missing the three essential leaves from the great book? Would he then understand that she had not left her religion and her faith once she had this part of the wholy book with her? She knew of course that her father would find copies of the missing pages and replace them in his Torah, still it would not be the same as the original pages that belonged to the book, this book that had been in the family for generations. In her heart she knew that he would forever love her not giving up her faith. But how was she to hide her true identity for the rest of her life?

But she had made her choice. She had chosen her Trygve. But maybe, once they had children together, then maybe Trygve would let her come out and worship her faith? There had to be other Jews in this her new country and maybe there even would be a synagogue where she could come and pray?

Right so, but there would be a new era, new times, where Jews would die for their blood.

THE SECOND BOOK,

LARS'S ROAD TO GERMANY AND DIVISION GROSS DEUTSCHLAND

THE HIPPODROME

Thursday June 30th 1941. Lars had just sneaked out from campus, skipped a lecture on his favorite subject: Gastro. Precisely this morning the lecture was given by Professor Heiberg, his specialty, twist of a bowel. Would his absence be noted? Of course, it would be. Would his fellow students be questioned about him? Evidently. And what about the Nazi-controller at the university? Would he denounce Lars? It had been necessary to tell the guy that Lars was off to the Hippodrome to enlist. But would he keep it shut this guy?

And what would happen to the two fellow students, Terje and Loke, sharing flat with him if this got public, that Lars had joined the Nazi party? Of course, he would be labelled Nazi if he went to hear Himmler's speech at the Hippodrome. Not to forget this Quisling, the Norwegian Führer.

His fellows would call him a traitor to his country, and he would be asked to leave the apartment on the double. Maybe not Loke, following his path like a dog. And what about the university? Would they accept that one of their students openly flagged Nazi, he being one of their smartest students as well?

But the reason to it all was quite simple: In order to enlist to fight it was compulsory to be a member of the party. Lars was convinced about this and so was his roommate Loke. Lars was going to enlist, not to support Hitler, but to get to the front and fight the Russians, having now conquered his mother's land, Karelen in Finland. It was as simple as that, however conflicting.

Hefty discussions as well at the student's pub as in their shared flat. All five in their colloquy group had their meetings in their flat, plenty space there. None of the five were excessive drinkers, but Terje, the one from Oslo west with easy access to his father's dentist liquor, he could be heavy on the booze.

And the others in the group they were jealous on him, not because of his easy access to liquor, that as well and it benefitted them all. But Terje was handsome, really handsome and women fell easily on him. Terje was to take time off from the med-studies and become a fighter pilot. "In Germany?", Loke had asked provokingly. But it was not taken as a provocation. Terjes' brother had been shot in the battle of Jøssingfjord and they were all convinced that it was from an English bullet. This might tip the balance to choose Germany over England. His brother Yngve had only been at the wrong place, at the wrong time.

He was on a stroll with his fiancée from Ånefjord, near by the Jøssingfjord. They had become curious as to what was going on, was it a real battle between Germans and the English? So, they descended right down to the fjord and then they got caught in the crossfire. His fiancée died immediately, while Yngve was brought to surgery at the Ullevål hospital. Staying there for months, but in the end all hope was gone, punctured lung.

Terje was adamant that this murder on a civilian should not be forgiven and these murders of his brother and sister-in-law to be, beautiful Maren, should be revenged.

"Ideological Terje, you did hate Germany for their march into Poland. That was an unacceptable provocation to you. And what about the Bolsheviks conquering of my mother's land Karelen in Finland? And now England, murderers of your brother and his fiancée? Could you see yourself on the English side, this England now even supporting Stalin? This murderer that just overrun Poland as soon as his ambassador left the meeting with Hitler?"

Terje looked dismissingly at his fellow students. This was the night when he learned about the final of his brother there at the hospital, so they stopped arguing. Two bottles of booze later, they decided on wishing good night. Lars heard the clacker of a door in the night. It was Vera coming to Terje and no doubt he needed her this special night.

Terje did not show up at the lecture the next morning, nor did Lars and Loke. But Terje came in the evening to say his goodbyes. Anyone who would like to join were welcome with him over to Vestlandet (The west country). To Fosnavåg and the boat waiting for them there to take them over to Shetland (UK). He could not tell them anything more, secretase, background being that only 10 days earlier a denouncer had eliminated a resistance group in Florø. For the party involved, court martial and death to some, the prison camp Grini to others, so no passage for them over the North Sea to Shetland and later military training in Scotland, sadly enough.

But Terje had made his decision. He would never forgive the murder on his dear brother, still no forgiveness to the German invasion in Oslo, however peaceful, more like a parade than occupation, up the main street. It had to be England then and further off to Little Norway in Canada for training as a fighter pilot. Understandable, but still foolish was Lokes verdict. "This is a battle that the Brits are bound to lose. It will only be a matter of days till it is over".

Terje searched for arguments to back his choice. "Don't you forget that England is now the protector of our king and our government". But Loke was on the offensive now. "Terje, our dearest friend and fellow student, why should you leave us to protect our government, a government that did not wish to stay and defend us against the Germans. They did not even call for a mobilization of our troops. Where is your logique. And now you are leaving to join up with the English, those who shot your brother and your sister-in-law to be? And this king of ours, nothing wrong to him. He has just gone home to his family over there". Loke had himself a big laugh now. "Why should we have this so-called monarchy and with a former Danish prince as our king? He does not even speak our proper language. Why could we not have elected ourselves a president like in the States. And do you find the monarchy more unifying than having a president? Our flag, that is what is important to us, the only sacred symbol, something to rally round".

Loke was adamant on this. But this last night together was not the night for hefty discussions between the great orators Loke and Terje. He had lost his brother. Terje did not even want to participate in the funeral. In Terjes world, his brother had been dead ever since Jøssingfjord. He had been in coma most of the time thereafter. During one of his bright moments, Terje had managed to reach out to him telling him he was soon to leave for England to become a fighter pilot.

Terje had made his decision, and if he were reluctant to fight as part of an English force, no worries, USA would soon be involved and there he could join up, once he had his pilot certificate in place. His mother was an American so no problem with dual citizenship.

No more discussions that evening, Vera soon came to visit, and they were all crying a bit following the bottles being emptied.

"What about me then boys if you all leave?" "You will manage Vera, only one fault to you!". Terje suddenly awake; "what the hell is wrong with

Vera Loke?" "Just relax Terje, I was just quoting Gaute from our colloquy group". "And what did he have to say about my Vera?" Terje was really pissed off now.

"Well, Vera would be the sexbombe of the ages, with a blonde wig!" "Meaning what Loke?" The atmosphere had become really amply by now and Vera, in ultrashort shorts, pumps, and deep, deep neckline had stood up ready to fist Loke if Terje did not do it.

Lars opted for peace: "Vera don't you listen to all this shit, but to be honest you are even more beautiful when you are angry". But no go, Terje asked Loke to come outside.

But Loke just sat there with a sheepish smile, sort of. "Gaute meant that all sexbombes have to be blondies. Fake or not." "And then you had to hang on to that Loke?" "Vera is by far more beautiful than all other chicks that I know of. Go get yourself a blondie you Loke". "I got one already as you know well". Quite so, he had his nurse from the Hospital, but she was by far no sexbombe.

What was the background to these arguments Lars wondered. Was it all about the evening that Loke had rejected Vera? The one night when they were both ever so loaded, there in Lokes bed? Must have been two years back. They had both kept shut about the episode and that was just what it was, an episode to be forgotten and thanks Loke to that. She had been ready for it. Rather loaded and in rage for Terje's flirting with a cheap blondie at the students pub. Vero and Loke had then just left, she in rage over Terje. Soon after they were both naked there in Lokes bed. But Loke could not get his penis up. She suggested to suck it, to his irritation. She had turned mad, help yourself then and he had tried masturbating himself, to no success. In a minute she had been fully dressed and was on her way out when she dumped into Terje coming home up the street, apparently quite drunk.

Maybe Loke was homo at the time, and would it pass? Just by pressing a button? Just like that?

They had all calmed down now, emptying the last bottles from Terjes stock, two bottles he had forgotten about, coming handy this evening. How were they to get new supplies, now he leaving for UK? "Do you want for me to talk to my dad about new supplies?" Loke and Lars looked at each other. They would not be in need as they had decided to sign up both of them, but on the other side, with the Germans.

Vera tried to ease the mood with a question: "Are you both considering joining up with Terje as well, best pals and all?" The look on Terjes face was all sorrow, no doubt he felt they would be on different sides in this war. Loke chose to shut it. But one of them had to say something. Lars could not let go.

"Vera, for me this is exceedingly difficult. I am soon to leave as well. But I cannot join up with friends of Stalin, you get that don't you? Half my mother's family has already been killed by Stalin's invasion and it is going to get worse according to my father and his reports from the front".

"But must you at all leave to go somewhere Lars. Why not just pass your exams, stay at the farm, take care of the surgery, the farm and not least your mother?"

"I cannot just stay here and see my mother crumbling every day she receives another letter telling her that one more of her relatives have been killed. And beware, soon there will be no more relatives to write letters, that is if no one here stands up against the Russians".

"Then what about you Loke?" "I think about the Russians as well and not to forget about Finnmark. It might be just a matter of weeks until they invade Finnmark, our land Vera".

"But Loke, will not the Russians give Finnmark back to us once this war is over, a war that the Germans are bound to lose?" "It is good of you Vera to have such positive thoughts, but please keep them to yourself or you will soon end up at Grini Concentration camp for starters".

Terje had been quiet for long now, but then he cut in: "Loke has ever so right Vera. Do not talk about your feelings in this war, or you risk being taken at any time. There are plenty of denouncers just outside our walls".

"But Loke, how do you see the defense of Finnmark?" Vera was not quite done as yet. "Are you considering joining up with the Germans. Then we will all be enemies". She started crying now. She was one of us, had been coming and going to our flat over the three last years now. "Maybe it will be just like that Vera, Terje will be back trying to bomb us and we, Lars and I will do our utmost to shoot him down".

"I am glad I shall soon be a certified nurse, then I shall nourish all, irrespective of the side they may have chosen. But are you really to leave you as well Loke? And have you chosen side? At last?" "You can come with me Loke, I am ready for you". Terje still had a faint hope that at least one of the small group would go with him. "And what about you Lars, Vestlandet, then Scotland, Canada and training at the pilot school, Little Norway?"

"The war in Europe is not my war Terje. My war will be for my mother's land, Karelen in Finland". He felt sure about it now, wanted to leave soonest. "But this means Lars that you will join the German military forces and when England and Soviet fight together in the war against Hitler, then you and I will be enemies. You and Loke against me. OMG we are after all from the same med-class the three of us. Been friends for more than 5 years, shared everything, even girls at times".

It was all quiet now, slowly the impact of Terjes speech got to them all. Terje was of course loaded, still this was the moment of truth. So little or so much was all it would take to split a close friendship.

It took him hard this Lars, and throughout the night he had only one wish, yes that this evening should finish without violence between them.

"This is our last night boys. Just us boys together. Maybe in a couple of years I shall be back bombing you both to pieces".

"I am going to Karelen Terje, to fight the Bolsheviks, not Berlin or Paris for that matter. And as at now it seems like Germany is winning on all fronts".

"But you just wait Lars. Soon USA will join England in this war. USA will never accept England to be invaded and then it is done for with Germany".

"I do not say that you are wrong Terje, but please see that as for me I have no choice. It is my mother's kins that are fighting over there and even my father has been there fighting". "Yes, and returning home one arm short". Terje regretted his outburst the same very minute. "Beg forgive me Lars". "But Terje, this is what war does to all of us, and none of us have any guarantee for coming out of it alive".

"What about you then Loke?" Terje had not quiet given up getting at least one comrade to come with him. "You Loke. You have no relatives to fight for in Finland, why then this sympathy for Hitler?"

"No, I do not have that much sympathy for him, but I want a military training so I can do my best to defend our country up in Finnmark when the Russians come. And for sure they will come. Stalin looks at this war as a great adventure to get new land: Karelen, the Baltics, Pommern, Finnmark, get control over the Northern areas to the Atlantic".

The two friends looked at each other. "Where have you learned about all this Loke?" "Well, you should know that my elder brother is a researcher in this field and his conclusions are unambiguous".

"No doubt, but he is just one voice. But what about all we others that may have a different view? Maybe it is just Stalin that wants to protect himself from Hitler, Loke?"

Lars could not take no more of this: "Maybe you are right Terje, but this does not count for Finland and Karelen. Then we must talk about a brutal invasion, no less". It was all quiet for a while. Finally, it was Terje again, ever so drunk now: "So, it seems that I shall go alone my friends". None commented. "All right then, let us have the rest of this ass-cleaning alcohol before we all go to bed. When you wake up, I shall be gone!"

Lars and Loke sat next to each other at the Hippodrome. They both had sympathy for Himmler's speech, but they were clear on Quislings speech as well: all to pompous he was this Nazi figure.

This was particularly noted for his repeated reference to Vikings, runes and a national pride. This part of the speech was way over the heads of most of the audience, Lars felt. But many of the younger crowd gave the speech wild applause and were ready for immediate signing up to the Frontkjempere. The name to be the official notation later on.

Loke called it all a show, superbly directed and the atmosphere got close to hysteria when Himmler read the message from der Führer in Berlin, with the closure: "Victory over the Bolsheviks and coward England". Not least the final sentence which should be like a forever mantra: "Deutschland siegt am allen Fronten, Germany wins at all fronts". The threat against Finnmark was of course highlighted. Likewise, that all and everyone now joining up, they would be the core in the new Norwegian division with the Norwegian flag on their uniform's shoulders. Later when the war was over and Germany was the victorious part, then these young ones would be the core of the new Independent Norwegian Army. Away with the cowardly Norwegian officer-corps and the even more cowardly government of the broken rifle. Now hiding in England, leaving their people at will.

Quisling speech had made an enormous impression, especially on the young ones in the audience, many of them picturing themselves parading the main street behind the Norwegian flag once the war was over.

The young ones, some barely sixteen, many of them out of work or sons from smaller farms, they were all more or less in euphoria in their admiration. For sure they had listened to Quisling on the radio, but now hi standing here in front of them together with German officers in impeccable uniforms, talking about these Youngs as they were the ones to take responsibility for the future of Norway, was awesome. Could anything be greater than to serve this man and their country?

Lars felt the impact of the performance on the audience, but to him it meant nothing. All that mattered to him now was to get registered as a Frontkjemper, thus get his training, get to Karelen and fight the Russian soldiers. He totally recognized that should he stand a chance against the

Russian machinery, then he needed top training and be the best amongst his fellow soldiers.

But what about Loke, what was the driving force behind his enlisting, Lars wondered. Was it mere ideology or his close connection, say dependency to his best friend Lars? He often felt Loke to close and even if they were sharing flat, Lars was not always happy for Lokes approach, especially while in the bathroom, by Lars considered a sacred place, a place to be on once own. But every so often this did not coincide with Lokes wishes, more so when Lars had to tell him to stay out. Eva had on occasions mentioned that Loke seemed to be interested in boys more than girls. In fact, she meant interested in Lars. But he had just told her this was nonsense, only some fantasy on her behalf. But there were times, especially when Loke offered to rub his back after a runner, then he had felt some discomfort, more so after Eva's remarks.

He pushed the thoughts away. All great now that the two from medschool were to enlist together. Loke had not twinkled for a moment once Lars had told him about his decision.

But what about the people back home? Not least Eva's father now in charge of a secret resistance group, according to rumors. Eva's lips were sealed and so were his dad Trygve's? Well as a doctor he could not comment on his clients, not even to his son.

Terje had left now, and this was the day when they should go down Kirkegt. and do their formal enlisting. "What about your folks Loke? Have you got yourself into trouble now?" "Just leave it be Lars, my brother and I have of course had hefty discussions. I shall send a letter to my parents, inform them sort of. My brothers already consider me an enemy, now that I am going to enlist. But I have to do what I believe in".

Lars felt some discomfort. Did Loke join up only because now he could have Lars all to himself, no Eva around?

Once the papers were signed there were quite a few things to sort out. We cannot go back to the Uni Loke. We will have to mail them, yes separately. Our reason for enlisting differs a lot as you know. Whatever, we will never be excused by our fellow students for our action. Terje on the other hand is already considered a real hero.

I shall go home as soon as all the paperwork is done with, yes home to Eva, yeah and mom and dad. I fear that my father is leaving again". "Do you mean he shall be leaving for Finland once more?" "Yes, to Finland, as a doctor, he can be of great service even with one arm only".

"Do you want me to come with you Lars?" Right there he felt quite strongly this discomfort once more. Loke should of course have realized that he had no business back on the farm when Lars and Eva were to say their goodbyes. "No, no you stay here Loke, settle the business with the flat, but under no circumstances should you dare go to the Uni. Just stay in the flat and wait for my return".

He was getting short of time now, but Loke would not let go: "Did you know Lars that well into the thirties the royal family expressed great sympathy for the new Nazi Germany?" "Have you been dreaming sort of Loke, this must be pure propaganda?"

"No Lars, you know the Swedish people in many ways sympathizes with Germany, at least those in the industry. And this Gøring, he himself has close relations to Sweden. Not all that strange if the Swedish royals lean towards Germany, and then the Norwegian monarchy might have sympathies as well. You know our crown princess; she is a princess of Sweden's royal family".

"I did not know about all this, really Loke, but our King, Kong Haakon has definitely chosen England, let there be no doubt about it". "Pity for us and no doubt for him if England should loose, seems likely now". "But Loke I must be off to the train". "Not that busy Lars, you know I cannot talk with anyone else about these matters". "Be quick then, the train does not wait for a poor student. And if I miss this train, I may have to use the bicycle all the way home to Eva". I am sure you would, Loke uttered to himself. Have you not said enough goodbyes already. But he kept these thoughts to himself and then: "Did you know that Himmler, not Hitler, being an atheist or something, Himmler has given us another good reason to get rid of all the Jews". "No, I did not, come with it, but fast Loke I gotta run now". "Well, it was the Jews that killed Jesus. Ok, Roman soldiers and this chief Pontius Pilatus helped as well. But just as they had Johannes, the baptizer prisoned and later murdered, the same path they followed murdering our Jesus. And for this they shall forever be punished according to Himmler". "When did he turned that religious and Quisling never mentioned any of this Loke". "Maybe not as we have heard, but many Christians among the authorities, police and other official say right out that on this background it is ok to hunt down the Jews!"

Quite obvious that this wasn't something Loke had sucked from his own breast so to speak. It clearly was mere propaganda. "Not big news this Loke, it is all in the bible. It was a high priest or similar that got rid of Johannes and later Jesus, although with great help from the Romans".

"So, you agree then Lars that is ok to hunt down the Jews? If it were not for Henrik Wergeland and his continuous fight for them, Jews would never have been admitted to Norway". "Loke this an absurd topic to discuss right now, purely academic and I on my part I am on to Germany to be trained to get the Russians out of Karelen. You likewise, to be trained to defend our Finnmark when the Bolshevik hordes come to overpower us. We should leave the Jews to the Germans, we have bigger fish to catch, have we not Loke!" "But what about the Jews here in Norway then Lars, should we just let them have their way?" Lars felt that enough was enough, he was almost on the breaking point now. "Loke, what about our two fellow students, Benjamin and, in his excitement, he had forgotten the name of the other one. Does it seem to you Loke that these two fellows are always having it their way and Loke, whatever, I leave now, right now, take care!"

Loke followed him with his eyes for some hundred meters. Strange that Lars was that liberal or rather indifferent towards these bloody Jews. But maybe best to shut it until Camp Sennheim. For sure Lars would be lectioned there as well.

AND WHO IS LOKE?

Loke was the hobo of the three classmates. Maybe the most intelligent of the three, but also the one that ever so often did not give a damn about the studies.

Snobbish western Oslo-boy, he had hanged on to Lars from day one. In the beginning Lars had felt flattered, he that come from rural farm district-background, Terjes favorite expression.

Loke had roots from farmers himself, from Telemark actually and he was prouder to that than to his snobbish family there at Frogner and he often made a point of that especially towards his elder brother. And every so often he liked to put Terje in place, when he talked about Lars, the farm boy as he put it.

"You know Terje, and you really should give it a good thinker: If people in general did not have caries, then your posh dad would live in the gutter begging for food, and you had been some kid from a foster home. No white sweater with KNS on the front". (Royal Norwegian Yacht club)

But in spite of their differences, they liked to hang out the three of them and when Lars said he was looking for a small place to live, then Terje was on to him on the double. "What we need is a flat for all three. What about a celebration, I have one on hand till this evening. Let us just take that one".

Lars considered himself a guy not that tidy, but when he looked into Lokes room, he was shocked, no way space for two, hardly for one. But why all these clothes, Loke hardly put on other clothes than his black corduroy, yellow shirt and a scarf. He really looked like a gypsy and was content with that.

Now, Loke declared that he had enlisted to fight for Finnmark much to the mischief of his elder brother laughing out aloud. "Just you go for it Loke. Go there and have a good look, Lapp sledge and reindeer, something for you snobbish Frogner boy!"

Loke had never visited Finnmark; hardly knew how to get there. Some told him the shortest and best way was to travel via Sweden and why on earth should one go to Finnmark in the first place, this outpost towards The Bering Sea, Arctic north of Norway. If the Russian were interested, then let them have it.

Not only Finnmark. Let them have all the land south to Finnsnes, no doubt interesting for strategic reasons plus access to the superb hiding places for submarines in the deep fjords up there.

But still it was part of Norway and what would come next if one let Finnmark go to the Russians? Next then might be Svalbard and Bjørnøya. And finally, what about the rest of the people living up North and the fortresses that had been secured there for hundreds of years?

But his brother made a point of the Russians strategic interest and one more time started his lecture about Karelen, the Baltics and then northern Norway as the gem to the admirals. These provinces and Pommern was there to be taken by the Russians.

"Now what about you Loke?" His elder brother was on to him again under the latest parental dinner there in Frederic Stangs gt. the most super posh of all Frogner. "If you really want to enlist and go fight for the freedom of the people up North, which one army would you chose? The Norwegian one? Just pieces left of that one over in the Uk. How about the Yankees if they seriously got into the war? The Finnish army has fallen flat on the face and is totally to the mercy of the Bolsheviks. Well then Loke, no big choice then, just Hitlers army, victorious on all fronts according to their propaganda. But Loke would you really enlist and fight for this sottish Austrian with his mustache? And then follow him in the after tow when he has lost it all?" "Hush Bjørnar!" It was the father that cut in. "The walls have ears all over Bjørnar".

But Bjørnar was not quite finished. "Let the USA get say six months to get their fleet orderly and fit out their weaponry and from there on you may start counting months and weeks till Hitler is doomed. His only chance is if he and his generals brain up and make a safe alliance with Stalin".

But Loke had not listened to Bjørnars lecture at all. "You seem to be totally absentminded Loke". His mother had noticed his face and reckoned that he was all absent from the dinner and Bjørnars speech.

"Eh, what did you say just there Bjørnar, I am afraid I missed out on your last reasoning". "Just stop it, enough now". Their father was utterly clear. "Leave the questions of war, now!"

And Loke had been really absentminded, he had been far away, up at Hedmark, at Lars' farm. Wondering what Lars was doing to Eva right now, or she with him. Were they doing it in the back the two of them? Was she the one to have the pleasure of his big dick right now. Loke had longed for it many times, especially when he had sneak looked at Lars, he being in the shower. Did Lars ever notice him there?

But it was Terje that he had to be careful with. Terje one morning asked him directly if he was gay or not. And Loke then had to laugh it off, heading straight for his girlfriend Randi, she being off duty, and just fucked her there and then. She had been that waiting for longtime now, but Loke had all the time said NO, so she was quite proud when later that evening she came to the flat and declared that Loke now was hers, because now they had slept together. Terje then a bit shameful: "Sorry Loke, how could I be that mistaken".

It was later that Lars invited his two comrades with their girls, to the farm and Eva was super happy for Loke now having his Randi and that they were quite intimate as well. She had to beg her excuse: "Loke I have never seen you with a girl before, at times I kept thinking you being gay. So sorry Loke!" And she kissed him right on the mouth, exclaiming "Oh I am so happy for Loke!" The others looked at her, questions in their faces, especially Terje. "What is it all about Eva?" "Silly you, it's about Loke, now with his own girl!" Big lough from everybody, and especially Lars, he seemed to understand nothing of it all.

But Loke knew it was not at all over, in spite of Eva's outburst. No doubt she still had her suspicions. But Randi was over herself: "Maybe we can have a triple wedding as soon as this stupid war is over!"

It was all quiet among the boys as the girls went to change for dinner. "She came out of the blue this girl of yours Loke, did she not?" But Loke was well prepared. "Randi and I have been intimate for almost 3 years now Terje. But some of us are quieter about things. Not all of us have your way with the girls and what might have happened if I invited her to our flat? Would you have had a go at her, you could not have resisted, could you?"

Lars felt that this was it, there was a limit to everything even amongst friends. "You are pushing this quite far now Loke, somewhat out of proportion not so?" "Yea, and I am sorry". His excuse was there in split seconds, maybe too fast this one?

Terje and Vera had to leave early next morning, Randi and Eva made a stroll up to Øvre, making time for a close conversation between the two friends. They went for a long walk and when they turned back – it had been awkwardly quiet for a while, then Lars felt he had to put the question to his friend: "Are you bisexual Loke?" Lars red-faced now. "It is of course none of my business, but I was just curious from a medical point of view".

"And if so Lars, if I was keen on both girls and boys, would it really matter to our friendship?"

"I deserved that one Loke. Of course, it would not matter". But he lied and knew well that he had to do just that. No way, he had not noticed Lokes glances at him when he was just in his boxer or totally nude. But he could not quite cope with this, that maybe his best friend possibly was bisexual. Were they just best friends or was Loke in love with him? He had of course noticed that Loke at times had a strong erection, but that was the case to himself as well. All young boys had it like that.

The lectures on homosexuality and disruptors of chromosomes had been scarce at the university, more or less with reference only to the old-time Greeks.

But the professor had said something about both sexes might have what he called a 'Problems of orientation' in their teens, but this would go with age. So, all hetero then? But the professor had declined further questions.

Lars felt it became difficult to smalltalk after this, luckily the girls were soon back. The chatting during the night took the sting out of it, but finally Randi felt for asking if something was wrong, the boys being awfully quiet. "No, my dear Randi, nothing to it, it was just Lars questioning if I was gay or something". "Can you please stop it you guys or am I to give you intimate details from our latest intercourse?" Randi had stood up, Lars flushed, and Eva laughed. "So, there you got one right on your nose my Lars, but please don't give intimate details about us then".

It passed, however slowly, and Lars was happy that Loke did not stay till Monday but took the late Sunday train together with his Randi.

Damn it, Loke his best friend, why the devil did he had to come out with this, their private conversation! But could he trust Loke thereafter? Was it his attraction to Lars that made him enlist at the same time as Lars?

Randi was quite absentminded on the train back to Oslo. "Are you ok Randi? Did we not have a great trip to Hedmark?" "Yes of course we did Loke"; she gave him a mischievous smile. "I am just that happy we managed to sneak out to the barn and made love there in the hay, even if it stinged a bit on my ass." "Yes, it was wonderful Randi". But did he really mean it, and should she dare ask the question? "Would it be just as good with Lars Loke, be honest to me now!" "Lars isn't gay, not even bi and I, what am I Randi?" "But Loke, let us assume that Lars was keen, and you had fucked him in the ass and he you as well and you had then come with an outcry that could have waken one and everyone on both farms? And why didn't you scream when you came last night?" "I wanted to, but I feared someone might hear me dear." "But Loke, when you took me from behind, did you then think about Lars' white ass my darling?" "How do you know it might be white? Have you looked at him that closely in the shower or?" "No silly, but all boys have white asses, don't they?" She gave him her most innocent blue eyes.

"By the way, I never looked at your ass Loke, not so that I would remember it in this context. Is it white dear? Shall we sneak into the toilet here and have a peek? Just look you know?" "Stop it Randi, there is nothing more disgusting than the toilets on a train!" "Well, yes there is: another train toilet".

Finally at the main station in Oslo, "do you have the flat by yourself tonight Loke?" "I do not know really, maybe Terje and Vera are having a ball. Do you fancy group-sex Randi?" "Stop it then. And tonight, you cannot come to my flat, my cohab Siri is for sure off duty now". Did she feel a sigh of relief? "And what about tomorrow, will Siri be there?" "Not quite sure, but I think so Loke. Maybe we should venture a trip to one of the islands?" "Listen Randi, why don't I come by your flat, say sixish?" Thus, he bought himself some more time.

Whenever needing an alibi, Randi was super and he loved taking her from behind, fancying that it was Lars's ass glowing invitingly to him, except for the bikini lining being more into her bottom than with Lars. He had seen that much from the shower. Still, it was ok to dream, was it not?

Terje and Vera were out, so he was there alone with his dream! But up Hedmark it was a silent couple sharing a bottle of wine. "What is it Lars, please tell me, is something wrong between us dear?" "No sweetheart it is only this war getting so close to us. Come let us go upstairs. I need to have you close to me tonight". "But what about Trygve, your dad?" "Now Eva, this one is for you, and I do know the name of my dad!"

The mood got redemptive, for a while. But once he had kissed Eva goodnight there on her landing, then all thoughts about Loke came to him. Was it right to avoid an open confrontation with Loke? He was certain now. Dead certain. All this wishy wassy about Finnmark, maybe realistic enough. But that Loke was to enlist because of the approaching war and Finnmark? No credibility at all. So, then there could be only one reason: Loke wanted to be close to Lars, as friend or as his lover, maybe both. And what if Loke was wounded, more so killed? Was he Lars too feel guilty and should he be just that, Loke enlisting solely because of his attraction to Lars?

LARS COMES OF AGE

The celebration of this special day, his 21st birthday was shadowed by the war, the Finnish one. As Trygve had not yet returned from Finland, there would be no celebration. Better wait till his 22nd birthday, make it like one extra day coming of age.

Lars had wondered for quite some time, what was so special of finally being 21 years. But soon there would be revelations far more important to his young life than just another birthday. His father had told him long time ago about his studies in Leningrad and the voyage home via Karelen, Finland. He was done with his final exams, except more final formalities back in Oslo, so together with two fellow med-students they had decided to visit Finland from Leningrad. So, this was not at all news to Lars. What was to come then?

It was not that much his father had told him about Leningrad, the revolution, the murders and the purge of dissidents, so-called. The city was more or less closed to foreigners, so apart from the University the three med-students hadn't seen much. But Trygve had been over himself, when talking about Karelen, the Jewel of Finland, with its rich farmland and above all the beauty of their women.

But it was not his 22nd birthday as such that he came to remember for the rest of his life. Not because it happened to be on a Sunday, free of daily chores, but because this very day should change his entire life.

They were sitting there together, his father and Lars's beautiful mother. And she was a beauty, with her golden, almost sad skin. Maybe the skin wasn't at all sad, but could appear like that because her eyes, always radiant her eyes, they overshadowed everything.

"Mother has decided to tell you about her childhood in the beautiful Karelen, her motherland. What you are to learn now Lars, you must keep it in your heart and never, never ever reveal it to anybody". And he had sworn to it, not only on the Bible. But his mother had shown him some yellowish pages with different writing on. He had no idea what the text was about, but he knew it was in Hebrew. "You have to swear on these pages as well my son". Why should he do just that. What secret were they to confide to him?

"We have been uncertain whether it would be right to impose on you what you are now to learn, even you have just sworn. But we have concluded that we have no right to keep this a secret to you, now that you are of age.

Try imagining your mother there in Karelen as an 18 year, sitting in a flower field down by the lake. Picture yourself as a fresh med- student that after three days visit to her family were to leave her forever. She is being engaged to a super-rich merchant's

son in the nearby village, ten years her age and a Jew. Did she love him? No, but she was given to him.

That day down by the lake she denounced her faith and her family, chose me and Norway". "But could you just elope Dad?" "It was not easy, but I succeeded in bribing a Finnish guy to take us back to Leningrad in his boat. A doctor at the hospital got hold of a priest, an orthodox of course and we were married. It was all documented by a Commissar, bribed as well. All necessary papers, a kind of a wedding certificate were issued there in the chaos, and we left for Norway and the farm here".

"But what about your parents and your kins, mother?" "I cried myself into sleep, sent a letter to them and asked for their forgiveness. But I never got any message from them, not even from my baby sister who most probably got married to the rich merchant in my place. But now your father reckons they are all exterminated". "But you are a Jew then mother?" He almost whispered. She could be taken by the Germans and /or the Nazis any time now. "So are you my son and you know the Germans kill all Jews. That is why I now have to burn these pages from my families Torah and no one, no one will ever know about my ethnicity, nor yours my son. Officially I am Finnish and as such you have a Finnish mother". She opened the door to the big stove and the pages were about to disappear in the flames, before she composed herself, crying over once again to denounce her origin and her faith.

Lars's father had been siting quiet during her confession. He now took her hands and kissed them vividly: "I love you my dearest Sarah, now as I once did". Lars left the room quietly. How was he to keep this secret to Eva, to Loke and not least to his German fellow soldiers when the time come?

THE WINTER WARS

His dad had come home from Finland with just a lump where his left arm should have been. It had been cut off right below his elbow. Now, a few months later it looked all ok, until one saw the prothesis with the iron hook instead of fingers.

"Are you to tell us about the war in Finland now Dad? You have kept all silent about it this far". "Well yes let us do just that Lars, get done with it, although done is a wrong expression as now the second round of this war is raging. It is now we have the real winter war, favorite expression among the Finns".

"You sound that excited Dad, are you planning to go back there, only one good arm and all?" His dad acted like he was already back in the war. "But didn't mother tell you Lars, and what is wrong with only one good arm as you put it? I work just as well with my right arm and the hook serves me well when needed. No longer sleezy fingers losing their grip in wounded bodies. No probs getting a good holding". His mother was in tears now. "Yea, I shall stop it my dear girl".

His father adjusted his prothesis sort of. "I shall spare you to the details, still some knowledge about your mother land and what happened to the family over there will be good for you". He counted on their interest and continued: "This new war started with the Finns taking back your mothers land, in fact most of Karelen, and the survivors returned to their land, their dearest Karelen. But after the counterattacks from the Bolsheviks, the casualties were enormous and there were many wounded as well. The lack of field-medics led to indescribable sufferings".

"But Dad, how did you come to know all this?" Well, you know we doctors have colleagues even abroad, doctors I got to know during the first Finnish war. Now they beg for me to come back, even knowing that I have only this claw on my left arm, so in short, I could not resist. They have agreed to keep me posted and the colonel here in the main house, well we are more or less on the same side when it comes to Finland, so he keeps me informed about the developments.

But listen closely now: The other powers are now on the scene with England supporting Stalin, thus declaring war on Finland. It was then that I realized that the outcome would be a simple one: the Finns would lose all that they had reconquered in the first round. But the Finns were not opted to admit this and now the demand for field-medics got really crucial. So, I felt that I no longer had a choice, but get back to the front.

Stalin is struck by hysteria to build a safe zone round his Leningrad, so that the city would never be conquered. And just you wait, the punishment for the Finns will be gruesome if Germany is not successful in the siege of Leningrad".

"Ok, but when are you leaving Dad?" "It may take months; I shall be notified about when and where. As at now it is all very complicated, much pending whether the Germans will allocate substantial resources to aid the Finns".

So, it was all mapped up to Lars now. Germany had to be the winner if Finland was to prevail as an independent, free nation. Yacta es alia. "Father, I have signed up and I am leaving. Tomorrow!"

Sarah had been sitting quietly under her husband's orientation, some sighs was all she mustered. She was no doubt wondering if any of her kinfolks at all were alive. Now she pulled her great scarf closely to her head and hurried out the door. What if she was going to lose them both, father and son?

THE GOOD-BYES

"Quisling was on the radio Eva, did you hear his appeal about getting married, have children, children to serve the great German empire?" Her father was enraged. Just think about it, think that this rabble, not only shall he decide over life and death, but more so over who is to live and how the children shall live".

"Mind your heart, Dad!" But she was even more worried for her own heart. This should be the last evening before Lars left and then what about her and the baby, well if she was at all pregnant then? She did not have her monthly last week. But maybe it was all about nerves. Nerves and worries for her sweetheart who was leaving for the war. Her best friend Marte, safely engaged now with her Ola further down the county, she had maintained that one week's delay, that could be just natural. And had they not been precautious? Just forget it all, was all she responded to Marte.

But this night, four weeks back, when Lars had told her that now it was decided and he had gotten the exact date for the departure, then they had clinched to each other more than ever there in the barn.

It was final and none of them were in control, she knew that now. Why the barn? Dad was away somewhere, and no one had cared if they had been together up at her farm.

Her monthly, well if her mother had been alive, then they could have talked it over, woman to woman, if she had dared to. She had lost her mother from one day to the other. Heart failure according to the doctor. Now what if she really was pregnant? Would her father, once he knew it was Lars, would he insist on them getting married before Lars left for Germany? Her mother would never have kept it secret. And what about herself, would she have said YES there in the parish church? Yes, to the boy she loved and who were to leave her tomorrow morning? Leaving her then to die in this meaningless war, but then the child would have a father at least, written in the church annuals. Not as of now, just a changeling born outside marriage.

Would dad ever forgive her? Would the child be a lawful heir to the farm? And if Lars was killed in this war, never to come home and she got married to someone else? Would this new man take the child as his own or would it be a changeling with no heritage rights? What if the child would be a girl and she later got a son with her new man, a boy that would automatically inherit the farm. The new man? There would never be a new man to her. She had sworn everlasting faithfulness to Lars and that is how it was to be, no question to it.

She was close to crying now, but she had to be strong for Lars and more so for her dad. But she could not get rid of her anxious thoughts. Maybe they should have been married privately at the priest's house tonight. Both dads could have been witnesses. But what about formal announcement? Did the law require a formal announcement fourteen days before the wedding, yes in the church? If not, maybe this marriage would have been declared invalid?

But she could just as well leave with Lars and then get married in Germany, possibly at the embassy. But maybe the regular ambassador had been summoned home now or had taken his leave and now there would be a Nazi ambassador. Would that marriage, effected by him be legal after the war, if Germany were to lose?

There were many thoughts, maybe too many. She stroked her tummy, maybe she wasn't even pregnant. Maybe it was just her imagination and such. But what if she really was pregnant and there was a baby already in the making there?

Would she consider abortion? Definitely illegal and if it was to be known, then for sure she would be severely punished. But one of Lars's fellow med-students, this Gaute, he was almost certified as a doctor now, maybe he would help her?

She suddenly remembered what time it was. OMG, they were to meet down by the fence at nine, and it was already half past. What about her Lars, maybe he thought she wouldn't come?

She stumbled down the stair and her father were worried if there was a fire lose or something. Her dear dad, only should he have known. Of course, there was a fire - in her heart. Her cheeks were red when she saw her Lars already deep onto his third cigarette that morning, stubs on the ground.

"What is it with you my Eva, much later than usual and your dress half open, red cheeks and do you come straight from your bed?" Should she reveal it all to him, all her thoughts?

But no, he was all prepared, suitcase packed, first off to Germany for his training and then to Finland to the front to fight the much-hated Russians. Would they ever be happy the two of them if she told him all? His departure at halt and she would be the one to be blamed for being careless there in the barn. And what if it was all false alarm? Would Lars then ever forgive her? No, let him leave, I shall pray for him so he will come home safely.

"Sorry I am this late my dearest; Dad had one of his many enragements over this Quisling and I just couldn't leave him".

Lars contended himself with that and she buttoned her dress, all the way up. "So, so don't rap yourself totally my darling, or maybe I shall forget how beautiful you are". "You mean like naked?" For sure it costed her to say that straight out, but she could not risk for him to ask more questions and she, what if she by chance came to tell him about her absent monthly?

MEETING UP WITH THE RECRUITS AND FAREWELL NORWAY

Loke was already there in the flat when Lars arrived by the evening train. They had hardly been alone since the weekend with the girls and they both felt quite awkward about it now, just the two of them alone. Surprisingly it was Loke who called for an early night, everything packed, and all settled with the land lady, so now all to do in the morning just get into their uniforms and off. Thank heavens there would be no need to hear tales from Loke on the hatred Jews. He felt very uncertain how he would handle that, following his mother's revelations.

The landlady hadn't been overjoyed having rented room to Nazis as she put it, but they were allowed to spend the last night as well for a hefty extra payment. Money talks, always.

They were 182 men, most of them boys in their teens, lining up for Quislings words of departure and where he stressed that they must be prepared to give their lives if it came to that. Give their lives for the new Norway within the great German empire. And he should prove right, more than half of these youngsters later found their graves in the marsh land at Leningrad.

So, then it was off to the city of Holmestrand for physical training and indoctrination in race ideology. It was almost unbearable to Lars to hear the way they talked about his mother and her race. And what about himself, half mud rat to use one of Hitlers favorite expressions, an expression that should be some mantra within the camp. Did he at all look like a Jew? No, he did not. He had his father's looks, tall and blond. Nordic/Arian Himmler would have called it. But it hurt his soul every time hearing the lectures about these wretched Jews. Although it did not matter much to himself. This far he had not managed the transformation of himself from an ordinary Norwegian to now one-half Jew. His thoughts were entirely to his mother, yes it was his mother they talked about, as a mud rat. His mother giving birth to new mud rats at the conception. "We should be thankful that not everyone lives to be normal people. Many of them die as children or later in their teens", said Loke. But what about his dear little sister Ragnhild, she was not normal according to the definition from Quisling and the Germans. Ragnhild was born with poliomyelitis. Poor Mummy and Ragnhild. Lars had to swallow the insults.

Lars was no doubt the only Jew of the recruits. One was not only half-Jew or something as long as one's mother and grandmother were Jews. That is how it was written in the Torah. But Quisling and Hitler may have their own definitions.

Most of the youngsters had poor education, only elementary school, so for Lars and Loke it was imperative not to brag about their education from med-school and thus get classified as Oslo snobs.

There should soon be a confrontation this very first night at the camp there in Holmestrand. Oslo snobs, was the mantra of three rather rough boys from up country Trøndelag.

Lars now had heard enough of it, time to speak out. "Loke and his family come from the rural district of Tuddal in Telemark and my home is on a farm in Hedmark, so maybe for you it is time to stop this whispering about Oslo snobs. Worse than small girls you are". It got quiet for a while. "But why do you both speak Oslo-language, or should I say dialects?" It was the boy from Verdal speaking for the three of them. "When you have been attending med-school for 5 years, then it comes natural to speak the way that the professors can understand you". Loke felt this was going into ridicule now. "But shouldn't you rather use your medical degrees instead of going Frontkjempers as the rest of us?" The Verdal boy just could not let go. "Maybe so, but we have a just cause for enlisting and fight". Soon they were all listening to Lars. "My mother's land in Karelen, Finland has been occupied by the Bolsheviks and can you imagine then, me sitting passive at the Uni in Oslo, just reading the news about the atrocities done by the communists? And more so, it may be that one or more of you would be in need of medical assistance once you are at the front".

OMG, he had almost "tramped in the piano" telling them that he himself was half Jewish. There would not even have been a court martial for him. No, shot on site, having joined up on false premises only to spy on the real Ariens. He better keep it shut in the future.

But the lads from Trøndelag turned out to be a nice crowd wanting to hear more from the front in Finland. "Later boys, I do not think I can take more of this today. I get really pissed, whenever I think about how the Russian terrorize the civilians over in Finland". "But do you think they will let you come to the Finnish front then?" "Yea, they shall set up a new Division Wiking to be sent up to this front. The Finnish people need all they can get of soldiers and materials".

But the one guy from Verdal, quite forward this one: "I am certain that you have to rethink about all this. It is Lars is it not?" Lars just nodded. "I have a brother who is a petty officer, and he has been quite adamant that this new division shall be sent immediately to the front at Leningrad, alternatively sent as support to the Rumanians, fighting at Stalingrad. So, Lars if you want to get to the front in Finland, your chance will be to go there as medic. The rest of us are not likely to go there".

Neither he nor Loke were so happy with this information. "Maybe just fake news", Loke mustered. But even he felt bad about this. "I think we should try to get to Berlin for the final training as field-medics Lars, get our exams instead of being sent to the East front as cannon-fodder". "What is eating you Loke, have you suddenly gone chicken, taking a veering. No lust for fighting?"

Loke flushed. "You know Lars I just wanted to give you support. If we are two of us stressing for Berlin and field-medic training, then it might be easier to have the admission". He tapped lightly on Lars' shoulder. "You know Lars I only want to go to Finland and fight together with you".

For the very first time Lars felt real discomfort by his friend's nearness, so he showed his arm away. Right so, Eva had hinted on Loke being gay or at least bi. Sheer fantasy, he had told her at the time. But what about now, right now? Could it be mere imagination?

"No way we could get away with less than six months at Sennheim, Germany, Loke. Neither you nor I". He pulled himself together, better look ahead and get rid of these thoughts about his friend being homosexual.

"And whatever Loke, it will be useful to learn weaponry and survival under dire situations. And that is what we are to learn at Sennheim". Should he have added something about Lokes overriding mantra: defending Finnmark? No, leave it be for the moment. But neither of them knew what was in the offing there in Sennheim. And what about Berlin and training as field-medics?

They all looked at their stay there in Holmestrand as a complete waste of valuable time, and their earch for getting on to Germany and be close to whichever front got increasingly strong. To some of them, especially this guy from Verdal, thoughts about the front overshadowed everything.

So, he went straight to the commanding officer, presenting his complaint. This was not what he had enlisted for. He wanted to have proper weapons and more so, learn to fight with the same weapons. So far, they had gotten no weapons, just wooden copies, used when training, marching and such. Arnvid was his name, and he even threatened the sergeant to speed up. If not, he would write a letter directly to Quisling. As a minimum he urged for them to have bayonets.

The sergeants took a small group to the side. "I might be shot for telling you all this. Quisling is nothing to this case, he is good at recruiting, but here guys, or comrades, yes, we are comrades, even if I have this degree as sergeant or Oberscharführer as is my degree with the Waffen-SS. Here comrades the Germans are ruling everything, just forget about Quisling!

Norwegian flag onto your shoulder, ok with that and no SS-runes, ok as well. But this is a German unit, and you shall be trained to be German soldiers". "But will there not be a Norwegian division then?" "Well yes, eventually". He felt that he had told them all too much. "Maybe there will be Norwegian petty officers in time, possible also officers leading companies. But do not make yourself illusions. You are and shall be totally under German command".

Monte Rosa, the transport ship left three days later and then they went further on with train from Hamburg and westwards almost to the French border, to Sennheim. Stonehard discipline from 06.00hrs. in the morning and at times up at 01.00hrs. in the night and "Ein, Drei, Vier," and tight marches. Sometimes orders to be ready for night-marches in 45 seconds. The punishment for not making it was 24 hours punishing exercises.

The duty sergeant was devilish hard, although it was not the intention to have this type training there at Sennheim, but at Klagenfurt. Here in Sennheim re-educating was the main task, according to Loke. He had gotten along well with a Norwegian petty assistant, having lost one arm, but then he was allowed to keep his rank, now as interpreter at Sennheim. Physical training was not the top item at Sennheim. It should all be about indoctrination, race ideology over the few weeks there. Above all learning about the pure Arian, Nordic race, Himmler's main subject. He even joined the camp one day to give a lecture about the obligation of them to lead on in the fight for the pure Nordic, Arian race in the great German empire, Das Reich.

"OMG Loke", he whispered to his friend, "are we not Nordic and maybe Norse more than all others? What are we to learn about ourselves?" But Himmler carried on, until in the second part of his lecture he came to focus on Untermenschen, gypsies and even Poles. But the latter were to be tolerated as long as they worked as slave workers in the German weaponry industry. But one race not to be tolerated was the Jewish one. Mud rats, Hitlers favorite expression.

According to Himmler there was some thirty million Jews in Europe, Jews that was the poison to the society, Jews only caring to themselves. The brain of these pestered Jews was such that it poisoned all and everyone in their nearness. And he continued: "The same goes for half-and quart Jews, a crime in itself to be defiled with Jewish blood, even these quart-Jews as well as the eight part-Jews, they were all as dangerous. Think about it, even this criminal Stalin, he had expelled all with just a portion of Jewish blood, expelled them far East of the 49th longitude, to make sure they could not defile the communists.

And we", he continued, "our foremost task is to beat the communist to East-Siberia, and then have them exterminate the Jews totally. Der Führer is working day and night with a plan of mass extermination of them all before it is too late. Our SS shall be the most important instrument to find all these Jews hiding as mud rats. Get them out in daylight and into a special exterminating machine. We cannot allow ourselves to spend proper bullets on these swines".

The lecture was over. "What did he mean with this expression extermination machine Lars?" But Lars was far away, very far away, in the part of Hedmark with his mother the Jew, and more so with his kinfolks over in Karelen, Finland. He pondered, what if he had stood up in the midst of the lecture saying: I am a Jew and I am proud of it, 50% Jew is that good enough? "What did you say about the Jews Lars?" Loke was uncomfortably close to him now. "I said what?" "Yes, you were mumbling something about the unfair treatment of the Jews, the Russians and Stalin". Thank God he had said nothing more. He got the color back to his face.

"You must have misunderstood Loke, I was just fantasizing about Hitler's idea of expelling all Jews east of the 49th". "And then Lars, then what?" "Yes, but listen Loke, all Jews now expelled east of the 49^{th,} and they were to hunt down the communists all the way over the ocean to the other side Loke. Be kind of allied to us?" "So, we should be allied to the mud rats Lars? And is it not America there on the other side of the ocean?" "I might be babbling now Loke, but I got really confused by Himmler's lecture".

"Yes, no doubt you sounded confused Lars. But we shall exterminate all Jews, did you not catch that. Exterminate Lars, a super medical expression! I wonder how Der Führer will do just that. For a moment I wondered if you had gone soft Lars, having sympathy with the Jews. You would then gotta hide yourself as here you would have been dead no later than in half an hour, if this had come out into the open". He gave himself a real big laugh now. "What if I were to lose you Lars, and just because of your slip of the tongue". Was there un underlying sting in his words, wasn't there?

Lars felt he was on dangerous ground now, so he felt he had no choice. He gave Loke a real bearhug. "Thanks, Loke for saving me from this misunderstanding dear friend. I must have been completely deranged by all this geopolitical lecture Himmler invited us into. The two of us shall never be separated Loke". He could feel Lokes super excitement, hugging Lars back even stronger and they both joined in the Heil Hitler as the train of cars left with Himmler.

It hurt, for sure it did hurt, especially at night when he tried to be rid of the indoctrination, and the hatred towards the Jews, lectured throughout the day and he now craving for some sleep. What if he would start sleep-talking, then it would be over and out on the double. After weeks with anxiety and bad sleep he had lost 10 kgs and had to change to a smaller size uniform.

Then one day, the petty officer came to the barracks pointing at Lars. "You shall report to Hauptsturmführer Reichelt, having honored us with his visit, now on the double!" Should this be the end of it. Had he been sleep-talking and then some of his fellow aspirants had reported him as a Jewish spy?

"Now you speed up, check boots and shoulder belts, all must be shiny". "May I go to the bathroom first?" "No, immediately on to the Hauptsturmführer and stand at attention!" What if it all got into his pants, Jewshit? His fellow room mates were watching him, face pale, as he walked out in front of the petty officer. Was he to be detained for something and to what? Luckily Loke was not present. The talk about Jews would have been brought up, no doubt to it. But his nerves relaxed when he saw this SS-Hauptsturmführer Reichelt. He seemed to be a nice man, doctor as well, Lars learned later when he was having private tuition.

"The commandant has checked up on you and your background and it doesn't seem like you take pleasure of staying here in the camp". What was this all about. Did they know he was Jewish. But Reichelt's smile made him calm down. "We have looked thoroughly into your background, and we now know that you were tops at the University of Oslo. Now, you are blond and have the right Arian look, you may call it the Norse look that we want, not least amongst the leaders." Reichelt himself, was tall, blonde possibly in his thirties. Were they to send Lars on some expedition, maybe Berlin?

"I am responsible for all the activities at our school for cadets in Bad Tølz, and not alone that is. As the commandant has managed to slim you down some ten kgs, then you shall leave with my people to Bad Tølz in the morning. It seems evident that you need a different menu". He laughed now to the commandant.

But Lars was preoccupied by his thought about Loke. "Am I the only one to go Hauptsturmführer? I have a friend, a medic as well". But the commandant cut him off. "You should be ashamed of yourself and your impudent behavior. You have to accept here and now. No choice, you are commissioned to go".

He was fast to beg his excuse having thought this much about his old friend, expressing his thanks to the commandant. "No problem", Reichelt said. "But another time and place, then be careful".

"We have looked into your friend as well. But sorry, he has not gotten your blonde appearance, and does not at all look Norse. He might even have Jewish blood in him, I mean maybe an eight or less". The commandant wanted to have a say he as well.

"I beg you excuse me Herr Commandant, but Loke comes from tenth-generation farmers in Telemark and Jews have been given access to Norway only since 1814".

"Very good Lars, you know your history. This shall work out just fine. We leave at 05.00 hrs. in the morning". This was it; the audience was over. Worst then with Loke. How should he put it to him that he was rejected because of his Jewish looks?

GOOD-BYE LOKE AND THEN BAD TØLZ

Taking good-bye with Loke had been heavy, real heavy. "It was as simple as that; they didn't want me?" There was like an undertone in his words; had Lars really stood up for his friend?

"I asked them if you could come with me as well, both of us being med-students. Sorry, no go. And the commandant was really pissed since I did not accept on the spot and Mr. Reichelt warned me to skip non-egoistic thoughts at the next crossroad. So, what more could I have done Loke?"

But Loke obviously was not content with this explanation. But Lars felt he could go no further, give him the real story. He still feared that Loke might think more closely about the babble from Lars in his sleep. He might even have said that he was 50% Jew and right so.

"But why you Lars, why did he want you and no others?" Loke did not give up that easy. "Listen Loke, they quite obviously wanted people with education, so it should have been the two of us. But I got no more option, told to be ready at 05.00hrs. in the morning".

"That soon?" A sad sigh from Loke. Lars felt he could be generous now, gave him another real bearhug. "We must write to one another Loke, and then we might meet in Berlin or at the front. But do not forget, I am going to Finland sooner or later whatsoever".

Lars did not have to show up at the evening's anti-Jewish lecture. He was exempted to get his gear ready for an early leave in the morning. But he did not have much to pack, so he just sat down, and his thoughts were all about Loke. Maybe best get to bed before Loke and the others came back.

He had agreed with the night watch to have him wake up at 04.00hrs. to be on the safe side. But it did not take long till he felt he was not alone in his bunk. Hairy legs crossed his and he was soon to feel that his guest had an enormous erection.

Lars had been lost in some sort of dreamland, but now it was rise and shine on the double. It was still early, only half past three, and here was his friend Loke with an iron erection between his legs.

"What is it that you are doing Loke, have you clicked? If seen by the night watch it would have meant directly off to the East front, best case, maybe even shot on sight, right here in Sennheim".

Loke moved himself to the top of the blanket, his erection was still just as strong even when he was sitting up. "I just wanted to say goodbye Lars". "But what about this then?" Lars pointed to the enormous erection. "No go to that one". "It is like that with me during nights Lars, and isn't that quite common with all young guys?" He tried to smile it off sort of. "But you must be really careful Loke, so you are not taken by the nightwatchmen".

Yes, Loke could pick a lie, but this one was an ok one. "Make sure you hide it immediately Loke. I shall come over to your bunk before leaving". He gave him a consoling smile. Soon this nightmare would be over. But it took him hard to leave his best friend, more so in a distant country far from home.

Poor Loke, what if he had been seen by the nigh watch, not to speak of himself, been denounced as a Jew. And Loke, not only gay, but caught while trying to have sex with a Jew?

Lars had seen pictures of this beautiful Bavaria, southern Germany with its hills and its forests, beautiful green-clad mountains and valleys. A kind of Norway, but by far more fertile it was here in the southern part of Germany. And here it was, his new quarters, Bad Tølz almost at the border of Austria.

A former sanatorium, and a very popular one, now it was a senter for education of elite soldiers, handpicked and soon to be officers. Well, they were cadets from the moment they walked through the door to their new home. On the ride down from Sennheim, Lars had gotten a substantial orientation about Himmler's idea with it all.

The aim of the cadet school was to be a trainingsenter, producing the best young officers in Great Germany. This was Hitler's ambition. It was clear that they were to become the best officers, but in contrast to the officers in the regular army, these new officers should have the correct faith, meaning being ardent Jew-haters.

Many of the cadets here were young soldiers having been promoted at the front, taking the positions as petty officers, when the regular ones had fallen. At times they were only corporals having stepped up as platoon leaders, even leaders of whole companies.

This was not much appreciated by the officers in the regular army, Die Wehrmacht, officers with the correct, traditional education. They considered themselves as the real officers, not someone picked up from the frontlines.

But there was change on its way. With the rapidly increasing number of these new officers of Himmler's, yes, he was credited to this, and the Waffen SS getting bigger and bigger, soon to be millions of well-trained soldiers, then all the harassment from the Wehrmacht was dead. No doubt that these new officers in the Waffen SS achieved results, much envied by the officers from the old guard.

Himmler had early in the thirties been direct about his opinion of the traditional officers corps. Their way of life in their clubs and even on camps was the direct reason why the great army was stiff legged and not very mobile. Even though most nations had come to admire it in the successful Blitz war against France. But Hitler himself took the credit for that one as well. All coming out of his military genius.

But now it was time for the new generation of officers. This became the everyday mantra there at Bad Tölz. "You my cadets shall soon be the backbone in our new proud armies!" This mantra was of course backed by the everyday slogan: "Germany is victorious on every front"

But under one morning's lecture, there was one of Lars' new comrades who desperately wanted to raise a question to the groomed instructor. "But sir, am I not to be a soldier Captain?"

"My Cadet, first and foremost you shall be a first-class officer. And do you know why? It seems that you don't. I shall therefore give you private tuition this evening, so you can stand here tomorrow morning at 08.00hrs. and give all the others a lecture about what separates the soldier from the officer, keywords being Duty and Honor. And just you all remember that!"

It was not only the landscape that was beautiful there at Bad Tölz. The intern maids were all beautiful and so were the girls they observed on their marches throughout the days.

His longing for Eva grew stronger by the day and her letters did not quite make up for the loss. But Lars had regained his weight, the lost kilos from Sennheim and now carried his uniform bravely, elegant, tall and blond he was.

He was more than once eyed by the intern maids and his closest friend Friedrich had on several occasions asked if Lars would join for an outing with him and his Gretchen, she happened to have another girl as her closest. "Thanks Friedrich just you go, I have a girl back in Norway to whom I have sworn forever faithfulness".

"But Lars I am not talking about infidelity, only having a night off in pleasant company. It would not hurt, would it?"

But Lars was not used to do things that he could not write about to his Eva. For sure she would not like to read about her Lars being together with his mate, going partying with two girls here at Bad Tølz. Still, when Friedrich and a third mate Herman left for partying, Lars felt depressed. He just sat down by himself, reading Eva latest letter and then he started to write his own to her.

But the four were soon back. This other girl, Lisa had not enjoyed Herman's company, she talked about stomachache, possible food poisoning or such. "It is you Lars that she wants to be with. Don't you see that Lars?" Friedrich was on to him again.

Later, Lisa approached him and asked if he would join her just for a small walk and this time, he could not say no. "I got the key to the backdoor", she whispered. Lisa was looking quite a bit like Eva, and he intuitively felt that this could get wrong. Lisa knew whom she wanted, and that it was Lars, she said it openly.

They had stopped by a small suspension bridge over a stream. "Don't you like me, Lars?" It was difficult to get across on this bridge without dumping into one another and of course she slipped and for fear that she would fall into the stream, he had no other option than to grab her, and in seconds she was in his arms. Lisa with her sky blue- eyes, the red tempting lips and she smelled from lavender as well as from her freshly ironed uniform, and she wanted to have him there and then.

The only thing he knew would stop her was if he told her he was a 50% Jew. But for sure that would have meant death, executed secretly, no one were to know. Not least that the Cadet school was a camp also for Jews, the hatred people that Hitler desperately wanted to exterminate. Maybe she would be executed as well!

But when she pressed herself on to him, she recognized the bulge in his trousers, and it was too late to withdraw. She wanted him desperately and he longed for her sex, almost figured it could be his Eva.

Soon they were naked there in the moonlight by the stream. And Lars felt almost unconscious when he came the second time and they then slipped down from the suspension- bridge, down in the shallow stream.

The very next morning he asked to see Captain Reichelt. He now knew that he had to get away from Bad Tølz soonest.

"German soldiers at the front are suffering Captain. And I, I lack the last part of my medical education, Field- medicine. So, I should concentrate on that part, become a complete medic and then off to the front to save lives, German lives. But then I first have to get to Berlin, the university hospital, to combine theory and practice, then final exams and off to a division at the front.

Following Sennheim and now these months her at Bad Tølz, I have had tuition to the fullest in ideology, weaponry, and exercising. But I feel it, that I am about forgetting essential parts of my profession as a future medic and Germany desperately needs field-medics now Captain".

"Well, you have said that twice now my young Norwegian. Some lecture you gave". Reichelt had lit his cigar, stood up and walked about from window to window in his spacious office, shiny booths, sharp pressed uniform and the Ridder Kreutz round his neck.

"Might there be something behind this seal of yours to get to the front, or is it merely this intense craving to serve, Duty, Pride and Honor that drives you?"

Should he dare mention Karelen and risk investigation that worst case might reveal all about these Jewish families? No, he could not.

"The picture might be a little more complex Captain. But I enlisted first and foremost to serve at the front. I have never hidden my urge for just that".

"But my dear young Cadet, Germany is strongly in need for an efficient officers corps. That may well be our foremost need". Lars kept it shut. Stood at attention, saluted his Heil Hitler and left.

At luncheon he could hear happy laughter from the kitchen every time the revolving doors opened. Lisa was one of the happy ones and the way she eyed him left no question of her attraction to him.

But in his heart, Lars felt only bitterness. In a romantic setting he had betrayed his fiancée for life, Eva. Of course, he could never tell her about the incident and for sure, no way he could marry her following this sex adventure with Lisa. How he eventually was to convey this incident with Lisa to Eva, he really did not know, but for sure it would be a sorrow moment.

As a rule, captain Reichelt dined with the cadets only on very special occasions. But at the dinner this very day, it was commanded "at attention",Heil Hitler and all formalities.

Everyone was curious about the occasion, but Reichelt did not say a word about it, he saluted them all at the beginning of the meal. The main course, veal brisket had been served and everyone around the tables seemed in good mood. Then he knocked at his glass, saluted to the picture of Hitler, everyone followed closely. But he did not sit down thereafter, no, he left the table and stood tall there in the middle of the large hall. Made certain that he was seen by all the cadets, he standing there in his impeccable uniform and shiny riding boots.

"Cadets, at attention", they all raised. The tension could be felt. "I want to introduce to you our commander, Brigadier General Lothar Debes".

"Thank you, Captain. Heil Hitler! Now at ease! My Cadets, you are all handpicked, you the future of Germany, the honor of the officer's corps to be. But one of you, he is leaving us tonight by train to Berlin. He has chosen to leave us even before the education here at Bad Tølz, education to Duty and Honor is completed. In spite of this I have decided to let him go and I have given him my strongest recommendation to Berlin where they shall make the final decision".

Lars felt the chill down his spine, could it be that his request had been accepted? No one dared look at the next cadet, they all focused on Debes.

"Why will this cadet leave us? Is he fed up with our mantra, Duty and Honor, so often repeated, our craving for precisely that, not least to the discipline that must be every officer's hallmark right to the end?"

It had become totally quiet there in the large hall. One could almost feel the famous needle falling. Even the intern maids and those working in the kitchen, they all stood quiet, listening.

The cadets, all and everyone feared that maybe this was someone to be punished for the most serious misconduct, resulting in him being expelled, then off to Berlin, further to the front in the East and then being assigned to the well-known Strafcompany (Punishment company). Survival of the officers, 10 days, soldiers six days at most.

"No, our man does not fail his Duty and Honor. On the contrary! Our cadet has another 6 months education in field-medicine to catch up with there in Berlin before he gets his Medic certificate and then off to the front at Leningrad, where he shall be strongly needed, saving many of our wounded heroes. So, this cadet has no more time for us, he desperately wants to get to the front, Duty and Honor. You listen well cadets, he has not gotten time for us! Our soldiers, the wounded ones they all need him more! Heil Hitler.

Cadet Lars, our Norwegian, come forward and stay at attention. Here you have a diploma showing that you have served with us here at Bad Tølz. Berlin and the East front salutes you heartly welcome. May you help save many hundreds of our wounded. Heil Hitler!" The sound of the boots, when standing at attention sounded from the big hall. The following acclaim was enormous.

At the door to the kitchen, there was a big bang, when a tray with twenty caramel puddings banged to the floor along with the unconscious maid.

Lars got a short hour to make ready for the train. Then he was off in a staff car to Munich for the night train to Berlin

And his Lisa, what about her. Were they ever to meet again, maybe in Berlin?

BERLIN

He had plenty of time to dwell with his new situation there on the night train to Berlin. Why had he been the chosen one at Sennheim, and how come Reichelt just changed his opinion and let him go? But it was not a change of opinion. He had not been decisive to the one or the other issue there in the meeting. Still, he could not let go that someone had pressed on to get him to Berlin, finish his med-studies and then off to the front. Could it be his father, or Quisling or even Himmler himself? Wild fantasy, what was he to Himmler? He let go of the thoughts, or didn't he? His father? No way he would have anything to do with Quisling, and the big shots would not care the least for the career of one single cadet there at Bad Tølz.

Captain Reichelt was a rising star, but Lothar Debes talked about strings he had pulled there in Berlin and who could that be, he just an insignificant cadet?

Skip these thoughts Lars, still he missed someone to talk with on this matter. Yes, he missed his best friend Loke, not least the matter of same-gender attraction. Where would Loke be now, already at the front? Suddenly he felt like a chill down the spine, remembering the words from his Eva. "Maybe your best friend is gay or at least bi, Lars."

But when the cold of the chill was gone, then it was not Eva that was on his mind, but Lisa. He had not even found her to say goodbye. Following her fainting and the bang on the floor of all the deserts, she had vanished. He felt sorry not being able to help her when she fainted. He had to write her and explain everything and why not do it right now in the night. How to start this letter then? My darling Lisa? No, crazy you Lars! How about My sweet Lisa?

The fact that he could not ever come back to Eva made him think that it would be a good idea to keep the contact with this lovely Lisa. But would she wait for him? But the incident was nothing but an incident, however pleasing. So why not start with something neutral. "My dear Lisa," well yes that would be it. But eventually he would have to write to Eva, tell her that he could never come back to her following his mischief at Bad Tølz? But no, he could not do that, better tell her about Berlin and that everything was ok. But would it not after all be better to come clean and tell her how it all had happened, betrayed her in a weak moment? Wasn't that how the boys usually talked about things? And why did girls never have a weak moment?

No, he could not tell her about Lisa. He should continue with Eva as if nothing had happened. Get rid of Lisa and that was it. But what if she came to Berlin? For sure she could get a travel permit from Munich.

Berlin looked like he had seen it on pre-war postcards. No signs of a war going on. There were talks about English air raids, but many of the Brits' planes were shot down, so, little harm on Berlin itself. Decoration in the streets for Christmas, yes it all looked pre-war.

Only at the Hauftbanhof, the nerve of the city, yes at this railway-station there were soldiers all over. Still, this was the only sign of a war going on.

There were of course many wounded from both fronts, East and West, but they were not shown in parades in the street. No, the Germans wanted their wounded back soonest to the fronts, so they had set up rehab centers in the old baths in the South, as well as in Austria, all far enough from the showcase for glorious Germany, Berlin.

And Berlin bleibt doch immer Berlin (Berlin forever).

He ditched the letter to Lisa in a trash bin. He should write her a far more neutral one, give her his thanks for the fine time together and wish her best of luck. As for himself he had no idea where he would be stationed after Berlin, hopefully, eventually Karelen, Finland.

His letter to Eva was a true love letter, still he had spent most of the first four pages to talk about his selection to Berlin, his sheer luck. Now he could finish his med-studies and go straight to Finland and Karelen when there still was a Karelen free of the Bolsheviks.

Would he get leave to come home for a short visit once the exams were over? For sure no. It was all about getting to Karelen now. But once that fight was over, he might get a short leave. As for now it would all be about getting top grades, make the stay in Berlin as short as possible and then off. No doubt he would be working long into the evenings on practical issues, possibly also at night. All theoretical studies would take place during daytime. This was how the program was laid out from the officials, no problem to him describing it and thus no point for her coming to Berlin.

But he had liked a sting in his heart when the next day after checking in he was allowed time for a stroll down the Unter den Linden, the street to look and get looked at. The atmosphere was vibrant with all the cafés more or less crowded, despite the war. The wintery weather had not made all the Berliners stay at home, no, behind the protective glass wall in the cafés, there were still many having their usual coffee and snaps or whatever.

He noticed that apart from an elderly gentleman, much of the clientele were officers accompanied by rather young women. The younger men were no doubt already at the fronts.

It did not come as a surprise that the personnel at the registry of the Berlin University Clinic, they were all in uniform. He was greeted by an SS-Untersturmführer who took his papers and then gave him a summary of the subjects and the educational program. First the studies and hand in hand so to speak, the practical, taking place at the Clinic building three blocks away.

The Clinic turned out to be a freshly established one with only 50 rooms, a pure University Clinic. Adjacent to the top floor, was a separate wing for professors, their assistants, doctors, and surgeons plus hospitant med-students, Lars being one of them.

Initially he was to share room with a Herr Günther, but he had already dropped out and was off to the East front. His elder brother was in charge of a full company and needed medical personal. So, he got a new roommate, a Belgian professor, having field surgery as his specialty, nothing the better. Sheer luck again he felt.

So, no hard feelings, nor of betrayal to Eva. It was more or less a round-the-clock operation, these 6 months studying and training. Michel, his roommate seemed to have no negative feelings of splitting room with a student, even him being a seasoned professor. On the contrary, he was happy for Lars, an officer educated from Bad Tølz, Himmler's own baby, although his stay there in the south was cut short for Berlin and field-medic education.

At the Uni as well as at the Clinic there were many hot young women, nurses, and younger interns, but thanks to Michel there was never time for social escapades. Michel insisted on being available to discuss whatever intricate medical question.

Theory, blood, and shortage of sleep might well have been the heading to this field-medic study, but in June it was all over. The six months intensive study in Berlin would correspond to 1.5 years at the Oslo Uni. But he was now a fully fledge doctor and had papers to prove it.

Papers might be good enough per se, but during the six months he had taken part in more than a hundred amputations, sorted splints and bullets from breast-and stomach regions on the wounded soldiers, sewn up intestines hanging on the outside, following explosions by the Russians, often caused by hand grenades.

No way he would have been as qualified following the 1.5-year termination at the Oslo Uni, theoretically qualifying him as field-medic. And he kept thinking now that he was ready for his mission. What would be his father's reaction if they met at a field hospital in Karelen?

DIVISION GROSS DEUTSCHLAND

He got only 24 hours to take his leave with the fellow students and not least Michel at the Uni and the Clinic. Then off to the depot for his new uniform as SS-Untersturmführer.

If he got lucky, he could enjoy a few hours at Unter den Linden there in sunny spring weather. He stopped at one of the many cafés where chairs and tables were already out on the sunny sidewalk.

It seems like all of Berlin was there now, wanting to enjoy pre-war times before the military took command of the streets.

Lars was the only one in uniform, so he asked the waiter: "Is there no longer no war?" But the waiter quieted him down. "Hash, Untersturmführer, two tables further there is the Gestapo in civil."

So that was it and maybe the girls were Gestapo as well, just decoys they were. He felt for a provocation and approached the blonde one, a bit too much makeup to his liking. But yes, she would like to join for a glass of sect. She had once been a beauty, no need for makeup then.

He noted from the corner of his eye that the Gestapo-guy followed closely. But Lars really had to concentrate on her sort of interrogation. "Where do you come from, where are you going, which regiment?" Lars was playing with, broad smile and "cheers sweet you, but you should know that as an officer I have total confidentiality."

Clearly it was stupid of him to engage in this flirt with the blonde-haired girl. He excused himself, having an important appointment and left. But one Gestapo guy followed at 20 meters pace. OMG, what if he was brought in for questioning and they managed to uncover that his mother was a Jew and he as well then? He got to get rid of this Gestapo guy. You have been nothing but an idiot Lars!

So best go back to the Clinic, change to civilian clothes, and then get out by the backdoor. But hold it, there was the other Gestapo guy from the café. This one covering the back of the Clinic. Soon there might be special forces ransacking the Clinic.

He had to get out of there, off to the Hauptbanhof and then board the train to Warsaw ready to leave in the evening. But what then, somebody would no doubt search all the trains, would they not?

Damn, but he knew that the first stop for this Warsaw-train was the little station at Friedrichs Berg. If he managed to get on a local train to this station then he could join the Warsaw-train from there, all control probably done with. But how to get out unseen from the Clinic when the Gestapo was covering both front and back? He had his bag with the uniform all ready to get going now. No doubt he had to be dressed as civilian in his escape.

Almost half an hour now since he left the café and plenty time for the Gestapo to call for assistance. Search for this officer who might be some spy.

There was a small window down in the cellar, at the morgue. No people on duty down there at this time of the day. With a sharp knife he might be able to open the door to the morgue even if it might be locked.

15 minutes later he was at The Hauptbahnhof, found the local train to Friedrichs Berg, ready to leave in 10 minutes. No problems at all.

But there was a guy there in a black leather coat, and was there not something fishy about him? He also saw the controller coming towards his wagon, accompanied by a uniformed Waffen-SS.

But Lars had all the answer ready. He had always wanted to see Friedrichs Berg and now he had some five hours to spend there before picking up the Warsaw-train in the evening. On his way to the front, this was his only chance to visit this little village.

If the Gestapo- guys from the café had managed to circulate a search warrant, they had not bothered with the local trains, least not their priority. But for sure the Hauptbanhof would be under close surveillance, sheer luck he had gotten on to the local train.

Suddenly he saw a big Mercedes with blinded windows coming in high speed into the station, all the way up to the platforms. But his train was already on the move. Nobody focused on the small train to Friedrichs Berg. He went to the restroom and thanked God; somebody had let behind a well-worn copy of Hitlers Mein Kampf. No doubt someone in a hurry.

A superb disguise this, put the book in his jackets side pocket, the title showing quite well. When arriving at the little station he went to the kiosk, bought coffee and Berliner muffins, then sat down in the small park to wait. It was way too early to change to boots and uniform.

The long-waited spring endured a setback and even now when the sun settled there was an ice-cold draught and he had to find himself a café. The waiting room at the station had not much to offer. Now what about his bag, should he change to uniform right there? He was no longer a civilian once he bordered the Warsaw train.

But he was still worried, and should he be? Some decoy from the Gestapo, this blond one and two more Gestapo-agents following you, Lars? So, what, you have nothing to hide. Why this paranoia, you have the best papers and you have been handpicked to Felix Steiner's renowned Division Gross Deutschland. Who would ever find out that you might have a Jewish mother? She was at the time adopted in Karelen Finland, the others were Jews and as at now they are either dead or expelled. Just think about your own stupid behavior. First inviting this blonde-haired person to a drink and then ever so arrogant say no comments to her questions. If you have told her that you are a field-medic, just coming out from the Uni Clinic, papers ready and all, and then invited her friend for a drink as well, then there would have been no problems at all.

The Warsaw-train was due in an hour, so he might as well get changed. He finished his so-called coffee and then on to the toilet. Occupied and what about the man over in the corner, wearing a leather greatcoat. Tried the restroom once more, still occupied. But it was locked, so it was for him to go to the restroom on the train and get changed there, then throw the civilian clothes out of the toilet window.

He calmed down now once he had a plan. But what about the man in the leather coat, what was his business here, was he to go with the train as well? Some coincidence was it not? Best forget about him, so he opened Hitler's book and started to read about the dangerous Jews. At least he pretended reading, seemingly extremely interested. It was already fifteen past 22.00hrs. and the train was due in 10 minutes. Now he really had to go to the toilet, but no one had come out, so no doubt it was sealed off.

"Interesting this book of yours, don't you think?" It was the leather coat man. "For sure and I try to read every single chapter at least three times. You can see it is well used." The leather coat man looked closely at him. "Berlin, no?"

This was too obvious. Lars laughed; "No, it is my dialect from Bad Tølz you may note. You know Bavaria and Austria, different dialects, but sorry, I gotta dash, my train is coming in now and I must run for the restroom once I have bordered".

He gave the leather coat man a friendly nod, off to the platform with his bag. Carriage nr.7, seat nr.2. There was the carriage nr. 7. and he made way directly to the toilet.

Luckily, he was in there now, had spotted only 2 Waffen SS of lower grade, together with the conductor. No one from Gestapo, at least not in uniform. The train had only a short stop and within minutes he had changed into his boots and uniform. The conductor was twice on to the door, but Lars cried out about a diarrhea and asked for another 3 minutes.

The man coming out of the restroom was no civilian, but one Untersturmführer in an impeccable uniform, well pressed and shining riding boots. The handsewn Division Gross Deutschland embroideries on the uniform's arms, they were no doubt envied by many, those that never would be admitted to this Elite-division. The soldiers on this train were regulars off to help a commander risking death or being captured.

Lars could see no danger to him in his compartment, an elderly lady, a young attractive brunette and one man in civilian suit, looked like a travelling salesman or whatever. Two seats were not taken, nr.2 next to the brunette and nr.4 next to the elderly woman.

Lars through his bag, much diminished now, up on the shelf and was off to find the restaurant wagon, possibly still open. Luck once more, it was open, but crowded, so he had to content himself with a seat, right behind a table with higher officers. Was not too happy with that, but managed to order a Schnitzel and a carafe of red wine, but only a half. Anyway, it would do him good enough for this night travel.

"Is this one free?" It was the leather coat man, no doubt he was recognized. "Yes of course it is free." Right behind the leather coat man were the two Waffen-SS guys he had seen when boarding. They came right up to the leather coat man, fingers on their machine guns ready for action.

One of the officers at the next table turned and asked what this commotion was all about. His grade was SS-Obersturmbannführer. Lars had been sitting still, but now he rose, clicked his heals: "Heil Hitler, I don't know what these guys are after."

"Ah, you are one of us," he pointed to the embroideries on the sleeves. "Yes sir, Obersturmbannführer." He was ever so calm, no nerves at all. Even now knowing that the leather coat man was Gestapo in disguise. Confidence he knew came with his uniform.

"And you are?" The officer pointed condescending at the leather coat man. "Security Police, Herr Obersturmbannführer." He produced his papers. "And then what, what do you want from this Untersturmführer?" "Berlin thinks he might be a spy sir." "Your papers please," he addressed Lars.

"Well, well, a field-medic isn't that just fabulous my General," he turned to the highest ranking at the table. This one had not cared much for the commotion, still with his back towards it. "What is it about Walther?" "Well sir, here we have a freshly educated field-medic, having served at your own Bad Tølz as well. Now this security guy accuses him of being a spy. Ridiculous!" The general rose, looked intensively at Lars: "Are you a spy?" "No, Herr SS-Obergruppenführer Steiner, I am a doctor, field-medic to be precise." So, it was the legend General Steiner he faced, yes in the flesh, and Lars was not mistaken. "Come sit with us, we can always find use for a field-medic"? He laughed to the others. "And you," he pointed to the leather coat man. "You just get out of here or would you rather come with us to the East front? Yes, you would like that, would you not? We may well have a place for you in the first line at the Stalino front. Interested? Herr Walther will of course supply you with uniform and weapon." The leather coat man almost kneeled to the general in fear that he would really commission him to the East front. He started with a speech to defend himself: "Berlin...." But then he just shut it until he suddenly clicked his heels. "Thank you Herr Obergruppenführer. Yes, Herr General. Heil Hitler." Steiner's lips had gone blue now. "Leave us now!" And the leather coat man left with the two Waffen-SS.

It turned out to be an ever so nice evening until Lars dared to ask about how to be commissioned to Karelen and the Finnish Front. "When the supreme command wants to strengthen our forces in Finland or the commanding general asks for assistance, then maybe we, Division Gross Deutschland may come to assistance. But we are until further notice attached to Army Groupe South for clear-up- actions or to be ready once/if there is an alarm from one or the other fronts."

Lars obviously did not know when to put a stop at it. Should he dare take it one step further? But General Steiner was well aware of what would come next, so he nodded to Walther who quickly got up and made Lars do the same. "Thanks for this evening Untersturmführer and again, welcome to us." The audience was over, and Walther accompanied him back to his compartment. The leather coat man was gone, but no doubt, Lars' bag had been moved.

"Herr Untersturmführer, please don't challenge fate another time or I am afraid you will be sent to a punishment company in the East." Lars looked wondering at him. "You may well be assigned to one or more regiments in Finland when needed, but not as yet. Should this leather coat man show himself again, then you will find me in compartment 8, right by the restaurant wagon. Good night."

The brunette was the only one awake. She gave him an intimate look. "This man in the leather coat, he opened and looked through your luggage." "Did he find something of interest?" "No, but he looked through some letters there." So, this swine had seen the letters from Eva and had confiscated one.

He did not wake up until the light came on and the conductor announced Warsaw in 30 minutes. He was somewhat confused, where was he? Had to sit up to compose himself. The brunette laughed at him. "Yes, you were lying with your head in my lap, all through the night. You were most welcome to it Lars." "Oj, did I speak in my sleep, how do you know my name?" "Not that difficult Lars, the man in the leather coat was quite persistent, wanting to know if we knew the owner of the bag. I did not notice your last name, but it was something with 'Gard' or something. But Lars, your first name, yes, I remember that one, handsome man." She laughed. "I have been sitting here all night holding the head of this handsome guy in my lap. Don't I deserve a thank you at least?"

Lars had to laugh as well. "And you are?" "I am a nurse, specialized in surgical operations and you, you are such a freshly promoted officer shouting and crying to your poor soldiers, like shown on the weekly film revue?" "No, I am not, and since you are asking, I am a doctor, a field-medic. I have trained for field-medicine the last half year at the same time as I did the final theoretical studies at the Berlin Uni."

She appeared quite surprised. "But why do you wear a Gross Deutschland uniform. Must you wear uniform at all when you are a doctor?"

The conductor was at the door, wanted them to leave. Lars looked closely at her. Tall, maybe like 1.75, slim although not too slim, he could see her full breasts and perky buttocks. Would look stunning with heels this one. But the most amazing was her hair, chestnut, now in long braids, real long. Were there not regulations for this in the hospital? Now doubt her lovely hair would reach halfway to the buttocks. But it was her eyes that took him like a storm. Green they were, like he had seen them at Bad Tølz, yes Lisa's eyes. Even the ones of this brunette had the same intense green-bluish color, like the water from the icebergs. Her green blue dress matched with her eyes. He felt that he got all red with the memories of Lisa, although this brunette had fuller lips and higher cheekbones. He had to compose himself. Did he want to meet with this sensational girl in Warsaw?

But the conductor was getting impatient and Lars felt this could be the moment. "Hi there, you beautiful woman. We cannot stop at this. We are already at the station", he nodded to the conductor, "and I for sure shall be on my way to wherever already this afternoon. And how about you, where shall you stay?" "Here in Warsaw? I don't know, I have just been told to meet up here". "Why not exchange names, addresses and such so we may write to one another?" "You really want that Lars?" Her voice was ever so soft and who knows, he said to himself. At least they could have contact on a professional level. What a silly excuse! Kisses on the cheeks and then he was off to Division Gross Deutschland.

Herr Walther from the train came to meet with him. "You shall stay with us". Felix Steiner looked much nicer now in the morning. "How was life in Bad Tølz my young one. You may know that I was Commandant there two years back". Lars had of course seen the picture on the wall in the great hall. But most important, Steiner was considered a hero to the young cadets. But he best keeps quiet about that. Maybe no point getting on too intimate a level.

Walther was on to him. "Were you not to join the regimental staff in Lviv?" "Yes, right so". "But if you care for it, then you may stay with us for the next two days here in Warsaw, and then we take the train together south to Lviv. Felix has a liking to you, not least since you have been at his Bad Tølz. But whenever he calls you the young one, make certain you don't consider this a family reunion and do mind the formalities. I shall send a message to Lviv telling them that you will arrive together with us".

Lars had not at all been prepared to this. The room was over luxurious. Totally different from the expectations he had after his dad had told him about the quarters at the front in Finland. Out there at best he could expect to have his own tent or more so sleep in the surgery tent.

"The Imperial hotel" was Reichelts nickname to it. The correct name was Hotel Leopold. He had managed to get a sneak-look into Steiner's suite, the living room alone was no doubt more than 200 sqm.

He wanted to see Warsaw once he had a chance to it. "Stay away from the Ghetto" was Reichelts advice. "We shall have dinner at 19.00 hrs. sharp at the Rathouskeller, mainly German officers in that restaurant".

Two sickly looking musicians, a pianist and a violinist provided the entertainment. Steiner had no liking to the noise, so they had an early breakup, and they were back at the hotel short to 22.00 hrs.

"A sweet brunette over there", Reichelt pointed at her. "For sure I have seen that one earlier, maybe on the train. Oh yea, she sat next to you, seat nr 1 there in your compartment Lars. Why don't you go say hello to her, then I shall leave you to it, while I join with Steiner. Good night to you and please don't miss breakfast at 07.00 hrs. sharp. We are strict on routines here, as you know".

Lars had wished for an early night up in his room, writing to Eva. But Birgitta had already seen him so no way he could just leave. She told him that she didn't want to intrude, but after a full day, she was badly in need of a shower. "Yes Lars, I really hoped that you hadn't left Warsaw but were staying here. So, you think I can ask you a favor?" "Well, you have been my nurse all through the night so tell me what I can do for you. Are you in need of cash?" "OMG Lars, what do you take me for. I have my things in this small suitcase, and I only want to ask you for the possibility of having a shower, then I shall change and be out of here on the double".

He flashed a bit, Lars. "Sorry I didn't mean to insult you. Here take the key and off you go. I shall stay at the bar for a while and then be up in the room".

She was all gratitude and then she was gone.

What are you up to Lars, another adventure? But Birgitta no way was the type for that, he mustered to himself. And after all there was a war going on, so no harm helping a colleague in need. But it struck him; would he have been up to this if he hadn't already committed adultery with Lisa? A deadly sin it was. But now, second time all much easier?

He gave her 20 minutes then off to his room but run into Reichelt in the corridor. "So, this was just a short meeting I gather?" Lars couldn't help it, but flashed once again "Well yes, up early tomorrow morning and then off to Lviv in the night". "Right so, but you are just a young one?" Walther laughed and he was off with a "Good night!"

No one answered when he knocked at the door, so he had to ask one of the servants to lock up.

Now, where could Birgitta be? He checked the bathroom, but no, so he switched on the light in the far end of his junior suite and there she was, laying on the canape covered with a blanket. She didn't even wake up when the main light came on, so he was really quick to switch it off. What now Lars? Should he wake her up? No, let her sleep. But what about tomorrow morning? None of them could bear a scandal, at least not he.

It turned out to be a restless night. No, he didn't bother at all about her presence in the suite, but he had an urge to get her over to his bed.

He was up at six, the room was totally dark due to the compulsory blinds, so he sneaked out, and rested in the reception area to wait for Walther. This must be done cautiously, if not he would have had it, risking trouble, new on the job.

"Now did you sleep well?" Walther looked fresh and fit. "The General shall soon be with us, at 07.00 hrs. on the dot as I know him".

"But Colonel, I must speak with you first". "Don't be that formal Lars, are you in trouble?" "Yes, and I don't know how to handle it". "We can't have Steiner waiting, so we shall have to sort this out later. Is it about ladies?" Lars got totally read and then pale. "Yes, sort of, but not the way you think". Walther laughed at him. "Really, and what are my thoughts then Lars?"

"What's up gentlemen, our young one looks pale to me this morning. A as a doctor you should be capable of solving any medical problem to yourself, right?"

This was close to getting awkward, but Walther saved his neck. "Our young one, as you put it General, he has got himself a problem, ladies take a liking to him as they do with all fresh Lieutenants". He had himself a diverting laughter.

"Not so with me", said Steiner. "No one dear talk to me, looking like a Christmas tree in this uniform. But as you know I am committed to wear all these decorations. I really look forward to getting to the front and become one of the boys in field attire". And they both knew this was a fact. Steiner was loved by all his soldiers, all the way through his regiment.

The breakfast had come to a close. "Is it ok by you Herr Steiner that I go with our young one for a 5-minutes consultation?" "Yes of course but make sure to be in my suite at 08.00 hrs.".

Lars wrapped up the situation and Walther meant he better come with him to his room, thus they would be two when the young lady was wakened up. Then they would give her ample time to get ready and leave the hotel. No more to it. Walther should have a word with the clerk at the reception.

Lars gave it a knock. No answer. Tried again still no answer. So, he unlocked. Knocked at the door to the bathroom, no one there. No Birgitta.

"Come now Lars, it seems to me that it is time now for you to find you a girl, so we are rid of such hallucinations." "Right Colonel, but here is the proof". He pointed to the letter on the sofa. "My fantastic Lars", Walther was reading out loud. "A million thanks for the night and the shower and I hope we soon meet again".

Walther had a broad smile. "I shall not ask you for any explanations Lars, but I am happy for you that it was no hallucination. You may always come to me or Felix whenever you have problems. Now you have three minutes to get ready for the morning meeting". "Am I to be part of that?" He was almost in shock now, he a mere lieutenant. "Yes, you are to meet, now in two, and then the general will decide if you shall stick with us throughout the day or meet up with us at the train station tonight. Heil Hitler!"

The general's adjutant presented the report from when they last marched into Lviv and explained why it would be necessary to come back. Maybe they had been too keen on saving the old, beautiful city on the last encounter. No doubt it was still a partisans' nest, and no one knew how many of the Jewish rats were still hidden in the souterrains. Especially in the city center, where there were numerous underground tunnels linking the Cathedral and the Castle heights. This far no one had succeeded finding the entrance to these tunnels, not even from the crypt in the Cathedral.

Lars felt ill at ease right from the way the participants in the meeting spoke about the Jews. And it shouldn't be any better by the tale to follow: Before the Russians left the city, they had mutilated a large number of German prisoners and thereafter given the Jews the blame for this misdeed.

The partisans had willingly joined in this carnage, killing all the Jews they could find, neighbors, old friends, they were all considered enemies now. And the reward for the partisans were the free confiscation of all Jewish homes.

"Herr Lieutenant, you heard the summary presented by my adjutant. This is what we have to stand up and fight against, not regular troupes, where one fights with honor. And what carnage and mutilations you will see! Germany will be ever thankful for your decision to choose Berlin and the course in Field Medecine instead of finalizing your studies up in Oslo and then home to your father's surgery out in the country". Lars kept it shut, but he was surprised that Steiner had put an effort to find out that much about him Lars. Maybe it would be Steiner who were to save him if he ever was badly cornered. Punishment company at the East front for the least misdemeanor was kind of a mantra in the officers 'messes.

THE LETTER FROM EVA

She had long felt something was wrong Eva, missing her monthly and now sitting biting her pencil trying to find the write words to write to her dearest Lars. "I shall soon be with you Dad, just trying to find the right words to my boy".

"You don't need do that Eva, because now you have me here and that must be much better than this med-student soon dead like a herring when he comes to the front. So, you didn't know what to write Eva?"

She got quite uneasy by the monstrous figure of Nazi Jens who had made his way unannounced into the living room. He must have tip toed that man. And her maid and her father and the hire hand, where could they all be? One of them at least must have seen Jens coming. And his car, strange that no one had heard the sound from the big Mercedes, nor had she. Had she been that deep sunk, pondering about Lars?

"Should you not have knocked at the door before storming into one's living room Jens?" "As we know one another that well Eva, then I thought I would come with some chocolate as a surprise to you". "Chocolate now there is a war on. So where have you got your chocolate?" Tore was finally at home. "You know Jens that none of us here at the farm don't want to be unfriendly, but should it come about in the county that you and even we ordinary people are sitting here eating German chocolate, then?" "There is a war now Tore, so one takes what one can get". "So, now you are here to take my Eva while her Lars is gone fighting a war?"

"Not that literally Tore, but yes I am here for your Eva". "This is too much to me right now Jens, so you should better leave. Some other time maybe!"

Jens got the message, no point in getting unfriendly with his future father-in-law. But when he stood up from the chair, there was a rattling sound, it was from his uniform pants torn at the seam back there. This was a bit too much for everyone, especially to Tore who had decided to play sick, but luckily Jens got himself a big belch from coffee and chocolate allowing for all to laugh, although slightly disgusting it was, not so for Nazi Jens himself, holding on to the torn pants back there.

He had sat down now Tore, holding his hand to his heart. "I didn't know of your talent as an actor Dad. Well-hidden it has been. But you were fantastic, thanks heavens to that".

"My child, we must be careful. This Nazi Jens has become quite pushy and smells blood as they say. And for sure it must have been quite a while since anyone helped him with washing of laundry and such. That pant we got a glimpse of must have been white once, only long back".

Well, that's the way it is my dear Lars. And now I am sitting here all by myself in the blue hour thinking about you. There is spring in the air and one can smell the new seeded soil from our fields and from yours as well down at Elvegård. Our hire hand has been with your father all day helping to get the seed in the earth. I think your dad is fantastic, he with only one arm managing it all.

Are you soon to be home my Lars so you can squeeze me till I cry out loud?

She was on to it now and kept going till her father came to hug her good night. "One more phrase now, and then off to bed with us all father".

Oh, we miss you tremendously both of us, Lars my own. Both of us? OMG, how should she be able to correct that? She didn't even know for sure if she at all was pregnant. Rewrite it right from the start? I mean daddy misses you as well, we were just chatting about you. So, goodnight then my dear boy. Yours Eva. Forever.

But he had no more tears to Eva, the breach was too deep and would it at all help crying?

THE LETTER FROM HIS FATHER

They came at the same time, the two letters; some coincidence. He wasn't quite through with the one from Eva, but put it aside eager to read the news from his dad.

"My dearest son". The beginning of the letter from his father almost made him cry. It was very rare that his father wrote such an intimate address in his letters.

"Your little sister has passed now. Her sufferings came to an end 4 weeks back and a week thereafter your lovely, but frail mother said her goodbyes as well. As you know well, she had suffered a lot over the last months, and it was like she knew that her latest goodbye to you was to be the final one".

Poor dad and both of them gone, within the week.

"So now I am all by myself here. Still living in the annex together with our Tanja. She is getting old she as well, our Finnish elk-dog. But I shall let her live in memory of the flower of Karelen now buried in our county church yard. Two funerals in 14 days Lars. A heavy burden to me, but your Eva was at my side as much as she could till it was all over. Now it is all on me and for sure it is just as bad for you having to experience it from a note on a simple piece of naked paper".

He had to take a break, having read but half of the letter. Why on Earth hadn't Eva written about this in her letters? No, for certain she had wanted his dad to break the sad news about the departed. Now what about him Lars having whored with a woman in Bad Tølz and now almost doing the same here in Warsaw? The punishment from God would for certain be heavier than being sent to a Strafbatallion. He wondered if he could get a short leave now if he went to General Steiner. But no, he couldn't ask for it now, shortage of doctors, and soldiers dying all around. You are no ordinary soldier, he said to himself, you are not here to fight and kill, you are here to save lives.

He felt the atmosphere a solemn one when thinking about the Doctor's Oath he had sworn to, grasped pen and paper and immediately started to write a letter to his father now sitting there alone on the farm in Hedemark, Norway. Never had he felt such nearness to his father sitting here in a pub in Warsaw while the war raged on the outside.

Later, out on the street his brain cleared, and the afterthoughts got to him. What was going on, occupying his mind? He had enlisted to be able to fight for his mother's land Karelen, but now he wasn't up to asking for leave to go home and console his poor father as well as his fiancée. No, he would rather stay here and save wounded soldiers from dying, the same soldiers that had invaded his own country, taken over his childhood's home, now a HQ for German officers. It went around for him for a moment.

But then he came to think only about his Eva. Was it all just a deception? Was the real reason for not wanting to go on leave his fear for looking Eva into her eyes. Then having to confess about the whoring in South Germany with this waitress? Fear to Eva's reaction, maybe their binding love then would be at stake? Yes, that could be it, he Lars a super coward. It struck him terribly that as at now he had no choice; he had to get to the front soonest and then off to Finland to Karelen and fight the Ruskies. But he was realist enough to know that no way General Steiner would let him leave Division Gross Deutschland till 6 months later in the least. And then what about Karelen, would this his mother's land forever be lost to the Ruskies?

Having posted the letter to his father he went back to the hotel and the sidewalk cafe. He just sat there with the two letters, feeling lost kind of. The waiter looked closely at him, time to order. Even an SS-officer couldn't just sit there without ordering? Not even a bier? Lars finally excused himself and ordered a glass of wine. Looked at the letters one more time, then he saw it, In the envelope from his father there was a clipping, a pic of a flashy Nazi Jens at his father's house together with colonel Von Klepka.

On the back of the clipping his father had written another message: "This Nazi Jens has become more and more bothersome according to my neighbor Tore up at Øvre. Had you only been publicly engaged now, then I could ask Eva to move in with me, but now it is not possible. Just think about the gossiping. Not that I would care, but for sure it would have been no good to her. So, I think the best now would be for you to get a furlough, come home and the two of you should go to the parish minister and from there on be publicly engaged".

OMG, his poor Eva with her cheating fiancée and the fight against this Nazi Jens. He had to do something, talk to the general about leave before their ways might be divided and he losing his chance to a possible special favor.

"What is it you want for me to help you with dear boy?" The general had power, but if he could intervene for Lars, that was another matter. "Well could you possibly send a wire to Terboven (supreme Nazi chief of Norway) and have him instruct the Nazis up my county to stop harassing my fiancée?" "So, you are engaged then?" Lars red-faced now, "not publicly as I didn't want for her to have bounding vice to me if I should come home crippled or maybe fall there at the front". "Noble dear you, very noble and you don't even want a leave?" "No, Herr Steiner, that would be like deserting those having given me my education with the aim of saving lives. At least not now General, now I want to get to the front to a field hospital, and then later to Finland to fight for my mother's land, Karelen".

"I value your thoughts about my position and my grade, but do you really think that Terboven, supreme commander of Norway, reporting directly to the Führer, would he be impressed by an inquiry from a mere SS-general?"

Lars looked down; "Yes Herr General, I feel confident about it and maybe it would be a good idea to involve the Colonel Von Klepka who has besieged my father's house and made it his HQ. He at least gave me the impression being a man of honor".

They met later in the dining car that evening. Walther took him aside. "You have got what you asked for, but please don't come with any more wishes Lars". "Am I to thank him then?" "No just forget about it for now, leave it be till he comes back on it".

LOKE AND LVIV

Army Groupe South on its way towards the Caucasus needed doctors and he was dismissed from the regiment with the promise of a swift return once Operation Finland was clarified and approved.

Lars felt himself discouraged and down now as he was to leave the two high ranked officers and be on his own, bound for the Caucasus.

But before leaving for the Caucasus, he was attached to the German quarters in Lviv. The local hospital there in Lviv served as a regional field hospital and there was an ever-increasing demand for field-medics, mainly due to the continuous attacks from partisans during nights.

They could attack wherever and whenever like a guerilla. It was the task for the Rumanians to counter this guerilla, a challenge clearly to heavy, they weren't trained to this. But the forceful attacks from the guerilla made it necessary for the German site commander to allocate separate German soldiers to halt and possibly stall these attacks.

Number of casualties turned out the same to the Germans as the Rumanians, but with one big difference: The Germans were adamant that the guerillas was not just partisans, but included groups of Jews not yet exterminated. Following this, a large-scale hunt for Jews began. They told their new medic Lars that during the earlier hunt, close to 30.000 Jews had been killed only there in the Lviv-area. But Lars wouldn't hear about all this. He just wanted to be gone with his assignment and then move on to The Caucasus and eventually to Karelen, Finland.

"You never dreamt about this when enlisting", someone said in Norwegian, and yes it was his old, best mate Loke speaking to him there by the open door." Is it not customary for a private to knock before entering the office of an SS-Untersturmführer?" "Well, I am not a mere private, but a Scharführer or sergeant in our Norwegian grades".

A heartly laughter followed and they had dinner together.

The major in charge for the field hospital found it very strange that his closest, a fellow officer had dinner and was familiar with someone not belonging to the officers' corps. It was almost a case to be reported. But to whom, he was the one in charge and almost without any military training. He Major Klemk, Friedrich Klemk, Chief surgeon from the main hospital in Dresden. Drafted to serve in these barbarian surroundings, although Lviv or Lemberg was an extraordinary beautiful city.

He called upon Lars the following morning. "My dear lieutenant. No damn it, I rather say Lars. Don't make this a habit although you are old comrades. If you do, I might have to send your friend to a different post, close to the front. Would you like that Lars?" "No of course not and by the way, I shall not stay here myself for very long". "What, by whose orders?" "Felix Steiner's". "Really and who might he be Lars?" "If the Gestapo or Himmler himself had heard that question from you, then you would have been shot, on the double, no court Martial, Sir! Felix Steiner, Brigader, he is Himmler's and Hitler's golden boy. And in some sense, I am happy to have him as my protector".

"But Lars, just go out on town and have some beers with your old comrade, but stop seeing each other intimately here in the barracks"." Now what are you hinting at major, intimately? I am engaged to be married back in Norway. Are you implying that I might be homosexual?"

He had acquired a totally new confidence now having spent time with Steiner and his staff over the last days.

The fat Major just clicked his heels, up with his arm and "Heil Hitler" sounded through the thin walls. Officers came asking if there was top brass coming. But Lars just laughed, waved to Loke and left for town. "Meet me at our regular café at the Town Hall in 15, sergeant"

It was all over for now, he told Loke, but for sure he couldn't risk another incident, let alone a possible report to the Gestapo. He told Loke about Berlin, about Friedrichs Berg and how he run into Steiner and not least Walther, proving to be a real friend. But he kept quiet about Birgitta, after all to private even to tell his old friend Loke.

"But your turn now Loke, how was Sennheim and how come you ended up here and as a sergeant?" And Loke talked willingly about Sennheim. "It was rather tedious after you let, except for a couple of Danes. All the others were just negative". "Even the other Norwegians?" "Well, they were all poorly educated and maybe that was the reason for their enlisting. Get oneself a uniform, Sennheim meant employment, proper housing and food, especially in times of war. Maybe even look a local hero to the folks back home. None back home had any illusions about the real life of a soldier, as we came to experience it on our march into Lviv.

But many of them had heard of Himmler's promises and just as much the big words from Quisling that after the war, we would be the core of the new Norwegian army, maybe several of us would be promoted to officers, having fought well at the East front. Several of the boys in my room were adamant that after a short training course, promotion to sergeant was the first step and quite likely the road to having stars on the uniform could be very short. Not in the German army, of course not, but in our new Norwegian army where all the old officers with their stars would be kicked out, maybe even shot, having proved themselves totally inefficient or worse, found secretly tied up with England.

Please don't interrupt me now. Sennheim should have lasted for 6 months, but all of a sudden new orders, off to the very training school in Klagenfurt, southern Germany. This stay there should have lasted for 6 months as well, but after 4 months with excessive drills and learning about weaponry, it was clear that the brass needed more flesh at the front. We were then attached to regiment Nordland, three Norwegian officers there, the rest Germans. This was no way what they had promised to us, but the excuse was lack of Norwegian officers with the right "Weltanschauung", Himmler's mantra."

"Meaning what Loke?" he just laughed back. "Memory blackout Lars? In Sennheim they told us over and again, lack of Norwegian officers with the chin", Lars. Very few Norwegian officers hated Jews and there were not many of them ready for new teaching to the right "Weltanschauung ", meaning that Germany and the German race, build on Nordic ideals, would soon be in possession of all Europe and later the whole world. And that all enemies of the people, such as Jews and "Untermenschen" were to be exterminated. This should be particularly true for Holland and France, real Jewish nests they are these countries. Not to forget the worst country of them all, Ukraine.

Himmler gave us a speech and that day the farmers' sons almost got wings when he told us about the fantastic plans for farming in East Europe, particularly in Ukraine where big farms should be created and then given to Norwegian farmers and their sons. And on these big farms, they would have Polish workers as well as Ukrainians, not to forget all the Russians they would be free to take on. But special attention should be given to the Polish workers; there were too many of them, so some were to be exterminated, not least to avoid food rationing for the troupes; but first, away with the Jewish swines and the gypsies, all to be exterminated".

"But Loke, did our fellow countrymen, the farmers' sons believe in all this Loke?" "Yes, it all became true to them when Himmler talked about the upcoming farm-week in Leipzig, to which all the farmers' sons would be especially invited.

'You must never forget, the leader of my platoon addressed me: Even though you are not a farmer's son, for sure you have a farmer's blood in your veins from ancestries back in time. The battle lying ahead of us now will give you and your likes the rights to take over whatever land you may fancy in all Eastern Europe, all by the order of Herr Himmler.

Himmler has decided for a new city in Eastern Poland, there on the border to Ukraine. It has already been named Himmler Stadt and it is going to be the meeting place for all the big farmers of the Nordic pure race".

And Loke continued: "This business about farming soon came to an end, no more talk about it. We were soon to conquer one village after another and with substantial losses as the resistance from partisan groups and remains of Russian troops were hitting back during the dark nights.

With all the casualties, we finally were almost done with as a regiment. Although we set double guards during the nights, come next morning there was the most dreadful showdowns. Of course, there were dead Jews all over as no one managed to bury them. But every morning the same horrible things were revealed to us:

German soldiers, stripped from the waist down were hanging by their legs in the nearest tree. Their heads max half a meter above the ground, no helmet and their wombs being sliced up by bayonets or knives. The entrails? Already food for the crows. Penises and testicles cut off and seemingly tried to be forced in behind". "Behind? What do you mean Loke?" "Well, yes, stuffed into their asses and if ever so tight, their assholes had been widened out to make room for penis and the testicles, screwed in if necessary.

Sometimes their teeth were knocked out and the genitals pushed in and down their throats. All this, apparently done when the poor soldiers were alive, or just dying.

Some men were badly hurt in their heads and their faces bitten in pieces by dogs who happily took their chances for free meals. Most likely these soldiers weren't even dead when the stray dogs attacked. Some of the guys had their tongues bitten in half".

"But what happened here in Lviv Loke?" "Well, Lviv was the first largest city to fall to us, next to Warsaw. The Ukrainians and the Russians were holding up the defense. Our plan was that our Rumanian friends should do the hard work, the first tough fighting, but as always, they had but weak leadership and we had to join up and get the job done.

There were smokes from fires all over the city, the Russians eager to burn documents. In the basements we found thousands of dead bodies, beastly murdered and with the standard Russian visit cards, genitals cut off and stacked into mouth and throat.

The Jews got the blame, of course they did. But this wasn't some Jewish sport. But they got the blame falsely and now it was free road for the Rumanians and the partisans, those captured, to start the big hunt on all Jews. When it came to hunting down Jews, no moral codex was followed. Soon, not only Jewish men, but their families, old ones, wives and children became legitimate preys and those of them that there was no room for in mass graves, they were buried in new graves digged by the Jews themselves on the outskirt of the city. Thereafter poured gasoline on and set ablaze.

The very next morning all the captured partisans were gone, set free by their fellow partisans during the night. At that time, we were ordered into the city, truly expecting trouble. The Rumanians had celebrated their assumed victory all through the night. Now the streets were empty. But it turned out to be a horrible ambush.

Soon, very soon it was now that the drunk Rumanians and some of our soldiers becoming the victims for slaughtering. But this should not last for very long. When we mounted our newest Machin Gun, rounds of 1200 pr minute, it was all soon over, and we could send the Rumanians on recognition patrols in the outskirts of the city and the woods. Some 35000 Jews and about 500 Romanian troops were killed, the number of partisans, well we have no idea. Our staff mentioned that maybe 300 partisans were killed in this ordeal. Our losses were minute".

Lars looked him intensely into his eyes. "Loke to me they have referred the number of 100.000 Jews being killed or rather massacred". Loke tried to get out of the squeeze, but Lars held on to his head with both hands: "100.000 Loke, and of all Jews,60.000 being women and children, so the count you have got ok, that's only for men? Wives and children not worthy of being counted, isn't that so? And how much do you know about all this Loke?"

"I don't know about all this Lars, only the official numbers and they say nothing about wives and children in the official bulletin Lars". "But where do you think they are hiding or being buried all these women and children Loke?" "Honestly Lars I don't have the clue, I only cited the official bulletin".

Lars was enraged, had immense problem calming down now. He was definitely sure, very sure that his old, best friend Loke was lying him straight into his face. But he had to press on to know more about Lokes swift promotion and how it had come about. "Tell me now Loke how about this promotion of yours, quite sudden was it not?" "Well, our lieutenant and the sergeant were taken out by snipers". "And then you were there handy to be their new sergeant then?" "Well, yes, I was a bit puzzled as they had several corporals that could have been promoted instead, but that was the way it happened Lars".

Some beers later, and 2 hours only left before the curfew, then it was time to "think about the refrain", as his dad would have put it. The thought of his dad gave room for another question: "Do you remember the two students in our group at the UNI Loke, Levi and Benjamin?" Loke looked questionably at him; "Yes, what about them Lars?" "Do you think they are still alive, or have they been captured and possibly killed these our colleagues?" "You must be joking now Lars, don't you?" "Well, but you should know that the Germans together with the Norwegian police are hunting down all Jews in Norway now, not so?" "No, this was quite new to me.

And Lars I don't think any of our student group were Jew-haters!" He pondered what Lars was aiming at. "But if some of our fellow students have joined the NS, then they might have become denouncers." "But we as well Lars have joined the NS Lars, right?" "Right so Loke but we had no choice, if we were to get enlisted". "But Lars would any of us have denounced Levi or Benjamin, our fellow students? We might possibly have asked them to change their given names". He gave himself a small laughter.

"You will have to answer to yourself Loke. I would never have done it, denounced them I mean". "Well Lars, then you know my answer as well!" Lars looked intensely at him. "Is that because we, you, knew them both, really knew them? But Loke what about the 100.000 executed here in Lviv when we marched in, many of them by killed by the Russians on the run, many of them by the Rumanians and in part by the Ukrainians. And quite likely some were shot by our troops".

"I don't know Lars", Loke was clearly uncomfortable now. "The so-called Einsatzgruppe have been on to our heels here as they have with the Army Group South, slaughtered all they come over. It seems like it has got prestige into Hitlers new Command. Not only were adult Jews to be slaughtered, but women and children as well, old people, pregnant women all were to be exterminated. The order for the last weeks has been to make vast areas and Lviv in particular Judenrein.

Hitler has threatened to bombe this fine old city into gravels if there was ever a single Jew to be found here. So far, the city has been spared, honors to the partisans as well as Einsatzgruppe D". "You said Honors Loke?" But Loke didn't face him and just fell silent.

"So, your sergeant stripes have been won by shooting women and children then Loke?" His comrade looked questionably at him. "We don't wage war at defenseless women and children Lars, neither do you?"

For the first time bad blood seemed to have come between the former best friends. They were both quite loaded and well aware of it, trying to avoid any bad words that may just slipped their tongues under the special circumstances. But words slipped easier now and for sure Lars had his suspicions. Were the guys in Lokes regiment that innocent in the slaughtering, or had they been killing women and children without knowing who was who there in the grey light of the morning?

It was almost unthinkable that as many as 100.000 could have been killed in so short a time without the Germans playing an active part in it, with their brand-new machine guns. And maybe much of the killing was done by the German Regiment Norland, one third of this regiment being Norwegians.

It topped up for Lars now, sitting here with his best friend, having bears and cozy talks about the great number of Jews killed in the morning by soldiers from his friend's regiment and other German units as well.

Could Loke have achieved his stripes without so called heroic action? Probably not. But could it be that his story was a true one, he had got his stripes following the killing of his leaders by snipers? His half-finished medical educations gave no credit for fighting in field. "What are you pondering about Lars? Don't you believe the story as told you by your old comrade?"

"No Loke, I don't. You may not have gunned down Jews or partisans yourself, but in my mind, there is no doubt you have been in charge of soldiers doing just that at your orders. You tell me about beastly down shootings in the field, but you not being part of it. Who has given you details about pregnant Jewish mothers been slit up the abdomen, the unborn baby taken out and its head smashed by an ironclad boot, its mother still alive watching it all?

Why don't you tell me about women having their breast cut off, or other women still alive having their vagina stacked up with genitals from other Jews?"

"How have you come to get such detailed descriptions Lars? You haven't been at the front yourself have you then?" "The regular Army, the Wehrmacht and its regular generals take a clear stand against this kind of misdeeds. Their reports were conveyed to us under my time at the med-school in Berlin.

The intention with letting us in on these reports was to underline our duty as doctors to report such atrocities to the Wehrmacht, not only to the SS".

"Do remember your position, Lars. Your papers mark that you are an SS-officer as good as anyone. The moment you stand up as witness of proof of such atrocities to the Wehrmacht, you will be liquidated by your own in the SS-regiment".

"Quite possible Loke and thanks for warning me, but you must realize that I cannot be befriended with a butcher!" He got pale now Loke. "Simply swear to me Loke that you never have taken part in, nor commanded your men to carry out such atrocities.!" Lars was shifting between a deadly white face and a completely reddish one, but Loke didn't react, kept his grey color. "Is it difficult to you Loke to be completely certain that you have no part in this?" But Loke just stood up and left, no comments at all.

He had gotten really sad now Lars, just paid the bill and went home to the barracks.

Next morning at 07.00hrs. he presented himself to the Commandant.

"Heil Hitler, Herr Commandant". He saluted back, looking questionable at Lars. "Something the matter, we did have a chat yesterday afternoon did we not?" "Yes of course you are right Herr Commandant. But I have strongly considered your advice and want to ask for immediate transfer to other units. Rumors are that several battalions will be deployed to Army Groupe South, and I ask for being attached to the field-medical unit there".

"You have to bring the matter to Colonel Walther. He is the one allocating our resources, he and the Gruppenführer".

"In that case I ask your permission to bring the matter to Colonel Walther immediately". "Of course, approved. But what has happened, you changed your mind that sudden?" "I am aware of my lack of experience from the front, and this fits well in with your advice to not be befriended or intimate with old comrades of lower ranks. So, the problem is resolved once I leave from here, Herr Commandant".

Lars knew this was sort of a clumsy approach, but quite obviously the commandant seemed flattered by his request and how the matter had been brought on the table.

On his way out he run into Loke. "Goodbye Loke, I shall leave from here this morning". Then he was gone, but for sure he noted Loke's wondering looks.

And it should be ever so long until their next encounter, the final one.

THE GREAT MARCH SOUTH

Lars felt like being in a cinema looking at the wide screen, seeing how it slowly was filled up by the enormous number of soldiers, panzer weapons, tanks and anti-tanks weapons, supply services, field hospital and a long train of horse-driven wagons, all spread out on the enormous plain.

It was like a look alike from the times of the Roman armies when they displaced themselves to the outposts of the great empire or on the move to conquer new territories.

As the Romans had their platoons of engineers, so did these German regiments. Rivers were to be crossed, blown up bridges to be repaired, undermined bridges to be secured.

Casual attacks from groups of partisans especially after nightfall required huge platoons of guards even here, but the march Southwards towards Kerch and Crimea proceeded according to plans.

Over the Bug-delta they had to build pontoon bridges and while this kept most of the brigades waiting, a small battalion was detached to strengthen the defense of Odesa following the uprise in that city. The Rumanians were in charge, but following the retreat of the Russians, a bomb with timer had exploded, killing the Rumanian Platzkommandant and some regular soldiers, even four Germans.

But General Steiner's adjutant was not at all certain that the damage and the killing was done by the retreating Russian, he rather blamed it all on the Jews. But how could peaceful Jews at all have got hold of demolition material with build-in time lag? Lars was quite curious about it all, not least the allegations about the Jews. But the leader of the med-corps, coming from the traditional Wehrmacht corps of officers, he sticked to the book and when the adjutant of the Obergruppenführer had implied that it must be Jews behind the plot, then the matter was closed. "In Odesa you would find at least 100.000 Jews, Herr Untersturmführer!"

Lars had this far had no confrontation with his major, but they were soon to come. The major had been participating as a private in the First World War, had endured the Capitulation and was later discharged as were most of the soldiers in accordance with the treaty.

Conductor job with the Munich traffic company, not much to his liking, still happy he got a job at all. Wife at home as well as his daughter, still single and he lamented she would be so for a long time, all young men now at the front. Von Ruden made his complaint over the situation to Lars in the evenings.

The major was the only one in his large family that hadn't been promoted to top ranks. His degree as major wasn't well earned, simply inherited from his father. A pretty uncertain situation to him, so in a desperate attempt to avoid degradation, he applied to the SS. And the army was quite content letting him go. In fact, he was to be degraded to lieutenant there in the Army, lacking exams from the war academy. And the SS, they took him with open arms, no checking on his background. In fact, they were only happy to welcome a trained officers to their ranks, free of charge. And Von Ruden had sweared to himself that come what may, he should live totally by the book as someday a title as Leftenant Colonel would be there to him, but admittedly a long step ahead.

Partisans as well as Russian snipers would no doubt help clear the way to his goal. Lars had a vision of majors as short, fatty men with a huge belly, a sort of ridiculous looks. And this was just like Von Ruden looked on a photo of him when in Die Wehrmacht. Von Ruden had shown it to Lars on several occasions just to underline that in the end it was all about determination. As at now he was a well-trained man, almost none pointed stomach and a maigre face. Given the daily rations that Der Führer laid out for his soldiers at the front, a slim figure would come easy. But Lars kept his thoughts to himself.

However, Lars was no longer acting as field surgeon. The battalion had no use for such a position. Von Ruden took him aside one day while he was reflecting over his situation, what he was trained for etc. "Herr Doktor, I suggest that we get started up with some shooting practice, I mean before we drive on into Odesa. We cannot tell for sure what we shall be up to once we are there. Our first platoon is right now questioning gypsies and partisans. Maybe it would be beneficial to you to be present as observer during these interrogations". "To observe what Herr Major?" "Well to put it short, to observe whether our enemies are truly dead, if not let them have a shot in the neck". "But did you not say that our first platoon is interrogating the prisoners?" "Yes, but afterwards they will of course be shot dead. But no atrocities as we have had from them, limbs cut off etc.".

Lars gave him a query look. "But what about the Geneva Convention?" "Do you mean the regulations about how to treat POW's and their rights?" "Yes of course".

"Lars, when you see the dead bodies of our comrades in the early mornings, delivered voluntarily by the partisans and the Russians onto our doorstep, then you skip all thoughts about the Geneva Convention. All our soldiers, those thus delivered to us, all without exceptions have been mutilated.

Decapitated by a rusty sable or an axe while they were still live. Their bellies slit up when they were still living. The entrails taken out and instead the hollow room is filled up with remains like the head of a dead comrade or the genitals cut off and stashed into the empty womb. More so the Classic here on the Eastern front, genitals stacked into the mouth, onto the throat or pressed into the enlarged anus. And at times we have even found our dead guards being skinned alive. You want more Doktor Lars?" No, he couldn't take no more, ready to vomit. "This isn't war Herr Doktor, not war as you read about it from the First World War where armies stood facing one another. This is a type of slaughtering and butchering totally undignified, to all of us. But it is evident that our men get pissed off or worse when they see what the enemy is doing towards us and then they sometimes respond in the same way".

Was this what Loke had been part of at the march onto Lviv and thus earned his stripes? Could he ever be friend with Loke after this showdown, this debacle?

The platoon commander had finished off the interrogations. But the inquests had been without results. No information was passed on by the prisoners and now it was time to give orders to the proceeding. The prisoners were waiting as well, the seven of them in their strange habits. Some of them wearing the traditional brown Russian uniform, jacket and ragged pants others in totally civilian clothes. Two women, they in Russian uniforms as well, shouted gross words to the German guards and spat at them.

"Let's get done with this so we can get on the move!" Von Ruden was clear in his command. An Mg 30 was mounted and two soldiers manned it. "Now Herr Major?" "Yes, on the double!"

Lars looked at the weapons they had found on the soldiers, a couple of sables, a brand-new Kalashnikov, a really old rifle with a rather old-fashioned loading system. But in the midst of it all, two brand new German army rifles. He and everyone knew that these rifles were once the rifles of the two skinned comrades. There was hatred in the air. A short round with the Machin gun and it was over or was it not? "Make sure they are all dead Herr Untersturmführer and if they are not then you know your duty!" But Lars was like in trance. What if they weren't all dead? What if one of them took a shot at him. What if one of them lie there in deep pain just waiting for the neck shot to let him go? But Lars had never killed anyone before, not people not even animals at the farm.

When the slaughter boss came to the farm and the cow or the oxen was taken into the barn, the shooting mask mounted, then Lars was long gone. But one time he was forced to stay in the barn and watch it all; "you are to learn", they told him. So once the animal was hanging there in the ropes, the slaughter man cut the main artery and skewed the pot under for the blood to run freely, should be blood puddings, possible sausages as well from this blood. But Lars wasn't able to eat anything came dinner the next evening.

And now he was the one in charge. His job to be the slaughter, to control that death had come to the poor and if not, he was to set the final with the neck shot at close range. OMG think about it if he should miss.

The major had come close to him now. "Don't put shame to the officers' corps Lars. Look closely now". All the guards were looking at the scene, what was the major up to? But he just took his own pistol and whispered to Lars, "just see what I am doing now". He put the pistol at the back of one of the prisoners and pulled the trigger. Brain mass flowing out of the head. Lars had gone pale. "But was he not already dead Major?" "Does it matter Lars? He felt nothing of it and now you take the 6 others, but be careful, pull the trigger and be prepared, one or more may still be alive, just faking dead!"

He touched the warm body of the first woman. The poor one, hardly 17. Long, dark brown hair curled up and with an elastic band to keep it in place. She had lost her bonnet by the MG-firing. She had taken several shots from the MG this one. Was it really necessary to gun down prisoners, why not just a normal execution with one shot to the heart?

And what about her, maybe she wasn't at all 17, but only 16 like his little sister? This was murder, even child murder. He looked at the neat trait in her face. Black eyes with an empty look at him. He had to close them immediately, but felt Von Ruden coming on to him. OMG now it was done for to this young girl. No doubt she had a mother and a father, and he dwelled with thoughts about them. Maybe they were partisans too and they might be soon to die as well? Maybe one of her parents was among the other 6 prisoners?

"Aber schnell! Make it quick now!" He heard the command from behind, stood up and leaned towards the other woman, a youth of his own age she was. Maybe they were sisters the two of them? Then there was a gun shot and he felt the bullet passing through the collar of his uniform. What happened? Had he just pulled the trigger to early, just by reflex and might it be the recoil that he had felt to his collar? But for sure he had heard two shots and none of them came from his pistol.

But he didn't need pondering for long. The lieutenant responsible for the platoon, kicked away the body of the dead woman, picked up the gun she had now lost from her hands. She had fresh blood coming from the bullet hole in her back.

"Lucky you that I managed to shoot her, or you would have been dead by now". He looked at the bullet hole on Lars's color and laughed. "She really almost had you there, Herr Untersturmführer, careful with the next one then!"

But could he blame her for trying? Trying to take with her into death a man in the much-hated uniform? She knew for certain that she was going to die this woman. If she had tried to escape, she would have been cut to pieces by one or more rounds from the MG. Maybe even blown to pieces by a hand grenade? No, act like dead, and take one officer with her was no doubt the best she could have hoped for. But still strange that she wasn't instantly killed by the rounds from the MG. Maybe the MG-shooter had got second thoughts? She was after all incredibly beautiful this young woman. No Russian traits to her face, more so Slavic as he had seen on the women from Odesa coming there in Lviv. And she had curves, not that she had been busy hiding them. And maybe it was the open blouse that stopped the MG-shooter from giving her the full load? Her right breast nipple was almost hanging out there. Was she at all wounded? Except for the shot from the lieutenant there in the back, straight to her heart region? He was to tell Von Ruden about it. This would have to change, round by rounds from the MG to kill a few partisans.

All the other prisoners were dead, except for the last one of the seven, a very heavy build guy of at least 2 meters height. Lars could clearly se he was alive in spite of the MG rounds. He closed up on him, carefully this time. "No prob. Herr Untersturmführer, I am right behind you".

Lars knew that it was now or never, but would he ever get rid of this picture of himself as a murderer? Because this was nothing but murdering.

No excuses for skinned German guards, no court-hearing, no prosecutor and no defense lawyer, just plain murder. But Lars, just like they would have murdered you, he said to himself

But was that a good enough excuse for what he now was to do?

No way this was part of the education at the Uni in Berlin, nor in Bad Tølz. One exception though if the man had been a Jew. Then it would have been one's duty to shoot him down. "Jew shooting Jew", some exclusive clipping on the Wochenshow (review from the front) there in Berlin!

He felt the nausea coming as he sensed Von Ruden coming on to him. Strafcompany ringed in his head. He pulled the trigger and shot him. A short movement from the man and Lars felt for his main aorta. For sure the man was dead.

Following the incident with the dead woman, Von Ruden had instructed the lieutenant to follow closely on Lars.

They were making ready to leave now, but first they were to line up to Von Ruden. "Soldiers, as from now on, all liquidation shall be done with an execution peloton. No more episodes like the one this morning. Our snipers shall have one prisoner each, shots to be placed in head or chest. And do remember, on these special expeditions we don't keep prisoners. We have nor time nor capacity and not least supplies to keep partisans alive". And Lars was soon to experience this slaughtering at close range.

HUCKLEBERRY FINN

Major Von Ruden had summoned to staff meeting at 06.00hrs. the next morning. There were no dead guards outside the tents. Double guards plus the killing of the partisan group had served its purpose. So now they could move on.

But at Rostov the battalion had lost contact with the main division. They were initially attached to Army Group 17 heading for Sevastopol in the Crimea, this city had long been subject to intensified battles. But then came this dispatch from Odesa, Germans almost failing to hold the city as the Rumanians to be responsible didn't live up to their orders. They were to keep the fort, but no way they could, so what now?

Lars didn't catch all the fuzz about strategy, not his favorite, but he as well as the other officers got their wake-up call from an orderly on motorbike rushing into the camp. He just fell off his bike, the latter spinning in the air. Blood poured from his neck under the helmet and Lars was on to him in seconds. He threw the Depeche-case to Von Ruden, off with the helmet and touched the main aorta. The man was already dead. Oddly enough a splinter from a hand-grenade explosion mysteriously had hit his main blood vessel, blood just pumped out and now he was gone.

"This man shall be decorated with the Iron cross, first order", Von Ruden declared, and his aide took immediate notice of it. "Got to be postumt", Lars mustered, "the man is already dead".

Von Ruden picked up the Depeche-case and took out a map showing the lines of the Russian forces. He soon got totally pale. "Gentlemen", he barely whispered now to avoid panic among the privates. "Double guards immediately and patrols in all directions! I want 4 MGs, North, South, West and East and two men for each MG".

"What is going on?" Lars was as curious as the other officers. "OMG we are trapped behind the Russian lines. A full division of Russians lies between our camp and Sevastopol. Our only chance to get out of this alive is to retreat back towards Odesa, and we are badly needed there according to the messages brought by the poor orderly. It is an incredible job he has accomplished this man getting through the Russian lines. He must have taken a road via Nikolaev, but still just as incredible!" Well yes, Lars thought to himself, but he had lost his life in the effort. But Lars didn't speak up.

Von Ruden had now composed himself: "Gentlemen, we have to cross two rivers and have to force ourselves through a terrain of marsh and all, and we are short of time, not to forget that there are Russians and partisans all over this terrain.

This means marching only after nightfall and we have to get rid of our antitank guns and our air protection weaponry as well. Only the Mg's, Panzerfaust and standard hand weaponry we can take with us. We must walk a minimum speed of 7km per hour. No prisoners, let alone wounded comrades can come with us".

"Excuse me Herr Major, but we shall be shot at Court Marshal leaving weapons behind!" A leftenant had finally manned up. "Leftenant Genke, well put, you shall be responsible for dismounting and destruction of all the weapons we leave behind. Best hide the essential parts into the ground, so have someone start digging. And for your information about us being shot, it shall be you leading our advance, come nightfall!

That shall be all, march starts soonest it gets dark, i.e., 20.00 hrs. Make sure all meals are done before we start. There will be no stopping till we seek cover next day at the break of dawn. All contact with enemy soldiers will be with bayonets. Shooting shall not be responded to. Hand grenades will be the one and only last issue.

Doktor Lars?" But Lars was in his own world right there and then. What was all this about. He now found himself as part of a guerrilla group far behind enemy lines. Here was no field hospital, no lazarette where he could use his knowledge, his education as field-medic. Crazy? Yes, that was the proper word. He had almost no training in being a soldier and what if he got his hands hurt in battle, then not capable of doing the most minor surgery?

"Herr Untersturmführer, if you have problems with your hearing then you better cure yourself immediately. We are in an emergency situation, this means that every man as from now on is a soldier, disregarding rank and education.

All officers, you as well, shall from now on have their own machine pistol. Herr Doktor, now it's the time not to save lives, but to kill as many Russians and partisans as needed to get us through to Odesa.

The Russian forces may well be of more than 10.000 men, but not all of them have weapons". He gave himself a laugh. "It is well-known now that the Russians are short of weapons so not everyone can have one, many have to wait for the soldier in front of him to fall to get his weapon.

But gentlemen, these forces have commissars. Their task is to shoot their own men in the back if they are not up to fighting the enemy. This is not how we wage war. Our soldiers know their duties. It will take 100 Russians to match one of ours. So, we shall show our superiority".

The roll call was a short one and Lars wondered how many of the men believed in this crap. Now the most important was grub and sleep before the night expedition.

A sergeant came to him with a machine gun. "Have you any experience with this weapon Herr Untersturmführer?" No, Lars had never touched such weaponry. But it didn't take him long to realize that this one could be his life savior.

"How many rounds do you want?" Lars looked at the sergeant. "How many do you deem necessary?" He himself hadn't the foggiest. "I suggest 500 and then a few hand grenades to your belt", said the sergeant.

Well then, he was a soldier now, no longer a field-medic. No one were to be saved if seriously hurt. And no prisoners were to be spared. In short no use for a medic. Now the General (Steiner) stood out as his only hope, to get to use the job he was educated to, trained to do and then off to Karelen, Finland.

Lars was told to stay in the middle of the long train of men, no longer marching three alongside as usual, no room for that. Suddenly he almost stumbled over dead bodies. They lay further up the narrow path all five with cut throats and fresh blood pouring out on the brown Russian uniforms. Some moved in cramps, so he figured the executions must have been done only meters up front from him. This must have been a Russian reconnaissance patrol and when not showing up at their post of command, hell would break loose.

Von Ruden no doubt was fully aware of this, so he commanded forced march up towards some huge rocks higher up in the terrain.

Lars and his aide, the sergeant had for some mysterious reason come to head the train now. "Be quiet", said the sergeant and then suddenly he was gone in the mist and the dark. They all stopped waiting for his return and there he was with a bloody bayonet. It felt like he had been gone for five minutes, but he really was back in few seconds.

"The Russians have like an advance posting here, some twenty soldiers, so what now major?" Von Ruden looked at him. "No way we can circle them and get on without them knowing about us?" "No way Herr Major, their one guard is already dead and missing and soon they will be searching".

"Ok take them out, all of them with hand grenades and bayonets, no firing if you can avoid it. Maybe we get lucky as their leaders might think it was one of their own releasing the hand grenade. Lars, give him cover".

He almost glued himself to the back of the sergeant, ready to fire with his new weapon. The sergeant ushered him down behind some bushes. "Shoot at anything that moves Herr Doktor, but not at me!" And then he was gone.

And soon there was a big bang. Splinters and pieces of bones and rocks came out of the cave in the mountain. But there were no cries for help, no cries in agony or pain, no shooting, all totally quiet and they all sought for cover, waiting for the Russians to look for their comrades, now blown to pieces literally. And right so, a Russian patrol came to the scene in forced march. "I can hear them talk about some accident, that one of their own has come to loosen a hand grenade and that they are all in Ural or whatever heaven the Ruskies have". It was the sergeant once again.

Passing the opening of the cave, they were literally walking in entrails and blood up to their knees. Cut off limbs, twisted weaponry and helmets. This was Lars's first encounter with the horrors from hand grenades. Von Ruden came up close to him. "You did learn something from this encounter Lars, did you not?" Learned? Were they on an excursion or something. "Herr Major, I learned that following a hand grenade explosion, there is no need for a medic, just body bags and possibly not that either".

The crossing of the Bug should turn out to be the ultimate test. They didn't care more for the Russians. Having been under cover for the whole day, the major was certain that they now were well ahead of the Russian lines, so now they only had to worry about the challenge crossing the huge river and maybe some partisan snipers.

All the men had made it through the night, but they were soon to be out of food supplies, and they had no engineers to help them with the crossing. If they were to walk further north, all the way up to the city of Nikolaev, then their relieve of the Rumanians in Odesa would be delayed for at least 2 days. And who were to know if the bridge up in Nikolaev was still in place or it had been blown as well. So, the major didn't consider this at all an option.

Lars wasn't trained for long marches, but he thanked his maker having been brought up on a farm with a forest. His physical form was then excellent.

So, what would happen next? Major Von Ruden was at loss. "Herr Major, I suggest we think about Huckleberry Finn and how he solved similar problems, I mean the hero from Mark Twain's book". "Come on Lars, you got hallucinations now?"

"No, Herr Major, you see Huckleberry Finn was an expert on building rafts even from lumber. We shall have to build rafts if we at all shall manage the crossing Herr Major". "But Lars we have no nails nor anything to link the lumber together!" Seemingly irritated now the Major. "Well then we have to use willow branches like Huckleberry Finn did". "So, draw me a design of this idea of yours Lars".

And Lars was on tops now. "We haven't got time to build a large number of rafts, so we have to make enforcements so some of the rafts will hold for several crossings. Each raft should take 6 men and the crossing must be done where the current is at its strongest and water up to the waste max. No doubt there will be long stretches with shallow water and if we get lucky then we shall find us a rowboat or something on the other shore".

"But what about the partisans? And we cannot do this crossing in the dark Lars?" "There must be some real shallow ground in the middle of this river, some place where we can mount our MG, maybe two at best". "But don't you forget that the partisans have snipers able to kill at 1200 meters Lars!" But he chose to ignore the comment. He was on to it now, proud to lead the operation. He looked at his sergeant; "How wide is this river?" "800 meters Herr Doktor".

The suppliers had left a handsaw for the cook, and with this one they were able to cut threes and start the work for 5 rafts. They hoped for the Russian camp to be at some distance so no interference was to be expected.

The Major was scouting over the Bug for partisan groups, but it was really hard to observe anything in the wake of day, not least with the mist drifting over the other riverbank. Luckily this far in the morning no signs of hostile groups. But there were some high grounds on top of the other riverbank, making good cover for eventual snipers, according to Von Ruden.

The Major was back in charge now. "The first platoon will go over soonest and secure the heights". "But what about the possible mounting of the MG in the shallow middle then?" The leftenant was clearly worried. "Mgs will be mounted by the second platoon by first real light and then it is full speed towards the heights. And I repeat, there shall be no prisoners!"

Lars wondered who the Geneva Convention was written for and not least signed, by whom? But he kept it shut.

He got a queer look from von Ruden. "Herr Doktor, our counterpart doesn't wear uniforms, no doubt they are partisans acting like civilians or they might be dressed up like Russians. Please go inspect the rafts and the seizings".

The first one to be set out into the river would take 4 soldiers, the sergeant and the two Mgs. The other rafts needed extra reinforcements. This was taken care of by Lieutenant Genke, while Nr. I with its crew started on the crossing.

The first stretch was quite shallow, making it possible to wade for quite a bit. But then Lars saw that the one seizing up front was about to loosen. He couldn't warn the men by shouting, no doubt it would be heard by the partisans if they ever were on the heights, so he had no choice; he run towards the raft with his machine gun over his shoulder and a long rope to do the fastening.

Von Ruden tried to call him back, but he was soon at the raft and did his job securing the timber. But this operation delayed them considerably, so when the mist had gone and the sun broke through, then the first bullet smashed in the water too close for comfort. It was obvious that they would be well beyond reach for the sniper before they reached the shallow, sandy ground in the midst of the river.

"The two of you take care of the Mgs. We others mount the raft on edge and carry it towards the midriver and the dry ground sort of". They looked at Lars, clearly in doubt if this would at all be possible. The raft was huge and the timber all raw, but finally they managed to lift it while the bullets now were hammering against the protective timber.

Lars knew it was just a matter of time before the first bullet would make its way in the glipe between the timber stocks and if the snipers had access to explosives, then they would have been killed instantly anyway. But the rounds from the sniper weren't very frequent. He was obviously alone, and it must have been old weaponry he was using, took time to reload. But there was no hustle when the first soldier slided into the water with a bullet hole in his temple. It was tough now with only the 4 of them to push the raft, but finally they made it to the midpoint and dry ground and could take cover behind some willows.

One of the Mg-detail was gone as well and Lars was the first to mount nr. 1 and then came their second, both aiming at the high grounds and the cover for the sniper. All quiet at the top now. "Save on ammo!" Lars was suddenly in charge for it all.

He ordered the four others out into the water with the raft and told them to speed up. Reinforcement to the sniper could be expected at any moment, he being dead or alive, no matter.

Von Ruden had seen how shallow it was over to the middle and soon a long caravan of rafts was on its way. The first raft had reached the other bank now and all four were climbing up. Suddenly they were only three, but the first explosion from their hand grenades gave a big blast up on the top and they seemed to be in control now the three soldiers.

But the partisan gang was numerous now and the three of them would require assistance soonest, so Lars got the sergeant and five more men plus the MG on to the raft and soon they had managed to secure the bridgehead on top of the riverbank.

But Von Ruden was mighty pissed. "Who the devil allowed you to go in front Herr Doktor?"

Lars truly didn't get it. "I have an extensive training in leading men, Herr Von Ruden. Not to forget that I am an officer, and we were soon to lose. Plight and Honor were what it was all about at Bad Tølz, Herr Major Von Ruden".

To counter the major in a staff meeting was regarded as a most dangerous challenge, it was like asking for immediate transfer to a Strafcompany.

But Von Ruden may have known what could be in the offing with Lars's close relation to General Steiner, so he just closed it all: "We shall continue later gentlemen, Heil Hitler!"

In the wake of the meeting, the sergeant, Lars's bodyguard got an offer he declined, to be transferred to a Strafcompany for neglecting duty. He had no way followed orders. As a bodyguard he should have stopped Lars from taking the lead. And as soon as they were back with the regiment, then there would be a court martial to decide upon his doings. Von Ruden, being the only higher officer could not decide, he alone, in this delicate matter.

"Just you relax Sergeant. If they should find you guilty, then I promise you that I personally shall bring the matter to General Felix Steiner". "Then I trust you completely Herr Untersturmführer". But Lars did not respond as a sniper almost downed them both and they had to run for cover. So, all partisans weren't done with then?

THE THIRD BOOK,

ARMAGEDDON, WOMEN, DRAMA AND TRIANGLE

ARMAGEDDON

Little Chaim, his nickname to his closest, he had left nothing to chance. During the six months he had stayed up in the mountains with his Uncle Ezra he had grown from being a lenient twenty-year-old with no experience with guns, to now being what his uncle called a fully-fledged partisan. This guy will reach for the skies and make it big; he had told his wife Esther.

"Yes, my husband, if he will live". "What do you mean?" "As most young ones, taking risks comes natural to him, doesn't seem to care for danger".

"No, Esther, this is truly the token of a forward person!" "But look for a moment at yourself my husband. You have certainly taken your chances. But you have carefully examined the situation before attacking!"

"The youth Esther, the youth, it has always been like that". "So, teach him then Ezra, no need for more training on the shooting range. Your nephew could be done with only one exercise, you hear!". "Well, yes", she had a point. "I can hear you talking to yourself again my Husband". Ok then, she had not only one point, but many, his Esther.

And little Chaim benefitted from Esther's advice and his uncle's experience. He had tried out the escape route twice now in the course of the night to make sure nothing could go wrong. The pistol as well as the knife he first had left for Rebecka, he now had taken away. The risk that the weapons could be spotted, and the escape route revealed was too great a risk to take. The heavy concrete lid on top of the way down the sewerage was in part removed, quite heavy for the skinny Rebecka to move in the emergency. The flashlight, two in fact were in place and were controlled before he took cover by the window on the first floor of the huge administration building.

He had used the last minutes to a final goodbye with his two elder brothers. None of them would change their opinion; they would leave their fate to the soldiers and certainly die together with their fiancées and the rest of the families. They knew of course that joining their father there on the Parade square was for certain saying yes to the immediate death. "Go with God you my brothers and your fiancées, no way I wanted for you all to die here, but what can I do!"

How dreadful a way to go, die only by stubbornness in their interpretation of the Torah, let alone the Torah said nothing about willingly accept murder to oneself.

But it had become like an obsession to say yes to the murderers and death and more so to the most horrendous method of killing, hanging, by the feet, or being burned alive. Was he ever to forgive them all these of his race, now voluntarily letting the race die?

"You know well little Chaim that it is the murder of their Platzkommandant that the Rumanians use an as an excuse for the mass murders and then finally they can send the long-wanted message to Hitler himself, his goal now reached: Odesa is free of Jews, now Judenrein".

His uncle Ezra and himself had spent many nights discussing his brothers' stubbornness.

In a way it was understandable that his father as well as his uncle, both Rabbis and responsible for one congregation each, that they would not leave their people, but join them in the coming certain death. But not to understand that both of little Chaim's brothers should sacrifice themselves and accept hanging and thereafter being shot or burned to death? No sense to that at all! And who was to know if they would be hanged or just shoveled into a mass grave and set fire to, like the Rumanians now were doing with the gypsies.

"Uncle Ezra, was it like that in old times as well, that the people of Israel suffered in silence and then accepted to be slaughtered down?" "No, it was not my nephew. Just think about Masada, the fortress in the desert, the fortress that never was conquered by the Romans. It never fell, Masada. When the defenders saw nothing but defeat, then they killed one another, the few of them that were left on top there in the desert".

"But why is there no spirit of resistance in our people any longer then uncle? In Odesa alone it would be no problem to raise an army of 50.000 men and weapons, no problem at all. We are known to be rich on gold as well as cash, so we could buy whatever weapons we wanted. Then we could defend ourselves till Stalin and his army came to save us all". "Do you really think he would come save us my nephew? Would he at all care for us Jews? In the Soviet Union he has disposed of our people years back to the east of the so-called Jewish longitude, so I doubt the realism in your suggestion little Chaim".

"But Stalin will never give up!" Little Chaim was on the offensive. "And with help from the Americans, and that help will come for sure, then it will be the Bolsheviks taking over from the Germans and the Rumanians. When we join in the fight with the Bolsheviks, then we will live in peace ever after uncle. And Stalin has not published any decree about exterminating the Jews, as Hitler has done it. And don't forget he will need us and our craftsmen to rebuild Odesa as well as the rest of the country. We Jews are the best craftsmen. But look at the situation now uncle, my people and my family chose to die, freeze to death, get beaten to death, get shot or burned alive and then shoveled into mass graves. Why uncle Ezra. Why?"

"Our brethren in New York ask the same question. Why do you all choose to die and how can you accept these gruesome slauthering methods?" "You see Little Chaim, there are hundreds of years for this tradition, to bend, be subdued, all in spite of Masada, but I tell you this: There will come a day when the people of Israel will stand up and get together in the country that is ours. And our leader shall come from Odesa. His name is on many men's lips already: David Ben Gurion shall be our great leader my nephew!"

Little Chaim was in place at the window in the Administration building already at 05.00 hrs. this special morning. He had found his way through the narrow streets. All empty due to the curfew. Now he followed the preparation on the Parade square closely. The German soldiers didn't mix with the "Rumanian hounds", the nickname used by the partisans. Now the Germans stood closely together right by his window enabling him to follow their talks. The Germans were quite cocky, but here as elsewhere the dirty work was left to the Rumanians.

Some two hundred Jews, old and young, even women with babies on their arms were stacked together in the midst of the ground. The women folks were hanging on to their men, wanting to meet death together. Was it? Yes, it was, had to be; the women of his brothers with small children, all together. Strangely enough they had been allowed to meet death together as a family. For sure someone must have bribed someone. It was all about gold for the Rumanians.

Two of the most recent MGs were mounted at 10 meters distance from the group of Jews and the Rumanian soldiers were ready with fingers on the triggers; Quite obvious they were afraid of a last minute's revolt.

The Germans with their Schmeisser machine pistols were more or less relaxed. Jews were Untermenchen, nothing to worry about.

It was still early days. Little Chaim's hand watch showed only 05.30hrs. and in the frosty mist, the floodlight didn't quite make it turning night into day. The Germans were not reluctant to use much energy, so better wait for the coming break of dawn.

An SS-corporal waited for orders from SS-Sturmbannführer (Captain) Podolski. The latter wondered why he was ordered to run this show as he called it. The killed Platzkommandant was a simple Rumanian, not a high-ranking German officer, so why couldn't the Rumanians do this revenge killing on their own? Maybe the top brass didn't trust the Rumanians to the job, maybe they would fail again as they had done on other occasions?

And right so, his colonel had said just that. "We cannot trust these Rumanians. Der Führer had been utterly clear, all exterminations shall be methodical and correct, hanging, burning, but no massacre with bayonets and dogs tearing out entrails.

And what more Captain, we must spare on ammo and as I have said already, I don't trust these our fellow soldiers. No doubt they would have found pleasure in spending that many rounds from the MGs, neglecting that each round takes 1200 shot pr minute. Ammo we shall need badly in the great fight against the Popov's and Stalin. And Sturmbannführer, maybe some of these Jewish swines have managed to escape?" "No, Herr Obersturmbannführer, here we are doing everything by the book." And Captain Podolski had learned his lesson well now. And he was to be the one in command for the entire operation.

He addressed the corporal and Lars who had joined for support as required. "We shall make Himmler proud with our action and of course Der Führer. Now, Herr Doktor you will be responsible for the report on this action". "Of course, Herr Sturmbannführer, of course", and heels were clicked. This would be the lowest meanness ever, he thought to himself. He who had accused Loke of being part of the death commands. Now, what about himself? A voluntary toll to carry out the extermination of his blood brothers? But could he have refused, denied orders? Von Ruden had been adamant that Lars's presence as a medic was needed to make sure that none of the prisoners were undue tormented by the Rumanian hounds. Would he have to do neck shots here as well? That would be the limit, no more of that, rather take the deportation to a Strafcompany. Von Ruden checked his watch. Little Chaim looked at his as well. It was six o'clock sharp.

"We have been hunting Jews all through the night, so let's get started. Fire up generator nr.2 so we get light as needed and then tempo, tempo.!" A corporal, obviously an efficient minded one, wondered why they didn't speed up the electricity and then hanged the Jews directly on the electric cable between the masts, effective and clean.

"We shall not waste electricity on them and with all these fat swines, he looked at Rebecka's father, then we risk that the cable will break down, so tempo, tempo, all according to plan!"

Strong ropes were spanned between a number of the masts, and in some places, they had used real wires as well. The Rumanians had made the Jews set up gallows and large crosses earlier in the week.

Some Rumanians couldn't let be with gross jokes about the poor Jews, but the commanding officer immediately cut the crap.

150 Jews were ushered close together, even the two women and their babies. A big truck drove up close, the load of barbed wire was dumped and rolled round the group. Hooks were fastened to the last roll and this once again fastened to the big truck starting to circle the group, round and round, tighter and tighter and the painful cries increased as the barbed wire fastened more and more by each round and the cries toward Jahve filled the quiet morning.

Lots of urine stemmed from the group, like a little stream until it froze on the outside of the barbed wire. Von Ruden seemed like he wanted to threw up, turned and faced the wall of the administration building where Little Chaim managed to take cover last seconds.

Finally, the Rumanian sergeant was content, no more rounds and the cries for Jahve had now turned in to quiet sobbing. There were no longer hopes for being freed and the hooks were unfastened from the truck.

But right behind came a big lorry. Little Chaim chanced on looking out of the window, fully aware of the risk that he might be spotted. The cover was taken off the lorry and he could see a great number of jerrycans, at least 50 there on top. The lorry had made its stop on the far end of the Parade square. Now the focus should be on the remaining Jews. The soldiers manning the MGs were on tip toe. Maybe the Jews would mount an attack? But the remaining Jews were as passive as before. Little Chaim tried to look for relatives next to his father and Rabbi Melchior. The latter should have become his father-in-law eventually. But the rest of the big family was no doubt already in the group stacked together by the barbed wire, just like cattle.

Most of the Jews were no doubt exhausted, having had to seek hiding and short of food as well during weeks. And many of them in fear for their families, wives and children and grandparents, maybe even grandchildren and now their fiancées. Those not being captured and assembled here in the square, were no doubt already part of the big train of people on their way North, possibly freezing to death in the bitter cold and the strong wind.

Little Chaim heard Captain Podolski getting more and more impatient to get the operation going. "Tempo, tempo. No doubt there are still some 50.000 Jewish swines under-cover here in the Odesa region". Lars wondered, why Jewish swines? Maybe this captain came directly from the front, and maybe he had never even met a Jew in his whole life? At least he wouldn't know who was Jew and who was not until Hitler made them all wear the star of David, the yellow one.

At long last the Romanian officer commanded action and soon the first Jews were hanging from the light masts. The gypsies that had been hanged there yesterday were already lying on the ground ready for transportation to mass graves.

"We will hang the next Jew on the cross", one Rumanian shouted and seemingly the German soldiers took a liking to this, high shouting followed. But Little Chaim heard the voice of the German commander: "No dying on crosses. No martyrs for Jesus! Don't you forget that it was these people actually killing Jesus!"

Little Chaim saw that the hanging went very slow. Two comrades, friends of his brothers were waiting in line, like at the slaughterhouse kind of. How long were they to be tormented before it would be over? Would his two brothers meet death together? Maybe he should venture a shot with his gun, aim at their necks and get it over with? But the shotgun wasn't the appropriate weapon at this distance, and he knew he himself was possibly not the best marksman.

Next to be stringed up was a little boy and an elderly man. It just had to go wrong and the rope with the little boy of course flew straight up as he couldn't balance the weight of the old man. The Rumanian leader got really pissed off. "Through them with the rest inside the barbed wire". And the soldiers did just that, straight on to the cramped flock.

Little Chaim saw that the next up, to be hanged by his feet was Chaim, his father. So, his father hadn't been spared after all, and how could he at all have arranged to be spared?

Now he was no longer little Chaim. He was Chaim now, the only remaining of his big family. It was his father hanging right there, hanging sprawling at the light mast while the SS yelled about getting the next guy up to balance the weight of his father. The two brothers, were they to meet death together?

"Look at that fat Jew, he really deserves being hanged by his feet. The fat Jewish pig, how many has he cheated on?" "Hang me by the neck and I shall pay you handsomely, in gold". He hardly recognized Melchior's voice. He knew of course what was to come. They had been through the whole operation a number of times. But the 4 Rumanian soldiers only shouted back: "We shall have the gold, but you shall be hanged by your feet like the others you grey-haired swine".

He could see Melchior show them more gold, but Little Chaim could not hear what was being said because of the cries from the flock enclosed by the barbed wire.

"Ok, ok, but get done with it!" The sergeant responsible was agitated. "String him up whatever way you like, but get done with it". He could see Melchior be lifted from the ground, the rope round his neck, then he fell one meter down and his head was bowed to one side. But what about his dearest Rebecka? She must have felt something, felt that her father now was dead?

Little Chaim heard the sound from the lorry well before he saw it driving close up to the barbed wire enclosure. The four Rumanian soldiers entered the truck hold, opened the Jerry cans and started to pour gasoline over the hundreds in the enclosure. The cries were louder now that everyone knew what was coming to them.

But the German captain was already tops irritated over the Rumanians' slow progress, so he ordered a number of his own soldiers to take action.

A Steiner Personellwagen raced round the corner, closely followed by yet another lorry; on the benches there were but SS-soldiers with their machine pistols ready.

In split seconds, two SS-officers were down on the ground and one MG was mounted ready for its round of 1200 pr minute. The SS-soldiers had in no time formed a circle round their officers.

Things accelerated now, the Rumanians were sent off, SS was in charge and in no time the last 10 Jerries were emptied on the Jewish flock.

The corporal leading the SS-soldiers took one hand grenade, drew the splint and threw it on to the middle of the crowd.

The Fatal Choice

An ocean of fire blew up against the red skies of the morning and then there was an enormous blast when 1000 liters of gasoline ignited. The hand grenade had blown those closest to pieces and the pressure on the barbed wire was enormous, but all the rounds made it stick.

Entrails, body parts and blood whirled through the air, but the Rumanians managed to get most of it back inside the fence. Little Chaim, now Chaim had witnessed a mini-Armageddon.

Those having looked at the scene from the administration building were all gone in seconds. No one took the chance of waiting for what was to come. For sure the Germans would hunt down any witnesses, nobody should live and talk about this dreadful morning. Chaim could hear the clacking of many feet down to the cellar, hiding, but the smell of burnt flesh and gasoline would no doubt follow them even there.

But it wasn't the Armageddon in itself that drew his attention. When the hand grenade blasted, there she came out of Melchior's great coat his darling Rebecka. She was like an arrow heading for the corner of the Parade square to the sewer and salvation. There was no time for him to wait, so he run towards the harbor and the opening of the sewer tunnel. For sure he heard the sound of the Schmeisser bullets shot after Rebecka, but he couldn't stop to check, she just had to make it on her own now, all according to plan.

The cries from the still surviving Jews were faint now, only a few were still half-standing up, but it shouldn't take long before they were all massacred. Following a round from the MG plus some extra Jerries with gasoline, then the pyre sank together. Finally, there was just ashes with some embers that smoldered. And it was barely 10.00 hrs. in the morning.

THE ESCAPE FROM ODESA

Chaim was to wait for her at the other end of the sewage tunnel, there should be a ladder taking her straight up to daylight by the harbor. She could see a faint light there when she finally reached the very end of the tunnel. But what if there were soldiers there waiting for her, having guessed where her escape route would take her? Or would it be her little Chaim as agreed?

There was no time for celebration once she was up the ladder, just a short embrace and then off to narrow alleys and streets hoping to get through not spotted. Not only was there a risk with the soldiers, but who was to trust these days, Jews on the run all over.

"We cannot go on like this my Rebecka, we have to seek a hiding place till it gets dark enough to continue towards the Carpathians. To go by motorcycle or car would have been far more pleasant, but it would be too dangerous as I don't think the Germans will stop hunting you for some time. No doubt they consider you the only witness to the massacre".

"But my little Chaim, I cannot leave from here not seeing my mother for the very last time!" "And where do you think she is right now then?" "Rumors have it that she and my cousin Sarah were forced up to the Plaza north in the town and from there all were to start the long march North. The Germans as well as the Rumanians tried to lure them by saying that this should be a march to freedom, so they should take with them all that they were able to carry, bags, food and clothes as much as they could take. But mother was convinced that this was nothing but lies; they were to march North in the terrible wind and the cold until many of them just froze to death. Those manage to get through the icy hell would be stacked into a deathcamp, later to be burnt alive or simply shot to death".

The wind had got stronger now, a stiff gale at least as Chaim judged it and the drifting snow made it difficult to walk. Maybe there was little risk to be hunted down in this kind of weather. At last, they reached the house of her mother's friend. But there was nobody there, except for the cat sitting alone on the breakfast table.

They looked for any food in cupboards and yes all over, but there was nothing to be found, all gone. So, had these women been able to take everything with them or had there been looters already? But they found wine there and water and above all, a lot of warm clothes. "But little Chaim, can we just take my mother's friend clothes just like that? It is like stealing is it not?" "My dearest Rebecka, the truth is she shall never be back". "So do you mean that my mother and my cousin are doomed as well?" She cried quietly now. "Yes, that's the way it is, I shall tell you about my father, my uncle and my brothers as well as their fiancées, they are all gone forever. So now it is just you and your own little Chaim remaining of our big family. Big Chaim is gone forever dearest. It lasted more than an hour the hanging, the killing by Schmeisser and the big fire and the explosions from gasoline and the hand grenade. Nothing left of them, and the ashes of our family and all the others there at the Parade square spread by the strong wind. So now my Rebecka, we are the only survivors here to carry the race and the family onwards. Provided we are not caught as well and that we must fight against with all our might".

"I hear what you are telling me my darling Chaim and of course I know that my dad is dead as I was the last one to recognize his heartbeat and the sudden stop". She was crying loudly now. "But Chaim, we cannot leave from here without a last farewell to my mother and my little sister Sarah"

Then suddenly they could hear the dogs. It was all about survival now, so they rushed down to the cellar; beyond it was an even lower cellar and a shaft out to the backyard.

Chaim knew this place quite well. It was here in the house of his mother's friend he had met Rebecka on the wake of the massacre, and it was here he usually took hiding himself so his family wouldn't know he was in town, no one were to see the two together. The shaft was mere half a meter deep but there should be a railing on the outside. Hopefully it was easy to get loose, not frozen fast to the brick wall. But this was their only escape possibility, the German soldiers were already inside the neighboring house.

There was an iron plate covering the opening to the lower cellar, and a device to lock it to the beams. But would it stand against bullets and the Schäfer dogs?

He pushed aside the big stone covering the entrance to the shaft and pushed Rebecka ahead of him, then in with him as well and he then drew the big stone after him to seal the entrance. It would be difficult for anyone to hit the right stone to pull out, but what about the dogs? They were ever so good at smelling Jews, this having become Himmler's mantra and then of course adapted by the SS.

They could hear the soldiers now coming down into the cellar. The clicking of the ironclad boots was overwhelming, and she was shivering now his little Rebecka. The soldiers soon found out that there would be a lower cellar beyond, but as soon as they figured out that the iron plate was locked from underneath, then they started shooting fervously to the beams around the plate. Soon the timber was shot to pieces, and they were able to kick the iron plate down. Next second the dogs were down there, and their intense barking signified to the soldiers that bingo, there were Jews hiding beyond the big stone.

"We gotta get out Rebecka, now!" But she was stiff from fear, helpless she was, and he had to pinch her bottom forcefully to get her going. Finally, she got away from the iron railing and they were out, replacing the railing and locking it with a real big stone, but were they safe now?

THE DEATH MARCH

They finally were out of the back yard. The barking of the dogs followed for some time, but the dogs hadn't managed to get through the railing, and soon they were inside Chaim's second cover apartment. It was from here they escaped, the Jews, up to Uncle Ezra and his fighters in the mountains.

From the windows they had a good view to the long avenue where the train of half frozen Jews were lining up for the march. The train seemed endless there in the drifting snow. She knew that her mother and her little Sarah were out there in the biting 20 below, the wind making it feel maybe minus 30C. Much too early this winter coming on to them.

She felt she had to get out, to see her mother and for her to see that Rebecka had made it and was alive, and not least have the chance to hug little Sarah, her cousin, more so like a little sister.

"I have to get out Chaim and you cannot stop me!" "But Rebecka, think of all our efforts to save you and all the gold taken from our holy shrines. Should all this be in wain if they catch you, Germans or Rumanians?"

"They won't get me Chaim". "But don't you see that you may even put your mother and little Sarah at risk once you show up with them? The Germans as well as the Rumanians are no doubt searching for you all over Odesa, you their only witness to the gruesome massacre".

She had gotten really pensive now, sitting by the window, looking at the train of Jews out there. Again, she heard the barking of the hungry dogs, scattered shooting and she noted an old man falling to the ground as the train moved on. An old lady, totally exhausted, could take no more; some tried to help her, but she was shot on the spot. Falling, clearly meant that one was done for, goodbye to this life. But who would help an old mother from falling, no helping hand to her? But the Germans no way were to accept concern for others and the young boy having tried to help the old lady, he was shot as well. Soon the snow was no longer white, but red.

The aim for this train of people was probably not to have as many as possible to reach the camp, wherever that might be. The goal was clearly to make Odesa Judenrein, nothing but that.

She then saw an elderly man with two bags, he not able to keep the pace with the others in the train. Then the soldier tripped him, so he fell straight on to his face, fluttering like a crow, face buried into the snow, one bag on each side. This time no one dared come to his help. He was lying there like an island, the train of detainees, passing on either side. Two Rumanian soldiers emptied his bags on the sidewalk and took whatever they felt for. The old man tried to get up, but now the German solder with his machine pistol put an end to it and his torment was over.

But the train had moved slowly forward, not stopping for the incident at the sidewalk. No, it didn't stop for a split second as one and everyone now knew that stopping meant the immediate death. Even the Rumanian soldiers that had been allocated to keep the train moving, they had picked up some German lingo like "Schnell, Schnell" and "Los, Los", they shouted as best they could. And Rebecka she was never to forget what now happened, and later, much later she was to write about it in her diary exactly like it happened:

When mammy died from us!

Suddenly I saw my mom, bent and frozen, carrying her worn bag, the so-called Jew-bag, small and brown, cardboard with two attachments and two hinges. Or was she not my mom? The strength of the drifting snow had gotten to me, almost impossible to have a clear view. Yes, there I saw an elderly woman and a child. It had to be mom and little Sarah and before Chaim could stop me, I run down the staircase and over to the train and embraced them strongly the both of them. But "Los, Los" they shouted the soldiers, and all had to speed up to catch up with the train. But one German soldier had spotted me, wanting to know wherever I came from. Where had I been, had I been with the train all the time or? I just looked down in fear, maybe the soldier had been at the Parade square and remembered me as the girl running away from the fat Rabbi, they had stringed up? But my mom, she had her way. "Mein Tochter", she cried. "Ok then you whore of a mommy!" and he turned to walk away. But the two Rumanian soldiers wanted their part of the show so one of them kicked my mom hard in her back, so she fell crying in pain down into the ditch. She couldn't make getting up from the ditch and I knew that if I tried to help her up, they would shoot me as well, but I just couldn't let go. He shot at me the German, but he missed, and the bullet went straight to my mom's head, killing her instantly.

But little Sarah cried out too and then she got her bullet as well and the Schäfer dogs were barking and it was like hell there in one instance, and next minute in the chaos there was my little Chaim. I waved goodbye to my mom and to little Sarah, maybe she wasn't quite dead, but now I had no choice, but sneaked up to the train of people that could hardly stand straight in the strong wind. The snow covered me, escaping this time and I saw Chaim gunning down the two Rumanians with a pistol he must have got hold of and we run. Oh, my Chaim, we were suddenly around the corner of the next house, then run back to the hiding house and up the stairs to the loft. There was a secret passage to the next house Chaim said. All the houses were built really close to each other.

Chaim removed some planks and we eased ourselves into like a big locker. He then put the planks in place again and locked them by boards across. We decided to wait take the planks away onto the neighboring house. Thank heavens to Chaim keeping his cool. I was totally apathic after the gruesome happening out in the snow, the murder of my mom and my Sarah, my two most loved ones.

Did I for a moment think about Chaim killing the two Rumanians and what a terrible sin that was, taking lives?

The entrance into our new hiding was a narrow one and we were cramped together at the far end. This box opened the way to the neighboring house Chaim had told me. And now we just stood there waiting. We didn't dear move to kiss each other, but I could not stop the silent flowing of my tears in sorrow of my mom and my Sarah. All other sounds would reveal us to the Germans that no doubt was searching all the houses. They knew who we were now, a partisan having shot down two Rumanian soldiers with his pistol and the girl, no doubt the one that fled from the massacre.

We were standing there throughout the day. Being that tight, it prevented us from not falling to the floor. But we couldn't get to the bathroom, couldn't sit down even. But I had to pee, and the cold didn't make it any easier to hold the urine, I was amazed about Chaim not having to pee, some bladder? Or was it just his stamina? If we peed with our clothes on, the urine would freeze eventually, and we would clearly freeze to death during the night. No doubt it would be easier for Chaim to just let it go onto the floor, but if they came with dogs then they would smell it and more so if the urine dripped to the apartment below.

Finally, there was only one way. Chaim got one of his long boots off and he managed to lift my dress up to my waist, so there I was, only in my panties. What now, we had of course been naked with one another previously, but this was all different. But Chaim was the man for the moment. He pressed my panties down, put the top of his long booth up to my vagina; and what happiness didn't I feel when I peed right into the boot, and it never seemed to stop. But it did and then it was on with the clothes again, still in my cramped position standing up. Next, Chaim had to pee as well. I closed my eyes when he took out his penis and I heard the splashing in the boot! "Not quite blood brethren my darling", I could hardly whisper for fear of the sound.

Many hours must have gone by, and I didn't know that I was able to sleep standing up, but then I woke feeling Chaim's lips to mine. "I don't hear any dogs nor soldiers no more my Rebecka, but the wind is stronger; I wonder where the train of our people is now, all the 20.000 caught in a strong snowstorm. But we my love, we must get out of Odesa, soon after nightfall. Tomorrow when the wind is down, then they will no doubt start a search from house to house in this area, soldiers with dogs".

"But Chaim, we shall need food and warmth for our frozen bodies and what about my mom and little Sarah, probably left in the blood-stained ditch there!" My tears started rolling again. "You can do nothing to them now Rebecka, except make your utmost to live and survive". Painful as it was, I knew he was right. "We have to get out now my love".

He emptied the boot with the urine into the corner and started to take down the planks. "In half an hour or so it will be completely dark in this month of October". October, yes, the 23rd. And it was my birthday. Did I at all think about the big party I always had on my birthdays?

No, my mind was elsewhere. I had but one thought in my head; what about the train of Jews, all the 20.000 or maybe more, were they all gone? I ran against the wind to the ditch where they had gunned down my mother, the bullet meant for me. But by now there was only huge snowsheds all the way. No clothes blaffing in the wind, nothing but all white. OMG, mother was gone, and so was Sarah, both their bodies, stiff frozen now. End to the torments. But I couldn't let go of it: Would they both had lived now if I hadn't stirred it up all together causing the guards attention? Maybe so, but who was now to know?

I was tormented by this thought that maybe I was the one causing the death of my loved ones. Well, not directly, but I was the one creating the hopeless situation, so it had to be me being responsible. But then suddenly

Chaim was there. "We gotta go Rebecka, here is nothing for you. Standing here you will freeze to death and why should you do just that? Don't you forget that your dad so wanted for you to live my love". "But what about my mom and little Sarah, would they have a chance to survive if I hadn't caused this horrible motion?" "Tomorrow Rebecka, they would have been dead, all of them, even those who had made the march to the camp up North". "You are that horrible Chaim!" She boxed on to his chest, but there was no longer any power in her hands, she was but a skeleton, as she was supposed to be to fit into her father's ingeniously constructed harness. "No, not me my love, but the Rumanians and the Germans. I spoke to one of my contacts, the one to help us getting up towards uncle Ezra's place and he told me about the end-station of this train of Jews. A huge building up at Dalkin was made ready for the surviving Jews and alongside it they had prepared a deep ditch where the few who had made it this far would find their final death. But first, all that had made it so far would be stacked into the huge building. MGs would start firing and finally the building was to be set a blast".

"But Chaim, cannot your people, the partisans set a stop to this endless murdering then?" She looked at him reproachingly, but at the same time in deep distress as she knew his answer. But she had an urge to question him after all.

"There is no such thing as my people Rebecka. I am but one in Ezras group and they are located at least 4-5 days of strenuous march from here".

Her tears were flowing like a stream now, but soon froze to her cheeks in the strong, cold wind.

"All of our family and all our friends, shot, killed and now mom and little Sarah gone as well", She had to say it out loud once more. But it was only the wind hearing her lamenting now and it kept blowing even harder and colder and the snow kept pouring down.

Lack of food and water had weakened her skeleton body; she was maigre earlier as well, but there was no choice if she was to be saved. Even Chaim had to accept that it never was their choice, but that she had to be skinny to fit into the harness and thus save their race.

A maigre comfort it was that no longer was their fate in the hands of Rumanians nor Germans, or the ruling partisans, but it was all given to their own God now, their father up there who turned the switch so that the wind pressed whoever was out there now, friend or foe, flat to the snowy ground.

But there was no stopping Chaim. Staying put would be the certain death come tomorrow and he knew it.

"We simply have to get out of town, and you need food and water. It will take its toll on you this weather darling, so let's get started. You have to come up with your last forces to make it, sweet you". "Yes", she believed in Chaim, but where could she find enough force in herself to survive?

JOSEPH'S FARM

They were finally on their way now. The contact man, Joseph knew about the plan and had asked them to come to the old barn. It was empty now following the Rumanians' confiscation of the animals. The farmhouse itself was closed with scudders on the windows.

The doors to the barn were closed and with extra padlocks as well. But Claim was optimistic, went round the back and there was a small door, still not locked so they bolted it real fast once inside. They could of course not lighten a fire, but there were still coals glowing in an old pan. Chaim almost lifted Rebecka's half frozen body over the glowing pan and slowly she felt life coming back to herself. There was no smoke from the glowing coals, so they felt pretty safe now.

Joseph had left food for a week for the two of them and there was even linen to the mattress in the corner. "Thanks to our kind Joseph we shall live Rebecka, for sure we had perished without his kindness". "But where is Joseph and his family then Chaim?" "Joseph is with uncle Ezra or on his way to him". "But the family then Chaim?" "His wife Lea was extremely beautiful, and they had two boys". "Chaim, why do you say was and had?"

"When Joseph came back from a fishing trip one week back, then his house was emptied for all food, wife and kids were no longer there, neither were the animals. Doors and windows were not properly locked, and you can imagine with the wind and all". "But where does this food come from then?" They had an extra storage for supply outdoors, not found by the Rumanians". "But what about the family, wife and kids?" "The two boys for sure are murdered together with other Jews on the run". "But what about the wife Chaim?" She looked wondering at him.

"I am certain she is in a place you would have been sent to as well had you been captured". He fell silent thereafter.

"But tell me then Chaim what do you mean by that?" "I said she is beautiful, if she is still alive then". "But where was I to be sent then?"

"To the officers' brothel". "But Chaim, I am a Jew". "Only the Germans care about that Rebecka". "I for my part would have taken my own life Chaim, wouldn't you have done the same?" "It is not as easy as many seem to believe, taking once own life. Now we have to eat and get some much-needed sleep. Soon after midnight, then we must be on the road north". "But what if anyone comes here and finds us?" "Not very likely, our footprints will be long covered by this horrendous snowstorm. And I have bolted the door". "But what about the dogs then?" "This is a horses' stable and it smells from horse and manure, but we still have to be awfully quiet my love".

He wanted no further questions about weaponry and such. Wouldn't tell her about the machine pistol and the hand grenades till it might come necessary. No way they should be taken alive.

But it wouldn't let go with Rebecka, her thoughts were with her mom and little Sarah, but finally she fell asleep in Chaim's arms, tears running down her cheeks.

He woke suddenly at 1 o'clock in the night. It was bitterly cold now and Rebecka was no doubt still exhausted. But first they had to eat and then get going. Chaim learned the escape route by heart and then swallowed the bits of paper.

And Rebecka, was she dead? Was she already in heaven? But then she heard a familiar voice. But if she was dead, how come he as well was in heaven? But then she came to her senses: She wasn't dead. No way! She was laying freezing in a stable. But she was to freeze even more, much later. I have never ever been that skinny, she said to herself as she got out of the crummy bed.

TO ARI AND THE CARPATHIANS

It had been a terrible march up towards the mountains and without the mega forces of Chaim, let alone the fabulous hiding places Joseph and his friends had arranged for, they would never have made it, at least not she.

According to Chaim the trip should take like 4 days, and they could only walk after nightfall and till the dawning. The second night was the worst one and it was still a long way to go to reach uncle Ezra's place.

But the third night, then she knew they could make it less there would be new storms and flocks of wolves. Make it both of them, for sure Chaim would never leave her on this march. She was adamant about that.

They run into wolves twice, but there had only been three of them, so Chaim managed to scare them away.

She wasn't but skin and bones when they started on the long march. Now when they were to sleep the third day at one of Joseph's contacts, she could see that her skin had fissures. Over the knuckles as well as down her tummy, her skin hangs in patches sort of. The skin fat was more or less gone. Even Chaim noticed it and he asked the woman on the farm if by chance there was some sort of fat to be found in a creme or whatever. It turned out that the only remedy would be speck that could be melted, but no doubt it would give a horrible smell according to the woman.

Rebecka had eavesdropped to the farmers woman and her conversation with Chaim, pretending she was fast asleep, but she had heard every single word. Who were to anoint her in places where she could not manage herself. This farm woman? No way she wanted some strange woman to touch her private areas, so it would have to be Chaim after all. If he was keen on doing it though. But one thing she was certain about: Once this ordeal was over with, he would no longer have interest in her as a woman, his woman.

The smell of the animal fat made her want to vomit, but she had nothing to throw up. Food had been very scarce on this escape route.

When he came to her with the bowl filled with fat, she was just lying there, apathic in a way and she didn't even react when he stripped her naked.

It was ok when he did her back, but when he approached her intimate part, she gave him a long sigh and she mustered: "I am no longer a woman to you Chaim, I am just a skeleton that you will help get up to Ezra, our uncle".

Then she was gone and Chaim who only had seen her naked in the dim light back in Odesa, he stroked her gently with his tender hands, all the way down to her vagina. This was too much to her, so she twisted slowly: "Oh Chaim, please stop it right here!"

But her skin was in the poorest state over the kneecaps and the ligaments had sparsely little to hang onto.

Chaim realized that come the last night, then he would have to carry her. But no way she pushed more than 25 kilos and he simply had to manage.

But now they were to face their third night and the farmer looked at him: "Chaim she won't make it another night, we shall have to make a little sledge of some sort so you will be able to pull her. For sure it will take its toll on you, but much worse if you were to carry her and you cannot stay here any longer. Besides, Ari is waiting at the next farm".

"But if she just sits or lay still on this sledge, yet to be seen, then she will freeze to death, isn't that so?" "Yes Chaim, but you will have to stop every hour in the least, get her to stand up and work on her circulation, less she will be doomed".

There wasn't enough time to heat up planks to construct the sledge to make sure it would run on top of the snow. So, when the farmer came with a wooden box, Chaim had no choice but to thank him and hope he would be able to muster the forces that would take them through the snowstorm; a storm that still was raging, but come nightfall they had no choice but to get on with it, and he simply had to pull through, literally.

At three in the night, he spotted a road, cleared of snow there in the scarce moonlight. No doubt there could be patrols on that road, but he had no choice now. Rebecka would have to try walking and he would give her pauses by carrying her.

The wooden box was no longer of any use. No doubt she would have frozen to death sitting still in it.

He heard the rattle from the tanks long before they came on to them. Had to be a whole column of Tiger tanks. Then it was no snowplow that had prepared the road, but the tanks that were moved during the night, no risk for air assaults. But Chaim, no tanks without infantry, so?

He had no choice but to carry Rebecka over the snowdrift, where they both would take cover in the snow ditch behind. But first back again to erase their footprints, ignoring that the wind could have done the job just as well.

They were closing up now, the tanks, so he digged into the snow trying to cover them both. And sheer luck, the wind did the job. He checked on Rebecka, she looked almost dead, but he still sensed her weak breathing.

"Five minutes now my darling, and they will be gone. But she didn't seem to hear him and in the violent blows by the storm not even the sound of the tanks belts was detectable. He counted the numbers by himself, 17, 18, 19, 20. That was it, all gone, but what about the infantry? He opened his eyes to the drifting snow still no sound of soldiers. Maybe this was just a deployment of tanks?

"Rebecka", he digged her out of the snow. "It is over, they are all gone". Her lips were even more pale now, but she was still breathing, and he managed to have her drink the last drops of the milk provided by the farmer. Milk almost frozen as well.

"Where are we Chaim, in heaven, all is but white here?" Fever? No, she wasn't feverish hot. "Get up Rebecka, you have to try stand on your feet!" But she didn't manage, and Chaim realized that he had to carry her down to the road and maybe even a bit further. He didn't know what time it was, could only hope for the promised break of dawn soon to come. And that the bleak black- grey soon would turn blue, and then yellow by the sun coming up over the ridge.

He knew he couldn't have made it another 100 meters, when he recognized the path leading to Aris' farm. When he thought that all his forces had gone, then they weren't and he fought his way through the snow, but now with the violent wind to their backs. He had to stop for a moment lifting Rebecka on to the other shoulder. When he looked back there was no trace to be seen, not a single footprint indicating that someone had been walking just here. This gave him new optimism and a forceful drive through the last snowdrift and onto the barn door of Aris. And praise the Lord, they were then in the warmth from the herds. He carefully placed Rebecka on a load of straw and then back to the door, locked it properly and bolted it. Off with all her wet clothes, then back into the straw with a horse-cover over her and then lots of straw on top.

If she were to move, then the straw would pick her, making sure the circulation would be back and she would live. He could do no more for her, not now.

Ari and his wife were just doing their chores, happy that the Germans have already picked up the milk and that they were gone, following their routine even at this early hour. The door onto the sleeping quarters were open to secure the warmth from the animals. Ari pointed to his part of the large bed and Chaim just dived into it fully dressed except for the big overcoat and his booths. "And the girl?" Chaim pointed at the door to the cows: "Let her sleep!"

The storm was now raging for the fourth day and when Chaim woke in the afternoon, he got convinced that Rebecka could not take another night in this weather. Ari agreed. The girl had been awake just a short spell, drank some milk and that was it.

They had another 60 kms to go up to Rivne and there was a crossing of a river as well. Hopefully it would be frozen on top. The strong wind kept blowing. And for every 10 kms they would approach Rivne, then they had to count on increasing traffic from Rumanians and Germans, probably some partisan groups as well.

It was Ari that came up with the solution. "This coming night she may stay her with the cows, but no later till 04.00hrs. Then she must have left from here. The Germans are early birds, they just love to hit before sun-up so there is only one issue to this". Chaim looked at him wondering what would come next. Rebecka had to be saved, no efforts had been spared to this so far.

Ari Looked at him: "The muck cellar Chaim". "You must be crazy, is this serious Ari?" Yes, and I do know that the smell is terrible, it is soft and really bad smelling this cow muck coming down all the time, but I can see no other option and listen, in this cellar there is little height so she will have to crawl over the worst part to get to a dry spot at the end". "But is there no a hatch, an escape way to her if she has to get out?" "Yes, in the summer, but now that one is way down under the snow Chaim".

So, this was it then. He had to tell Rebecka about it all and that she would be left here for the next night, then he would come back for her. And he was gone out into the dark.

He pitied her enormously, Ari. But he had heard Schäfer dogs outside the barn and now it all had to be done quickly. Up with the hatch and into the muck cellar with Rebecka, no time for questions. Did they have to come this early he wondered, 03.30hrs in the early morning and they kept banging at the door. But he had to give himself time to wake up as he should have been sound asleep now. But first he spread some fresh muck on the hatch and shouted back that yes, he was on his way. The standard shouting's, "Los, Los", and "Schnell, Schnell" and he opened up.

"Papers, papers! "The same every morning. The sergeant was like crazy, waving with his arms, no doubt swearing over the cold out there as well and now he wanted back to the warm barracks soonest. The dogs were sniffing around making the cows restless and some of them got truly panicky. His wife tried to cool them down as best, but it wasn't easy with the barking Schäfer's around.

The sergeant slapped Ari to his face: "Tomorrow we shall be back for those cows that don't give milk. Understood? Our soldiers need fresh meat!" Ari just nodded, but that wasn't good enough. "Have you understood what I am telling you?" The sergeant was getting tops red now. Ari shouted back a "Heil Hitler!" as a last attempt, hoping that would calm the man down a bit. And then it was over for this time.

But soon thereafter he heard Rebecka crying out: "My hair, my hair is completely ruined, may I come up now?" "Sorry Rebecka, not till the evening. You just have to wait; these guys may be back whenever".

And the Germans sticked to their threats. When the wind was down a bit later in the day, they were back with a lorry having a sort of snow plough mounted in front and two motorbikes as an extra force to back up the operation. But even the snow plough got stuck in the large snowdrifts. They couldn't get the lorry up to the barn, so out with the smallest cow and it was a hell of a job to get her on to the lorry. Ari was tops red of rage while his wife was crying. But the Germans told him to shut it, or they would take with them his wife as well. "Just make sure you produce and deliver milk every day, then they won't harass you any more", he whispered the interpreter".

Then it was all over and come nightfall the second night, Chaim was back together with a younger comrade, some extra warm clothes and more important, a small sledge.

"Where is Rebecka then?" "Still in the muck cellar and the Germans have been here twice and last time they even took one of the cows". "Yes, I get that Ari, but show me Rebecka please". Ari nodded towards the hatch, off with it and there she was, possibly fainted from the gasses. So, Chaim had to pick her up and carry her upstairs. She woke only when up in the barn. "Lots of hot water Ari and soap. See here Rebecka, clean warm clothes for you". "Men's clothes?" "Yes, you have to go along with that". She looked desperately at him. "But are they clean and look at my hair. My beautiful hair, and now the soft muck has been dripping onto it between the planks!"

Ari was soon back with lots of hot water in some tubs. "Look here Rebecka, first you wash yourself in one of them, then out and roll yourself in the snow and then back into the other tub. But start with your hair, that's the worst part". Chaim couldn't hide a laugh. "Sorry my dear, but we shall leave you to it, alone. I shall go outside and watch. We leave as soon as you are done, and we have eaten a little. More grub on the way".

Soon she sensed something, something awful, her nose functioned at last, cleaned for the cow muck and OMG as she was stinking.

But her hair was a mess, she had to deal with it, called for the woman to come with scissors. Chaim heard her shouting and wondered what was going on. "Please come back Chaim, I need your help right now!

Just cut it off and let me look a man, but fast, fast get rid of it all". "Do you really mean that my Rebecka?" She looked up to her beloved Chaim: "If I am to be a man in men's clothes, then just get it off, the hair I mean. It would never be clean after this terrible ordeal".

She didn't even cry a little, no tears when he cut it all, tears all gone following the dreadful days. She had to go along with Chaim seeing her totally naked as he helped her out into the snow, rubbing her as clean as he could and then back into the hot tub and the wife was there with towels and helped dry up and she wasn't cold anymore and started get into the clothes. But they were of course far too large to her. But they were warm, weatherproof and above all clean. The boots fit her well and then they were ready. "Burn it all", Chaim pointed to the hair and her dirty clothes. Ari just looked at him. "Yes, Ari burn it all!" And they were on their way, two men and a manikin. She would have to walk as long as she could take it and then it would be the sledge.

Late in the evening, they arrived at uncle Ezra's. "What is it you have there on the sledge Chaim. Have you picked up a man on your way up here?"

"Uncle Ezra", she stood up. "You are the only survivor of the three of you, dad and uncle Chaim are both dead and so is mom and little Sarah". She hid herself under Ezra's big overcoat, a quiet sobbing followed and then she dropped off.

"Rebecka dearest, don't you forget that you are no longer Rebecka but Sergei. You cannot hop around here with all these men, a young and beautiful woman, and remember my Esther cannot look after you all of the time. We shall deal with you once you have got your female shape back, but as for now you are just a boy, with a non-Jewish name.

And Little Chaim is no longer Little Chaim following his father's hanging and later being burned on the big fire there in Odesa. Now he is Chaim.

We shall get through it my Rebecka and we shall have good use for your education as a nurse. Welcome my child, now we shall start fattening you". She had to lough over the expression, her first laugh in weeks. "Fattening to what end uncle? To the offering?" Ezra turned serious. What was on the little one's mind.

LIVING THE PARTISAN LIFE

She had envisioned training in weaponry, fast deployment to new hiding places and not least attacks on the Rumanians and the Germans. But it wasn't to be like that, not at all. And what about sex? No feelings when he touched her, neither on his part. No bone erection as when they met in Odesa, he then would get a hard one merely when touching her. Now, no reaction no more. Had this war managed to kill all the fine sentiments and all their fine sex life? She didn't see him much; he being out on missions, and it was just as well.

This march together to the mountains and all the things happening between them had erased whatever sexual feelings, now replaced by a bond like between brothers and sisters. Chaim had seen her totally naked body, he had washed her, anointed her and dressed her when she was naked. But she had not reacted sexually, not then and not now, strange it was when she came to think about these moments. She remembered him having anointed her down to the pelvis and her vagina, now just a faint memory evolving nothing but kind feelings. That he cared for her and wanted her to soon get well.

She never thought of Chaim having another woman, not at all. Nor were there any attention from the other men in the group. Maybe they didn't think of her as a woman, this boy Sergei. And if they did, then they no doubt thought of her as Chaim's girlfriend. But she was not even that, although she would have liked to be at times, but she just couldn't get that feeling.

Life as a partisan was not like she thought it would be. There were the chores, helping Esther and dressing wounds after shooting raids. But no one to talk with except Esther in charge of the cooking. She was considered far too young to participate in operations, so her life was limited to assist Esther with the chores and for the rest simply be there as Ezra's niece.

She made small tours to the river, her only distraction and every time she had a swim there it felt like just another layer from the muck cellar disappeared.

"But Rebecka", Esther always used her real given name whenever they were alone the two of them. "You have tried a hundred times now to get rid of the muck layer as you call it. But be aware, every time you use this strong soap, your skin fat is hampered and maybe if you keep going at it the skin itself will crack and possibly dissolve. So please, no more of that soap and let me rub this cream well on to you".

But Rebecka could not get enough of the fresh stream from the Carpathians. There were tails about this water having a healing force. But she wasn't sick, except for her mind maybe.

Then one day by the stream, she had just done some stretching after a good swim, touched herself down there, felt some excitement and even more so when she held her breasts now fully ripe. But to what end, having this beautiful, ripe body up here in the mountains when Chaim was so distant to her? Then suddenly she heard like a cry, and she was quick to get the dress over her shoulders and cover herself.

"No, there was absolutely no one around", Esther replied. "I kept watch all the time and for what's it worth I always carry this one with me". She waved with a Schmeisser machine pistol they had taken from the Germans. When Chain came home next morning after a nocturne raid for supplies, she told him about the incident at the stream. "It had to be someone watching her there and maybe just this one time". He was puzzled: "All men here were with me and Ezra on this raid Rebecka, so no one from here could have been watching you".

"But I am adamant Chaim, somebody was there". "And what about Esther, did she see anybody?" "No Chaim". "Well then don't go skinny dipping the next time". No, she shouldn't do that. But a few days later she had once more this feeling of being watched and she told Esther. "Must be some tramp here" she said and reported to Ezra. "I think there is someone around here, Rebecka is right. While we were down by the stream some meat and bread had disappeared from the outside depot, the one right under the rocky shelf here". Ezra sent the men to scout the terrain, but there was no trace of anyone at all. Still, he had noticed like a fresh path down to the stream from the other side, but was it really fresh?

"Tomorrow Rebecka, you go down to the stream for your bath again. I shall take cover on the other side". He told his men that he would stay at home the next day. But nobody showed up, but she skipped bathing for some days. Extra care was given to the outside depot, properly locked at all times now.

No more thefts and Rebecka concluded that the person she had felt observing her by the stream, he must have been a loner, now gone.

They lived rather primitively up in the big cave, fearing that they might at any time be revealed by the enemies, not least those partisans with a profound hate towards the Jews. Rebecka's greatest pain was the loss of her mom and little Sarah, she could not stop thinking about them all through the days. Not so with the loss of her father. She had for some nonspecific reasons come to terms with his death, however brutal. He was gone for good, but she cherished the memories, all good they were.

More than anything else she missed her dear colleagues from the Jewish hospital. No doubt they were all dead now. But her conviction to nursing, her education, it haunted her that she was just stuck away in some cave, the one thing that she was permitted to was dressing a wound from a bullet, and that was it. Yes, she missed her past terribly. And she knew that she had to go on, learn more, do more to help sick people. But the Jewish hospital for sure was no more. The building would be there, but now it was filled up with wounded Germans. How am I to get there? She wondered, and was it to her, a Jew, to save German officers? But were there any other options then? Go over to the Russians, but surely, they would find out she being Jewish? So, should it be her fate to end up here, hiding in the Carpathians. Never get to finish her education? "Never, that's taking it a bit far is it not Rebecka?" Ezra was looking at her, sort of reading her mind. "This war may last for maybe two, maybe three more years Rebecka. If Hitler won't give up or get killed, then all of Germany shall be destroyed and then it will be three years at least till there will be peace".

"And then uncle, what will be next, our future, what about it?" "The Russians my dear girl". "And what will they do to us Jews?" He looked at her and reddened. "Well, I guess they might put us in camps or something, I mean us men. But on the other hand, they shall need our skill and the manpower to rebuild the occupied territories".

"Don't talk yourself out of it uncle, I saw you reddened". "Well, what do you think happen to women in war then Rebecka, do I have to draw it to you my dear?" "No, not at all, but do you mean that we shall all get raped or? Just tell me uncle!"

"There are more and more talks about getting to an agreement with the Russian authorities about emigration. But they want us to pay for it, pay pr capita so to speak. But most of us have nothing more to sell, and we are all short of cash and gold, let alone that our houses have been confiscated. But we hope for the Russians to be serious about this and then we may get money to pay them off from our kins in the USA and then leave Ukraine". "But do we have close relatives in the USA then uncle?" "All Jews are related Rebecka, so no worries".

"But emigrate to where uncle Ezra?" "To the land that Chaim has on his mind, The Palestine, or Israel our Promised Land and then proclaim it as our own state, together with the leaders south in Odesa".

"But uncle the war is still going on, and wouldn't it be best for me and us all if I got out of here and back to the hospital in Odesa so I can fulfill my education and practice on what's my vocation, help the sick and the wounded? Yes, I know it is filled up with Germans there now. But I could work there as long as possible while we wait for this war to come to an end, and then I shall be a fully-fledged nurse, ready for this new country Israel. And if there is one thing that will be in high demand when we come over there, that would be doctors and trained nurses". She was looking anxiously at her uncle, would so have his consent.

"And dear uncle what about the people living there now, possibly all nomads drifting from place to place with their herds? Yes, I shall have to talk about all this with Chaim".

"But Rebecka, going back to Odesa that's a tall risk and you know how many have struggled to get you out of the devils claws there and now you are considering going back? Think about all the good people having taken great risks for you". "Yes, I know uncle, but I am perishing here and Chaim, he is rarely here anymore".

"We all have high hopes to survive this occupation, this war Rebecka. But what we don't know is what will happen the day the Russians are here as victors". "But then uncle, then it may be the best option to stay with the Germans, not so?" "But what if they recognize you one day Rebecka, I mean down at the hospital and someone calls on you using your real name. How will you react then, what will your answer be? Denial from people once close to you?"

"If there are only German nurses and doctors there and all patients are Germans as well, then there would be no risk at all uncle, provided you can get me false papers for a new identity. I know my profession and no blood samples will tell if I am a Jew or a Russian from Ukraine for that matter.

And dear uncle, if we are pressed further west in line with the development of the war, then I shall become part of the deployment of the medical personnel, and then I will be like bombproof about my true identity". They both had a laugh at this expression. "But what will be Chaim's reaction when you tell him about your plan to go to Odesa?" "We are but first cousin's uncle, but as of now we might as well be brother and sister, nothing more to it". He looked at her slightly embarrassed. "But are you not a couple then Rebecka, boyfriend and girlfriend, that's what they all think about it here, I mean the men". "So, they no longer think I am the boy Sergei then?"

"I should have told you about it all two weeks back. It then became evident to all and everyone that you are a woman". "And how come uncle?" "Well, you were right about this guy looking at you there naked in the stream. He was the guy that helped Chaim picking you up at Ari's farm that stormy night and he admitted having seen you skinny dipping twice. He is mere 17 and simply could not let go of it". She felt the chill down her spine now. "But where is he now and what have you done to him?" "His father, one in our group asked Chaim what the punishment should be, but Chaim had only told him to take the boy back to his mom to grow up. Learn how to behave, no more fuss about it all. He was gone a week ago Rebecka".

"Some kind of a play to nothing then uncle, all waste". "But let them carry on calling you Sergei to be on the safe side. But now Rebecka, back to my question, are you a couple or not you and Chaim?" "Well sort of, but as I said, we are more like sister and brother and maybe it was only this war and the circumstances that brought us once together as lovers. We do love one another dearly, maybe so because we are the last ones of the family out of Odesa. The two of us that should be the foundation of the new family as your brothers put it Ezra".

Suddenly she fell to the floor and Ezra felt her cries were horrendous.

"My duty uncle, my duty as an individual and the duty towards your dead family is to be the one foundation to take this race further on. I just cannot make it go haywire uncle and should I be saved only to be like a breeding cow?"

"Shame on you Rebecka!" He was angry now using her real name, no Sergei this time. "You have no right to talk like that. Duty is what you have towards the Lord, no one else!" "But he has given me no answer uncle". "And what about Chaim then, he might be facing the same difficulties as you in this challenging question?" He cleared his throat slightly troubled. "But you have slept with each other then?" She blushed, but it was soon over. "Yes, twice in Odesa, but not later. But during the escape he was wonderful to me, cared for me, washed me, ointed me and dressed me, I being totally naked. So, he has seen me naked a number of times". "But no reaction on his part then?" "No, I mean I don't know, I was far too blunt and worn out to notice, but no, I don't think so".

"I must talk with Chaim once he is back, maybe he will open up. May I say that you struggle up here since you cannot work with your profession?" "Yes, do that, but don't you touch upon our personal relation, I mean the intimate side. I would have been a coward not to talk about it myself directly with him. Promise me that uncle Ezra!" "Yes, I promise".

She could see that he had gotten lye as he walked away from her. Maybe he was sick? There was no doubt a reason to it, he staying in the camp and no longer participating in the raids. Maybe he wasn't just old, but reel sick? But suddenly he doubled back. "Rebecka, what are your inner thoughts, I mean going back to Odesa and work for and save lives of those having brutally killed your friends and all of your family? Some of these officers may have played a huge part in exterminating millions of our race. Have you thought about that?"

She was only 17, so maybe he set her to a test hard to overcome. But she responded immediately. "Yes, I have uncle, but we cannot turn the clock back. I hope for the Russians to be back, take over the hospital and then they will need qualified nurses like me, I mean except for the German staff. And officially I am Russian/Ukrainian, and they will need me". But he had to think a little, then: "But you are young and beautiful Rebecka, and would you not be a tempting object to violent men there?" "Just as much up here in the mountains dear uncle, don't you think?"

When he had left the second time she was soon down on her knees and prayed for an answer from the Almighty God. But maybe his answer was that there was no answer to her prayer. Maybe this was the challenge for her to find out what she stood for, a challenge to her own judgement, her capacity to choose the right direction to her life. But she was agitated now and felt the knocking to her chest and her brain was just making her turn in circles all the time. Would she take better care of the children of Abraham staying up here in the mountains with Chaim and the partisans, subject to rape whenever, or should she risk her own life as a nurse to German officers south in Odesa?

But the days went by and no Chaim. Her hair had grown long again, but now she decided on having it short. Her face grew greyer by the day. She didn't seem to care at all for her looks.

Would there be no answer from the Lord, or should she just be hanging around here by the cave, slowly pass away?

But Esther, Ezra's wife, she had an eye for what was going on in Rebecka's brain. "Would you consider going to the stream with me one day Rebecka and then we will help each other with water to the tub as well? You know Chaim is finally due back in the evening." So, she was to be the lamb for the offering now?

Oh, she hated herself for her caliginous thoughts, but her auntie read her like an open book. "Sorry dear Esther!" And she hugged her auntie, "Sorry."

Esther helped her cut her hair and after a hot bath in the tub Rebecka got a brighter view on life. Chaim would just drop by, leaving later for a new raid in Lviv according to Ezra, just home from some mission.

"I found some kind of an ID down the road here Rebecka. It is from a nurse, Svetlana and there were even some papers signed by a field-medic, he probably been dead now up at the front in Leningrad and maybe the nurse on the picture as well. These papers could come handy if something happens to our camp and we all had to run for it. Don't you think so my dear niece?"

Absolutely a masterpiece they were, made with a lot of stamps she had never seen before. A clever craftsman it must have been.

Then Chaim and his group came, he being NC now. "Looking good Sergei" and he kissed her straight to her cheek. You are good at lying dear cousin, she thought, so she returned his kiss, prone to lying she as well.

They had moved away from the others and sat down further on to the path. "You are looking good you as well Chaim, but you seem a bit tired of it all if I may put it like that". "Not tired, but maybe a bit fed up sort of. Life goes in the same rhythm more or less day out and day inn. We kill some Rumanians and now and then and we hide for the Germans when looking for food to our group and others in need. Kind of Robin Hood way of life. But we don't get any further. For the others it is all about surviving, but I am restless, cut for something more challenging. The Ukrainians have gotten a sort of authorization to take over our properties, our goods and valuables and at the same time it has become like a race ideology to them to kill as many Jews as possible".

"And what about the Russians?" "Stalin would best see us far East to Ural or maybe to the Crimea as well, but there you have the tartars, and they despise us. So, we have no place to go Rebecka". He was fed up with this Sergei fuss he called it. "Careful now Chaim, you may come to reveal my identity". "Well, you are right Rebecka", he pulled her on to him, but no kiss and no reaction from down there. "And you Chaim, what future do you see up here?" "I really don't know, but this has become too small to me. I had rather we mobilized all the Jews and form a regular army, craved our rights and got ourselves a large territory".

"But the Germans would have bombed us to pieces and then let their tanks finish us off Chaim".

"The truth is that I want to join up with Ben Gurion. He thinks big, thinks we should have our own land, Israel. But to quote him, he says that we must do our utmost to survive now, women and children alike, so when the war is over, and it will be in a couple of years, then we can stand up and go to our Promised Land, Israel, craving what is rightfully ours.

You should know Rebecka, our people here in Ukraine, maybe several millions of us, and in Odesa and western Ukraine alone more than half a million, we have only turned the other cheek to our imposters and accepted extermination. Think about the million in Kyiv, marching straight on to death in the mass graves. Our future in Israel shall be totally different, we shall stand up for our sacred rights and with the help of our kinfolks in the USA we shall build up defense systems making us invincible. There will be no more Armageddon to the people of Israel. We Jews cannot survive as a race by continuously being on the move, like nomads, from one place to the other. We have to get back our Promised Land and stay there".

"But what about those living there now then Chaim?" "They have to move, go to their Arab kinfolks where they belong or stay with us on our conditions". "But where is this Ben Gurion now then Chaim?" "I don't know, but our people in Odesa knows". "So, then you are going back to Odesa you as well then Chaim?"

He gave her a small smile and then he stroked her new cut hair. "I read uncle Ezra like an open book dear you, but I have to go now". "But you are just back after three weeks Chaim?" "Yes, I know, but there is something hot going on somewhere and I shall be back this evening, but only to leave again at first light". She accepted his kiss, this time on her mouth. Was this to be his good-bye kiss?

"So, you couldn't stay out of it uncle?" She smiled openly to him. "But dearest Rebecka, it was Chaim that came with the ID-papers". She got embarrassed. Please excuse me Chaim, she said out in the air. "Your man thinks big Rebecka and I hope he shall succeed with some of his views".

After supper, Esther took her aside. "You may be sitting up for quite a while and wait for Chaim, you know he shall be late, and he will be off early morning. So why don't you take our room, uncle and I can sleep with the others in the big room".

She reddened, angry now. So, the offering lamb was to be prepared. But she kept it to herself. "Thanks, dear Esther", and she composed herself

Come midnight and still no sign of him. She could not withstand the urge for sleep, so she let the little lamp down and closed her eyes.

Then she had a sensation from times back, when she felt the naked body coming to her from behind. Should she pretend sleeping, or should she give him the farewell he no doubt expected? But it was too late to consider, he had entered her from behind and she felt totally lost in the delight. It had been so long, so long since Odesa and then all the gruesome that they had experienced together. Still, she was able to think one sentence: What if there would be a baby? But her thoughts were drowned in the lust of the moment.

"Dear Ezra, we must plan for my departure. I think the best way would be if I suddenly show up at the hospital say in the middle of the day and simply ask them if they need help from a nurse". "But will they not question where you come from and who has sent you, and what will you answer to that?" "No more worries uncle". "But still please listen to this possible explanation then dear Rebecka:

The field hospital up in Rivne was to be moved to the main one in Lviv. Your old boss had been moved to the front at Leningrad, North Army Groupe and you were not keen on going there as your interest was to specialize in surgery before once again to return to a field hospital. So that's the reason why coming to Odesa to a proper hospital to learn and get adequate training before once again returning to the front".

"Ok, but who was my former boss, and can they not reach him to check my story, either via field telephone or Depeche?" "Rebecka, stop worrying, but to your question. As I said he is at the front, his rank is captain, name Weber, a rather common name". "But this Svetlana, the nurse, what about her?" "She was the only Ukraine nurse. The others were German or Polish. Svetlana chose to leave in connection with the reorganizing and was free to take whatever position in Odesa. This is backed by the papers signed by Captain Weber".

"So, when am I to leave then? Tonight?" "Well, you may go with the night train, or you can hike with one of our drivers going south for supplies. Personally, I would have chosen the lorry, less comfortable, but on the train there would no doubt be several control posts".

"But what about control when we come to Odesa?" "You have hiked with a supply lorry, totally legal that. The driver is of course one of us and his mission is to collect goods for the supply service here in Rivne".

It proved hard to say goodbye. "Chaim reckoned you would leave now Rebecka and him being that restless, then this is probably to the good of you both. But for sure you will meet again". "You really believe that uncle?" She was crying now.

"But what about you and Esther, will we meet again?" "It is not for us to decide Rebecka, it is all about fate. We have decided to stay here in this camp and fight and then we will see how far this will take us. I don't blame your father nor your uncle and their sons who chose death by hanging and burning. But we up here we would rather die fighting. That's our choice". "But uncle Ezra, I don't think you are soon to die. I think we shall meet in a year or so, right?"

Then she was off. The driver had already gotten impatient wanting to get South soonest. He didn't speak but a few words and she was happy to that.

She was half asleep sort of when they arrived at the first control post. The driver handed it professionally, presented her papers as well telling them she was on her way to the Odesa hospital to work.

Halfway south he took off from the highway and off to smaller roads, lesser risk for more controls. "Where is Chaim?" she mustered next time; she came to herself. "I am Andrej and there is no Chaim here". He yawned a bit. It had been a long night and finally they were at the hospital gate. He just wanted to get rid of the girl soonest, then get his loads and be on his way home. "Bye!" was all he said and then she was on her own. Was she frightened to that? Not the least. Getting afraid was something she had put behind. She had convinced herself that following the escape in the sewage tunnel, fighting the big rats, then nothing could ever make her frightened.

"I have greetings from my old boss Herr Doktor Weber, now at the front in Leningrad". She introduced herself to the Matron as the nurse Svetlana. But the latter pretended that it wasn't all about showing up in broad daylight, taking a new job for granted. She wasn't to make it easy to the newcomer, even though she lost one of her most skilled nurses only yesterday. It took a while and then finally: "We have to hear what the doctors say".

ODESA AND THE HOSPITAL

There were no more letters from Eva, nor from his father. Most likely there were problems with the welfare service. So, he didn't write he either.

He was happy to have missed the march towards Sevastopol and that he now was formally allocated to the hospital in Odesa, making use of his education and training as a field-medic, no longer a guerilla soldier.

But there was a constant lack of medicines and more so of nurses as they were badly needed at the front.

But one day there was really too much for their capacity. He as well as his Chief surgeon had worked with saws and knives all through that night. His coat, the last clean one was like bathed in blood. Then came this girl, maybe 18, or 19 at most. Skinny, but she still had curves. "Who are you and why do you come here?" The boss was really tough on her, and Lars saw that she looked frightened.

"I am the nurse, Svetlana; they have sent me down from Rivne. All and everyone had talked about the imminent need of more personnel here in Odesa, so here I am". Lars didn't understand much of what she said, only that she was a nurse applying for work.

"Papers, papers" shouted the boss, but Lars took him by his arm, "later?"

So she was in business, and she was fast and clever. "What am I to call you?" "Svetlana, my closest call me but Sveta".

That night she got supper and uniform and even her own room. She was to share it with one nurse Nina, but she had just left, couldn't take the workload anymore, 24 hours shifts at worst.

Her papers were good enough. Educated and trained up in Lviv, and then half a year's practice in Rivne. Russian father and Ukrainian mother. Quite common that, but Lars felt she had more of Jewish looks than Russians.

The boss was of the same opinion, they were looking at her papers a couple of days later. "Her credentials are ok", Lars commented. "Hope for her not having yellow fever then", he laughed the boss. "Well, be it as it may, but this one, this one must be for keeps, if not we shall have to ask for reinforcement from Berlin and that may take long".

Lars was happy now, finally he could make use of his education, no more long marches and no risk for bullets from snipers. No court martial and no neck shots to be done. But he missed his Eva as well as his father and he couldn't wait to get to Karelen and then maybe have a leave to go on a short visit home to Norway, if the war wasn't over by then. But Lars you cannot go home to your Eva! His inner voice was powerful now. No, off course he couldn't do that. Not now and maybe never? First, he had to concentrate on the job here in Odesa, then Karelen and later maybe his father could bring him up to date about the farm and everything, not least all about Eva.

Still, the evenings were dull and heavy sort of whenever at rare occasions they had the nights off. Then there was the longing. The longing for a woman to share it all with, not just his thoughts, which became more and more predominant.

"What about a night out Sveta?" Lars could no longer hold back. I only pity her, he argued to himself. Alone in town, loads of work and the German nurses they sticked to themselves. Would hardly acknowledge that Sveta, not being German could do the job just as well as they could. "Thanks to the offer, but I shall devote myself to study to be a specialist nurse trained for surgery. In a few months' time I may be ready for going back to Lviv and do the final exams".

"No way you are to leave from here Sveta. What are we to do without you? By the way, I can help you with your study, just let me know and I shall be there for you".

Yes, she was stunning and tempting the little one, especially out of uniform, the latter always bloodstained. A clean one lasted hardly more than a couple of hours from the morning rush, badly wounded patients incoming at all times.

It was after the third or maybe the fourth talk they were together that Lars found it best to inform the Chief surgeon to avoid gossiping from the other nurses.

"Very good", was the comment from the super, "but make sure to meet in the canteen to avoid any gossiping and whispering, women love intrigues you know".

Fair advice, not only to her, but just as much to him. No way should he start on a new relationship right now.

"Doktor Lars, are you married or engaged to someone up in Norway?" He was taken aback by the sudden question. "You never go to Norway on leave I mean?"

Lars knew he flashed and of course she saw it." Sorry" she whispered, "really sorry for prying". "And what about you then Sveta?" He had to get out of the trap. "Well, yes I have a boyfriend sort of, up in Rivne, but we just spend time together, we are not engaged or something".

Lars had managed to compose himself now. "It is like this Sveta, I once was engaged to a girl in Norway, but…" "But?" He shouldn't slip away. It wasn't his furloughs that was on her mind. He felt this quite intuitively.

But Lars had gone silent. "She had a name this girl?" She had to help him back on track. "Eva", he spoke softly now. "Herr Doktor, if you don't want to talk about it, so let's skip it, I am sorry for prying". Her German was quite impressive now.

"No, it's ok. But we are not together anymore and that's ok, I mean she being far up in Norway and me here by the Black Sea".

"I guess she was quite pretty, was she not?" She should stop now, should she not, but he laughed openly, kind of relieving to her. "Yes, she was, just like you Sveta". And now she became the one with red face. She was in a squeeze now. "Thank you, Herr Doktor,". But the female cunningness got him. "I guess you will be going back to Norway then, once the war is over?" "Pending who wins this war". "Who wins the war? Raising such a question Doktor Lars would be looked upon as high treason and a shooting peloton would come next. Of course, it will be Germany, and you are here in a German uniform working for German soldiers and officers. How could you at all raise the question of who wins the war? Of course, it will be the German Reich". She was in shock now and couldn't hide it.

She then whispered to him: "But should it be the Russians coming out victorious, what then Herr Doktor, will you then go home to this Eva, the girl you know up Norway?" "Your question Sveta is based on a defeatist attitude not allowed in these quarters". As an officer he felt he had to put her right. "Are we done now?" Following this inquest sort of, small talk came easier and to his surprise she then accepted to join for an evening walk.

But Lars on his part was far from done. Sveta had risen in him a fear to be arrested if the Russians should be the winners. Deportation and confiscation of all goods. 10 years in camp up at Bjørnøya in the North some said or was it to be Svalbard or even the Norwegian possession in the Southern Ocean, Bouvet Island, close to St. Helen, Napoleons deportation island. Quite fitting that would be.

Marked as Quislings, traitors to their country, which was the comments from the other Norwegians once in Sennheim. And these guys were just privates while he was an officer in the SS and should have known better.

And the Germans were to lose this war, he was almost certain about that now and for one particular reason: Stalin had no respect for human life. If his generals needed some 100.000 more men, well then, they just sent for them from Siberia or wherever and if these perished, well then, the generals called for another 100.000; as simple as that.

But what would happen to the farm he wondered, and not least what about his father? Only one arm and then the surgery plus the farm? And his father had already suffered the loss of his one daughter, stricken by polio. Not to forget his darling wife Sarah, the flower from Karelen, the one and only woman to him. And what if there was a message to him one day that his only son, the heir to the farm and the surgery, that he was now dead at the East front and probably shoveled into a mass grave. Would this be too much and thus taking his father's life as well?

Maybe there would be an amnesty some time, maybe ten years after the end of the war, but maybe even some 20 years later? But by then his father would be gone and what about the farm then? Would it be merged with the farm up at Øvre as written in the old documents, according to Eva? And what about her, would she be there unmarried still waiting and who was then to take over the two farms? Some distant relatives maybe?

Just forget about it all Lars, he said to himself. This isn't about gold and green acres. It is all about your father and Eva, his Eva. But was she his and by what right? He had cheated on her with the first and best of the tempting German girls south in Bad Tølz. But I didn't cheat on her with Birgitta, he said to himself. I was firm then. Yes, and what an idiot and to what end? The Eva-train was gone then and Birgitta was a great person, they could have hit it big the two of them.

But where should they have stayed? His inner voice was on to him again. In captivity in some Russian camp, but not together? So, were there really no free harbors to them? Maybe England? No, let go of that. England had once declared war on Finland. Then there was but the Iberian half island left to them or Switzerland of course. But Switzerland wouldn't be evident, less he could play his half-Jewish background. But what about Birgitta, would she be on the run? She could probably do well in the regions to be taken by the western powers, could she not? In contrast to him, SS-Untersturmführer, member of the most hated of all the German forces. The penalty would be a long one and his right to practice as a medic, what about it?

Stop it Lars, your brain has gotten crazy. Whatever you chose, you cannot go back to Norway, it is as simple as that. Not now because of your cheating on Eva, not later as you once chose Germany over England.

What then would be the best issue? Live in hiding in some country, hoping to be officially gone, not a wanted guy ready for exchange with regular prisoners? Better so, officially been declared dead, missed in action or something? No trace, no shame to his loved ones back home. Only a sorrow memory to both of them, memory fading with time.

Yes, it had to be that issue. He wasn't but 24 years of age and he could sense the bitterness of a possible fate that he never had envisioned. But this issue would be the consequence of the choice made at the students' flat back in Oslo.

He had consoled himself with his life now and did his best to help the halfdead and the lesser wounded as well. But one day there was a Depeche coming in, motorbike with side wagon and the driver was in a hurry, needed a signature only and then to hurry back. "Where they come from?" "HQ of Division Gross Deutschland, sent by the aide de camp of General Steiner".

"Maybe we are to move from here then?" The Chief surgeon looked at Lars. He was worried and combed the little hair he still had, picked up his glasses and started to read out loud: "I would of course have been delighted to be present and lead this ceremony". That was the beginning of the letter to the Chief. "But unfortunately, I couldn't make it as I was summoned to Berlin, to meet with our Führer".

The letter continued: "SS-Untersturmführer Lars Nedregård is with immediate effect promoted to SS-Hauptsturmführer (captain) and is simultaneously decorated with The Eisenkreuz Ritterkreuz of the second class for his bravery when crossing the Bug delta.

This promotion and the decoration were mentioned in the "Announcements from the Eastern front" and Steiner would personally inform Der Führer about it all. The Hauptsturmführer will no doubt be summoned to Berlin later".

Furthermore, I Felix Steiner am convinced that in addition to Lars's personal qualifications, the fundament of the Nordic race, then the education at my dear Bad Tølz has been of decisive importance to his heroic bravery, saving an entire battalion. Heil Hitler!" (Signed Felix Steiner, Obergruppenführer)

There was a small note next to the letter, marked "Personal to Lars".

"My dear young one, your sergeant and escort on the crossing of the Bug delta is promoted to first sergeant and to be decorated with the Eisenkreuz first class. The question of having him transferred to a Strafcompany is flatly refused. Yours Felix"

"You never mentioned nothing about this Lars. I figured you were an ordinary medic and that was it". Lars felt slightly shameful. "The General may have exaggerated a bit Herr Major. And we don't wear uniform here, nor decorations, do we?" The Depeche had been signed and they got on with their work the two of them.

One day at lunch the Chief surgeon wanted a word in private: "Be careful now Herr Untersturmführer. The German girls, the nurses have started like a whisper campaign against our girl Sveta, darned stupid and this may in part be by your doing, not so?"

But the growing sympathy to one another wasn't to go further. Three days later in the park, at night, the shock came to her: "Sveta I shall leave in the morning". "Will you leave?" Panic-stricken then and she just burst out: "What about me then?"

Then suddenly she realized what she had just said; OMG what was he to think about her. "What I meant was that hopefully there will be a replacement after you and then I will still have a job, right Herr Doktor?" She was no good at it and he saw right through her.

She had put on some weight this little flower and now in her own dress, green to her copper-black hair dropping to her ass, God forbid that the Matron should se her in that outfit, she was a sight he couldn't resist. Her dress was open at the neckline, not only one button but three, and the soft tissue couldn't hide stiff nipples, clearly, she wanted to have him, just as openly as Lisa south in Bad Tølz. So, when she let go of his hand and faced him, tip-toing, then he knew there was no way back. It had to be now or never and when they were in hiding behind a big maple tree, he pulled herself even more forcefully against him and there was no resistance in him, none whatsoever. She was just there for him, mouth wide open. OMG, he longed badly, but for Eva. A woman to love, he said to himself.

She came to him that night and then quietly went back to her own room, fiveish in the morning something. When she came down for breakfast at six, there was no Lars.

She asked the Chief surgeon about it. "No, he has left for Finland to fight the Bolsheviks. Amazingly clever that guy, being that young. But maybe it is to the best that he has left Sveta?" He didn't need say no more. She blushed and looked down. "At your service Herr Major".

But she knew in her heart that one day Lars would be back.

KARELEN AND THE FAMILY FARM

He was bidden welcome a hero by the crowd when arriving in Viborg. He had brought a huge stock of medicines and bandages. But the deception by the Finnish was overwhelming when they realized that all the help, they would get this time was a platoon of sanitary workers, medics and nurses.

Lars tried to soften the commanding officer by telling him that really, such decisions were not for Lars to take. He himself was but a voluntary from Norway and had joined the Waffen-SS only to help the Finnish people, his kinfolks. He also made a point of how important a role it played that Germany had advanced towards the Russians. If they hadn't done just that, then the whole of Karelen now would have been Russian.

"And where do the captain go from here then?" "Well, following my promotion to Hauptsturmführer I have been promised two days furlough. I now want to look for my mother's kins in Karelen if there are still anyone alive out there". "Satan, why did you not tell me you are half Finnish then?" Now there was vodka on the table, and it was arranged with driver and escort for Lars. But no way he got on the route this morning, the impatient Lars. The commanding officer insisted on them having a Finnish luncheon. Lars didn't have a clue to the local way of drinking and then it was suddenly late afternoon and no way going for Karelen in the night.

A list of supplies for two days was arranged for. Should keep driver, escort and Lars going. He felt he could spare no more time and maybe there would be a chance for going back to Karelen later if there were kins to be found at all.

A late and "damp" dinner and then departure at the break of dawn. The jeep was of acceptable standard, not so the narrow roads so it was almost evening before they approached the farm of his grandfather, or at least they were in the area where it might have been located, all according to his mother's rough sketches.

But there were no houses left there, only the remains of the stone foundations and barely that. Well, the church was still standing there like his mother had said it would. But now it served as horses' stable according to the church clerk, the only living soul in the area. The walls of the synagogue were demolished and dispersed out on the fields.

And there were no dead either, the gravestones were taken away and the Russians had plowed the field and used it for potatoes right there where the graves once had been marked. His mother's map was correct except now all was barren and abandoned.

"Not much sense coming here", he looked at the clerk, "I mean now the barbarians have turned it all upside down". "Well not everyone were barbarians, many of them were orthodox, but they didn't dare to declare their faith. The children of the revolution have Marx and Lenin, not to forget Stalin as their gods.

But who are you actually looking for? Maybe you aren't German, are you?" "No, I am from Norway, a Norwegian doctor being here as a volunteer to the Finns. More precisely I am on leave from a German division fighting by the Black Sea". "But do you have a name to the family you are looking for?" Now, he was just on the edge to reveal himself; his grandparents being Jews and all and even if his mother now was registered as adopted, still there was no point in shedding light on her and indirectly on himself.

"I have been here for more than 50 years", the clerk went on, "baptisms, weddings, funerals, I have seen them all", he still wanted facts this man.

Lars felt a thrill to his stomach now. "I have to check further on my papers, but I seem to remember the name, Anna Jahujærrvi or something like that". "Yes, that is a real Finnish name! But you see the farms up there, they were owned by Jewish families, so naturally I had no dealings with them." Was he getting too clever now this church clerk?

But he was saved by the driver, Lars. "But Captain this is not East- Karelen".

"East Karelen?" The clerk looked at him.

Lars played with, looking apparently surprised. "But where are we now then?" The escort came up with a well-used field map. "See, here is the Karelska neset, and this is where we are now". He was proud of himself the escort, showed off his content, at least someone was able to read a map.

Lars composed himself. This one was close, too close. "Then we have to move on immediately". "Now, it is getting dark soon?" He was ready for getting rid of this nosy clerk. But this one wasn't quite finished. "Then I hope for sake of God that you have good weaponry, a lot of things going on in this forest at night, hard to tell who's who. But there is an almost smashed inn some kms further down the road. Be cautious and don't go any further than that this evening".

The driver and the escort shared room at the end of the corridor. Lars had been very adamant that they were to leave sharpish at 06.00 hrs.

But what was the point in going further into the Karelen. The Karelen he once had decided to come to and fight the Bolsheviks did no longer exist. The cemetery with the graves of many of the parish's elderly and people alike was but a field for potatoes according to the church clerk and if there had been a Jewish Cemetery at all, then it was ruined as well, possibly totally destroyed. No plantations, no sign of human beings, only deep tracks from tractors and shovel dozers.

The same would no doubt be the case for the farmhouses. He hadn't the slightest doubt about their location. This was where his mother had been raised. Here she had probably played with her little sister, maybe even been fishing trout in the little stream running towards the lake. He was stunned by the beauty of this place. And how more beautiful wouldn't it be with the red painted main houses and the big yellow painted barns here at the fruitful Karelien soil. Not strange at all that the farmers from this area were in high esteem.

For sure there was no poverty here compared to the barren land further up in Finland, not to speak of the North where the forest was predominant, the cultivated fields were all small and the soil was mostly boggy land.

But here it was like a divine beauty and Lars felt a deep sorrow in his heart. Naturally this was due to his mother, but may as well be by the vandalizing of his mother's beautiful landscape and the parish she had come from.

He tried to remember from his father's tale about the visit in the twenties and how beautiful it had all been with mother, then a young woman in her blossom sitting there in the sunshine by the lake. Were there tears now, well yes there had to be.

But now it was destined to be large collective farms, people and machinery coming for the spring seed; once done, then leave again until it was time to come back for the harvest. In the meantime, this wonderful land just lay there, no more farmhouses nor people. That was the way the Russians did farming.

He wondered, would the Finns be up to holding Karelen against the Russians and would it at all be sensible to spend time in Viborg looking for more kinfolks, previously farmers and ask them to come back to their land? No, he didn't feel for that. No sense at all as long as there was a war on and who were to know about the outcome? Russia or Germany? And these kins being Jewish, well he might not even be allowed to meet with them and then he best took care for his own sake, the suspicion of him being a Jew might well be fostered.

This adventure about Finland and Karelen came clearer to him now. It was no longer about fighting together with his fellow Jews. They were all gone now, possibly in camps in the Ural or exterminated. Now it was all about helping the Finns against the Russians, work as surgeon and done with it, no more sentiments.

He was ready to go already at 05.00 hrs., wake-up call for the driver and the escort. "We are not pushing any further boys. Back to Helsinki and my commission by train tonight".

What about his father, would he still be in Finland? What about train? Maybe there was no train at all. But the Commandant would certainly get him to Helsinki where he was to report, the leave soon over.

The drive back was a real sunny one and Lars couldn't refrain himself for looking up at the once beautiful land of his forefathers as they drove by. He felt at peace with himself in a way, maybe more so thinking about his mother who never was to see the destructions of this her childhoods beautiful landscape.

The local commandant was utterly surprised by their swift return. But Lars was adamant that he wanted back to the front and the lazarette soonest. So, it would have to be Helsinki willingly during the night, but then he would need a driver that could do the distance during the night. The commandant wasn't too pleased by having to allocate another two men, but maybe it was all to the best to get rid of this Hauptsturmführer soonest.

"What was his mission in Karelen then?" "He talked a lot with the Church clerk but said nothing to us Commandant". The escort had nothing to add to the driver's comments.

Lars was well received in Helsinki, but much to his surprise he was to be allocated to a lazarette at the Karelska Neset. So back to where they had driven the other day. And it was here at this lazarette that there should be the surprise of the day, say the year for that matter.

The lazarette consisted of two large tents and in one of them a surgeon was operating together with an assistant. Remains of legs and hands having been saw off were laying outside the tent. Some assistants were busy clearing the grounds. But the field-medic was a one-armed man.

Following the sad feeling having left his mother's land, it was an indescribable feeling to meet up with his father out here. It really was his father working on a patient there, well telling his assistant what to do, not much he could manage himself, the one-armed.

"I don't know if I like your attire my boy. But get out of that uniform and find yourself a coat so I shall be able to hug you".

And things developed ever so rapidly. Mere 5 minutes went by and then the two of them were operating together. "This is to be my last trip over here Lars. I want home and then it will be for others to take my place here. But I hope I have been able to save some lives. Many of those I have operated on here, they won't thank me for being one arm or one foot shorter. But with time I feel certain they will appreciate that I did it to save their lives".

But to Lars this sight wasn't any worse than what had been witness to on the South front. On the contrary. The Russians here in Karelen had been much more human to the prisoners. Almost none of them had their genitals cut off. But maybe that had happened to soldiers not making it to the lazarette?

"What is it like there South Lars, all bad?"

"Well yes, from a medical point of view. Every so often it was the partisans to blame, let alone the Rumanians and some Russians. But there is no war in the old traditional way, least where I have been. It is guerrilla warfare, terrorize, frighten and brutalize". "The women soldiers as well?" "Yes", and he thought about the execution of the partisans where the bullet just missed his head.

"But worst of all is the extermination of the Jews. By the tens- of thousands father and I think Loke has been part of the murdering as well. I haven't seen him for some time now, we didn't split as friends".

"Women, what about them?" But should he talk about Eva having been courted by Nazi Jens and that she now had a son? No, he couldn't do that, not now when there was a war going on. He better try get Lars to come home at some instance. But there would of course be questions about Eva and what was he to say then? Best come on the offensive himself when the time was right.

It was late in the evening when they finally could close down. They were to sleep in the same bivouac the two of them. "I am going home in three days Lars. Will you come with me?" No, he couldn't do that. He was summoned to this lazarette to do a job here, an effort in memory to his mother. "Did you see the farm, Lars?" "Yes, I did, but there was no farm no more. I have seen the burial place as well, now it was just a field for growing potatoes".

"Yea, it is all gone now, and if they weren't in need for a stable, then the old church had been gone as well. Think about it, Karelen one of the pearls on our planet". His face got suddenly saddened. Lars tapped his shoulder where there was no longer an arm. "She is gone Dad, and I thought about it yesterday when I was out there, praise the Lord that she never was to see the destruction of her beautiful land. And her kins, all gone Dad? Do you know when and how it happened?"

"They fled from the slaughters, first to Åbo and then over to Sweden, many of them. But it is dangerous to ask about it, people may think that you sympathize with the Jews. Almost as dangerous as to be linked up with the Bolsheviks".

Not much sleep to father Trygve. Lars had been unwilling to talk about Eva, so what was Trygve to tell her once he got home? And what about Eva's son, was Lars the father, or had Nazi Jens forced himself on her one of his many visits? If Lars and Eva had slept together before him leaving then it would all be much simpler, Nazi Jens was dead and the boy looked quite a bit like Lars. But what if they hadn't slept together, what then? No, was it at all right of him Trygve to put questions to this matter? Shouldn't the young ones sort it out by themselves?

"Eva has a child Lars, a boy". "What did you say father, you were sleep talking, are you in pain?" OMG had he babbled while asleep? "What did I say Lars, did I speak incoherently, maybe tongue tale?" He tried to brush it away.

Lars laughed, "no nothing to worry about, at least nothing dramatic. You said something about Eva, but I didn't quite catch it". "Maybe the next night Lars, just listen more carefully then. But now we really need a couple of hours sleep the two of us. Sorry waking you up my son".

But Lars didn't get to sleep, the sun was already up and the rattling from the train of wounded coming in, made sleeping impossible.

He made the round to those they had operated on yesterday. One had already passed; his cot was empty. "He passed round midnight", the corporal said, "very quietly he passed". "Well, I had my suspicion, the loss of blood was too much to him".

For sure it was primitive out here, no lab and no possibilities for blood transfusion, but this soldier had been too weak to be moved and with the two legs gone, then maybe it was all for the best? Stop it Lars, you are here to save lives, not to take lives.

Father and son spent two more days in the surgery tent and Trygve was astonished by the capacity his son possessed after less than a year since finished med-school. "You should know father, during my six months at the university in Berlin, I studied during daytime and the evening was spent in the operation theatre saving heavily wounded soldiers, less they would have died in a waiting line somewhere. So, there was no option but to develop one's skills as fast as possible. It was all about saving lives".

"But now my son, you are here in the midst of your mother's land, have you then thought about your decision, enlisting to this purpose. Are you happy with your choice?"

"That's a big one father. You know I couldn't have helped these brave Finnish soldiers if I had stayed at the Oslo UNI, then intern at the Ullevål hospital and given time had my final approval as a medic. From there on covertly gone to Finland like you have been doing father. Looking back at all this I feel my decision was the right one, now I am helping our Finnish friends every day".

But his father wasn't quite through as yet, he wasn't stupid, was he? "But when this war is over, what then Lars? Will you come home to us? Of course, you will if Germany wins the war. But what if they lose, the Germans?" His father had no doubt thought a lot about it all and the Home Front had no doubt been persistent, telling one and everyone that there would be a time for revenge and God help those having chosen the wrong side.

"I am not to talk about this now Dad". Should he tell him about the rumors, that when coming home he would be deported, lose his citizenship and his legacy to the farm? Maybe he would lose his right to practice Medecine as well? No doubt his father was familiar with all these rumors.

No, he couldn't take way from his father the dream of having his son come home safe and having him take over the farm as well as the surgery. And he knew that if they digged deeper into these matters, then the relation to Eva was bound to be on the table. He wondered what his father's dream was about. He definitely had said something about Eva, but he was no way going to pick up the subject. Better wait until his father might come back on it.

It was soon time for his father's departure. A new Chief surgeon, a Swede had come to replace him. He wasn't too happy to work with a Norwegian Nazi he had said in the camp. Lars for once could not hold back. "Although you are my boss, please bear in mind that I am a damned good field-medic. I joined the Germans to finish my education and then get over here to Finland to help defend my mother's land. This wouldn't have been possible without first joining the NS and later the Waffen SS. That's the way it is. You don't have to like me at all, but I shall not accept you talking crap. On this camp we are both equally doctors".

Not a word to the matter from the chief, not then, not later, but Lars had the bivouac to himself that night.

It hadn't at all been easy to wave his father goodbye. Lars had this feeling that this could be like a goodbye forever. No way he thought the Germans would win this war, now that the Americans had joined the western powers.

They were deeply moved the two of them. Trygve made no further attempts to get his son home with him. No doubt he knew it would have been in vain. "Give my love to Eva Dad and do your best to take care of her". Then it was over and there was a new leg to be cut and a shoulder to be put in place.

But his sorrow wouldn't let go. Even the chief recognized it and kept shut. At long last the evening was over, and he just dived into the sleeping bag, hoping for a well-deserved rest, but sleep should not come to him. There were only tears, but who was he crying for? Himself and his incredible misfortune. His beloved mother who had been happy and young and in insane love right here? Over Eva sitting there waiting for the rest of her life. Oh yeah, he cried for both of them, even to himself, but the deepest sorrow he felt for his father. His own dad, with all his dreams, dreams that would never come through.

Now it was time to read the letter from Eva.

"My dearest Lars! Thanks a lot for the greetings brought to me by your dear father. I am glad the two of you had some time together. He bragged about your skills in the operational theater. No doubt you have spent time well in Germany as well as at the East front".

Well then, if she were to know about his womanizing, and maybe there would be a child following the episodes in Bad Tølz and Odesa?

Episodes? Had he grown totally cynical? He had after all had serious liking for the two girls, just as much to both of them, even though his attachment to Svetlana was much deeper.

Was her real name Svetlana and was she really half Russian, half Ukrainian? He as well as the Chief surgeon had meant she had Jewish traits. And what about it, he said to himself. But he let it go, if she had been Jewish then she would have long been killed.

He membered one night when he came to pick her up in her room, he then had seen a stamp on her suitcase with the name Rebecka. Should he ask about it and was she not a bit careless, Jewish or not? No doubt she had found this typical Jewish bag amongst the leftovers among Jewish refugees. They seemed to have all that baggage following orders from the Rumanians and the Germans.

But their attachment wasn't all due to their profession. Oh yes, they worked extremely well together, but there was something more to it, not only a flirt or fierce desire as with Lisa in Bad Tølz. And this Lisa, she had been ever so excited, and maybe nothing but that. But delicious and tempting she had been his Lisa. No doubt she would soon be over with Lars and find herself a new cadet. Sveta not so. Fair enough, she had this friend up in Rivne, but she had been quite quick to say that there was nothing serious between the two, not even engaged, so.

Let go with his thoughts, the corporal suddenly stood there at the opening of the tent. "Sorry to disturb Herr Doktor, but we just had a transport, incoming with two very badly hurt, shot in neck and head and the new Chief surgeon, Johansson, he wouldn't take it all on him".

THE NEW CHIEF SURGEON

Ok, the letter from Eva would have to wait. Lars was up in no time. Well then, the Chief surgeon asked for help, assistance from a Norwegian Nazi? For sure he should come to his assistance.

He just nodded to Lars when he got into the tent used for operations. "This one", he pointed at the one on the stretcher, "he shall have the rest of our morphine and then we shall wait with operating on his leg till the morning". "And what about this one then?" Lars pointed to the man with wounds in neck and head. "Shall we just let him die?" "What's the opinion of the captain then?" The Swede consequently denied using Lars's German title and grade, and no way he wanted to be on friendly terms using only their given names.

"With no more morphine we shall not be able to stabilize him, but the bullets will have to be removed. Just as bad the two wounds, the one in his neck may have damaged his spinal cord". "Is he able to move his legs then?" "Oh yes Captain, but what about the bullet in his head?"

"Let's be over and done with this rubbish talk, Captain etc. Here we are both field-medics, at least this very night, so better leave the military reference till tomorrow." "Have you treated such damaged neck and head previously then?" then He looked questionably at Lars. "Well yes, at least five of them during my training in Berlin, and for sure another twenty in Odesa".

Johansson bet to his lip and got quiet. "Ok, then we shall have no morphine to the man with leg wounds". "No problem, just give him something to bite on so he doesn't damage his tongue. The corporal will look to that".

"Alright then, I best assist you when you start with head and neck?" "We shall start with his head, maybe it is just a splinter from a hand grenade". "Only that?" Lars chose to overhear the remark and was on to the job. Right so, the Swede was a first-class assistant. Scalpel and suture came instantly. But they were almost out of wound wash.

For sure the morphine was to some help, but in the end the corporal and a private came to assistance having him strapped to the operation table.

The wound was a simple one, just a little splinter from a grenade. He was lucky this soldier, had the splinter from the grenade forced its way under the scalp, then the soldier would have died instantly. He was merely twenty, one of Finland's many young heroes.

Next, he started on the neck, and this one was a very demanding one. The bullet was stuck between the two lower cervical. If he missed out here, paralysis would be inevitable.

"Have we got vodka, corporal?" "Now then the captain wants vodka?". "Just skip the crap Johansson. I shall need vodka for cleaning and may be our patient should swallow the rest of the bottle".

Johansson seemed like he wanted to leave the tent, but Lars ordered wound wash." With vodka?" "Well, do we have a choice?" No, they didn't. "Scalpel!" And with the greatest care he opened up with a cut in the same direction as the bullet had entered. Strange it was that it hadn't gone right through and smashed the cervical. Something must have taken the first shock and then the bullet had just swerved, till it finally stopped.

"Where are the clothes he was wearing the poor one when you brought him in?" "We don't understand Herr Doktor?" "Precisely what I said, his clothes, bring them here!" The corporal speeded up now. "Here, Herr Doktor, here they are all of them". "Is the corporal sure about that?" Johansson had stood up and wanted to have a say as well. "What in the world do the captain want with the clothes of the poor man. Are we not to start operating?" "Corporal, who undressed this man?" "It was done by our assistant out there". Shivering now the good man. "Well then, get him in here on the double!"

A vice-corporal appeared at the opening; extremely pale he was. "And what about the rest of what you took from this poor guy vice corporal, your grade as at now, but maybe not for long. Where is the rest of what you took from the poor guy. Nothing but his clothes you say? This man could have died while we waited for your answer. I repeat, was this all?"

"No, Herr Doktor – Captain", he was trembling now, the vice corporal. "Oh yes there was one more thing, this medallion here, laying in an iron capsule. But it was smashed, I mean the iron capsule".

Lars looked closely at it, clearly marked by the hit. But was one allowed to have medallions on one's back? Then it got to him: "Where is the Death Mark". "Right here", the vice corporal showed it to him, clean and no marks on that one.

Then Lars realized the tour of events: The Death Mark had been on his breast according to regulations and the medallion back on the neck. He had to see the girl or maybe it was his mother, before he carried on. Maybe he should have had one himself with his mother's picture? But no way the Germans would have accepted this type of ornaments.

He opened up the medallion, almost like sacrilege this. Yes, there was a woman, but no way a relative. The picture was of the Virgin Mary. Johansson had become curious now. "What has happed you think?"

"This bullet has come from long distance, maybe it could have been a ricochet, losing much of its speed when hitting the iron capsule and the medallion, before it swirled into the neck. This should leave us with the cervical undamaged, but it is the nerves and the spinal cord I am worried about. If this guy should make the smallest movement during the insertion, this may be catastrophic. So, you must hold on to him as best you can, the last resort would be to make him unconscious". "With vodka?" Mustered the corporal. "Be that so, if he cannot lay absolutely still".

Lars wondered if the Swede would report him for this unconventional treatment. Crap or shit, a local expression from his parish. Now it was all about the life of a Finnish soldier. One that believed in the powers of the Virgin. The bullet, he could see it now was right there in the middle of the cervical. This wasn't to be an easy one.

Half an hour later; "you may do the sewing now Johansson, but make sure you wash it first, wash it really good with vodka".

He slept long this morning, far too longue. When he finally got out, the operation of the man with the leg wounds was done and yes, here as well the wound was washed with vodka. No car with supplies had shown up.

"What happened to our neck patient?" The corporal saluted. "He is in the next tent Herr Doktor, wide awake and hungry".

"Good morning, surgeon", it was Johansson. "Good morning ", he nodded back. Where could he have left the letter from Eva? "My coat corporal, the white one". "No way it was white any longer Herr Doktor and our Marija Lena took it with her together with the rest of the linen and now it is no doubt getting cleaned there boiling in the big iron pot". "Did you empty the pockets, Marija Lena?" "No, we were all in a hurry Herr Doktor. Was it something of importance?"

He looked at her. The poor Marija Lena had no doubt deserved a better fate than staying here out in the wilderness boiling and cleaning bloodshed linens and bandages. She must have been beautiful once, very beautiful.

But now dressed up in far too large men's clothes and with her hair cut short by the neck? "No Marija Lena, I was just curious, no worries". "Thanks, Herr Doktor". Obviously relieved she went back to her chores.

He would have to write to Eva once back in Odesa and give her a full recap from the operation area.

"It was an amazing job you did last night Doktor. I was certain the man would die. Congrat! But listen, we don't need tell the commandant, I mean the Head surgeon I mean that we used vodka for sterilization". Lars recognized the devilish smile from Johansson. So that was it, the Swede was trying to get him by his balls now. "That will be totally up to Herr Johansson. If he shall need a witness, then just let me know. But you best not to forget that I report directly to Obergruppenführer Felix Steiner, General would be his title in Sweden, he being one of Hitler's most trusted men".

He turned his back to the Swede and then back to the biuvack. Catch some sleep now before the next train of wounded was due and maybe the long-waited supplies would finally be coming.

But this letter from Eva, was there something special about it. He couldn't quite let go. Could it have something to do with this Nazi Jens coming on to her again?

BIRGITTA

He was done with Karelen now Lars, done with Finland as well and not least with this Swedish Chief surgeon, Mr. Johansson, no way should he let him make his life sour no more. He had an orderly send a wireless to Felix Steiner: "Done with Finland, wants back to Odesa, cancel further furlough. Urgent!"

And it all went quick now: Two days later a jeep was coming up, a young Swedish intern was there to replace him.

Did he shed tears or get melancholia seeing Finland disappear in the mist when leaving Helsinki? No way, but he knew inside himself that this stay in Karelen had been necessary to come at peace with himself. His mother was buried in Norwegian soil now and the farms from peaceful days were no longer there and the once fairy tale that his parents had drawn to him, that fairy tale was no more either. But it had its price and it was to cost even more. Karelen was no longer green pastures and fertile black acres. A wonderful landscape was now painted in red Finnish-and Russian blood. But come next spring, following a harsh winter covering all the fields, then the pastures and the acres would again be plowed by men and machinery and in between, remains from the people once living there would come to the surface. His mother's people, his own.

From Gdansk to Warszawa, there was a direct train giving him a night off in the big city, before the morning train south towards Lviv and then change to the train directly to Odesa where he was to report.

Now what about this evening off? First and foremost a hotel and then a really long shower before dinner. He was taken by car to hotel Leopold, totally crowded by German officers.

But this time he was on his own, not part of General Steiner's entourage. "Room just for the one-night sir? Not likely, no reservation then?" "No, I come straight from the front. You may not remember me from last time, I was part of General Steiner's entourage".

"Ah! Der Obergruppenführer!" The outcry from the receptionist was that loud that many officers standing with their back to the reception automatically clinked their heals, up with the right arm, shouting "Heil Hitler". Lars had to follow suite as well, up with his arm. They were all looking around now, where was the General?

Finally, a colonel from the Wehrmacht came over to Lars. "Was it you that just now talked with General Steiner, Herr Hauptsturmführer?" "No Colonel, but the receptionist here shouted his name, me being part of the General's entourage on my last visit".

"The Ritterkreuz?" Lars felt that the skepticism between the ordinary army, Die Wehrmacht and the SS was quite predominant.

"Yes, Herr Colonel. I am a field-medic, but I was decorated when I led a full battalion over the river Bug under constant fire from partisans. The major meant I saved the whole battalion. I personally felt it a bit much, but Obergruppenführer Steiner insisted on the decoration and then one is thankful". "And where do you come from right now then?" "I have under my furlough served in Karelen Finland as part of a field lazarette".

So, it was all clear now, what might be the problem? The colonel looked at the receptionist. For sure he himself was the highest-ranking officer present. "No, no problems at all Herr Colonel". He had eavesdropped the receptionist. "But officers coming directly from the front shall of course have our best rooms. And as part of Obergruppenführer Steiner's entourage on his last visit he shall of course have the absolute best quarters. Heil Hitler!"

It was still early days, only six in the afternoon. He delivered the unform to pressing and was pondering, what now, should he try contact Birgitta? But maybe she was at the front or wherever. Still, it might be worthwhile to search for her at the hospital for officers. "You got a name for this lady; I mean except for just Birgitta?" The girl at the switchboard wasn't that helpful. "And who might you be?" He told her and explained that he was just back from the front and that Birgitta and he were well acquainted.

"Be it as it may, and you still have no family name to her?" No, hadn't as yet had time to unpack his gear from the front as he was off to the hospital in Odesa tomorrow morning. "So, you are a doctor then!" Quite more amiable in her voice now.

"Yes, field-medic in fact". But by golly, he wasn't in for a date with the switchboard girl.

"Then why didn't you tell me about this right from the beginning. You are looking for Birgitta Schønfeldt then?" "Yes, Schønfeldt is the name".

"Could you please stop interrupting me Herr Doktor?" "Yes sorry". He just had to play along with this nosy girl. "Well then, Miss Schønfeldt is off duty at 20.00 hrs. You got it or was it a bad line? Tell me are you married or engaged?" She never seemed to stop this one. "No of course not, I am a young Doktor and a Captain, educated from the University clinic in Berlin and for the record, my dad is a Doktor as well. Although he can only operate with his right hand, his left just an iron claw, but you now, duty first".

"Yes, duty and your mother?" Well then, he thought, let's get done with it, he would be more than happy if he could tell this girl to just piss off. "She died last fall", he said quietly. "My condolences", the voice at the other end was gentler now. "Where may Miss Schønfeldt get in touch with you then?" "Hotel Leopold, madame". "You are well behaved I hear. Goodbye Herr Doktor". This had been some ghost on the line and think about it, cross-exam in the midst of the war here in Warsaw.

Well then, he went to the bathroom, finally to get the long-wanted shower instead of the bucket with cold water as up in Karelen. But OMG, here there was a proper bathtub and he fell to the temptation.

He was wakened by the phone, the tip of his nose just above the bath foam and water was pouring onto the valve in the floor. He realized it then that he could have had the entire hotel flooded.

"I need someone to talk with. Yes of course it is Lars. Checked in this afternoon, leaving first thing in the morning. You are busy then. Ok, but at least we got to say hi to each other. Very sad that is, no, I mean very pleasant though, so till next time then".

What was he to expect. A great girl like Birgitta, of course she would be busy once she had time off. She might even be engaged or having a close boyfriend as well.

Then there was another call, and he got to hope for her to come to him still. But no, it was the clerk telling him that his uniform was ready, cleaned and pressed. "May they come up to the room with it now?" "Yes of course". Maybe he should just spend the evening right there in the hotel room or the mini-suite it was. Not mini, but Junior- suit here. He smiled to himself, Junior, yes quite so.

When room service came with his uniform, he ordered a bottle of bubbles and wanted it served right here in the bathroom. "Yes of course Herr Hauptsturmführer. For you only or more glasses?"

"Can you see anyone else here in the bathroom then?" "No, sorry, I only asked to be helpful. Be back in no time". "Please, wait a sec, bring two glasses, who is to know…"

"I am lying here, right in the bathtub, having a bottle of fine champagne and two glasses, will you join then". "Is it sex you are after?" "Did I say just that Birgitta?" "No, but it was the strangest invitation, if it didn't imply sex as well, don't you agree?" She just let it hang there in the air. "But Birgitta I just came from the front in Karelen this afternoon. I have lived in a bivouac and at times even slept in the operation tent, when I got some sleep at times. Now I hungered for luxury and above all someone to talk with, to reason with. Sounds dull does it not?"

"But Lars I can be there, but in uniform, let's say in half an hour. If I were to change first, then I would need like an hour and a half". Lars just laughed. "The shower is free this time as well, only this time I shall stop you from going to sleep".

"I did have a shower", those were her first words. "So maybe we can now be decent Lars?" "Well, if you consider me wearing my dressing gown, that being decent. But I might as well change to uniform, if you like. But I offer you my second dressing gown as an alternative".

"Ok Lars, I did lie to you, I never got to shower, but hand me a glass of bubbles and leave the bathroom to me. Please note that I haven't had time to eat since 12.00hrs., so maybe you could order something from room service less you want us to dine out" "No thanks, I want to talk and that is not an option in these restoes. I experienced that clearly on my last visit here with General Steiner!"

Bloody beautiful she was, this Birgitta. 5 foot 6, or something, brown eyes and she now had her hair down. Thank heavens she was not a blonde. He guessed she had a body quite as superb as Eva's. But now he had to pull himself together, away with the physical attraction, they simply were to talk.

"Lars!" she cried to him through the bathroom door. "This is real luxury, I want to go into the tub as well and we may keep the door open so we can talk, right?" "Ok, but we cannot speak up, remember the walls are thin here, big ears all over, I guarantee you".

"But Lars I forgot my glass". What was this about? He wasn't ready for some naked scene, not now at least. But no worries to him, only the tip of her nose could be seen in the foam. "Disappointed now Lars?" "No, not in the least, cheers and welcome. Just let me know when I shall fill up". Did he recognize that she got turned down sort of by him holding back? For sure she was. "Birgitta we were to talk and eat, and the meal will come in half an hour, but you only have to wrap yourself into the dressing gown, so now worries, plenty of time".

"But why me Lars and what do you want to talk about?" "We got along real fine last time we met and don't you forget I spent a full night in your lap there on the train. But kidding aside. I want to talk with you because you are a woman". "Are you sure about that Lars, I mean that I am a woman?" She laughed innocently through the open door. But Lars carried on. "I only meet with men day out and day in, and they either outrank me or have too low grades or they are just dead men on stretchers".

"Poor you Lars, just you come to Birgitta and I shall get things right whatever your troublesome thoughts may be". "I am not too sure about that Birgitta". He had gotten really serious now. "See Birgitta, I don't think that I ever shall go home, if Germany should lose this war". He just whispered the last part and was quick to draw a finger over his lips. "I think we must have some music here now".

"You think that you cannot go home, or you don't want to?" "Maybe both". "Ok then, let's get it all from the top. Can you take that then?" He didn't want to expose the intimate part of it all, but she cut him short: "Did you sleep with Eva or didn't you?" "Yes, I did twice". "And what now, does she sit up there in Norway waiting for you?" "Well, yes, I think so".

He then told her about the letter from Eva, lost in the washing by Marija Lena up Karelen in Finland. They both had to laugh a little over the incident, and when having another cheer to the bubbles, Lars felt it all seemed easier to talk about the real matter, going home or not, and consequences.

"But Lars, why can you not go on leave while the war still is on and you can't tell the outcome of it, not so?" "Go home yes, but let's eat first and we shall have Wagner to the entrée". He waved her over to him. "Go to your Eva and tell her about the possible sad outcome, you being sent to internment camp somewhere for maybe 10 years, denied your right to the profession as a doctor, losing the farm and all?"

He was saved by a knock on the door. The waiter was there with the rolling table, Russian caviar for starters, then sole Maria Waleska and another bottle of Moët Chandon. Maybe this would be the last time to enjoy such luxury.

But Birgitta wasn't quite done. "There is more to it Lars, is there not?"

He pulled her closer to him and whispered I her ear, "just you come closer and we can speak lower". "Check trick Lars?" Her dressing gown had opened up and although he was fast looking elsewhere, he couldn't miss seeing her beautiful breasts and the crown of hairs beyond the flat trimmed tummy. But she didn't seem to notice at all, just tightened the belt twice around her waist.

"Now Lars, shall we take it from the top", she almost whispered now and the setting was getting ever so intimate. "Have some of the fresh Caviar and let us drink to the nicest evening Birgitta". Did she give him a flirting smile or was she just radiant by friendship?

She got the story of the two farms and all about Eva and why he was holding back because he was going to the war. "Yes Lars, I follow, but why did you have to go for this bloody war, what was your driving force, just to fight? I don't believe it for a second".

"I don't quite know Birgitta, but I think it might be rooted in shame, shame that no one stood up and went to Finland to my mother's land and fight. Shame to Norway. Allowing just a small group of volunteers to go and help the Finns fighting against mighty USSR. We should have joined with Sweden and declared war on Russia the two of us. Instead, we just let Karelen go, let Finland to cater for itself. We, the Knights of the broken rifle, we trusted that our commy friends leave as at peace". "So, you believe Lars that the Swedes would have skipped its line of neutrality to help the poor Finns? I don't believe that Lars!

But there was something more that you haven't told me. How could you mount that much aggression on behalf of your mom?" He looked at her, hesitating sort of. "I cannot tell you all about it Birgitta, not tonight, but you will have to listen and trust me in all I am telling you.

My mother was kidnapped sort of by my father, she left Finland with him voluntarily, but still kidnapped. She never got to see her kins again, not her parents, nor grandad and grandma nor her siblings". "But did you not say that she was adopted?" "But she still was family and what about it if she was not adopted?"

She stood up, found pen and paper and wrote: "In that case you are half Jewish and OMG what then?" She then took the paper went to the toilet, teared it in bits and flashed it down.

She had gone all pale now and Lars he shifted from red-faced to pale, put Wagner on full strength and wrote his message: "You have to swear to total secrecy about this or I cannot have you leave from here alive". "I swear", she wrote and together they went to the lew and flashed it. But Birgitta's face was still totally pale.

"I chose to believe in your father, that your mother truly was adopted and now they are all gone, the rest of your kinfolks?" "Yes, and my mother has passed as well". "So, the finale then?" She tried to lighten up with a cheer, but no success. "Your Eva then Lars, how much does she know about all this?" "Nothing, nothing at all, she wanted for us to engage officially before I left. I was holding back, but in the end, it became impossible and we came to each other, yes, we made deep love". Tears were running now. "But I denied her official engagement Birgitta!" "Why then Lars?" "I wanted for her to be free in case I was killed or badly mutilated, more so the latter" "Noble my friend, utterly noble". "That's how Felix Steiner put it too.

But it had nothing to do with being noble. I was dead honest, didn't want for her to drag with a cripple, maybe a blind man, just an example, if I lost my eyesight".

"But Lars, what if she got pregnant following this heavenly encounter, or two as you put it?" "Well, then she would have written to me, would she not or my father would have told me about it". "You really believe that? Maybe your father wanted for her to tell you about it, and maybe that she wrote about it in the letter that was gone with Marija Lena?" "Stop it Birgitta, then the child would be almost one year old. And in that case why hadn't she written about it long ago?"

"But down to the bottom of this Lars, why should you not go home on leave to her, find out about it all?"

"Because I have promised her forever to be faithful to her". "And you haven't lived up to that Lars? So let me hear it, come out with it, tell me about your womanizing".

"Well, yes, I fell for one, the night was light and beautiful as well, and there was this odor from beautiful flowers there in the Alpes in southern Germany". "Oh, how romantic, but there was this odor of her too Lars?"

But he didn't catch the irony. "I don't know, I was lost in my longing for a woman. I pretended she was my Eva, but when I realized this lethal sin in the course of the night, I immediately asked for transfer to Berlin, never met this girl again". Now Birgitta got the full story.

"And what about this girl then Lars, did you or she use protection?" "No, I don't think so and if she had gotten pregnant, no doubt she would have searched for me". "But then you have been a sweet repenting boy thereafter Lars?"

"Her name is Svetlana". "So, you didn't go home to your Eva and you couldn't behold to her and the dire, sacred wows. Once one has stepped over the line, cheated once, then the next time doesn't matter that much, is it not like that Lars?"

"Must you be that infamous and cruel Birgitta? I thought we were friends, no?" "Yes of course, I just listen and try to understand you and possibly help you. You wanted help from me did you not?"

Her dressing gown was wide open now, but none of them seemed to care. And it wasn't just the beautifully pointed breasts for him to see now. But he Lars, he wasn't there. Not at all he was. Not now.

"We worked closely together for four months and I helped her in the evenings, she studying to become specialized surgery nurse. She was educated and trained as an ordinary nurse from Odesa and Lviv. Odesa? Did I say Odesa?" "Yes, you did". But was this merely a slip of his tongue. She had said she came from Lviv, he said to himself. "According to the Chief surgeon she had typical Jewish traits and if she was educated from Odesa, well then, she might have been Jewish".

"OMG Lars, there are no Jewish women with the name of Sveta or Svetlana. Are you just losing it now". "No, of course you are right", he put his fingers to his lips again.

"No, Sveta came from Rivne and she was extremely capable. But the German nurses they didn't like her sacrificial behavior, working day and night and for sure they were suspicious on us having an affair. And so was the Chief surgeon.

One night, we went for a trip in the park". "So, you did that, you did, right?" "Well yes, ever so innocent it was". "Didn't you even hold hands?" "Well at times maybe we did". "Get to the point now Lars, this fish is getting cold now".

"Ok, the last night in the park I kissed her, couldn't hold back and then..." "Did you sleep with her there in the park? How stupid could you be, you an officer and all, you might have been reported the two of you!"

"No, no we didn't, not in the park, I came to her and she to me in my room that night". "And the next morning then Lars? How was it to wake up look her in the eyes at work knowing that it had been that delicious, but then what about Eva and your solemn woes? Broken forever or was it ONLY one more episode?

You wouldn't know Lars how many offers I have got from the officers here in Warsaw. Do you recall the switchboard woman?" "You mean your mother?"

"Call her with whatever name you like, she protects me against the likes of you, keeps me well apart from the lot being married.

But what did you feel Lars and what happened thereafter? Are you still together?" "I felt extremely happy with her and would have loved to continue, but then it was Finland and of course Eva".

"What was the strongest obstacle Lars, Finland or Eva?" "Please don't make it difficult to me Birgitta, I think they were equally important". "So, then it was not just Eva?" "No, it never was". "I don't get it, how about Bad Tølz then? So, I guess I am right then Lars that following the second cheating, the picture of your wonderful Eva fades away?"

"My mother's land has always been the most important to me, I think. But let's turn to the most vital issue Birgitta, but we have to first open the second bottle". He then made face to the no doubt hidden microphones and the boyish expression to his face made her splash.

"I love Wagner, so listen, now comes his "The ring". "Come sit with me". And none of them had the slightest thought about making out when she sat on his lap and he whispered: "If Germany loses, then I cannot go home, ever. If I should go home then, I would be internated, get a sentence for 10 years. No longer possible to carry on with my father's surgery, gone with the farm and what then with Eva? She would never have waited for a Quisling, a traitor to his country, a jailbird with 10 years behind bars coming up. And the children that may have come, forever labelled as Nazi children, and my dad, father to the Nazi swine. Yes, this might have killed him".

Her mouth was quite close now and then it burst. The dressing gowns were quite thin and she felt his erection through the garment. Was it the spur of the moment or maybe the champagne? In split seconds they were naked in bed. "Wait, please wait!" she cried. But Lars wouldn't, couldn't wait. He came in seconds and then came the crying and the tears and the sobbing, and she stroke his body, stroked it until he was gone, in a deep, deep sleep.

Was she ever to be there and enjoy this boy awake, he had slept on her lap at the train as well.

SVETLANA

The chief physician's comments had been nothing but unpleasant, as they were meant to be, she figured. He could do well without discord and envy. Fully understandable to her.

She felt totally drained for energy, only wished for the day to come to an end.

She wondered if Lars had reached Gdansk by now and if he was lucky to get a boat to Finland right away. Nothing else mattered to her there and then.

At dinner it wasn't at all difficult to catch up with the comments from the German nurses. The expression from the eyes of most of them said more than their comments. "He is gone now your medic lover. Hope for your sake that he didn't knock you up before leaving!"

But she had to take it and soon it would be over when there was no more medic Lars to stick it on her. Lars had given her no hope, not even said a word about his possible return from Finland. He had only told her that now he had finally reached his goal, joining with the Waffen-SS, enabling him to go to Finland and Karelen to contribute to the defense of his mother land.

But she couldn't let go, thinking about the wonderful talk they had that special night. The night he had become her lover and only hers. She felt especially strong about his drive to be able to accomplish his dream; to fight for his mother's land.

"So, you are half Finnish Lars and the other half Norwegian then?" He looked her straight into the eyes and lied, he had to.

It pained him, but he knew he had to lie, even to this Svetlana whom he longed to make love to.

Now she had to come up with her story: "Yes, Lars but I have told you all about it earlier. I am the daughter of this alliance between a Russian businessman and a young Ukrainian girl. They even didn't get married, still I chose my father's name: Malenkova".

"Where is your mother now then Svetlana?" "I am not sure about it. She should have come visit me in Rivne, but chose to stop in Lviv. No news from her later, but rumors tell that she found herself a new man up in Lviv".

"So, you have no siblings then?" She laughed, "for sure I must have some over in Russia. But my father never came back to my mother. She heard nothing from him following my birth".

There were tears now, plenty of them, she was thinking about her dear father ending his life there on the Parade square, first hanged and then burned to ashes in the big fire, just a few hundred meters from the hospital. But her mother's death in the ditch on the way north was even more painful to her.

"No more crying now my love, I shall not pester you anymore". He had said the word, Love, and that should be the redemptive word to this, their last evening, and he came to her again. Where nobody had been before except Chaim and that wasn't that long ago. But this fulfillment with Lars, it had gone far too fast had it not? Well because there is a war on, she comforted herself and because she had left Chaim and now Lars was to leave her.

She wondered if the German nurses were right in their assumptions that she had been knocked up as they said, but by whom, Chaim or Lars? With the short interval it might not be impossible to tell who was the father.

Let it be, she said to herself, I am not pregnant and if I was, would it be such a tragedy? Dad would have been overjoyed as the race was preserved, be it as it may, the child being born half Jew or a pure Jewish one. No one was to know.

She decided to stay in her room and study now in the evenings.

"Rumors have it that you are not very social any more Svetlana", the Chief Physician commented one day when they for once had time for a lunch break. "But then, Chief Physician, then they have nothing to gossip about, right?" "Well, well my child, you aren't that old yet, so you still have plenty to learn". "Of course, you are right, but I study intensely every evening now". "Yes, and I am surprised by your progress. Maybe you should apply for med-school and real Medecine once the war is over. Yes, I mean study to become a real doctor, but as you know that's a long way to go and for women even tougher. Our work is dominated by men. But let's stick to my first remarks, you and your apparent lacking social skill.

Now, when our Doktor Lars is no longer with us and I doubt it if he will be back, then I really think you should mingle with the others".

"But I am short on time Herr Doktor, I still have many chapters to work through".

"Well, then, maybe it was a mistake having Doctor Lars help you with your studies, I mean he should have conferred with me first. But what about our new intern, well you know each other quite well already, you and our Doktor Zweig? Maybe he could give some lectures in the canteen on subjects you deem important in your studies? Of course, these lectures should be for everyone to attend, not just you".

Rebecka didn't like this, but she would have no choice. No way she wanted the elderly German nurses come close on her. Things might go really bad if they started to ask questions about her education and training up in Rivne, and how she got along with this Doktor Weber. No way she felt for getting closer to this new intern either. He was married, 2 kids at home, mere 24 and good looking. For sure he would be longing for a woman, would he not?

The Chief Physician made a fool of himself right from the beginning. He started by talking about Svetlana's wishes for further education and that she had suggested a couple of themes for the Intern to lecture on in the evenings, everyone to be invited.

One of the five subjects would be about the appendix, the second one, pancreas, and now it would be up to the German nurses to single out 3 more subjects. This came as a big surprise to Rebecka. "Sneaked in on the Chief Physician", she heard them whisper. Yes, for sure she would get worse eyes from the German nurses now. But what was she to do? She could only keep quiet, make her best not to draw further attention.

"When will we have the first lecture then?" The elderly of the nurses spoke up. The Chief Physician nodded to the Intern: "Our friend here suggests tomorrow evening at 20.00 hrs. But should we get more patients at that time, then of course we shall have to cancel. My suggestion was to have these small lectures every Wednesday the coming weeks".

"We do thank our Chief Physician for his statement and the offer". It was the same elderly woman speaking. "We shall have a small reunion and discuss whatever themes we would like to be presented and be back shortly". They then stood up all the German nurses and Rebecka and the two doctors were left there.

"It didn't go that well this meeting Svetlana, or how do you feel about it? You were quiet all the time".

"Herr Doktor, no doubt you felt the animosity and distrust. There is nothing I can do except trying with all my might to do an even better job and be polite towards everyone". "But would it not have been natural that you joined in their group meeting?" "I don't know Herr Doktor, I doubt that they would have wanted me to join. Maybe they think that me being half Russian, then I am not to be trusted". "Rubbish, you are born and bred in Ukraine and have your education from here. I really cannot accept such behavior in my hospital".

But it didn't seem to come to their mind that the war came closer by the day and that soon it would only be a matter of days before the hospital would have to be evacuated further west. It was common knowledge that Hitler had threatened the total destruction of the capital Kyiv and no doubt Odesa would follow suit.

There wasn't the slightest improvement in the relation between the German nurses and Rebecka, not least since the young handsome Intern flirted quite openly with Rebecka during the lecture. Luck to her that he was to be relocated to Kyiv, not to the Chief Physicians liking, now he would be the only surgeon. No more lectures either.

But things should go from bad to worse. It was obvious to all that the Chief couldn't operate during daytime and then be on duty all through the evenings as well.

The elderly among the German nurses and Rebecka were summoned to a meeting with him one late afternoon, the last patient had just been wheeled out.

"As you can see our operational system shows breeches. I cannot go double watches as you no doubt understand. The two of you are my very best nurses". Irma, the German one looked at him and then to Rebecka, anxious to know what would come next.

"I am totally dependent on the very best cooperation between the two of you, less German officers in our care will die. Thus, the responsibility rests heavily on the three of us.

The only solution is to free the two of you from daily routines and then have you responsible for one floor each of you from 19.00 hrs. till 07.00 hrs. the next morning. This means shifts of 10 hrs. and with complete responsibility for your respective patients". She had gotten pale now Irma. "But this is against the law Herr Doktor!"

"Nurse Irma, as from now on martial laws will be the rule. Don't you forget that we are located almost at the front. From the moment the Rumanians start to with withdraw, there will be only a minute German force back to defend Odesa and our hospital. And I don't trust these Rumanians, never did. Maybe they will escape during the first night of heavy Russian artillery. When the Russians come, they will blow us up. I have even heard accounts about partisan groups going from bed to bed killing wounded officers. So, what I ask of you is nothing compared to the sacrifices by our men, every hour at the front.

And you nurse Svetlana, what have you to say? Is my pledge acknowledged, well anyway take it as a command". "Yes of course Herr Chief Physician". It kicked hard down there now. Could anyone see that she was pregnant? No doubt Irma was the suspicious kind, but she might not have fancied that Rebecka was knocked up and now pregnant.

Back in her room she started on the math. 2.5 months gone if she was pregnant with Lars, more like three if Chaim was the father. OMG this was awful, not knowing who she was impregnated by. What would her mom had to say to this? And it was all tears now.

There was a knock on the door. No way anyone should see her, she was only in her underwear.

She could hear Irma knocking impatiently. "Sorry you had to wait". "Are you ill or something?" "No, I had such dreadful thoughts about my mother. Rumors have it she had been killed during a partisan raid up in Lviv". Lying came that easily, but she had to protect herself, not so? "No way there would be chances for a furlough to attend the funeral, Svetlana". Irma was now playing boss. "Oh no, I fully understand that".

"I just came to tell you that the Chief Physician has accepted my proposal for me to be in charge of the second floor". She gave Rebecka a triumphant look. Rebecka realized that this meant that all the heavy loads had to be on her watch, one more floor up.

"Thanks Irma, it was nice of you to tell me". But she knew instantly that this would be an impossible task, she had to cater for assistance. But where would she find an assistant and would the Chief Physician agree to it? The summer heat was on now and she knew that she would be totally dependent on an assistant. But from where and would the Chief accept it? But there was another obstacle: to ask the Matron to find someone, even with the Chiefs approval that would be risky, would it not? This was after all Odesa and the risk of being recognized was immense. No doubt there were no more Jews in the city, and if any, none of them would take the risk of coming here to the hospital for a job. That would have been absurd. What about here auntie Esther. She would possibly know someone fitting for the job? Someone with background from nursing and a strong one as well. No, that would be too risky exposing the whole group and not least her own auntie up there in the cave.

So, she had no choice, she had to speak with the Chief and then over to the Matron if she got the Chief's approval. Maybe then Irma would crave for an assistant as well?

But the Chief could only tell her that she should have been the first to ask, not Irma, she then had gotten the second floor now. "Too late for you Svetlana". "But could I have an assistant then, not necessarily a trained one, but one to take the heavy loads, helping with toilets etc.?" "That would cost us Svetlana and we don't have this in our budgets". "But what if I share my wage with this assistant then?" "Do you mean to split your wages?" Astonished now the Chief. "Yes, if that's what it takes then Chief". "But you are well aware that this will create an even worse climate between you and the others Svetlana?" "So, what, what's important is to provide best possible care for the officers, I mean the patients so they can come back to the front soonest possible". Or have them search for more Jews to kill, she said to herself. "I shall talk to the Matron about it then". The audience was over.

But luckily her proposal seemed to have been accepted. When she accidently met with Irma before the nightshift, she had to visit the canteen, then it was an all-poisonous Irma she run into. "Ok for you to lower your salary, no husband, no kids to support!" She was gone before Rebecka could respond.

A wonderful person in her 25's showed up at the surgery already the next afternoon. Real big and strong. The matron introduced her as Ludmila from Sevastopol. She was on visit to her cousin in Odesa when she learned about the vacant position. Irina, her cousin would have loved to be the one for the post, but having recently given childbirth, she couldn't leave home although she needed the money. Now it was for Ludmila to have a go at it and maybe she could help Irina with her economy as well.

Dear me, Rebecka said to herself, that many to live on my wage. To herself she needed no money, not yet. But for sure she would need it later when her pregnancy was apparent and she no doubt would be kicked out.

Ludmila was a fast learner making time for talks in between the chores. Rebecka advised her not to talk to the German nurses, them being strongly against her having an assistant. And more so, Ludmila being sweet and blonde she should be careful to get to close with the patients, many of them, they were mostly officers, had wives and kids back home, but open for an adventure here far away from the motherland. The chief as well had made it clear towards Rebecka. "Absolutely no fraternization with the patients!"

Rebecka had less pains in the mornings now, maybe because she was over the first 2 critical months, but more so as Ludmila was there for all the heavy burdens.

Every morning when she came off the shift, she locked the door, pulled the curtains and she even blocked the peep hole in the door before she undressed totally and looked at herself in the big mirror on the wall. Oh, yea she had certainly got herself a good hint of a stomach. Maybe she should have thought seriously about abortion?

The thought had never been on her mind and now it was too late. It was however absurd. If it was Chaim's child, then she could never, never live with such an outrageous action. "Let our race grow", were the last words of her dad, and now she was to murder the last one?

She was in her sixth month that morning when she came to her room and noted that someone had moved her things. Not much was it, but enough for her to be sure that someone had been in there. So, it starts burning under my feet now, she pondered. Maybe she should just quit right away while her tummy was still somewhat flat?

Her breasts were not the biggest ones when she first came to the hospital, but now they had the size she always had wanted. But she knew they would get even bigger and she had no bra to them. Maybe she could have Ludmila get one from her cousin. Of course, she was going to pay for it, but it didn't even have to be a new one.

"We have to change the lock", she said to the Matron. "But for sure it will be difficult to get a new one Svetlana and it will cost us". "No doubt about that Matron, but is it for anyone, free to go into my room?" "Something missing then?" "No, I don't think so, but I am adamant that someone has been in here and messing about in my private affairs".

"Svetlana, if I shall make a case of it, then I need proof and I must know that something is missing. You have no more to add, have you?" No, she had not. "Well then, you must understand that there is nothing I can do".

"Will it be ok if I have it changed myself then?" The matron laughed: "You are not from here, but fair enough. If you know of a locksmith, then just suit yourself. But I wouldn't bother in your place".

Once again, Ludmila should be the good helper. And she asked the guy to come and do the job while all others having room in the same corridor were at work.

But there were rumors. Somehow everyone seemed to have heard about the locksmith's visit and the next day when she came off the shift there was a note glued to her door: "Congrat with new lock miss!"

She showed the note to the Chief before she went on to her nightshift. But as she reckoned, he needed all and everyone, no one to spare, but he got really upset on her behalf.

You shall have to take it Svetlana, Kyiv fell to the Russians this very morning and then it may be only a matter of few days until we shall have to leave and regroup." She had to comply with that, some maiger comfort it was.

At the beginning of the seventh month, she knew that it was soon time now when she would have to run for it, with little warning. She only dressed in wide dresses now and even Ludmila complemented her with her good looks.

Be prepared, she said to herself. And she wasn't to get many seconds warning.

DENOUNCED AND ON THE RUN

This night, and it should turn out to be a special one, this Saturday night at 21.00 hrs. one of the officers, a captain had a visitor. It was strictly against the regulation, but poor Ludmila had fallen for his request and let this visitor in, a beautiful, German-friendly Ukrainian lady. Dressed in style and with reel high heels, her hair beautifully done, well-done makeup as well. Those were the thoughts of Rebecka when this woman came to the kitchen for a vase to the superb bouquet that she had brought with her.

Ludmila was to bring it immediately and the lady then just left the kitchen, with a half eye to Rebecka standing at the side.

"Ludmila I just have to pick up something in the canteen!" She run down the stairs and on to her room, grabbed the little brown bag, already packed and she was off. Change to ordinary clothes she could do later. Now it was all about time, time to escape before the alarm sounded.

She took to the back stairs and was out through a hole in the hedges as she heard the commotion from the hospital. So, she was already denounced then! She managed to get her long overcoat over her uniform. Rounded one corner and off to smaller alleys. Soon she was close to her father's synagogue. Yes, the front door was covered by planks nailed to it. But she knew of the small window on the backside, maybe she could get in that way. She acknowledged that she had gotten heavy now and what about the baby if she was suddenly to fall or was forced to make quick turns?

No one saw her on the backside and she managed to open the window. She heard some rattle and knew she wasn't the only one in there. Well, it might be rats as well. She was shivering when she got inside. Chairs were turned over and the alter was smashed, that was all she could see there in the dim light as she was looking for the door to the attic.

It struck her then, maybe the window wasn't properly locked? So, back again but it was ok. She was now hearing motorbikes racing through the narrow streets, all out looking for her no doubt.

Then finally she found the old entrance to the loft, but the handle was gone and the opening was plastered. But she knew there would be some button to press and have it opened so she could get through. But then there must be someone up there already. Someone in hiding. This was her only shot. "Help!" she cried out, "I need help!"

"And who might you be?" "I am the daughter of the Rabbi to this synagogue and they are after me. And who are you then?" When finally, up there she got a good look at him as well as of the two Kalashnikovs leaning to his chair.

"My name is of no importance. This is my hiding place whenever I am in Odesa. So where do you come from, why are they after you and where are you heading?"

"Too many questions, let me have some of the water", she nodded to his flask. He kept looking at her. "Well yes of course, but are you pregnant? I can see your tummy girl". Ashamed she covered herself.

"I have to go north to the Carpathians, a bit south of Rivne, well to a farm there". It came intuitive. She just knew that her hope was with Ari and his wife and maybe they even would take good care of her baby when it was time.

All through the night she heard motorbikes running up and down the narrow streets. Once they both heard someone trying to break their way into the synagogue by the main entrance. But then they had first to remove the heavy planks nailed to the door, but obviously they didn't care for that. And they must have wondered how she could possibly have managed to get in there, if she was there at all.

Strange that they didn't use dogs, they would for sure have smelled her even inside the synagogue. Efraim, that was his name, he had prepared for the arms in case the Germans would show up. He didn't fear for a fight, unless they threw in hand grenades. Then they would have been gone, he as well as this girl coming from nowhere, kind of. Strange this as the whole quarter was totally empty, no Jews, either they were exterminated or the few had managed to get away.

"What now then Rebecka or are you Svetlana to me? I don't care for either, you just make up your mind. The important thing now is that here we have very little food, almost no water and if you leave from here, you wouldn't get far on your own. Where is this farm you mentioned and are you sure there still are people living there? I for my part cannot imagine that the Germans have permitted Jews to stay in peace on this farm that close to Odesa."

"I don't know Efraim, but I am young and I am strong". "But you need food to both of you and what have you got of papers to show for yourself?" She showed him the ids for Svetlana.

"But these are the papers you used at the hospital, right?" "Yes, of course, less I couldn't have worked there! Are you tight there in your head Efraim?" He didn't react to her obvious irritation. "But now, they all know that you are not this Svetlana and that all your papers are false?" "Right so Efraim and what do you suggest we should do about just that?" "Now, I got to think, right now it is empty up here". "I figured that much", she smiled at him. "But my uncle Ezra, he had the answer ready to this situation." "Meaning what Rebecka?" She didn't care to answer him, just produced a small leather pouch, one she always had in a band around her neck.

The picture she pulled out was of a woman with a certain look alike to Rebecka, only her chinbones were more marked and her eyes larger. Her hair, now red was bangs cut. And this Eugenia Skripnikova was no longer a nurse, but a poor student out of work. Widowed by her late husband, a partisan, fallen at the battle of Sevastopol. Their home there in Sevastopol was shot to pieces and she was now looking for her family on her way up to Rivne. The address of her kins was a house totally destroyed now and all living there were killed, following bombardments from the Russians when they were withdrawing in 1941.

"Efraim, here you have make-up remedies. Will you be able to make me a look alike to the woman on this photo?" He laughed at her. "How are we to make your hair in Henna color Rebecka as we have no water?" "Yes, Efraim, but you have water", she pointed to his flasks. "And here is the Henna powder". "But we have only one full bottle and we shall need that as drinking water". "Then our possibilities are limited Efraim, less it starts raining!" "Meaning exactly what Rebecka?" She flashed now. "Don't you get it this time either Efraim or are you still that tight?" "Do you mean….?" "Would there be another choice then?" "Would you really do it that way, I mean make such a porridge or whatever?" "When in need one does what is required, right? And you don't have to take part in this dramatic change Efraim". "But OMG Rebecka, you shall stink that horrible!" "Efraim listen, I have spent almost 24 hrs. in a muck cellar, while the cows did their things on the floor above my head and there were plenty breaches in that floor. Just you get started with the changes to my face Efraim!"

She was a strange character this young woman. An incredible self-consciousness radiated from her and he decided to start with her eyes. "I am no way a painter Rebecka". "So, what is your occupation when you are not on the run?" "I just finished my studies to be an eye doctor, I still lack a couple of papers as the war came upon us". "So, I don't need to worry then being in the very best hands". Rebecka felt she had to lay down, the events had been strenuous to her. "But I shall need some more light Rebecka". "Don't be shy, come as close as you need. I am pregnant in my 7th month and is of no danger to you". She felt his hand shaking a bit, no doubt he flashed.

She dozed off until she woke by the sounds of the morning rush out on the streets and she could see the daylight sneaking in through the small, dirty window with the metal grid on the outside.

She felt his hand to her mouth and he whispered to her: "I think they are back here again". They heard the sound of someone crashing the glass in the small window downstairs. She was bitten by fear she as well now, as he handed her one of the weapons. "Just you lay still now and wait putting the magazine in place, they may hear the click from the metal. The only thing you have to do is pull the trigger. But pay attention to the recoil, it may force your gun to a different direction, pointing at me as an example. So, hold on to it by your hip with both hands. Shoot to kill and be ready to run for it as soon as the intruders are killed".

It became quiet downstairs, awfully quiet. But at long last there was this voice from a boy: "Crap, nothing to be found here, it seems all smashed and broken and I only see ghosts. Let's just get out of here!"

They both had to hold back an outcry of joy and Efraim kissed her right on her mouth. "Oh sorry, but I was that glad!" "It's ok, maybe now you can continue with the painting."

A mirror or rather bits and pieces of one, was produced and by golly she could hardly recognize herself, except for her hair. "Efraim, you have done wonders, but I am afraid it is at no end, less we can do the changes to my hair ". "We?" "Sorry then. You think we shall have rain today?" "I am not the weatherman Rebecka". "So, let's wait and see then". "But what will you do once this change is done, I mean finished? Are you just to walk down the street waiting for a bus or something?" "No, I am to get cycling north looking for Josef's farm and even if he might have been taken, I shall pass the night right there". "But what about water and food?" "I don't know as yet. We shall play it by ear. I mean we", she pointed to her stomach, "we cannot stay here for very long".

Of course, there was no rain this hot summer morning and the heat up in the loft became almost unbearable. But no way they dared open the little window as it pointed outwards when opened.

"But Rebecka, what if you get caught?" "That won't happen. Do you think anyone would care for a super pregnant woman?" "You don't look that pregnant, so?" "But that's easy fixed my new friend". He had no doubt about that.

"But now to your hair Rebecka, right?" "Don't you push it, or do you want to take part in the entire process?" He got all red once more. "Let's just wait till the afternoon, now you pray to your God, no to our God, pray for rain Efraim!" But the heat really crept to her now, but no way she could get naked to this unknown man.

Then late, very late afternoon, they were just dozing the two of them, then there was a breach in the skies and under an opening in the roof Efraim put his two bottles. But Rebecka pushed him away. "I first, find something to mix the Henna in if you may!" She gave him the little pouch with Henna and then she went close to the leak from the roof. Soon she was wet all the way through and she set the bottles back in place.

"Got a comb then Rebecka?" And yes, she had one in her purse and the change of her look could be finalized, now it was about her hair. She used her gown from the hospital to cover herself, less she would have been Henna-colored all over.

The rain kept poring for the next half hour followed by heavy thunder, thus making it possible to speak normally. What a relief, having but whispered for many hours.

"Now Rebecka, what's your plan for the colorization down there then? What if there was this Gestapo lady craving a full inspection?" It was her turn to flash now in the midst of the Henna. "Having fun now Efraim? Just you wipe off this grin of yours and get on with the process!" Some of the cream was still left at the bottom of the vessel. "What about the armpits then?" He wouldn't bend this funny guy. "You just get over to the far corner and close your eyes Efraim, and shut it as well!"

She then colored the hair in her armpits as well as the hair down to her vulva and it burned, really awful it was, so she soon gasped in pain. And Efraim had himself a laugh. "I shall murder you Efraim, couldn't you just shut it!" "But maybe you are soon to thank me then, you redtop!".

The rain was gone just as sudden as it had come. What now? They were both happy for this delay. Their thoughts hadn't been centered on how to get out of Odesa unseen. And now Efraim had concluded that they couldn't leave alone, she and her unborn baby. It would be much better if they left together like a couple. On their way to get married, only looking for a priest to do the action.

"They won't even care for me Rebecka, or maybe I shall start calling you Eugenia right away. By the way, you will have to leave all your other papers here in the loft and of course we shall have to get rid of any trace from the change process., even your clothes. Someone might pop up here and get a hunch of what has been going on"

"What exactly did you mean by unnoticed?" "Well, me just walking long side this redhaired bombshell, ready to give birth at any time, who would care for this guy". They both laughed now, clearly; she was the one most relieved. "What about your weapons then Efraim? You cannot risk having them in your sack when there is a control?"

Leaving his weapons behind was to him the hardest part. Be totally defenseless? No, he couldn't. But he still had to choose, Rebecka or the weapons. The combination was unthinkable.

"But Efraim, how had you planned to use these weapons if we were stopped?" She looked at him: "They will always be patrolling two together, never one man alone. Probably one on foot and the other in the side wagon of the motorbike". He realized that. It would be advantageous however if they spotted a control post down the road and then could sneak up to it and kill the two, or three Germans there and then.

"But Efraim, would you be ready to shoot them down in cold blood even before they have taken a shot at you? Maybe even have to shoot one or more in the back, are you trained to do just that like the partisans? No, Efraim, just forget about it. Hide the weapons here on the loft and then you may go back and pick them up on bicycle one dark night or come here with a friend in a car. You will get no way on foot with these weapons, not alone and for sure not by my side. We might have been better off with a couple of pistols, maybe.

On the road you will always be the weaker part compared to trained soldiers. Your education to be eye-doctor will be of no help to you". She gave him a comforting hug, but he pushed her away. "I am pissed, not at you, but at your damned analytic skills Eugenia".

Finally, it was over, the rain, and they had to get going. "You know where to find this Josef then?" "Well sort of. We must get on to the highway west and in some two hours we shall see a remote farm, long side a dirt road". "But Rebecka are you up to it, how much can you manage with the two of you?" "She gives me energy and power Efraim". "But how can you be that sure it's a she then?" "Don't fuzz around anymore, let's get going and Efraim, it is a SHE".

She skipped all the baggage that couldn't get into Efraim's sack, then down the staircase and out of the little window, now broken by the boys, still they got it back in place. Oh God, she was that heavy now and hungry.

They had shared the last carrots and one of the two bottles of water, now one bottle was all they had left, no food, nothing. She had pulled a scarf in part over part of her hair, looking ever so wifely now, even put some more clothes on to her stomach, so she waggled more than proper walking.

"Not one word about my looks now Efraim, not a single one or I shall have you to that". She noticed he having himself a laugh, but no words were uttered.

The afternoon sun was still very hot to them, her new haircut covering almost her eyes, but they were on to it through narrow streets and alleys. But ever so slow they moved on in the heat. Still, they made progress and in the right direction.

Soon they were at Stare Barzani and they managed to cross the small Plaza and on to the main road. No one to see in the streets, no kiosks or nothing where they could buy provisions. But all of a sudden, a very old lady appeared, loaded with vegetables she was. "Do you think we could buy some carrots from you mother?" She pleaded to her. "My poor kid, I would have loved to give you something, all for free, but my grandchildren need this food even more. When are your due little woman?" "In a months' time".

"If you have a piece of bread for us, then we shall pay you handsomely, not so my husband?" "Yes absolutely", and he gave her some coins. "Far too much", she said, but take this cabbage as well", and they thanked her and then they were off again, she disappearing into some alley.

They were closing up on the road cross now and Efraim meant it would be safer to walk in the woods along the highway, and then come on to it further up. But Eugenia didn't feel for it, not knowing if she could make it through the woods. Thirsty and sweaty, and hungry as well, and the one in her tummy, she was hungry as well, kicking all the time.

Whatever, she couldn't take the risk of a premature childbirth there in the woods. "We have to take it slowly Efraim. Let's just wait and see if there might be a cart going our way or maybe even an old lorry. Let's get a bit closer to the crossroad and have ourselves a small rest just there". The Henna had got mixed with her sweat now, and she felt it dropping in stripes down her face. "Please dry my face Efraim or it will all go bad for us".

They sat down in the grass by the ditch and then suddenly it came to her like a revelation. It was here, right here that she last saw her mother and little Sarah.

"How can you be that sure about it?" "I am sure", she looked at him, annoyed now. "Right here they were shot to death the two of them! Maybe we are to die on the same very spot!" So far, she had been brave, but now she bursted into tears and they were running down her face like unstoppable. She had to muster this on her own. "Just start walking Efraim, I shall join you further up the highway".

She was just about to start walking then, when she heard the sound of engines and a German patrol passed her, break-stopped, picked up Efraim and doubled back towards Odesa. If they had spotted her, then for sure they would have stopped? But poor Efraim, why did they take him?

She had no answer to that, but instinctly she knew that this was her chance, so she got across the road, off to the side where there were trees close to it.

Efraim, he had all her things in his rucksack and how was he to answer questions, questions about all this woman stuff when interrogated? But she couldn't think more about him and his capture, she had to use all her force moving forward. Luckily, she was the one to have the provisions from the old woman.

What if she would be attacked by wild animals' long side this highway? A bear or worst-case wolves? Then she would be done with, least if she met with a bear.

But she couldn't let go of Efraim, no way and she felt guilty. She should have let him be, thus he might have been able to take his weapons and be gone in the course of the night. Now he was in the hands of the Gestapo, or even worse the Rumanian Intelligence, known for their brutality, even torture when interrogating.

It would probably be easy to connect her disappearance to the stuff in his rucksack. Luckily there was no more Henna left there. That was the most important, the Henna coloring that might have disclosed her as well.

She heard sounds from panzers going north, maybe it was their belts that made all the noise. She had no choice, but on to the woods. But she was way too tired and stumbled and fell right into the ditch, this being filled to the top following the heavy rain.

Just as well, she said to herself, I am lying here with the tip of my nose barely above the water. First there were two motorbikes, then six panzers and to close it up a lorry filled with soldiers. They were singing that loud that they stifled the sound from the panzers.

It took like an eternity until they had passed her so she could try to make a twist and get on to her feet again.

The tiny piece of bread was all wet now, still, easier to chew on. But what about water? Efraim had of course the bottle in his sack. The dirt water in the ditch, should she venture it? Tempting, but she couldn't take the risk of an infection, now with the baby in her stomach.

She touched herself, yes everything seemed ok. This gave her energy and courage to get going again, shaking of the water like a crow, arranged her scarf and she was on to it again. She wondered if it was still long to go up to Josef's farm. As she remembered it, she would soon come to a sidetrack, and one more Km the dirt road should be there leading straight to Josef's farm. But it had been like a full blizzard when last she was here, so how much could she count on her own sense of direction? Not to forget that last time, Chaim was the one taking the lead, she being almost unconscious at the time.

It had to be Sunday, right so, no traffic on the roads. No military activity except for the panzers and the soldiers that had passed her. Luckily the Front itself was still far away; she hadn't heard a single shot of artillery.

There at the bend of the road, there was a patrol. Gave her no choice, she had to wait between the trees. Sooner or later, they would be replaced or they simply would pack up and leave.

She sneaked up on them and she could hear their chatter: "Only one more hour to go". One more hour to what? she pondered, to be replaced or to close for the day?

She heard the sound from the lorry long before she could actually see it. And she was fast retreating into a large hole in the boggy land.

It did of course stop at the bend and two soldiers got out. A lot of gossiping and craptalk, followed by laughter and five minutes later it was on the way towards Odesa. What now and maybe they had left one soldier to keep watch? No way, they were always two or more on guard, but there was no sound of talking anymore, only magpies flattering along. She had to hurry up now. The lorry had come from north and the two soldiers at the bend had been given a lift. But for sure there would be a new patrol coming, so she best hurry crossing the road. Didn't even feel worned out this time. She had made it and followed the edge of the forest lining up the road. She didn't dare stop till another 500 meters past the bend.

Was it the same lorry that came back? Two men just jumped off and the lorry disappeared north. OMG if she could have hiked with them!

The storm had raged and there was snow by the meters when she was last here, but by mere instinct she knew she was close to her destination.

She felt she could even smell Josef's farm. But his time it should all turn out totally different.

Silly you, are you losing it now, she said to herself, but it WAS Josef's farm and it looked even more battered now than last time. How was this to turn out the windows in the main house were just banging in the wind, the pit looked all dirty, but the outside shed, what about it? And what about the barn and the stable?

She found herself a cup in the crashed kitchen. The house was all empty and had been so for long. Some crows had made their nest right in the sitting room. Could she take a chance on the water in the pit? Well, she had to and it tasted just fantastic so she had herself another cupper before going up to the barn. It was totally barricaded as last time, but the door to the stable, what about it? The small door was overgrown by all sorts of wild bushes. But was it locked, if so, what then? Maybe she could find herself an axe or a hammer or even a solid stone could do the trick to break the lock, but she remembered it to be all solid.

But thank heavens it was not locked. But there was something stinking intensely from inside. She sensed it ever so clearly, same type smell as from the morgue at the hospital. But this one was worse, much worse and stronger. Stinked like rotten and she immediately felt for getting outside and relieve herself. Maybe there was an animal laying rotten in there?

But it wasn't an animal, but a man, a naked man lying there. Someone had cut off his testicles and thrown them away. On his chest someone had carved in the star of David.

A direct execution and it couldn't have been done that many days back. In this heat of the summer the body soon decayed. His face was no longer a face, some rodents had left him with only the naked scull. He must have been killed very abrupt, marks from a spade or something having almost cut his head from the torso.

Well, she had seen a lot of bodies, but not in rottening process like this one, nor maltreated like this body. It had to be the remains of Josef or? Someone had probably betrayed him in his work as courier. The kind Josef, now he had passed.

She covered his remains with the same old horse-cover as last time and made her way towards the small staircase leading up to the barn. If there was a hatch there, would she then manage to open it up? She tried and she managed. No way she could spend the night in the stable with the remains of poor Josef.

But first she had to inspect the outer shed, maybe there would be some bread or even some canned food there? And she was pleased, as there was an old bread, a bit molded, a can of sardines and one more can with brown beans. Her teeth ran in water

Once back she closed the stable door as best, she could, got the hatch up and she even managed to drag a couple of heavy cart wheels on top of it.

The bread was somewhat repelling, but she managed to eat it and even so the canned beans. The sardines she kept for later.

She heard them coming long before she could lay eyes on them, barking of dogs and shouting the traditional: "Los, Los, los!"

They made their way through the house, came to the nailed door to the barn and then into the stable. The dog whimpered; no way he wanted go inside. Then came the outcry from the first of the soldiers. "OMG!" "Is he dead?" it was nr 2. "Yes absolutely, this damned Jew. He stinks even in his death!" And should he not do just that? Rebecka whispered to herself.

The first of the two had to ran for it, out to throw up. Then he was back trying to open the hatch, but run right out to the yard again, vomiting and swearing. They almost fought the two, who would be the first out. The dog was still whimpering.

"Let's get the hell out of here! Leave the door open so maybe some wild animals will come and finish the job, just bark off the remaining flesh. Did you see that his dick and balls were gone?"

They were out now, got the dog into the tiny side wagon and off in a jiffy. What had they been looking for here, maybe Efraim if he had managed to sneak off and gone north again?

Would he possibly come here during this night? She wished for that and hoping he would come, made her happy. Possibly he had managed to get away from the enemy? Yes, it had to be like that. But once here, he would first have to dig a grave to Josef; she doubted she would at all be able to help him. But now she was done of all the thinking, she fell on top of a sack of straw and was immediately into deep, deep sleep.

She woke in the middle of the night by some man crying violently, long and grim. It had to be Josef standing up from the dead, had it not! Then she heard the stable door banged and someone run down the path, stooped and threw up. She tried to look through a breach in the panels, but it was all dark. "Eugenia!" someone was crying out there. "Eugenia!" Yes, it had to be Efraim. But he didn't hear her calling back and continued down to the dirt road. Then suddenly he seemed to have changed his mind so he doubled back, found himself a spade, and started to dig a grave right outside the barn. She tried to call for his attention, but he was too focused on his task. A bit later she had managed to loosen a plank, she now could see him clearly and he could hear her as well.

She had to admit to herself that she liked it when he kissed her in sheer joy over their reunion. But no tongue-kissing, she said to herself. That would be for the fathers' only, to my Lars and my Chaim, but to which one of them?

BACK AT ARI'S AND INNA'S FARM

"Let me go first, they know me, not as a pregnant woman, but still". Inna was at the door but she didn't recognize it was Rebecka. "Do you remember me Inna, I was here with Chaim during the winter storm?" But Inna just shaked her head. "Chaim, you were saying? Welcome Rebecka", Ari was at the door now and she told him about Efraim.

"It is quieter here now, but why did you come here? Is Efraim your new man?" he seemed quite reserved Ari. "No, he is just my helper and he has cycled all the way from Josef's farm with me on the luggage tray, and Josef he is dead, Ari. And many times, when there were transports, we had to go to the forest to hide.

"But Rebecka, where is Chaim, and Rebecka is this Chaim's child that you are bearing?" "I hope so Ari and I shall give birth in maybe two months from now".

"So, you are the scraped, bony, starved Rebecka from the muck cellar then?" Inna started laughing and hugged her warmly now.

"May Efraim stay here for some hours, get something to eat and rest a bit before going on up to uncle Ezra?" "Your uncle is dead, just suddenly dead; you may have noticed he was no way well when you left?" "Oh no, uncle Ezra has passed. The last one of the elders!" Now it was only Chaim and herself still alive from the once large family. "You forget about the child you are carrying Rebecka". "He shall be named Melchior in remembrance of my father".

She wanted only to keep crying, but had to pull herself together. And the energy from the child she was carrying helped her one more time. "But maybe it shall be a girl?" "Yes, I am positive it will be a girl" and then she started telling them about the life at the hospital down in Odesa right up to the time when she was denounced.

Lars? No, she didn't say a word about him.

"But what are we to do about Efraim then Ari?" "The Germans are back here now all the time craving for milk. Now, they might be here anytime". "So, no question about it, it has to be the muck cellar then Ari?" She laughed openly now. "I think I washed myself 100 times at least to get rid of the stench and not least this feeling of always being dirty". Ari smiled at her. "It is not that much filled up now, the bulk is out on the fields. But come on Efraim. You may take with you some bread if you think you will be up to eating down there. At three o'clock in the night you must be on your way north".

"Give my best to Chaim and auntie Esther then Efraim". Ari and Inna looked at each other, quite confused the two of them. "You were saying Rebecka, are you not going with him? You have to go!" "No, I cannot go north to the mountains and give birth". "But you cannot stay here, you are no doubt wanted both as Rebecka and Svetlana", Ari looked at her papers.

"Well of course you are right Rebecka, so Chaim shall have to come down here tomorrow night with new papers, and Efraim must tell him about it".

"So, those I got from uncle Ezra, they are no good then, me being this redtop, Eugenia Skripnikova?" "Well maybe Eugenia, or what you like to be called, but we shall not take any chances". Big laugh again. "And where am I to be hiding until Chaim comes down here then? In the muck cellar? Ok then Efraim, I shall keep you company".

But Inna had turned dead serious. "And what happens thereafter then Rebecka? I mean when you have your new papers?" "You mean when I am to be your half-sister, Tatiana from Kyiv, just escaped from the Russians?" "Yes, you said half-sister, did you not?" "Quite so and we have the same father, a Russian sergeant, he fell at Stalingrad. They were all wiped out there, all of the soldiers, only a few heroes surviving".

"When Chaim comes with the papers, we shall all sit down and have a good talk about this Rebecka". "Please say Tatiana from now on then Ari, best get used to it. You too, please Inna". But Inna kept it all to herself. No doubt she felt uncomfortable with the events she expected for the next evening.

Women always have this 7th sense, Rebecka thought and yes, we are raised to look after one another. She felt it really bad, once again go down into the muck cellar, memories of last time hadn't faded. This time even worse with the baby in her stomach. They couldn't manage to eat, nor she nor Efraim. Eventually she just fell asleep on a dry spot down there.

Efraim had left without her noticing it. But she was all awake next morning by the sound of dogs barking and "Los, Los, Los, Milk Ari, Milk!" A German voice, probably two of them as usual.

Ari had put fresh muck on top of the hatch down to the cellar, but now she heard him getting scolded in German, being told to keep all clean. They wanted clean milk, not a filthy one. "You are a pig Ari, nothing but a pig!"

They had him scrape away the muck on top of the hatch and once it was off, demanding a ladder to get down to the cellar for inspection. "But we have no proper ladder, we never go down there". But the private was ordered by the sergeant to get himself down and Ari had to come up with a ladder on the double.

What now? If Ari was safe outside, then she could draw the splint from the hand grenade. The two Germans would go missing and to avoid any catastrophe Ari would have to go up to the German HQ and tell them that there had been this accident. The private had played with a hand grenade, cows gone nervous and maybe they would give no milk for a while. But what about herself and the baby? Killed instantly, no pain!

She heard Ari come with the ladder, but the Germans complained that it was too long, only problems here. Fortunately, 2 steps were missing, so when the private tried to go down into the cellar, he couldn't reach the next steps. No way to make it unless he jumped down into the muck. Ari had gone outside now together with the sergeant.

"There is nothing but muck here", cried the soldier, not jumping willingly down into the muck. "Alright then", the sergeant was back and helped pulling the ladder away. "You are certain that you did a proper inspection then, maybe I shall have to see for myself". The sergeant tried to use the ladder, but skid reaching for the lower steps and the private had to pull him up again. "Damn, damn where is the milk Ari?"

She had been like a tenth of a second from pulling the splint all out and then, point of no return.

"That was damned close Ari". "Yes, I know, but let go with this hand grenade, stay put and I shall come for you after dark". "Right so, but please tell your wife that I need to borrow some of her clothes and do remember lots of hot water".

She confided her plan to Chaim when he arrived and they had some moments to themselves. She did of course flash when he asked her directly the very question. But she interrupted him half way through his stuttering. "You must get your math right Chaim, then you will figure out that there can be no one else fathering this baby". It was for him to get all red-faced now.

"But how do we proceed with all this then Rebecka? By the way here are your papers". And there she was the blonde Tatiana. "How do we get your hair done then?" "Just cut it as much as possible and then we shall use lye or whatever you brought with you to change the color". She was smiling now; her optimism was back.

"I always figured for Tatiana to be a brunette Rebecka?" "Well, once you come of age you will see that all girls want to be blondies!"

Serious now he was Chaim: "I shall have to leave in two hours Tatiana". He had to smile to himself over her new name. "Have you talked with Ari then?" "No, but his wife no doubt has a realistic idea of what will come next". "And women help women, right? Rachel is her real name and she would never let down a Jewish half-sister". "Meaning Rebecka or Tatiana? Have it your way?" "I shall give birth to my child, right here and then leave Melchior to her, but he shall of course have an official name, Sergei is a popular one?" She laughed to him.

"But what if it is not a boy, but a girl, what then Rebecka?" "Then her name will be Eugenia Chaim!" "And how long after the birth will you and our Eugenia be staying here?" "I shall go up to the camp soonest Chaim, if it is still there". "If not, you have to search for me. Now that our dear uncle has passed, it is I who lead the group. I hope sincerely that our auntie Esther will be with us for a long time, but she seemed very much down following uncle's death". "If she had been younger, then I would have taken Melchior with me up to the camp, but as at now it seems too risky". "I think you meant Eugenia did you not?

I shall go and have a talk with Inna and Ari while you have a proper wash, or several too you're liking. So, you just start this change into a blondie and then Inna will cut your hair. When the Germans are back here tomorrow morning then you will stay in your bed, totally exhausted following your long march from Kyiv, all the time afraid of running into Russians. And you can use some more clothes on the front of your stomach, making you look super pregnant. But be smart, skip this talk about Melchior. It's too dangerous. Just point to your stomach and say Eugenia, daughter and you will get used to it".

He was soon back with a large scissor. Inna had flatly refused to take responsibility for the cutting.

Her hair was almost damaged following his treatment. "You want for me to cut you down there as well?" "Get lost my boy!" What? Did she really say that, my boy? Well, she just did!

No doubt she had to get rid of the Henna color down there as well and not to forget her armpits and it was even more painful with the lye.

Ari was ok with it, but Inna was super nervous for the meeting with the Germans next morning.

"Good morning to you, maybe you will say hello to my sister-in-law, Tatiana, escaped from the Ruskies at Kyiv. Now pregnant, birth maybe in one month". "Then she shall need milk as well, right?" "Well not that much, maybe just a deciliter".

The sergeant just laughed, but the young private was to mark himself and shouted with all his might: "Heil Hitler!" and "Los, Los".

But even if Rebecka had wanted it, she couldn't get up from the bed. The mattress made from straw had a hole in the middle so her bottom was right down to the floor. "Papers, papers!" He yelled the young private, obviously trying to imitate the sergeant.

"Just you relax, all papers are here for you", Ari was his calm and the sergeant took over. "She must of course come to our HQ and get proper papers when the baby is born and maybe she even shall need medical help with the birth?" Ari had got a swung to his German now, so he got most of the message. "Yes, maybe a Doktor, yes, Heil Hitler!" It was for him to shout out loud now. And Rebecka she joined: "Heil Hitler, Popov kaputski" To this they all laughed, more so the sergeant, saluted: "Auf Widerseehen!" And that should be real soon.

A CHILD IS BORN

Not much time for privacy after Rebecka had moved in. Ari had mounted a kind of a hammock in the kitchen, he slept there at times, so did Rebecka.

Between the two of them all seemed easy and effortless, while Inna, she was holding back, clearly reserved, as being restless to what would happen once the baby was born.

No doubt Inna was worried for the provisions as well. Rebecka needed nutrious food now, still it was often 2 weeks between Chaim's visits.

Days became long to Rebecka now and Inna wasn't that happy to have her helping with the cooking. Should she really leave her newborn to this introvert and not very positive woman, Rebecka pondered. It was obvious that the two women would never make it together. Rebecka being large and heavy now, but still she felt herself a beautiful woman compared to Inna. So, it would be all about jealousy then.

And Ari did of course notice it all, as did Inna. Noticing his attention to the young, beautiful mother to be. And who was to suffer to this? Rebecka of course.

She didn't dare to be much outdoors, wouldn't challenge destiny and consequently went in the skirts of Inna.

One week before the estimated term, Chaim came and told them that the camp up mountains would have to be moved. Consequence, scares provisions for some time. This was real bad news to them all, as food already was running short. The Germans took every drop of milk now and they had even insisted on having all the eggs, but the worst blow was that they had threaten to take the ox calf, one that Ari had saved to themselves for the autumn.

They hoped for the Germans to soon withdraw further north, but there was of course a risk that they would kill all their cattle before leaving, nothing to be left to the Ruskies.

The partisans no doubt knew well about the milk deliveries to the Germans and it was more than evident that they would take charge once the Germans had pulled out.

Chaim was naturally well aware of all this and on the next visit he took Ari aside, wanting to have a separate talk with him.

"Ari, in 2 weeks I shall be back to look for Rebecka. She has already started having riers, so I think she shall give birth in just a few days. But she cannot stay here once the birth is over and no way she can take the baby with her as we now have no permanent camp". Ari looked at him, clearly astonished: "You mean she shall leave her newborn with us, well yours as well Chaim?" "Yes, for a while. When the Russians and the partisans take over here, then she would be the one object for rape, sorry for being that plump Ari.

And no offense to your wife Ari, we are all different, but with Rebecka gone and Inna playing the role as the new mother, then it is more than likely they shall leave you at peace. Newborn baby in her lap. Even the Russian wouldn't get violent then and why should they? Plenty of beautiful young women in Kyiv and Odesa".

"How do you plan to introduce this to Inna then Chaim and Rebecka of course, or have you already discussed this?" It was ever so obvious; Chaim reasoned that Ari would strongly oppose to any plot behind his back. His face was a proof to that.

"Absolutely not Ari. I would never have embarked on such an issue not having talked with you first. You have to believe me on my words, but I shall talk to the two of them once I am back, not to discuss, but to present this as an order".

"You think it will come easy to these two strong women to accept an order?" "Yes, Ari because the alternatives would be much worse. Rebecka with a newborn baby at the Front and Inna without a protective baby, a far too easy object for hungry soldiers". "So, Inna and I are finally to be parents then Chaim?!" "Yes at least until we know more about how the war develops up in Rivne, or, maybe both Rebecka and I shall fall in this war". "Tell me Chaim, how well do you know Rebecka?" "We have known each other since childhood, Ari". "But what I meant is how well do you know her as a grown woman and a mother soon to be?" "Meaning what Ari? I don't get your question, spit it out straight please!" "Pretty simple this Chaim; do you really think she will accept your order, your decision, no questions asked?" "Yes, I do because, as I said she has no choice. If she is to come with me and join the group, then it shall be without the baby.

And you know she cannot stay on here. The Russians may not be many weeks from here now. And for sure she cannot stay with the Germans; she is probably wanted both as Svetlana and prior to that as Rebecka the Jewish girl, she being the only witness to the massacre at the Parade square.

No way we can forget about the partisans hating the Jews either. Maybe they will be the first to come to your farm Ari, starting questioning about this Rebecka and her true identity".

"But what is to happen later Chaim? Once the Ruskies have taken over?" "I don't know Ari, but if we are still alive, then Rebecka has to start her new life as a nurse on the Russian side, in Odesa of course and come time, she may use her real name and come for the child".

"But what if we come to love her child Chaim?" "Yes, I know", he tapped his mate on the shoulder; "what if both Rebecka and I are killed then Ari? You see, this discussion, think if etc. becomes far too difficult. But if we both should make it, then nothing is more natural than we coming back for our child, right? Now, I have to get going and please don't talk to the women about this at all. I shall do that myself when the time is right".

He left to bid Rebecka best of luck and say goodbye to Inna. "Will we soon have more food?" Her only comment. Inna knew by her mere female intuition what was to come.

"Yes, I hope to bring new provisions when I am back in 2 weeks Inna". They both knew that no way it was the provision that was on their minds, more so the solution to the complex situation. He pitied his Rebecka now, but what was he to do? He knew that in spite of it all she was in the best of hands and the Germans had promised medical aid when needed.

The two German "milk pickers" had grown ever so familiar and three days later the water broke right when they were at the door. The night had been really bad to her and Inna didn't know what to do, wondering if they should call for the German medic. But Rebecka was adamant: "No, we are strong people and we shall handle this ourselves. Just provide lots of hot water, clean cloths and make sure you boil the scissor!" "The scissor? Oh yeah to cut the cord with, of course".

The young woman was surprised to herself how easily she took the leading role, took charge, not because she desperately wanted it, but because the situation would require it and it came natural to her.

"Your sister not stand up this morning?" The Germans as well as Ari were in place. "No, maybe baby today". "Doktor then?" No, Ari didn't think so, but was grateful to them in case they were to call for the Doktor.

He looked at Rebecka, "You may tell the Doktor that the birth will be in two hours", she mustered bravely.

But it in less than one hour a Jeep skidbreaked outside and a medic rushed in followed by the sergeant. "Hot water, lots of it and clothes", ordered the medic, "and you", he pointed at the sergeant, "you stay on guard right outside!"

Rebecka was moaning, but she knew she was safe now and she was truly grateful to have the mature medic by her bedside.

"Where is the father then young lady?" "He is fighting the Ruskies". "Jawohl, I can see the top of the head now, it looks all normal this birth!"

15 minutes later it was all well over, the medic cut the cord and having washed himself he called for the sergeant who shouted "Heil Hitler" with all his might. Little Eugenia was already lying calmly at her mother's breast. "What will be the name of the baby?" "Eugenia". "If there should be complications then tell the sergeant here immediately. Heil Hitler and best of luck." "Eugenia and I are thankful to you Herr Doktor!"

And her Chaim, what would be his reaction: All curly blonde, her hair!

RUBICON AND THEN BACK TO ODESA

She was gone when he woke; damn, only one hour till train departure. So, no breakfast, he just had to run for it and the letter from Birgitta, what about it? Read it once on the train. Grabbed himself some scones from a vendor at the platform. No dining car till after Lviv.

Birgitta? What about her? When had she left? He hadn't the faintest idea. He could only remember himself crying and she stroking him and kissing him. And what an ego in bed! How much he owed to this fantastic woman.

"My dearest Lars. Thanks for a wonderful evening. I don't know whether it was of any help to you, concerning this question about your Norway, but to me it seems utterly clear. You shall have to stay and find yourself a new identity in a civilized country. No return to Norway.

But Lars, I am part of this war too and I had truly deserved to have what you got. But you were just lost and shame to you. You have to come back or I shall come to you. Then we shall know whether we will be together or not, right? Let's try to get a weekend in Berlin at least, that would be the best. But don't call now, write me. Mother is ever so curious already".

Yes of course, he owed her a lot. He could feel the shame creeping on to him there and then, thinking of her outcries: "Wait, wait!" And he the ego, let it just come for himself, in seconds. She was entitled to much, much more and had gotten nothing, except having to play the comforting one all the evening. Beautiful Birgitta!

It was clear to him now, should have been all of the time, that now the train had left the station, it always had. All the way since the first trip to Vestfold and the first camp. Well before that, right since he signed the recruitment papers. It was then that the train had left, no return.

But who were to know at the time that Germany would lose this war? He ought to have known it following the dogfights over London. He then should have seen that there was only a one-way track as the Americans never would have failed to support England, once she had proven herself in the fight for London. But if England had lost that battle, then Lars, would the Americans still have come to aid this England, now under German control?

No, he didn't think so. The USA was fed up with wars, having saved Europe in 1917. It was now for Europe to save herself. Without the support of the Americans, even Stalin would have had to make separate peace with Germany. And the Americans would have their hands full, following Pearl Harbor.

So, the signs have been clear then Lars? You have only been blindfolded, all the time thinking about your mother and her land in Karelen, Finland. It was clear that Germany would lose and your way home would be a road to prison and loss of all you hold dear. That's the way it was and there was no way asking for forgiveness. Asking who? The exile government in London? How were they to treat an opportunist and what about the Courts once they were reinstalled and what about the people at large? What sort of forgiveness could he hope for? He an elite soldier from the East front coming home, rid of the Nazi stamp? The SS-doctor, Lars Nedregård asks forgiveness, asks people to forget about his war-past. Would he have patients at all?

And what about Eva now? He had to write to her and tell her about it all, that he never was to come home. But what if she offered to come to him in Germany and marry him to be his wife? Would that be a sacrifice that he could take and would they possibly be happy thinking about all they had left behind in Norway, their childhoods fairy land, the farms and the two old dads left alone with the scars and the everlasting gossiping from the community? They were absurd the thoughts he had right there. But what if he got killed there in the war? One of the many falling at the East front, buried in a mass grave? Would that make it all easier to Eva and his old dad? Then there would be no homecoming to a Nazi soldier, no one to put in jail, no one to scold by children and grownups.

Why hadn't he thought about all this before enlisting or was it that obvious at the time that Germany would be victorious? He himself had never had any ambition about fighting for Hitler and no way would he have participated in the extermination of the Jews, he himself being a Jew as well.

He had only had the one vision: Fight for his mother's land, get his medic degree and then come home, marry his girlfriend, join his father's surgery and look after the farm, well both farms eventually.

But your choice was the wrong one Lars. In hindsight Lars. You could have gone to Finland as an assistant medic, although last term student, worked as a volunteer at a field lazarette and then once the war was over there in Finland, you could have come home and finished your education there in Oslo. But you were that determined, on life and death, determined to learn how to be a soldier, learn how to best fight the Bolsheviks. It was there you made the wrong choice Lars. And now three years later and what about your train now Lars? The train is no longer at the station. This one being long closed. Never Norway no more. It was now time to get away from the advancing Bolsheviks and then look for a new, brighter future.

But what about Eva. Don't you owe her to tell her about it all? But then she might decide to come to Germany, or? Would it not be better to leave it all as at now, no letter, just let the war have its way? Maybe you are all wrong and Germany still is to win? Or the other scenario: You get killed at the front.

You are a coward now Lars, nothing but a coward! You simply have to write to Eva and you must answer to Birgitta's letter as well.

His mind was still in turmoil, but suddenly his night train had arrived at the station in Odesa. He had hardly reconned the change from day-train to night train there in Lviv. Now the Chief Physician was waiting for him there at the platform. Seemingly happy to have Lars back. "Welcome Herr Hauptsturmführer, welcome more than ever. I am alone here now. Even our surgery nurse, Svetlana is gone". "Gone?" he mustered. Something must have happened and he was about to lose himself if he asked for Rebecka.

Off with the uniform and Gerda, a new nurse from Linz in Austria was there for him with gown, gloves and face mask, all ready for surgery. "Ever so welcome Herr Doktor!"

No doubt the Chief was overjoyed having him back, but something was still wrong; The two of them were off to the Chiefs private office.

"Once again welcome back well and sound, Herr Hauptsturmführer. As I indicated we have a lot to talk about. But let's start with the simple chores first. We shall soon have to move from here, the staff, the patients and as much as we can take with us of equipment, all up to Lviv". Lars looked at him, saw the serious concern on the Chiefs weary face. "I do the realize that the Russians are not far from here. But what is the more serious then, are you going to leave us?" He smiled the Chief. "No way, not till everyone leaves. But Lars we have been tricked".

Lars just looked at him apparently all confused. "Tricked, by whom?" "By our nurse friend". He was close to saying your very special friend, but managed to hold back. "Svetlana, not being Svetlana, but the Jew Rebecka!" "But what about her papers then. We both examined them and yes, she was a first-class nurse?" "Right so, but she wasn't Svetlana as written in her papers, but Rebecka and not from Rivne, but from here, in Odesa."

"So, her papers were all falsified?" "Yes precisely." "Well then, but how did all this come about, how was it disclosed?" He told Lars about the necessary reorganization giving Rebecka the full responsibility for the third floor. "But did she not live up to expectations?" "Yes, totally. But Lars, obviously you need to have this spooned to you. Rebecka is a common Jewish name. She was, is a Jew!" Lars was sure his face would betray him now, only hoped for not getting totally pale like a corpse. "I do of course trust your story Herr Chief, but why should a Jewish girl choose to nurse wounded German officers, her enemies so to speak?"

"Old trick that Lars, rats hide where there is least chance to be caught. Ingenious but not good enough. Heil Hitler! Just think about it Herr Hauptsturmführer, think about it if there had become a closer relation between the two of you!" "Herr Chief physician, I am engaged to be married in Norway and such an alliance would have been unthinkable!"

Did he lie to himself or was it just the story to tell to the Chief. But Svetlana was gone and he was never to meet with her again. Should he, and would he wish for it?

FAREWELL TO EUGENIA

The little girl weighed almost 3 kilos. They had no balance, but Ari was usually good at weights. She was big to be a girl, almost 48cm but above all well shaped. But then it was her hair; Inna as well as Ari had been standing close like glued to her, looking at her blonde hair and they exchanged very telling looks. It was obvious what was on their minds, so attack was always the best defense.

"Quite some staring at the hair of my little Eugenia. Are you thinking about Chaim's raven black hair?" Well, yes, they had to admit just that. "Just you relax, in my family there have been dark ones and blonde ones. We the women influences the color of the hair by our genes. It is no way just the father's genes that are decisive, on the contrary".

But Inna wouldn't let go just like that as she felt that she had a grip on Rebecka right there and then. "What's your real color then Rebecka? But whatever she is a beautiful baby", she added. "I guess I was dark blonde in my childhood, later Henna-colored as you know and now a blondie. Are you to dwell long on this?" "No, but we do hope all the three of us that Chaim shall not be too concerned with this hair color?"

But Rebecka continued, no way should she be put down: "If he wants to have a part in my baby, then he best skips such thoughts if he has them at all. You folks should by no means nourish such thoughts. Eugenia is my child and Chaim is her father, basta!"

The sergeant and the private came every morning as usual. This very morning, they brought greetings from the German medic, curious to know if all went well with the baby and the mother. If she had enough milk or they should reserve some for her. "Just tell them thanks, but everything is fine here" she told Ari, and added, "the baby is asleep right now". They felt a little giddy now and what would Ari or Inna have to say the next time when both Tatiana and the baby were gone? Inna was not informed so far of what was planned to her, but Ari, knowing about it all, had a hard time to conceal it so Rebecka asked him if something was the matter. No, no he was just curious about Chaim's next arrival.

"What about the baptizing Rebecka?" Inna had been beating around the bush on this for some time. "Baptizing?" "Well, the baby must soon have a name, not so?" "She got her name several months ago Inna, her name as you know is Eugenia". "Name before she even was born?" Rebecka had to laugh. "Well yes of course, she is only a week old now as you know". "But who baptized her, a Rabbi or?" What was it with Inna now then, she tried to keep a serious look at her. "In a way you are right Inna. But Chaim and I decided on the name short to the birth and thereafter we felt there was nothing more to say in the matter". "But should you not give her a Jewish name?" Now Ari came in: "Are you totally crazy? Who is to talk about a Jewish child, a Jewish name and a Jewish baptizing? Have you not heard Hitler's Weltanschauungs speeches? Jews are to be exterminated wherever they are. Grown-ups, women and children. Now, you shall both stop this, you must be nuts risking this type of a conversation".

Inna was the one feeling most guilty. It was she that had brought the theme up so she said sorry and Rebecka nodded to Ari as well.

Then came Thursday and Chaim was finally at the door. Obviously worn out from the trip down from the mountains, still his sack was packed with provisions.

"Ari, please help me with the sack and in ten minutes time I want to speak to the woman folks alone. But first I want to see my son". Rebecka just laughed to him. "You should have listened to me, listened well. At long last we have a beautiful little Eugenia".

"Strange this, she has my nose, but your curls from when you were two years old. You wouldn't remember that would you and later hairs usually get darker". He kissed the baby on both cheeks, little Eugenia laying ever so calm in his arms and then there were some words spoken in Yiddish, hardly heard by the others. And Rebecka's heart broke to him. No doubt he would understand that this baby might have another father, not him and that Rebecka possibly had lied to him. But he had saved her from this embarrassing encounter with Inna and Ari. No one had prepared him for this situation, but he might have seen it coming.

She got pale Rebecka, death pale when he told her about the change of plans. But there was no way to change it. Military orders it was and there was no denial to it. He then turned to Inna; "have you any objections then or are you willing to take the role as mother to our child?" "What says Ari then?" "He has okayed it as he sees that this will mean better protection for you towards the advancing Russians at the same time as Rebecka can get away in time, from the partisans as well".

Rebecka had stood up now, raged in her face. "So, my child, our child, merely a week old, she shall be used in this fight against the victorious?" "I don't think there is any real choice to this my dearest Rebecka". "But could we not give it some more time, she is but 7 days old, maybe another week then?"

"The girl will have it just fine here and she will continue to be ok with Inna and Ari. Down in Odesa people are already fleeing from the Ruskies. Even the Germans have realized that now it is time to leave and the hospital and all patients will be moved up towards Lviv, where they will set up a field lazarette to support their troupes who are trying to stop the progress of the Russians. So far Army Group Center holds the town of Vinnitsa.

But even if the Germans hold Vinnitsa as at now, it will be of minor help as the Russians now are fortifying their breach into the German lines. To every German soldier, Russia matches with 100 and may even fortify their position by more men. No way they are short of manpower.

Rumors have it that the decisive battle will come in two, maybe three days, when the Rumanians just beat it and the German forces are squeezed back to Lviv.

So, maybe already tomorrow it might be too late to get out of here. I had no possibility to come here until now, had first to find provisions to you".

Inna went to the kitchen to her husband, leaving it to Rebecka to cry for her baby and get packing.

An hour later she was ready to go, the bitter goodbye was to be a fact. She knew to herself that this might be a goodbye forever. 7 days was all she was left with in her motherhood. Would there be more to come?

THE RUSSIANS ARE COMING

From Vinnitsa and west, the Russians had this breach into the German withdrawing. But for a while it looked like the reorganization at Vinnitsa might be followed by new successes to the Germans. And some non-commissioned officers had talks going about the new offensive eastwards. Hitler had made it clear that this time there should be no mistakes as he himself would be in command, no longer withdrawals ordered by incompetent generals and he should see to that these Russians once and for ever should be driven back to the land east of the Ural Mountains. His speeches worked fabulous as a vitamin injection to the worn-down German troops retiring from the East front.

But there was only to be this only counteroffensive at Vinnitsa and both the flanks of the German army were sealed off by the advancing of hundreds of thousands of fresh Russian troupes. Where did they come from, where did Stalin all the time find all these fresh soldiers, new ones all the time? This should be the word of mouth from the German soldiers.

It had been days now since the break up from the hospital in Odesa, staff already gone north. The tents they were to use at this new field lazarette had been supplied from Lviv. A detail from the Elite corps weren't too happy having to assist setting up this campsite. "We did not join Division Gross Deutschland to do this kind of work". "You shut it and work!" order from the sergeant. And a bit later Lars heard they got another order: "We shall join the division in one hour so you just get this job done or the whole detail shall be transferred to a Strafcompany. The survival rate has gone down there now, only 4 hours survival, you hear!" "Jawohl, Herr Sergeant. Heil Hitler!"

Who was this sergeant, or was it a sergeant major? Could it be the voice of Loke? He should find out later, now it was all about getting the lazarette orderly. It was situated on a height close to an abandoned farm. The living quarters were shot to pieces. A direct hit from heavy artillery. The family living there was probably dead in the gravel and scattered planks, many meters off the real hit. Maybe he should venture to go over there and check if anyone was still alive and needed medical help to survive?

But a man came crying towards him: "No one to look for there, just bits of corpses, all blown to pieces, I cannot take it any longer". The guy disappeared onto the barn, surprisingly undamaged it was. But why had the Russian aimed their heavy guns at this unsignificant height? It must have been "a blind one", when they were adjusting their cannons to the real battle. The family that had been home had just had bad luck, wrong place at the wrong time. But this guy, where had he come from and where had he been hiding? He should have been killed as well should he not. But he didn't seem to have the smallest scrape. No way did he look like a farmer either, Russian machine pistol onto his shoulder.

The patients who were able to walk by themselves or with crouches, or supported walking by help of the nurses were already sent north to Polish hospitals. All left was now five officers and a private they had picked up en route, left to die by his company no doubt having given up on his chances to make it. Not much that Lars could do to him. "Internal bleedings and it will soon be the end", commented the Chief Physician.

At this small height where the tents had been placed it was like an island on the immense high plain. From the sight they had on the top, all Ukraine seemed totally flat, miles by miles.

From far away they could hear the Russian "Orchestra" starting to play. But it was neither Aida nor the Mandarins in Madame Butterfly they heard, but the long-range Russian guns on their way to build the real offensive against the withdrawing German forces.

The night had been rainy and dark, now it was suddenly like a well-lightened opera scene in grand format. The grenades from the heavy guns shot great craters and there were cries over the whole of the German lines now when the "Stalin organ" followed suite.

The entire eastern sky was lit by the artillery-shooting so the light bombs sent up from both sides were totally wasted.

Lars could distinguish a grey mass of panzers moving slowly forward, while the air was shaking by all the explosions, even the sound from the belts of more than 700 panzers was stifled by the explosions. The reason to their slow advance got obvious to him once they got closer.

A detail, no several details run as crazy in front of the panzers, must have been more than a full Strafcompany. Every other soldier hit mine threads and it was now a complete inferno there down at the plain. He could only sense body parts swirling in the air.

He didn't want to see more of this, but he was hypnotized, like he himself was paralyzed by this gruesome, almost unreal scene.

The four-barreled machine guns and the fire spying from the guns of the panzers destroyed all and everything on the way. But what about the German artillery, all long-retreated west or north?

When the panzers increased their speed they sent dying, the more or less living bodies of the last ones in the Strafcompany. The panzers up front had now made it through the minefields. Stalin didn't care for human lives; it was all about saving the costly panzers from getting blown up in the minefields.

And at the rear there, came an enormous army, of hundreds of thousands Russian soldiers and they were singing songs of victory and at the end he heard the now well-known expression: "Germanski soldatski, kaputski".

It wasn't at all possible to count all these Russian troops. Could the Germans at all withstand these masses of soldiers? He heard German soldiers crying for help, crying to their mothers as well when they were taken out by the four barreled machine guns. But once again he wondered what had happened to the German artillery and their panzers?

It was all topped by a group of Tupolev bombers, normally not flying at night. From one thousand feet they dropped superbombs leaving the entire German front a burning hell.

The unfair fire ratio could have only one issue, but an infantry company, led by a lieutenant had found an escape route up towards the lazarette. But no way, they were soon surrounded, now standing with their hands up, but at no while.

It was like broad daylight now and the air no way stopped shivering. Lars could see the faces of some of the soldiers even at a distance of some hundred meters. The lieutenant, having led the detail was standing there in front. He was the first to be decapitated.

Lars turned to the Chief coming out from the surgery tent. "How many thousands have they mobilized for this offensive?" "I don't know Herr Hauptsturmführer, but there must be at least 2 to 1, Russians to Germans and we have no more artillery."

"When the Russians are done with their mass murdering there down on the plain, then they will no doubt come for us and what will we have for protection?" "Nothing Herr Hauptsturmführer, nothing!" And right so, the general in charge of the withdrawal had seen the events and knew the outcome of it. The evacuation of the lazarette was on its way. Fights men to men were ever so close now.

In the light from the Stalin organ, they could now witness the butchering of the entire company, some had surrendered, arms over heads. The Russians, no these were not Russians, least not all of them; only a few had Russian jackets, these were partisans, they killed with knives or bayonets. One of them was walking around in an old, rather comic officers' uniform from times back. He wore an artillery saber and beheaded at least two of the German soldiers still holding their hands high up.

The Chief handed his binocular to Lars. "You want you to see this, if you can take it? Maybe you shall survive and then tell the world about the atrocities carried out by the wild animals we are fighting". "Do you mean the Russians?" "No these are not Russians, least not any military units. Maybe they are Rumanians, shifting side or partisans or a mixed company of the two!" He handed Lars his binoculars.

Lars could see clearly now that they continued with the butchering. A Kalashnikov took the lives of maybe 50 German soldiers while they all had their hands up. "Lars, follow closely what's going on by the trees over there!" And then he saw the most grotesque and maltreating to be his worst memory from this war.

Right there by the beginning of the forest, 5 German soldiers were impaled to each one's tree. The bayonets or the knives were rammed right through their uniforms or what was left and into the tree. While they were still alive, the partisans cut the head of 5 other soldiers, kneeling on their knees, helmets off, waiting to be beheaded. The other partisans watched closely while this macabre operation took place. But one of the German soldiers he had it in him, he grabbed the Kalashnikov from the closest of the partisans and managed to kill at least 15 before his head was cut off from the torso by the bullets from other partisans.

The stomachs of those nailed to the trees were now slit open and the entrails taken out. The heads of the other Germans were instead placed in the wombs now empty. Lars had to turn away and vomit, while the Chief had produced a long-barreled Mauser, ready to fire. "The distance is too long Chief!" "No, just 500 meters", and he made himself ready. In the course of minutes, he had managed to give shots of mercy to all the 5 nailed to the trees. "You should have joined a company of sharpshooters Chief and of course been a Doktor as well". Lars was deeply impressed.

But this turn of the events shouldn't come unpunished. The partisans had manned a Haubitzer and in seconds the Chief was gone, only bits and pieces were flying in the air.

Lars had lost it now, following this slaughtering and the Chief gone, but suddenly he observed one regular Russian soldier trying to get to the remains of the lazarette. This soldier was thrown many meters by the Haubitzer's next shot, his entrails hanging out now. Lars started to run for him, but a colonel tried to stop him, shouting: "We are retreating, don't go for this Russian. Come back we shall leave the lazarette as it is!" "I can't, I am a Doktor!" Lars shouted back. "Idiot, come back this is an order, he is just a Russian!" But Lars had already reached to the soldier as another grenade hit the poor man and instantly there were but pieces of him high up in the air.

But what had happened to himself: his foot didn't move as it should have when he wanted to double back. But there was no foot where it should have been? His leg was cut straight off right under the kneecap. So, it had to be his own leg that was now gone?

REBECKA, BACK IN THE CAMP

She had to admit it to herself, admit that she was immensely longing for her little Eugenia. She hadn't had any choice when Inna told them she could take care of the baby and then it was off with Chaim to his new camp up in the mountains.

Her breasts were sore and at times very painful when she now had no baby to suck them. But her sore breast made her think even more how much she missed her dear child. Not a single minute at peace sort of. But they all talked about the fighting in Ukraine soon to end now. The Rumanians had long started their mass-evacuation to their homeland

The Russians were eager to put an end to it all, and now it was they doing the "Blitzkrieg". For sure they had learned a lot from the Germans, according to auntie Esther, she still doing the cooking. "Welcome back Rebecka, have you been down Odesa all of the time then?" Rebecka reddened. She couldn't lie to her only living auntie, could she? Half-auntie but still.

"Dearest Esther, Chaim must no doubt have told you about it all, what has happened". "No, he has not Rebecka and for sure there must be a reason to that, and only you are to know that Rebecka". "Not that fast auntie, are you psychic or?" "Just you start telling me all about it my child". Child, suddenly Rebecka burst into tears. "I haven't had anyone to comfy in about all this and at times it has made me tempted to take my own life. But you must swear to me not to tell Chaim or any other what really happened to me there in Odesa. I was denounced by a visitor whom I knew from childhood so I had to leave the hospital, just run for it to save myself". She told here about the run to the synagogue and Efraim.

"Did you sleep with this Efraim then?" "Oh my God antie, I was 7.5 month pregnant and you think I am the one to sleep around?" She had gone silent now her auntie.

"We found Josef and Efraim buried him". "An what then?" "Well, we made it up to Ari and Inna and I can tell you it was some struggle to get out of Odesa and up to their farm, me 7.5 months pregnant and all".

"But you stayed with them there and had your baby and our Chaim has a boy or a daughter. And in spite of this you wanted me to keep all this to myself, not let Chaim know anything?" "But you sweared auntie!" "Yes, and there must be more reasons to have me swear Rebecka. Tell me why then. Chaim is like a son to me". "I know, I know!" and she cried now. "But auntie I am not sure if little Eugenia is his child. I am not sure about anything no more, except my longing for my little baby, I miss her that terrible".

"So, you have given birth to a daughter and she is Chaim's? Why then has he not told me that he has fathered a daughter?" "Maybe he is uncertain, wants to wait and see, or maybe waiting for a revelation or a confession on my part. My baby was born with blond, curly hair", she continued. Didn't dare look auntie in her face.

"I met a Norwegian Doktor who was to leave Odesa to serve at a field lazarette in Finland, his mother's land. Yes, I know, but I am not a giddy girl. But eventually we got close and the last night before he left…

And he is a good man auntie". "But so is Chaim". "But I don't know if Lars survived at all". "Did he work for the Germans?" "Yes, I mean no, not more than I did. He had enlisted solely to go fighting for his mother's land up in Finland".

"But if you were to choose then Rebecka?" "No there will never be a choice. For certain he has gone home or maybe he isn't even alive any longer. And auntie, if Chaim should get to know about all this, then he would never take little Eugenia to his bosom again. You understand me now auntie, don't you?"

"But what will you do now as the war here in our country is almost over or at least we can see the end is near?

And your baby then Rebecka, what now?" "Ari and Inna have agreed to take care of Eugenia as if she was their own flesh and blood, least till all this is truly over".

"But why are you here and not with your child then?" "Because I want to serve my people and hope one day to help having a free Ukraine". "But Rebecka your place is at a lazarette or a hospital, they are however soon shot to pieces. The Russians spare no one". "Auntie I am still a nurse, but I have learned to handle weapons as well, Kalashnikovs and hand grenades.

The Fatal Choice

I am as good as anyone of the others in the group. I wear men's clothes and I don't stand back to nobody".

"But where do you come from now, I mean officially. What shall Chaim tell his men and what will be your answer if anyone asks?" "Auntie he is my only living second cousin and I shall of course be good to him. But I cannot sleep with him, not now.

And if he has this uncertainty in himself, then I guess he wouldn't be interested he either. The war must come to an end and then we shall find out about it all, not only I, but he as well, yes everyone.

I know in myself that he is not the father of Eugenia and he knows it as well. Life will never be as before to none of us, not even to us Jews at large and who is to know what kind of life there will be to us under Russian dictatorship?"

"These are Chaim's very words as well and I wonder if he will not join the group of David Ben Gurion when it is all over and then go to this Israel and Jerusalem".

"And maybe it will be to his best auntie. He is a man for great visions, ready for taking on great challenges, a real commander".

And that he should be, but not in Ukraine, but in the Promised Land.

THE END OF THE PARTISAN GROUP

They had done many great raids, with or without Chaim. Never had there been bad words between them. Chaim was the boss and she did her job according to whatever orders were give. She carried three hand grenades in her belt and her Kalashnikov onto her shoulder. Knife as well in her belt. The parole was clear to everyone. No one were to be taken alive and remember: Your comrades' lives are the most important. And the men, many of them boys merely 22, and even some 18-years-old, they had all come to appreciate Rebecka's readiness when in need.

When Chaim was absent, she often was asked about her opinion. Even if Levi was second in command. Levi come to ask her, he as well.

On their way back to camp one day he couldn't let go of it: Rebecka you are trained to save lives, and for sure you must have saved many German officers in your job down Odesa. Now here we are all taking lives".

"Levi, you know quite well that I usually stand guard, help carrying provisions we seize from our enemies and redistribute them to the most needed". "But you were with us when we released the elderly Jew from the interrogations down in Rivne. What would you have done if that Gestapo man had faced you with his Luger in hand?" "I had shot him in cold blood there and then Levi!" "Were you that cold in your earlier days or is it the war that have you be that way Rebecka?"

For sure she didn't want to fall out with Levi, but she had to put him right.

"I don't know Levi, but I have come to learn that the life of a Jew is worth just as much as that of a Gestapo officer". "How come?" "Because so many of our people have been butchered without a chance to defend oneself". "You think it will be to the better when the Russians take over then, the wolves from Siberia? They don't ask questions, they rape whatever moves not having a dick between their legs and sometimes they even rape men in their asses, if that's their only choice". "Why do you tell me about these gruesome things Levi?" "Because it is not a matter of the intruders being German or Russian, what's important is that as many as possible of our people survive and can tell the world about the butchering and the atrocities once the war is over". "But honestly Levi, do you think people will listen? People at large will want to be done with the war and all connected to it".

"When we have our own state, our own country, then they will listen, shall listen, all our allies and our kins in the USA". "Are you referring to the biblical wholy state in the heavens now Levi?" "Don't fuss it off Rebecka. I am talking about our Promised land, where to Ben Gurion shall take us. Whatever you do Rebecka, never give up your arms. We shall have to fight for our lives and our children's lives all the time, and never to give up".

She had to stepped aside now to have a moment to herself. What future was there for little Eugenia in this perspective? More war, more exterminations? Would life never be as in prewar times in her Odesa? Maybe she would have to evacuate, run away, she and her baby as well, go to Palestine or what was the name of the country over there, the Promised Land.

They had seen the Russian great offensive in the making now for days and there was no doubt about what was coming. But the first attempt to break through the German stronghold had failed. But maybe this first attempt was like a test to challenge the strength of the Germans? Chaim was adamant about just that.

One of the guys had lost one arm, and Chaim decided for all to stay in the cellar under the barn, best place to defend themselves.

But late afternoon the last of the transports from the hospital had arrived together with a detail of German soldiers and it was decided to raise the lazarette one more time, now in front of the barn.

Chaim's group had seen how the rest of the farm had been shot to pieces and they now waited for the barn to go as well, so the whole group had taken cover in the lower cellar. But there were no more incoming grenades, so Chaim concluded that the demolishing of the main house was just accidental. He then made a fatal decision: "We shall stay here in the cellar until the Germans have gone".

But the Germans didn't leave, they stayed on to support the lazarette. In fact, they set up posts and guards around the whole little height and then it was too late for Chaim and his group to escape. They had no choice than to wait for the Russians that would force the retreat of the Germans.

FAREWELL LOKE, FAREWELL TO LARS'S FATHER-LAND

The sound of the Stalin organ, mines exploding, and the grenades coloring the sky all red, Lars didn't notice it that much any longer. Nor did he react to the horrible sound when a T34 Panzer was blown to the heavens fully loaded with ammo.

Farewell Odesa. Farwell to Eva up Norway, farewell to all and then it was all black.

Loke, now in charge for the soldiers, took off Lars his Death Mark and a captain gave him extra magazine for the Luger. "Keep it going as long as possible Lars, you have been a trusted mate as you promised me in Sennheim". He woke for a second, wondered what all this was about, Loke and Sennheim? "Division Gross Deutschland is proud to have you staying here with us Lars". "But what about me, what may happen to me and my damaged knee when you are no longer here to look after me Loke?"

"Make sure to shoot yourself before the Popovs come close to you. They don't care for you being a medic. They butcher all and everyone from our division. But we are proud of our Standard, not so Lars? You want for me to shoot you? I don't think I could manage that Lars". Loke was in tears now. Tears to the Lars he never got to make love to, only in his fantasy.

But Lars was almost gone now, hearing or seeing nothing. The captain checked that the Luger was ready for firing and pressed the weapon into his hand.

They had laid a tourniquet up towards his thigh and another one right by the knee where the grim bone pointed out. But it didn't help much. There was less blood pumped out now, but it still kept running. "Shoot him if you are up to it sergeant, I have to go back to the company or what's left of it. Hurry back you as well". But Loke just cried, waited a bit and then he followed his captain.

Only Rebecka was waiting there now, waiting for the Germans to leave so she could get out of her hiding and see to the wounded officer.

"You cannot stay here, the Russians will be here any minute now, Chaim pointed at her with the Luger. The Popovs will take you for a group rape and thereafter you will be butchered. Get yourself out of here on the double!" But she stayed on in spite of Lars's pledge and Chaim's order to run for it.

It was hard to Loke now, leaving with his captain. Now his best friend had passed. They had first met at the admission to med-school. From there on they had sticked together and they were both adamant that they should go fight the Russians in a Norwegian regiment with Norwegian officers, thus helping the brave Finns. But Loke was never to fight in a Norwegian regiment and there were no Norwegian officers, all broken promises. But his best friend Lars had made it to Finland to fight for his mother's land there in Karelen.

His conscience took him hard; he should have shot Lars before the Russians would be there. He should at least have taken off the distinctions, but now it was too late. The barn that they had used as part of the field lazarette was already on fire. Better to be burnt than be massacred to death by the Popovs, and not least the partisans, they just loved to butcher German officers. Some had a great liking to cut off ears and noses before the poor victim was dead. They must be insane those guys carrying out such atrocities, or? Probably not. Vodka or Russian moonshine was consumed at large before a battle.

But now they weren't to have their fun time, Loke even heard explosions from the barn

It shouldn't be at all that easy to talk about it to Eva nor to Lars's father, if he made it to his next furlough, if there was ever to be one now when the Germans were retreating. He was cut short in his thinking by the captain. "All equipment is now loaded on to a half-panzred car. So off you!" and he jumped on to it in the last second.

"We shall have to retreat really far. Next there will be a train to Lviv and further on to Poland. There is no front anymore. Did you manage to shoot your friend?" "No, he was the victim of the fire there", he pointed to the barn, the fire was almost done.

How could the captain imagine that he would be up to shooting his best friend, his only friend. In spite of Lars's determination up in Lviv that it was over and out with their friendship, Loke had never believed this to be like a final. Their friendship was too deep, to solid and not least: He could never let go of this lust to once be able to sleep with Lars. This fire inside of him had been there all the time since the admission day, never left him.

Just think about it: Shoot his own lover! But you never made it that far Loke? No, but the dream he could always save to himself, could he not, would he not?

HE IS TO LIVE!

It was late the next day when Lars, half-waking up by a ram smell in his nose: "Where are we now Loke? You are Loke, are you not?" But how could Loke be here? He spoke to his mate in Norwegian. But it was a woman answering him in bad German. "Loke no more!" "Is he dead then?" Lars spoke German he as well now and she answered in German, however halted. "No, but they are all gone now, all the others. And you, you have been dead as well!"

At long last he managed to open his eyes, quite an effort since his face was covered in blood. Was it an angel in white clothes there close to him, but she was bloodstained she as well and angels were not. But there was something familiar about her voice. "Why aren't we all dead, wouldn't the Russians bother to kill us?" "Hush, not that loud, there are Russians and partisans all over the place!"

"But why are we here and where does it come from this bloody smell?" "We are deep down, deep in the muck-cellar beyond the cow stable. The top section of the barn is all burned down". Lars tried to move, but then the pain in his left leg became almost unbearable. He leaned forward to look at the leg, but it was gone. Where the heck was the leg and the foot.

"Stay still now Lars, your left leg is gone and I am short of morphine. You have been unconscious for the last 24 hrs.". He sighed heavily.

"But how have you managed to get me down here, two floors down even? And how come you know my name?" "But Lars, sharpen up, I had to knock you in your head with my Luger pistol. Then I got help from my cousin. He had taken cover here and was the only one surviving the attack from the Russians and the partisan.

We are Jews, but you must be completely confused and clearly you don't remember me. But don't be afraid, or rather be very much afraid. You are in part Jew as well Lars!"

"Just a sec, you are Rebecka are you not and I am not dead?" "Hush!" There were voices one floor up, the upper of the two muck cellars. Somebody was laughing out loud and had himself a rattle with an automatic weapon.

The Russians did soon leave and threw a couple of hand grenades into the glow pile on their way out. But this low in the muck cellar the two were not harmed. Rebecka was worried that the hatch had locked itself, so Chaim couldn't reach down to them. She didn't fear much for the glowing remains of the barn, soon there would be no more barn, just the stone ruins.

"Yes, I am Rebecka", she whispered. "But how can you be a Jew, you worked as my assistant as nurse for several months? You know what would have happened to you if the Germans ever found out about you?"

"I had no place to escape to and it was better then to deny our faith and survive as the only one of my people, least as I know of here in the Odesa oblast. Oh yes of course, not to forget my cousin Chaim!" "But what about your papers, your id?"

"You remember now Lars. Remember that I came to you with papers on a Svetlana looking for a job as nurse there at the hospital?". She looked at his face and could see it was all confusion to him now. Maybe all this talking was too much to him in his present state. But she couldn't deny him asking for truth when perhaps he was to pass away from her. But clearly, he was bewildered.

"But what about your education as nurse? For sure you seemed to know your business?" "Well, yes, I was halfway through the studies; besides my mother was a nurse and she taught me a lot of the ropes before she was taken away and shot to death. I finally got new papers and those were on Svetlana as presented to you in your office".

"But is your name Rebecka?" "Yes, it is, but my family name is not Kovskoia, even if that what's written in the papers. There I am listed as Tatiana, not Rebecka". "Many names that Rebecka, but I was your boyfriend when you were Svetlana. Was I not and didn't we sleep together?" "Hush now Lars, we will talk later, right now I am afraid all this will be too much to you!" Or to me as well, she thought.

"But Rebecka, I have to know, especially since I might die right here, then I must know if we have shared it all and been good to each other!" It was getting dangerous now, Chaim was on his way down the hatch.

"And your brother, is he your brother?" "No, he is my cousin and the last remaining gold from the synagogue provided for new ids to him and me". "So, the two of you aren't married to each other then, if he is truly your cousin or your brother?" She had to have him stop right there, Chaim was soon to be close to them now.

"It was Chaim that knew about this deep muck cellar, having taken cover here before the massacre on the Parade square in Odesa". "How come you know about this massacre?" "My father, the Rabbi, he had me hanging on to him in a special crib under his greatcoat when he was stringed up!" "So, you are the skinny teenager that run across the square while the SS was firing at you?"

"Well skinny, yes, but I wasn't just a kid, I was 15 then, but for no one to guess, I weighed but 30 kgs, maybe even less". "But how did you escape?" "By the sewage, the lock was half opened there at the corner. I lurked the lid in place and yes, the Germans weren't the worst part, but the big rats. But skinny me, not much for the rats to go after".

Once again, they heard footsteps, but this time it was Chaim's, her cousin.

"You don't know the least about me, but for sure we are one people". He was stuttering now Lars"

Chaim questioned his own hearing. Was the wounded man talking feverish? Lars tried to raise his arm, but was short of force now and he just slid into the dark.

"What about it Rebecka, will he live or do you think he shall soon be gone, maybe taken by gangrene?" "No one is to know, but we have to pray for him!" "Pray for a German officer Rebecka?". She didn't answer, couldn't answer. "But Rebecka if so, who shall we pray to?" "Our all God". Chaim had gotten pale now. "Meaning what Rebecka, please enlighten me!"

"There was a hole burned in his rucksack and a big envelope had fallen out". "Go on tell me, what was written on it?" "To be opened only after I have passed, written both in Norwegian, English and German!" "In Norwegian, and if you ever opened it Rebecka it would been grave robbery!"

"No of course I didn't open it, but as I have told you his sack had been partly burned and one corner of the envelope was burned or teared and you simply cannot imagine what I saw!"

"Money?" He looked questionably at her. "No something much more important than money! The edges of the sheets had letters in Hebrew. It had to be sheets from the Torah. But I felt it would have been wrong, almost grave robbery as you put it, to open the envelope". She had to lie now.

"So, what do you think?" "I don't know, but why should a medic, a captain in the German elite division, Gross Deutschland, have this sack with an envelope with half-burned sheets of the Torah? No doubt he would have been executed first instant if inspected".

"How do you know that he was, or is Norwegian then Rebecka?" He was thin in his voice now Chaim. Could he possibly have sensed something? "Do you think he knew about the content of this envelope?" "I don't know". This was horrible to her, standing here in front of her Chaim, lying about it all, while her beloved Lars was lying there dying.

"What was left of the field lazarette was made ready for departure. I witnessed it all leaving. But why do you think they just left this medic to die Rebecka?" "Maybe they had realized that he wouldn't make it, no more hope for saving him. You said yourself that the Death Mark was removed, so not a chance to survive."

"But do you think he knew about you being the girl that fled from the executions at the Parade square, you his close assistant, you being a Jew? No doubt this lazarette was what was left of the hospital in Odesa and he must have been the doctor you worked that closely with?"

"Right so, but if he were to know that I was Jewish, how on earth would I have papers and come to work with him?" "But do you think he is a Jew then Rebecka? Did he know to himself what was in that envelope?" "Maybe he had nothing to do with this envelope nor to its content Chaim?" She simply had to go on lying. But Chaim wouldn't let go of it. "If so, why then should the text on the envelope read: Open only when I am dead?"

Lars was moving a bit now, seemingly the fever had increased and maybe this could be his last efforts before his body could take no more.

"Who is this Eva, he mentioned her name several times Rebecka?" "What am I to tell to Eva?" He was just babbling now Lars. "Maybe she is his mother?" "No, I don't think so Chaim, he has been talking about his mom as well".

"Ok, so she must be his sister". "No, he never mentioned anything about a sister". "So, it has to be his girlfriend then?" "But he never said anything about having a girlfriend up in Norway either Chaim". The light in the cellar was pretty dim. Had it been real daylight, Chaim no doubt would have seen that she was well onto the road of lies.

"Maybe he hasn't confided that much in you Rebecka. Anyway, the Death Mark is sent home with his mate, so folks back home will soon get the message about him being dead.

And Rebecka, you should be the one to know what risk we are taking if we stay and care for him here. We might have a chance to get out of here the two of us, but if we are to take with us this crippled one, we wouldn't stand no chance! And honestly now, this medic is your friend from the hospital, is he not?"

"Yes Chaim, and I shall stay with him until he has passed!" She wasn't to see his face before he was off up the hatch, didn't even say Good bye. "Don't you forget Rebecka that you have a responsibility to your child, a responsibility to live!" And then he was gone.

Lars just made it to turn his face towards her. His blue-grey eyes, no doubt to her now; they were the same as Eugenia's. "We are Jews all the four of us Lars, you as well, as your mother was a Jew".

He looked at her seemingly confused. "Who then is the fourth one?" I don't know for sure Lars. The child might be yours and mine or Chaim's and mine. It all happened at the very same time. But whatever, we are all Jews. And Lars, together we shall make it, we shall survive".

But Lars didn't catch the last words and she started on changing his bandages. The spark in his eyes when he learned about Eugenia, was that not the sign that he would live? Even as a crippled one?

THE FOURTH BOOK,

LARS THE ODESA DOCTOR

THE NEW DOCTOR

He was bewildered now, Lars. Where had he been taken? Prisoner with the Russians? He was certain he could hear Russians talking. They got closer to him now, so was this to be the end? Some officer might just have picked up the Luger to send him onto his last voyage?

No, there were several of them and all speaking in quiet voices, no exaltation. He felt he was all naked under the sheet. Someone must have taken off his ragged clothes, washed him properly and dressed new bandages to his cut leg. It would have been Rebecka? But had she left and her cousin as well? Gone the both of them?

A doctor, at least it was someone in a white gown, came close, checked his eyes as well as his pulse. "All this being regular". He grasped this much from the Russian.

So, he was to be checked up, make sure he was well enough to be stringed up or stand to his feet to face an execution detail? Shooting officers was no doubt a delight to the privates.

Then the doctor started to read in German. He heard the crackling of the sheets, but chose to close his eyes, keeping at peace as long as possible. But what about Rebecka? Had she been taken as well and what had become her fate?

"Partisan, med-student from Norway, wounded in his left thigh. No problem, would soon heal when dressed properly. Left leg and foot gone. Must be cleaned up, and dressed properly. We shall have to offer him protheses". Wow, was he to live after all?

There were some words in Russian that Lars didn't understand, so? "Morphine!" was all he mustered. The doctor had himself another laugh. "No morphine since Stalingrad. But we shall see if there are any leftovers from the Germans. You have a name?" But Lars was long gone into his hell of pain so he didn't hear the instructions for the new Ukrainian nurse. "Go have a look if you can find morphine somewhere. The Germans might have left some before leaving". When Rebecka was back with the morphine, a high-ranking officer was at his stretcher together with the doctor.

"Off with his shirt, I shall see if he is a renegade. Maybe he is even SS!" Rebecka was glad that the hood of her uniform covered her deadly pale face. Now Lars would stand no chance. But suddenly a ray of sun came to her. Lars did of course have no tattoo on his arm! She was ever so fast taking off the sheet and off with his shirt. Lars was speaking incoherently now. Sometimes in Norwegian, babbling about Eva and was even crying out loud.

"Up with his arm", snapped the officer and she lifted his right arm. "No, you idiot, the left arm!" And there was of course no tattoo, of course there wasn't, but if there had been one, then her Lars would have been doomed. But Lars had told her all about the events when he joined up.

The very day when they were to be tattooed there in Vestfold, then the med-assistant had gone sick and when the last ones were to be tattooed in Sennheim, well that was the very morning he had left for Bad Tølz, and there, no way they asked for tattoos. It was evident that all cadets had long been tattooed with one's number and blood type. So, the risk of getting exposed was over there and then, and he was rolled into a hall for high ranking, wounded officers.

All with lower ranks than captains were shot. Those having the impregnates of SS were all shot, irrespective of rank, according to Rebecka. Rumors? No one knew for certain but some said that ordinary privates, not SS, they were the lucky ones to automatically board the train of no return, the train to Siberia.

But Lars shouldn't have stayed here among high ranked officers. Bad luck, he was lying next to the Rumanian officer in charge at the mass execution on the Parade square. So, what if someone recognized him? Maybe this officer? If there would be talks about the massacre at all, then his chances would have been zero to get out of this alive.

But would it be better if he was moved to the hall for wounded partisans, the ones that the Russians had decided were to live? Maybe so, they had after all been on the same side against the Germans. Least he could pretend to be.

He was still very weak, but the morphine had been of great help and his wounds were clean, no infection.

Should he play dead? Of course not, then he would have been dumped together with other corpses. But he had to get out of this hall, fast. Rebecka agreed and rolled his cot over to the Chief of the hospital, Colonel Gennadij Orlov. But they couldn't just walk into his office. A long, long wait, for hours. But this had given the two of them time to come up with a waterproof story to the colonel.

Lars was a Norwegian medic that had fought together with the partisans and of course he wanted to continue to fight Hitler, although now with only one leg. "Germans Kaputski!". The colonel laughed. "Dress him up like a doctor and here you have our Russian medal for bravery. Nail it to his right-side Svetlana so the backsrew doesn't hit his heart. And this red ban has already the color of blood, fits well to the job he is going to do, as there will be much bloodshed. Maybe you shall have the medal Hero of Soviet next time". "Meaning what Chief?" Rebecka translated: "When you lose your other leg as well, then you are bound to be a prime candidate!" Even more laughing and a bottle of vodka soon was on the table.

"But listen up you Norwegian, you cannot operate on crouches. Have you all gone crazy?"

"Just you tell him to relax, hand me a chair and place all patients on a low table in front of me, then more morphine to me and vodka to the patient".

Lars felt at ease now, quite safe that he was in control and soon there was a crowd wanting to watch. His experiences from Berlin, and above all from Karelen, in addition to his skills from helping his father had made him a first-class field-medic. The colonel was utterly impressed and there were cheers from the little crowd. "You Svetlana, it shall be your responsibility to have him work like this for a long, really long time. We shall need this man!".

"And now Lars, now we shall save the enemy? You will be ok with that; I mean your conscience?" "I am a pro Svetlana and you should be that yourself as well!"

But the danger wasn't over. But Rebecka was fast at it. She poured one full liter of blood over his face and thus he was not to be recognized by anyone. And who would think that the man lying almost dead on the stretcher close to the Rumanian Colonel, think that he would be the one right now operating on a wounded Russian officer? No way that it could be the same man.

"You had better look for him together with the dead ones or dying?" she commented to the Rumanian and it was over, at least for now.

It was to be a very long day, and his pains were coming and going so Rebecka had to go for another round, looking for morphine. "This shall be a very tough night on you Lars", they had a short rest waiting for the next transport of casualties.

"You wanted to live did you not, or would it have been much easier for you to bid good bye to all and everything there in the muck cellar? Chaim meant you had no chance to make it". "But what about you then Rebecka?" "Please don't use that name, dearest Lars, someone might be listening in, one never knows. But tell me now, what was it that made you want to live?" "I don't know kind you, and I cannot call you, my dearest. Even though Chaim and you are cousins, you still are his girlfriend are you not?" His voice was ever so thin now.

"This is very difficult to me Lars. Eva is like this ghost in your head as Chaim is in mine, but in little Eugenia's heart there is but a mother, me and a father, you Lars".

He felt warm and excited to this and wanted to get up on to his feet, now realizing that he had only one, the right one. He still wanted to cry out in excitement to one and everyone now, that he was a father.

"So, you are saying that you and I have a daughter of ours, really Rebecka?" "Yes, but Chaim may think she is his and I let him think that at the time as I was certain never to see you again. Yes Lars, the child should have a father, right?" "Rebecka the cynic one?" "Spare me for sarcasms Lars, without Chaim's dedicated help, nor Eugenia nor I would have been alive. I shall feed you details later".

"But were you not lovers up there in the mountains?" "Only once did we sleep with each other Lars, only once and that was because I felt that strongly that he needed me. We had after all been together as a couple, although in secrecy back in Odesa".

"Does Chaim think she is his baby then?" "No, but he is a generous man Lars, that generous that in spite of her curly blonde hair he accepted her as his own. I mean he was generous. Now having met with you, realizing that you are alive, then I don't know" "But deep inside you dearest, maybe he would have wished for me to die there in the muck cellar? Wouldn't that have served him best?" "Chaim is a soldier Lars, not a murderer!" "But would it have been murder if I was left there to die? Loke and his captain were both clear about the issue!" "To me of course and even to him it would have been murder, as long as there still was a chance for you to make it!"

"What are we to do with the two of you, come evening?" It was the Russian Colonel. "The medic here has his right to a private room, but what about you Svetlana?" "There is still a war out there, colonel and we may put an extra bed in to my room if it is ok by her?" "Obviously I can be of no harm to her or anyone for that matter". "Yeah, it seems like the two of you get along pretty well and we Russians don't care for a division between the sexes and I guess life is the same with you partisans. Only in western Europe people are concerned with this division". He laughed now the colonel. "So, it is settled then!"

"But what about Chaim then Svetlana, if he shall be back?" "Then we shall need an extra mattress as well and let's see to that right away".

"But this won't be right Svetlana and you know it you as well". "But Lars, you haven't made up your mind about your binding to Eva, have you? So, I cannot be yours, got it?"

"But my binding to her is ever so clarified. I cannot go home to her and endure 10 years in a labor camp following a sentence as traitor to my country. And I pledge for you to understand that I am not thinking about myself. But if I was coming home to imprisonment etc. what would that mean to my father, to Eva and her family and any child there might be. And don't forget, I am considered dead according to the list of war-casualties in Norway".

"But Lars, no way can I live with you as a number two. Whenever you have lost conscience or been dreaming you have cried out, sometimes even shouted out loud for Eva". "But that is the fate I shall have to live with and have to console myself with. No doubt Eva has already got the message that I have passed and nothing can alter that now or ever".

"So, you are no longer Lars, but a partisan medic now needing a new identity?" Tears were flowing down his cheeks now. "Who are you crying for Lars?" "For my father dear you! But now the line is drawn and that's how it shall be! But what about Chaim?"

DOCTOR LEO VOLGOV

Chaim was to return for sure, but couldn't say when. But one night he was at the door. "Do come in Chaim, but be quick and lock the door". Chaim looked at the two beds and the mattress on the floor. "Who sleeps in that bed?" "No one, it is there for you Chaim".

"So, we are to share everything now then Rebecka?" "Hush! I am Svetlana, there might be commissars all over the place". "Listen Chaim, you think I would be capable of any sort of action, if by chance one or more lusty women was to show up here?" Lars smiled to him.

"Welcome Chaim!"

"Please you shut it both of you, I am not some mare you may play with at will".

"I am sorry", Lars mustered. But Chaim kept silent, a bit awkward it was right there. "Now guys, pull yourself together and let's get on with what matters Chaim. I don't know how you manage to come and go here, some alias no doubt, but for sure you are in control. But your bed is right there for you".

But Chaim chose to neglect her totally and addressed himself to Lars. "You have decided then Lars to say Norway no more?" "Yes, that's how it is now. Officially I am dead according to the register and my folks there".

"And what about here in Odesa? What shall be your cover here?" "As you know, I have no contacts here, but I understood from your cousin that you may have a proposal ready for me?"

Chaim just laughed. "Right so Lars, but then you have to forget about your past, unconditionally. Those who are willing to step up for you, to your disappearing as Lars and to your new identity, they take an immense risk and want something in return. There are still a considerable number of Jews back here in Odesa, many of them lost whatever they owned before the war and most of them don't reckon they will get any of their property or belongings back, ever".

"This sounds pretty intricate Chaim. What do you have to offer, please be concrete now. I am still in pain and days are getting long even if I get the very best of help, and for sure I couldn't have managed without Svetlana". He yanked to his nose when he said her undercover-name.

"The proposal is as follows Lars. Leo Volgov", he handed him a picture of a man with a full beard, Russian-Jewish look. "Leo our dear Leo, I was never to meet him, he stayed with the parents of his Jewish girlfriend in Richevielska here in Odesa. Then the Rumanians came to the scene, went from house to house. They took with them those they thought might be of use to them, e.g., beautiful Jewish women were taken to their officers' brothels, the others were killed on the spot. No one was spared, even Leo was thrown on the bonfires".

"You have become ever so cynical Chaim!" "My dear cousin, this was only a short version of the real happenings. It happened just like that.

Our Leo was a medic, educated from the Kyiv university, where all archives were bombed out. The truth is, he was merely 10 days older than you Lars, given that your data are to be trusted Lars?

But there is a big question to all this, you shall have to learn Russian in record time. Meaning what? You will ask for sure. Three weeks, that's all you shall have". "And what about the Cyrillian alphabet?" "It will come in time, I mean being able to write in Russian, but by the end of these weeks you must be able to read Russian and above all speak Ukrainian-Russian". "And if I can make it, then what?"

"Then a partisan friend here will go to the Chief surgeon. He has some paybacks to do our Chief. Lars has so far been only your cover name. Your real name is Leo Volgov and you are from here in Odesa. Half Russian, half Jewish. Your mother was a Jew".

"And for sure she was, my dearest Sarah. But Chaim then there will be a couple of conspirators that can give me away at their will?"

"The Jewish partisans will never denounce you and if you accept this proposal, it implies that you shall be here in Odesa as a doctor to all Jewish patients here and at very low fees. And it shall be like that for the rest of your days"

"But what about the Chief surgeon?" "No way he shall crave for a holiday in Siberia Lars". "Is he that much involved in shady business or whatever?" "Yes, and he might not even make it to the train for Siberia".

"That's how it's going to be then my friends!" Lars looked at the two. "No doubt we are still friends?". He looked at Chaim's face but there was not a single movement.

"I shall need an answer now, this very minute, so I can take it further to my people. As from here, then there will be no looking back! Here you have textbooks. All with translations from Russian to German. Norwegian to Russian or vice versa were not to be found anywhere".

Rebecka had stood up now. "I have to go with Chaim tonight, but I shall be back if you will let me", she whispered in his ear. But Lars had only focus on Chaim now. "Thanks, Chaim, for giving me my life as your gift and best of luck with your endeavors".

And they were off, the two of them.

ABlars was on his own now with his new life and all that it would demand from him, above all that he should have to learn Russian, fast. Still, he wondered: Would Rebecka be back?

Come midnight he put the books aside and listened, not a sound, no one was coming.

He was promised a temporary prothesis in a few weeks and he so looked forward to get rid of the crouches. Maybe that would be his only consolation now that Rebecka was gone.

He came to wonder what happened home in Norway. But had to sharpen up: tell yourself Lars and tell it good; as from tonight you are no longer Lars, you are Leo tonight and tomorrow, yes forever.

Now he also wondered what happened between Rebecka and Chaim. All of a sudden, he was bitten by jealousy. Maybe Chaim, in spite of his tough appearance, maybe he was bitten he as well?

FAREWELL CHAIM

It turned out to be a bad night, pain increasing by the hours, but at three o'clock in the morning and still no Rebecka, then at long last he fell asleep.

He didn't have a clue as to what time it was when he felt a soft body, sneaking up to him. Ever so carefully he made room for her with his bad knee and embraced her.

"I am looking for Leo," she whispered to his ear, and he was lost, totally. "I am Leo and you know what that means". "The Lion", she whispered back.

"Dobre Leo. My own lion. Chaim is moving to Berlin. He wanted for me to come with him. But I couldn't leave all those suffering here, and no way I could leave you, now when fate has brought us together again. But please promise me one thing, one thing only I ask for".

"Yes, darling an what will that be?" "That we shall forever be together, always be there for one another here in Odesa. I cannot, will not have more of this gipsy-life. I want to stay right here in Odesa and forever be yours". "May I come to you now then?" "But you are with me now my love. Oh, you mean like that, and can you manage with your only leg then? And my Leo, can we get married now, right away?"

His kiss stopped here from all possible and impossible thoughts about who was to master what, he came to her and she took all of him there and then.

The next day she handed him the letter from Chaim.

"Dear Leo, I am certain that you shall manage perfectly with your new tasks, and that you will prevail in your new identity. As the lady no doubt have told you by now, I wanted to take her from you and asked her come with me towards Berlin. But she couldn't leave from here, neither could she leave you. But the three of us have a daughter together, but to be frank it seems obvious to me now that you two are her parents. It would have been a great mistake if I now were to go to Inna and Ari and claimed Eugenia as my own. She is but a spitting picture of you, no doubt whatsoever now when I have seen you. So, end of story, she is your child, not mine and I have felt that for a very long time.

But you mustn't forget about her, although Inna and Ari are keen on having her as their child. As at now she probably calls them mammy and daddy. But she has the genes of the two of you and if she was mine, then I should never have her grow up there at the lonely farm, miles to the next neighbor. And what would there be to her, should she at any time come to see herself as a Jewish woman, eager to confess to her faith? So, I reckon that as soon as you have gotten things orderly there in Odesa, then you will go north to the farm and take her with you to the good home I am certain that you will provide to her in our dearest Odesa.

My path in life has been laid out to me. I am to follow David Ben Gurion to Palestine, to our Promised Land. Maybe we shall meet before I leave then. Chaim"

He was crying now the One-foot, his nick name to himself. "I forbid you to use that expression, Leo. Now we go straight to the repair shop and asks for a temporary prothesis". "But it is way too early, the wound will still need time to heal properly!" "But we must have a go at it. Now I am in command. And Leo why were you crying?" "Well, you see Chaim wrote something special, yeah, he wrote a lot. But we shall have to pick it up later, but my crying was mostly because we never were to say goodbye". "And that would have been totally wrong Leo!" "Because?" "Because he loves me, while I love you!"

GERMANY AND THE NAZI-REGIME IN NORWAY CAPITULATE

Unter den Linden in Berlin was no longer the parade street. Hitler had taken his own life, Eve Braun's as well. Das Reich was no more. But what about Norway? More than 350.000 well trained soldiers were up there in what was known as Festung Norwegen; and what about his old fatherland, should the Germans endure there and then shoot his country to pieces in a prolonged war?

But luckily there was peace in Norway as well. There wasn't much about Norway on the news down in Odesa, but he had learned that the German High Command had capitulated to the Homefront. In the newspapers in Odesa there were pictures of the capitulation act, where the German brass was rendering over the command of the country to the Homefront in their "nickers" (more of a skiing outfit). The newspapers had pictures of the Norwegian Army, their soldiers also in "nickers".

This was what he had reckoned would be the outcome long time ago; now it was the Homefront and those on the winning side that should decide the destinies of the survivors from the so-called Frontkjempere, those having enlisted for Hitler. For sure the courts and the lawyers would be those administrating the process, but the opinion of the public at large would now have a far greater importance than if the capitulation had been to the regular, military Army. So, no doubt his decision had been the right one; there would be no amnesty in Norway to the SS-officers, medic or not.

Rebecka was reading his mind. "What now then Lars or should I say Dr. Leo?" "Darling, you may call me whatever here in private, but the by far most valuable I have to give you is our home and my love here in Odesa".

"My dearest, what was I to say if you hadn't said just that, because I now have great news to you". He looked at her. "Something particular on your mind dear?" "Yes, I am pregnant, super pregnant if that's the name to it. You are the doctor and it is for you to know!"

One day an old man, beard almost to his knees knocks on the door, wants to speak with both of them. He introduces himself as a doctor and now he has come to learn more about Dr. Leo. He smiles when saying the name.

He would find it interesting, yes more so, to have them both working together with him in his surgery and then they might take over it all when he plans for retirement in a year's time. "So, you are a Jew then?". Admittedly and he had known well both her father and the uncle of this woman that had escaped from the shooting, hanging and burning of Jews there at the Parade square.

What is your given name then? Rebecka was curious. So was he, made sure no one was listening." "Nikolayev is my present name, but I do have another one, Aron, the one I hope I shall come to use again, once this war is over".

"OMG, it was you assisting at the delivery when I was born then wasn't it?" "Yes, you are so right, but as you know well it is still very dangerous all this talking about identity!"

She embraced the old man. "You know I cannot retire just now, too many are suffering, but we shall see, in a year's time. But be careful with the baby soon to be born young lady!" How strange that he should comment on that; and how did he know she was pregnant? She wasn't that long gone in her pregnancy? Strange it was.

Leo and Aron finally agreed on making the deal. "And you do remember your commitment to Chaim then Leo?" "Yes of course. I shall take good care of your patients, those having means to pay as well as the others". This was a solemn vow he should always keep.

THE TOTAL COLLAPSE!

As the months went by, Rebecka got more and more worried. This pregnancy was totally different from her first one. It shouldn't be like this, should it? The first one was supposed to be the more strenuous one, right so?

She was now over the said term, at least with one day. One whole day she said to herself.

Maybe she had been stupid not going with Dr. Leo on to his new surgery. There would have been no heavy lifting and they could have helped one another when needed.

Almost without exception, she was always late in coming home to the tiny appartement Aron had managed to find to them. And her poor Lars, yes, she could call him that when private and they had yet to make a final decision about name.

Lars was just sitting there by himself, leafing through so-called important medical papers. But she knew it all too well. He was lonely, terribly lonely.

"It will be better soon my love, but tonight I shall not keep you company for dinner. I had some up at the hospital. Now I am only tired and worried.". "But must you really go to work tomorrow then, not much you can do in your present situation dear you?"

"I would rather go to work than stay back here alone with all the thoughts about things going well and that you shall have your son this time dear".

"Darling I'll be happy with either of them. What is important is that you will be ok as well". "But Lars don't make me uneasy now, I'm as fresh as a fish". "No of course not, but you know we doctors". "For sure I'm happy that we have female doctors as well, understanding their fellow sisters much easier". "You are so right Rebecka; it is all about feelings, so you are quite right".

They did not speak much more about it that evening. Day one, Lars wrote into his private diary.

A couple of days went by and Lars made a note to each one of them, summing up the status of the day. "More anxious today. Should absolutely confer with the doctor at the hospital".

"Day 4, uneasy, changing humor, should I dare talk with her about Caesarian?"

"Day 5, I have canceled all appointments today, Rebecka, will you allow me to come with you to the hospital?" "What on earth are you to do there. I shall call you when there will be some action. Our friend is just kicking and such. You must know about these things, you being a doctor and all, and honestly have you been assisting at any births my darling?" No, he had not. "So please darling, I shall be in the best of hands". "But I insist upon you taking a cab!" "Yes, Lars I shall do just that". "And both ways then darling?" "For sure!" She smiled at him, his flower, and kissed him straight on his mouth. But he had to say it now, however annoyed she might get. "Before leaving now Rebecka, will you please ask your surgeon to consider caesarian?" She got read in her face now. "How dare you start talking about that just now?" "Well since you have told me to stay away you must allow me to point to this possibility, darling you".

The cab was already waiting for her, so no more arguments.

12 o'clock, his nerves were already completely in disorder. He knew by himself that it was getting critical by the minutes now. He could not stay at home any longer, so he started to walk straight to the hospital. Fifteen minutes later he was picked up by a hospital clerk, on his way to fetch him. "Your phone was ringing time and again, but no answers". "Quite so, as you can see, I am on my way to the hospital". "We shall have to hurry up as she is in great pain according to the surgeon responsible for the birth". Once again, his intuition had been right. Dimitri, he could read his name on the lapel of the surgeon. Lars did not know him. "I am Doctor Leo Volgov, Rebecka's husband". "Yes, and she has cried out for you a number of times this last hour. We have given her sedatives, but the effect is short termed and we don't dare give her too much". "What about Cesarian then Dr. Dimitri?"

"We have of course been discussing that, but we felt we should wait a while. There is of course a risk to that as well". "Yes of course", he was well aware of that. "May I sit with her then?" "Yes, by all means. The nurse will find a gown to you". She almost crushed his hand when the pain was at its peak and then she would be gone ever so long.

Lars was certain now that no way should they wait, but make ready for the Cesarean. "Have you checked on the infant, I mean just now?" He didn't dare call it the baby. "Yes, and there is live, strong pulse, but not as strong as this morning".

Lars stood up and went outside. When leaving, "I should not interfere in all you are doing for my wife, but I ask you strongly to start the procedure for a Cesarean. I have my education as a field-medic and I can clearly see that this is not going the right way, neither does it for the infant from what you just told me".

The Chief surgeon stood up. "I can see a crushed man Doctor Leo and I have no problems whatsoever to understand your feelings right now. She was all good last night, in fact she seemed to be in extraordinary good shape. Today she has not taken part in any work and I was in fact very surprised when she declined to work herself. Not her usual self, she always wanted to participate. Let's go and see to her the three of us now. Yes, you can sit by, but as you no doubt understand….". "You don't need say no more".

But they had barely raised from the chairs before they were asked for. "She is asking for someone, Lars?" He had to pull himself together. "Yes, we have a nickname that we use when we are more intimate". He wondered if his explanation was good enough to them, no way was he sure about that, but now it was all about Rebecka and the baby. He was allowed to sit by her side, holding her left hand in his two. She looked like she was enduring the worst pains in the world. Finally came the order to take her into the operational theater immediately, and get ready with the anesthetics.

The two surgeons left for wash, face masks and gloves and soon there were eight of them in the operational theatre, so Lars felt he was just a pain in their asses. Rebecka, his most precious one was already gone. It all happened that fast now. The baby was freed from his mother now but the usual cry could not be heard. Its blue color was a no-good sign and the baby's pulse was very weak.

"We don't know what has happened during the night or this morning, but she has severe hemorrhages that we are trying to block. So far, we haven't found where the bleeding comes from". "And the boy?" Lars could not hold back crying now, but he had to pull himself together for the two of them. "The boy is fighting he as well Doctor Leo".

"We should have dared talk about it yesterday Rebecka and I, but then she would probably gone even more hysteric then when I touched upon it this morning". "Do you mean Cesarean?" "Yes of course, what else!" "Your wife and I have been working closely with each other and I think you would have heard of it if we were to do Cesarean yesterday!" "Yes, I know, but I still should have done it!"

A nurse approached them and asked if he wanted to see the boy. Yes later, but now it is all about my wife. She whispered something to the Chief surgeon. "Doctor Leo, I think you must see to your son now or maybe you shall not see him alive at all".

So, they were both to leave him now? Would you be up to it now? You might as well join on their way you as well. "I shall be gone for a minute, no longer". It was over for the boy now, as he had no more energy to fight with, maybe his lungs we're just collapsing?

"Is there anything we can do Chief surgeon?" "No, I am sorry but really there is nothing to do. He was lying the wrong way, so the cord must have been pressing towards his head, slowly damaging his lungs. Now we can only wait and pray".

Rebecka was gone now; extra blood transfusion did not have any effect and the surgeon was questioning if her abdomen was punctured. "If we start operating on her now, then for sure we shall lose her, she has hardly any more energy as it is".

"But what about it, Chief surgeon? What is the reason to all this?" "Dear Doctor Leo, there is no good answer to it, but she might have fallen in an awkward position and we both know that once she was on her feet again, she wouldn't even mention such a fall, never complained, did she?" "So, we are never to know then? But when she fell, something must have happened that got this bleeding started?" "Giving birth is either very simple or there might be extreme complications, Doctor Leo".

Suddenly she opened her eyes, could barely make it, and Lars bent over her to understand what she seemed to whisper to him with her last forces. She was going to die any minute now and they both knew it, all in the room knew it as well. "Our child, is he alive, is he to live?" Lars wasn't up to answering her, he was just crying. Next second, she was gone, but suddenly she was back again with a heartbreaking cry. Where did she take her energy from, he wondered. "Eugenia, Eugenia!" She cried out loud now. And then it was over. But Lars knew there and then that he had to live, live for the two now dead, and for all he could muster, live for their daughter with her blonde curls, their Eugenia.

Lars was beaten now, but not quite, he got himself a little while to say goodbye to the dead. Their son was laid by her side and they were gone the two of them.

But the Chief surgeon hastened to him. "Doctor Leo in the midst of your sorrow and all, I must talk to you right now!" Lars managed to leave his dearest, now passed and to join him in his office. "Make sure you close the door properly. Yes, Doctor Leo, this is all terrible. And we shall have time to talk about this later. But there is something very pressing on my mind right now". Lars' face showed that he couldn't take much more right now. "Yes, what is it about, you seem utterly tense?" "Your late wife", "Please don't put it like that, she has a just passed". "I am truly sorry Doctor Leo, but Rebecka cried out after some Lars, several times, one time very, very loud and later one young doctor came to me. "I thought her husband was Doctor Leo, Leo Volgov, isn't that so? Could it be that we are dealing with a bogey here now? His Russian was a bit strange as well, was it not?" "Western Ukrainian dialect", I tried to toss it away. "Maybe we should put it to the managing director of the hospital?" "Now stop it please Doctor Ivanov. This must be a total misconception, the two of them no doubt had nicknames to each other at intimate times".

"Doctor Leo, according to Jewish customs they bury their dead soonest possible, you know of course of all that don't you. My point is that we should be done with the funeral soonest and as quietly as possible, that's what I would have done and then you take one month's leave. Officially you are a way on a convalescence in your sorrow. Just make all the arrangements with your old colleague. Our new heroes, the commissars are all over the place now and this rumor can endanger us both!"

"What then, when can I come for Rebecka and the child? They shall both be prepared to the funeral here shall they not?" "No, not you. You must leave immediately, just give me an address to your cemetery. Now go straight to your old doctor, deal with him and stay with him there all the night. Don't even think about going home to your own apartment!"

So, this was how it was to be now, the dream of a happy family on this earth, full stop. Both his loved ones passed at the same time. But it was worst to Rebecka who had looked that much forward to her new life and had sacrificed herself throughout this horrible war to that end. And what about himself? What was he left with? Well, yes, of course he had curly, blonde Eugenia. He had to say her name out loud several times whenever he was going into a depression. Thus, he folded his hands and said her name loud for anyone to hear when people stopped looking. "Eugenia, Eugenia!" And he knew that he had to go to her if he was to survive.

LARS, THE FUGITIVE

He chose to walk all the way down to the surgery in Pushkinskaia, it took him more than an hour with the new prothesis. It wasn't well adjusted but he couldn't even dream of ordering a cab and possibly being shadowed. This could be very serious. More so use some time make some detours, coming onto the corner of Gretska and even drop into a café on his way. He had neither eaten nor drank anything this morning.

Both dead and now, "Eugenia" he cried out again. But then he knew he must be careful, some people might have recognized him and told the police that there was a limp, crazy man in the streets. He had himself a treat with borscht and a vodka. This should save him and vodka had no smell. Finally, he saw the signboard of the surgery. "Someone called for you Dr. Leo, no names were given but to me it sounded official sort of". "Thank you, my dear friend and what was your answer to their call?" "That you were on leave". "Precious you and thanks to that". "Do you have more news now? No?" He looked questionably at his pale worn-out friend. "She must be well over her set date now Doctor Leo?" "Yes, in all matters. Please draw the curtains and let's talk in the backroom". The old doctor had gone all pale now and he then got the full story about the events of the morning. "Her last call, no she cried it out twice ever so loud before her lungs clapped together was Eugenia". "And what was the meaning of that Doctor Leo?"

"We have a daughter together from earlier days. She is now on a farm up towards Rivne. A couple on the farm has looked after her as their own from when she was just one week old". "But why?" "Why? I didn't know about her until recently, but she was to stay there because Rebecka went to war". "But then you have a lot to live for and not to forget all the sweet memories Doctor Leo".

"Thanks for your comforting words, Doctor Aron. Today I shall not go back to the apartment". He told the old friend about the reaction from the Chief surgeon. "I might go there for you then". "No, you cannot, you risk to be taken, interrogated and maybe even beaten up. Not least if they accuse you of collaboration with the enemy. Then you are done for".

But Doctor Leo, I have some toiletry here in the surgery I'm giving it to you, and you may have as much money as you shall need. Now I shall find out when there is a bus going towards Rivne and then you stay put here until there is a departure that suits you best". "So, you mean I have to go today? But what about my dearest family that I have to bury?"

"My friend, you have a family to look after, look after Eugenia, didn't you just say that?" "But she can wait, can she not?" "But the commissars they don't wait. My two sons are coming here from Nikolayev already tonight and then we shall bury your two dearests in the same grave tomorrow".

Doctor Aron, can you make sure that grave will be that large that there will be room to me one day?" "Yes of course, if that's your wish. Now I have to make some phone calls. You have taken some great losses previously as well and now you should care for your little daughter up there at Ari's farm, that was his name was it not?" "Yeah, and where do I have this rough sketch on the place where I shall find his farm?" "OMG, have you left that one in the apartment?" No, thank heavens, he had it in his wallet.

"Don't open up if someone is calling and don't answer the phone until it rings three times then on the 4th call you pick it up and you will know it's me". "But I'd rather not you call as the phone might be bugged. Here you have the numbers to both my sons, I mean to use later when needed". "And for how long do you think this will last?" "Difficult to say, six months at least. Then the Russians will withdraw from here. They have plenty to deal with in Berlin and the new East Germany.

Sorrows may come easy, but don't you look for them. Here, take some medicines. I checked the bus times and it leaves at 22.00 hrs. from the railway station. But you can't enter it there. My oldest son will take you to the next stop about a mile further north and then you take the bus from there". "But your oldest son is he not in Nikolayev?" "Yes, he was, but now he is on his way here".

"But Doctor Aron, who is to inform the Chief surgeon?" "It is already taken care of. He knows that I shall look after everything and that you have left for a month, nobody knows to where, nor when you are coming back". "So, when am I coming back? As I said no one knows you simply couldn't manage with the funeral and all, and as for your apartment I shall look after it, so no worries".

"But you may just give notice, I can never go back there, too many memories". "And what about your personal things?" "You mean Rebecka's as well? Just give them the away except for money and the jewels and make sure you safeguard the Torah and my pictures. The rest you give away or have it burned, make sure there is nothing left, least not with the name Lars on it".

"You need say no more Lars, here you have money and there is more where it comes from, so please write me or call me. But hold it, don't call me or anyone in my family the first weeks. Here you have the name and number to our old partisan friend. Use him as a go- between, I shall keep him updated".

Lars wondered where the old man got his energy from. He was an organizational talent of the greatest. "Did you see anyone following you when you arrived here?" The older son had just come in the door. He greeted Lars and gave him a bear hug. "No, I parked the car in Gretzka on the corner, lots of people there, but up here no one. But why are you sitting in the back room?" "Doctor Leo will explain it all to you once you are off. Now you must go get the car and make sure that no one is shadowing you. When you are off the two of you, then drive down to the harbor and come up to the main road further north. If you're stopped, then you're going to Illichivsk. There might be routine controls, irrespective of our mission.

There is a small crossroad about 10 kilometers north of the city border on the main road towards Rivne. There, Doctor Leo shall leave you". "You mean now in the dark night?" "Right so! I shall give him a pistol now. If you are stopped and interrogated then your cover story is that you were on your way to visit your old dad and then this man here had you forced to take him out of town. You have never met him before and that's the truth. Now best of luck to you my brave Doctor Leo". "And to you too Doctor Aron. In this time of sorrow, you're help has been overwhelming!"

They made a round towards the office again, before going to the harbor and it was in the last moment that they got away. Two men in dark costumes were calling at the door of the surgery, but as there was no light there, they just turned back to their car and were off.

"I think we shall get out of town the fastest possible", he said to the son. "No way that there would be a control up in Katherynskaia and from there we head straight north". Traffic was light now and soon they were more than 10 kms out of Odesa. "But I cannot just leave you here in this dark wooden landscape Doctor Leo?" He had learned about the gruesome day now. "Yes, you shall do just that and go with God as people say and do great to my little family when they are lowered into earth tomorrow!" He cried openly now and then he was out and on his own. Sat down on a stone by the roadside to wait for the bus. Yes, this was probably how she had been sitting here his Rebecka on her first evacuation with Chaim and then later with Efraim.

He had gladly sacrificed his second leg as well now if he could have had her with him right now. But what about Eva then, there was another voice. Eva? But that's a different kind of sorrow. Eva and I are probably both just as miserable now. This was the life to be for us both. No way the voice said. You have much more than that, you have your Eugenia. Yes, if they would let me have her. But now you must be strong Lars, and if they don't want for you to have her, then you'll just have to take her; and be reported to the police? They have nothing to report about, they who have given shelters to Jews all throughout the war.

Right so, but it is no longer the Germans being the masters now, but the Russians and the partisans and they don't give a damn. Well then you have to make friends with them and win your daughter to you Lars. And if they still won't let her go? Then Chaim will be your only hope, they could never refuse Eugenia to him. And Lars, you must get hold of Chaim anyway, to tell him about Rebecka and the baby and their tragic death.

He suddenly felt better now having his mind cleared. Confident that Eugenia would be his had made him stronger and stronger. Who was to stop him now, if anyone at all?

BACK TO ARI AND INNA

There was no bus, probably it was very much delayed or maybe it was being held back in a control? Why on earth were so many interested in him? All those working at the hospital had been very fond of Rebecka and why should this junior doctor make himself a star sort of by starting an investigation to her husband's past? Maybe this doctor had feelings for Rebecka himself, but now it was too late. She was dead.

An old truck with only one headlight came hobbling north. Maybe it was worn down having been used in the war, but for sure it was moving rather slowly. Lars held his hand out. Would it stop? No, yes it did and he humped towards the car. His foot was no good now after all the events during the day.

The driver and his wife had been south delivering goods from the farm all this way to Odesa. "But why didn't you go to Rivne?" "Better prices in Odesa." But he was going towards Rivne. Although not that far now, he should stop at a farm and deliver a letter first, he told them. "But there aren't many farms up here", the driver said. They could be the Postman for him and then he could take the bus further north.

They were sitting tight now together and the smell from the wife reminded him of the same smell as in the muck cellar when he woke up and met with Rebecka again. He took his sketch out of the wallet and the thoughts about Rebecka came strongly to him again. The man had a pocket light, they could barely see the lines of the sketch. "You are fully aware of that you are driving with only one headlight?" Lars tried to get some attention. "Yes, I know, but I lost it just now in the night and this time of the year it hardly gets dark". "But are you not obliged to have one extra light and make the repair yourself if necessary?" "Are you sort of a policeman then?" "Lars had to laugh, no I just wanted for us not to be stopped by the police".

"How far from Rivne is this farm then?" "As you know we are not going all the way to Rivne". "I was told the distance is some 60 kilometers". "But up there is nothing but forest and boggy land. I can hardly think that you've got very straight directions". He was moody now this man, probably pretty much fed up from the long drive.

"For sure the farm shall be there not far from a dirt road on the left side of the main road about 1 km into the forest. They are said to have cleared the land by themselves". "You know the name of these people?" "No, I don't remember, never heard their names". "But what about the man then?" "I think it is Ari or something". "Do they have children these people?" "I don't know maybe that have got a little daughter". "It has to be Inna then, her sister gave birth to a small daughter, but just left her to Ina and Ari to take care of her. Lovely little girl not very much the looks of Ari and Inna, nor her father who was supposed to have raven black hair. I remember all the fuss after the Germans had left?" "Yes?" "Because these two are Jews and they even had a German officer, an elderly medic who assisted with the birth. Kind of a drama that could have been".

Lars had to give himself a laugh, the first one this day even as the word birth cut deep into his heart. Now Rebecka and little Melchior had probably been prepared for tomorrows funeral, now resting in the morgue.

"Sorry, what did you say, are they Jews?" "Yes, and the German medic was a high-ranking officer. They would all have been shot on the spot, even the doctor if this had come out. And no, I don't know Ari, but if you have met him", he turned to his wife, "then for sure you know where this dirt road is?" "Yes, I do, but it will take time before we get there, maybe five to six hours".

The ride got ever so long on the bumpy road. The man was asking what trade Lars was in and once he had delivered the letter at the farm where did he go then? But Lars told him that he was not to stay in the Rivne-area, but he was to go back to his wife and kids up in Lviv. They had left Odesa in his friend's car living in Rivne, but just outside the Odesa city border the car broke down. His friend was sure they would get help in the morning but Lars didn't want to stay, rather take the bus and get going. But then the bus never showed up. "I do hope to get a job in the optic business where I worked up to the war came". "But are you not half Polish?" "No absolutely not. You mean I have like a Polish accent? I have been living close to the border for many years so it just comes naturally".

Lars had slept a little on the trip there as well, but mostly he had been thinking upon this gruesome day and all that horrible that he could not even take part in the funeral for his dearest, the funeral to come in less than 10 hours.

But he had got suspicious now of the driver. For sure this man had a lot of questions that made Lars even more suspicious. Maybe this man would report him to the police? And what about Ari and Inna? Could they get into trouble as well? When this wife knew Inna quite well, then of course her husband must know Ari? Something really stinky this was.

He could see the lights from a small village further up the road. "I got to get off here, my stomach has gone wild". "Should we wait for you then?" "No thanks I don't think so". "But what about the letter to Ari then?" "I think I shall mail it in the post, have to get myself north to my home". "I can see you're quite pale in your face", the wife didn't understand nothing, getting off here in the wilderness in the dark of the night.

"I think he has Polish roots and you could see him getting pale when I asked him about where he came from. My guess is that he is a Polish Jew".

But Lars was ever so happy that he was rid of this meddling man. But the wife wasn't quite through with it as yet. "How do you think he knew about Inna and Ari?" "I don't think he knew about them at all", her husband responded. "But he did have this letter at least", he said. "Well, I'm sure he didn't trust us then". "All right, but who are we to trust these days? But let's just forget about him". "Maybe he really had stomach trouble", she tapped her husband on his shoulder and laid down trying to sleep a bit. There was more space for her now.

What now Lars, you are alone here in the forest land, no phone booth, no kiosk, no café only these two lights bluffing in the wind. But what about the bus? Could it be that the bus had passed while he was sleeping there in the lorry? No, for sure it had not, so he was hoping soon to get going further north during the night. He had after all got a good tip from the wife where to find this dirt road leading to the farm, so for sure he was going to make it.

And finally, the bus was there. "I have waited for a long time", he said to the driver. But not that interested in argument he was this man. "Shall you be going with us or not?" "Yes please, may I have one way ticket to Shepetivka, or do I have to pay for all the way to Rivne?"

"It is not my day today, or should I rather say not my night, three punctures, never seen the likes not even during the war. I shall let you off at Shepetivka, we shall be there in 2 ½ hours provided no more trouble".

No more punctures, all other passengers were sleeping, no questioning eyes. Maybe the hunt was over? He said thank you to the driver and got himself off and onto the dirt road. But at the end of the road, he saw the lorry coming towards him and he was quick to hide in the forest. His left knee was really painful now. For sure it was the same lorry with one headlight, turning onto the highway south towards Odesa. But why had they been visiting Inna and Ari this late in the evening or night rather?

He started to walk towards the farm and was soon met by a large sheepdog. For sure he could bark this one and the sight of his teeth were not too promising. Lars knew that the best thing to do was to speak calmly to him and avoid direct contact. But the closer he got to the farm houses, the more aggressive was the dog. Wow, such a dog and with a small child on the farm, not just any child, but his very own. He tried to get closer to the farmhouses, but the dog became much more aggressive, seemingly it wanted to jump on him, so he could only advance two meters at the time. But finally, a man showed up, shouted to the dog and the barking was over, so Lars took a few more steps towards the farmhouse. The man showed the dog aside and addressed himself to Lars. "Who are you coming on to private property in this late evening?" "Did you have a visit from a lorry with only one headlight a little while ago?" "What is that to you and how do you come to know about it?" "I was hitchhiking with them, but during the trip I felt that the man might want to hand me over to the police since he thought I was a Polish refugee or something".

"No, these are good people, kind of special though, but are you coming with a letter to me, the driver said so?" "No, more like a greeting from two that died yesterday and who were to come with me up here to your farm". It had become too much to him now, and no more energy, so he fell to the ground in front of Ari. "Be careful with my leg, it is a prothesis. And I might well be wanted by the police, at least in Odesa". He got pale now Ari. "Why would the police look for you?" "I am a Jew and a Norwegian", then he was gone.

"I figured the war was over now Ari?" "Doesn't seem like that my wife". "But who is he?" "I don't know, but he's on the run from the police, he's a Jew and a Norwegian he said." "But we can't just let him lay there in the road". "No, but do we manage to get him into the barn? He has a prothesis, he said". "Not too many options then my Ari, we leave him here on the road, or we drag him into the forest to let him die there, or we have to save him". "Meaning what my wife?" The muck cellar of course". "But do you think that Andrej would contact the police about a fugitive?" "Yes, I have never trusted him Ari, even if his wife and I have been doing OK together".

Two hours later, a black Volga sedan moved slowly onto the courtyard. Two policemen in civil stepped out, only the badges on their jackets revealed their profession and now slowly the driver from the lorry stepped out as well. "I beg your pardon Ari, but I got anxious for you". "For what then?" "Well, this Polish guy I talked about". Ari laughed at him. "Thanks for your concern, but we haven't seen any Polish guy around here".

"Who are these men and what is Polish?" The little curly girl had come out to the courtyard. She started patting on the dog, obviously they were good friends. "Have you seen any strange man around here tonight little girl?" She was chewing to her thumb, had not stopped doing that as yet. She didn't seem that afraid of this man but she looked kind of scared at the two others. "Well, yes, she had seen a man". "Where is this man now then?" "He is standing right there", she pointed to Ari. "No other man then?" "Yes, you as well", and she started to laugh.

The driver of the lorry talked a bit with the two policemen and then turned to Ari. "I'm sorry Ari, could we just get inside and have a look and get done with it?" "I figured we were good neighbors Andrej, but just you have your tour and get done with it, we are soon to eat. 3 minutes later the tour of the house was done and now they turned to the barn. "Be careful with the red cow she can get quite aggressive". Now there was nothing more that Ari could do, so come what may.

"No nothing found, so obviously he hasn't come this way. Should he show up here then please let us know!" They saluted and left.

"There you have our so-called good neighbor, so please stay away from the wife". "Nothing to worry about this Ari, they are soon to move". "Oh, is that so?" "They are fed up with living in this isolated area, the wife has told me, so they have already sold their farm and shall soon be moving to Odesa, maybe already this week". Strange, he didn't mention anything about that Inna". She just shrugged her shoulders. "They never were any good neighbors to us, were they? But what about the man in the muck cellar, we must look for him now Ari?" "You just take with you Eugenia into the house and then I shall get him up and talk with him". But Lars had already managed to climb up to the barn and he then gave Ari a recap of the whole day and the tragic death of his two dearests.

"I knew quite instinctively that this lorry man was no good. My name is Leo Volgov and right now my Jewish friends in Odesa are burying Rebecka and our newborn baby in a joint grave at the Jewish cemetery". He unwinded the whole story in-between tears. "But why have you come to our farm then?" "The last word Rebecka cried out before she was gone, that was Eugenia". Ari was the one to get pale now. "Have you come here to take away our child?" There was anger in Lars' face now. "Not yours, but Rebecka's and mine. Not Chaim's either!"

"Does Chaim know about this?" "Yes of course!" "But you are wanted by the police, you said?" "Yes, Rebecka called me Lars the last minutes of her life and a junior doctor got suspicious and reported it to the commissar". "So, what now then?" "Officially I'm on vacation and should take care of my wife and my child, but when she died from me there at the hospital, then I was advised to extend my holiday and let my Jewish friends do the burial, taking place soon now. We hope that in a month's time it will all be over. I am not on the run, my papers are ok, I am just on a long vacation.

But what now then Ari?" "First you have to change to clean clothes, you don't smell too well, neither did your wife when she was down in that cellar". "Please don't talk about her Ari. I was thinking about asking you to stay here, of course as a paying guest, get to know Eugenia and then go back to Odesa once the situation has calmed down".

Ari came back with a load of well-worn clothes, but they were all clean. "You may change here, Ina doesn't like all this, neither do I. Why hasn't Rebecka written to us about all this?" Please don't blame her, it has been tough to us and soon she shall be in her earthly grave".

"Who shall be in the earth?" Eugenia had sneaked up to them there in the barn. "Oh, there is a man here. Who are you? I am Leo". She gave him his hand and he as well. Ari felt totally silent, the little child didn't seem frightened at all. She hanged onto Lars's hand as if she had adopted him. Both men waited for her to say daddy. But there was no need to it, the expression in her face told it all, told all about the connection between the two. Lars in worn-out, but clean workmen's clothes from Ari and the little girl in a checked summer dress, braids and barefoot.

"But what is it with your leg, did you have a fall and hurt yourself?" "Yes, it is artificial". "Meaning what?" He lifted his pants so she could see the prothesis. He felt the cry pressing on in his throat now when she shouted, "Daddy I have to go into Mommy and show her the man with a strange leg, come on now man". Would he be up to this, being a stranger to his own child? His only holding now?

HOME AGAIN IN ODESA

It took him six months until he felt safe enough to go back to Odesa. He had written to the Chief surgeon and asked him if he knew if the manhunt was still on. At the same time, he thanked him for all his assistance in connection with Rebecka and his child's passing.

He felt quite comfortable when reading the answer. "The Russian junior doctor had returned to Stalingrad and the case was closed, a misunderstanding altogether. The Russian commissars had returned to East Berlin. We have to meet once you're back in Odesa. Looking forward to meeting both you and your lovely daughter as well".

Now it was time to think about this old colleague and run his practice again. They had kept regular contact during all this time via his elder son living in Nikolayev.

He was ailing now, so all his patients wondered when would Doctor Leo be back. "And the apartment what about it?" "Well, it was still there, but he had also access to another apartment around the corner from Richevielska. It was a bit more expensive this one, but Lars could get away with all the memories from the old one. And if he so wanted, then his elder son working as a broker, he could take care of it all. Am I not the lucky one, Lars said to himself.

But most important was what the old doctor wrote about a lady living there in the Richevielska. She ran a sort of a nursery with five Jewish kids and she was willing to take on one more. Lars could deliver in the morning and then pick up his Eugenia in the afternoon. And he had one more extremely good news, a Jewish woman named Judith was willing to work as a cleaning lady, both in the surgery and at the new apartment. And to top it all she would accept to work like a housekeeper to him a couple of days per week, once the cleaning job was done. She had accepted that she would go to the stores to do purchases of groceries and if he so wanted, she could also assist him with the cooking. "Who is to pay for all this?" Lars was wondering, "and don't you forget I owe you a lot of money already".

"Well, you can increase your small fees a bit and then you shall survive this as well. And if there is someone wanting to donate money to our surgery, well that's what they call it, then you just tell them they will be most welcome. But never forget your vows as well as mine, all Jews are entitled to use your services as well as mine as doctors as long as we have a surgery".

Lars had ever so often wanted to ask about the funeral. Who had been present, but no, this would have to come later. He wanted to hear about it altogether, look at photographs if there were any and then go to the grave first time on his own and later with his daughter Eugenia.

The break up from the farm was less painful to Eugenia than he had feared for, although Inna was having a bad time as she had hoped for keeping Eugenia all the time. Ari was far more pragmatic. Lars addressed him: "You should think seriously about adoption the two of you. Not just one kid, but two at the same time. Do you want me to talk about the matter back in Odesa? Please bear in mind that there are many poor children who have lost all their kinfolks". It was the night before the departure that they talked about this.

It was on the very day that the younger son came all the way from Mykolaiv to fetch them and Inna came to Lars and thanked him. "Doctor Leo, this was a very good proposal, and not just one kid, but two so they can have each other, not as with Eugenia being much alone here".

The reunion with the old doctor was extremely touching. He had dried up sort of now, more like a Methuselah, his beard hanging all the way to his knees. Neither of them spokes a single word, they just kept on hugging each other so long that finally Eugenia tapped on her father's leg asking, "who are those people, Daddy?"

This was at the Richevielska and next to the old doctor was his younger son supporting his father, and Judith was there, so was Maria in charge of the nursery and even the Chief surgeon was there. Lars was overwhelmed when he saw the welcome feast with food and beverages according to Jewish customs.

"The Chief surgeon so wanted to come, Leo and I felt it would be great to everyone". "I feel the same, and I have in fact a mission to him". "Oh, do tell me about it right away please". "The couple who took care of Eugenia want to adapt two kids, well so they can have one another, and this as soon as possible". One could see the glowing light in the eyes of the Chief surgeon, lights of happiness. "This is a gift doctor, a gift that will bring enormous pleasure. There are many Jewish kids here in Odesa, kids that have lost their mother and father during the war. Did they have any wishes as to the kids age?" "No, but from three years and up would be super. They have a big farm with production of grain and of course they also have cattle". "So, then we can go visit them Daddy, right?" "Yes, my child we shall do just that".

Everything went ever so smoothly now for Lars, and much better than he had dared hope for. His only wish now was that the old doctor would enjoy his retirement and have a long, happy life. He could never stop thinking about how fantastic Doctor Aron had arranged for everything.

But one day, it was just two months after that they had returned to Odesa, he wanted a private talk with Lars. "Doctor Leo, today we have to go to the cemetery, you haven't visited so far, have you?" Lars face reddened. "No, I haven't. I haven't been up to it as yet". "Well then we shall be off right now". "Now?" "Yes, we just hang up this poster saying 'back in two hours. I have asked for a friend to pick us up right now, the car waits outside".

The sky was still high and sunny and once again there was life all over Odesa. He thought about the damned war, seemingly far away now, in this beautiful weather they could have walked on the Deribaskaia, Eugenia at his hand and little Melchior in his pram, the little family of four. His darling Rebecka would have a white hat to protect against the sun and a flickering long dress, Odesa style in all the colors of the rainbow, wearing shoes with tiny high heels. But he was soon to leave this dream world of his. "We are here now", the driver said. "I shall wait for ¾ of an hour". Dr. Aron nodded accordingly.

"It was difficult times then Leo, so I had to take whatever I could get hold of". On the double grave there was only a wonderful little red- green stone, just big enough to make room for the inscription: Rebecka and her child, year and date. "For sure you will want to find something different Leo, but this was all that I could come by at the time, and I needed to find something?" The embrace was strong, but he had to take care not to crush the little man. Tears yes, like a little stream running down onto the top of the little man's head. "I shall let you alone now with your memories here a little while, dear Leo".

His emotions were that strong that he was soon to leave or he couldn't have made it any longer. He had to concentrate on Eugenia all the time now, as he had done previously. How would he ever come to make it without her?

Eva, back in Norway, his own home in Norway? For sure he no longer had any home in Norway. But still Eva was there with him in his grief although forever lost she was to him. And now his other lost love, his Rebecka. She was there in the cold mold together with the fruit of their love, they're little Melchior. They just made it to baptize him while his mother was fighting for her life.

Fortunately, Judith should stay with them the whole evening so Eugenia would not be left alone with her grieving father. And luckily, not so many hours to go till the patients were knocking on the door and he was back to his daily rhythm. He called his colleague telling him that he should be back early tomorrow morning just in case Dr. Aron was spending the night in the backroom. "All good to me Doctor Leo, I shall close the doors firmly, well you know the double ones.

But his morning shouldn't turn out quite as he had planned for, no, totally different it should be.

THE OLD DOCTOR ARON

He had taken a light sleeping aid and was then completely rested when he got up at 6 o'clock in the morning. Eugenia was sleeping in the room with Judith so he sneaked out, decided to have a coffee and something to eat in the café at Gretska.

It was just 7 o'clock when he was at his desk and started with all the paperwork. The door to the backroom was firmly closed. There was a poster on the wall: "I am at sleep, please wake me around 9 o'clock".

There was a fabulous man sleeping in there. What could he have done if Doctor Aaron had not taken all the necessary precautions, even managed to find a stone to the grave. For sure his sons had helped him, but still it was Aaron caring all the time.

But now he had to think about the settlement and the money, so he just got started at it. In fact, that was the reason why he had come that early.

The cash he had received when departing towards Rivne, numerous bills for cars and gasoline, picking him up at the farm and of course he now had to remember thinking of paying off his sons. He wondered how the two of them had managed to hide themselves during the war?

Next were the apartments and Judith as well as the nursery, not to forget his share of the costs running the surgery. The mere thinking about all this money made him totally sweaty. And had he not forgotten about the cost for medicines and electricity? He should have to talk with Aaron on the double about all this.

He went over to Aaron's desk, there was a big brown envelope there: To Dr. Leo. Maybe he should open it up right now? Well, it was for him and was placed in the "out basket", so named by the colleague.

"Dear Leo, for sure I knew why you planned to be that early at the office this morning, all about money, not so? I am here to help you if you will let me. This office has over the years received numerous donations as I prefer to call them. Many of our well-to-do patients remember well the days when we could not ask for cash neither for treatments nor medicines. And we still have a number of such patients and they shall come for free as long as they have no means to pay with".

And what then? Lars was thinking out loud. "This is nothing but the original deal and that's the way it shall be". What on earth was it that the old doctor had on his mind this time? And he continued reading: You should know that many here in Odesa have a high regard for you. But please stick to your mission, don't be tempted by charming offers, neither politically nor from our religious friends. We are doctors and that's what we shall be, ever. Nothing must stop us from being just that.

Finally, I have not been at my best for a while. Maybe it's soon time for me and I have had a rich life. You have contributed to make it even richer. My two sons have enormous regards for you, you should know that. Be nice to them when I have waved you goodbye dearest Leo. Yours Aaron!"

What was all this about? Was he gone already? Lars looked at his watch, 08.30hrs. but the time on the note was 09.00hrs., so he best waits till then. But what about the first patient which was due at 9 o'clock? He could make her some tea and ask for her to wait. She usually came well ahead of time, that old lady. But for sure he was not up to talking to anyone right now. He had to know and the minutes went by ever so slowly.

"Is there something the matter to-day Doctor Leo? The doctor seems quite strained". "I don't really know madam; I am waiting for some messages. So please have a seat and I shall arrange for some tea to you". "But what about yourself then, I have brought cake to both of us?" "Look, I was here quite early this morning so I have already had my breakfast. Please don't get offended now. I promise to taste the cake later on, it is always that good".

Yes, she seemed pleased now. "But where is the old doctor?" But Lars did not hear what she was saying, didn't want to hear it. It was only one minute to 9 o'clock now and for sure he couldn't take it to wait any longer. Kicking lightly on the door, but no one answered. Kicked one more time, stronger this time, had the doctor already gone home? Was the door really locked? No, Doctor Aaron never locked the door. He manned himself up and then he was inside the backroom where the old doctor was sitting in his armchair, with his back towards the door. But there was a strange angle to his head. God in Heaven, he must be gone already?

Lars lifted him up and carried him to the sofa they used as bed when they spent the night there. He closed his eyes and laid a carpet over him. "My dearest Aaron, farewell to thee, I shall cry over you sometime later.

You have been like a father to me, all these difficult years". So, this was the end. But he couldn't just collapse now with this woman out in the surgery. Would he at all be able to take care of her now? First, he had to make some phone calls and have all the day- patients delayed till the day after tomorrow, but more so his first obligation was to phone the sons.

"Will the doctor be here soon?" "Yes, the very soonest, Lars cried back. But I have to make some phone calls here from the office so could you possibly stay a while in the waiting room?" She looked offended now. "Dear you, if you feel that bad this morning, then I shall look at you immediately". "No, I just felt it was right to come here to the surgery this very morning Doctor Leo". "Oh, I am glad, so then there is nothing serious bothering you. No, she smiled, but there seems to be something serious bothering you Doctor Leo". "Nothing to me, but to the old doctor. He died here in the backroom this very night so now I need to inform his son's and also cancel all the appointments we had with the other patients today and tomorrow from the list".

She gave him a hug. "I knew instantly that there was something special here today. Take good care of my cake, we shall all be at the funeral".

They all die on me now, Eva. Was he talking out loud now again? How was he to manage all by himself as from now on?

EUGENIA

He could see her mother Rebecka in all his daughter's moves, in her moods, her way of talking, the way she hugged and embraced people, laughter and not least her smile. But she should have had cousins, children of the same age or someone like Melchior he thought. What age would Melchior have as at now? Fifteen? No, he mustn't lose himself in the past again. It should be all about Eugenia now.

One day he felt that the time was right, he could he could no longer wait. "You should go up to Kiev now and continue your studies there. It shall be good for you to get out of your father's shadow".

And it was true, the patients said it as well, something was happening with Doctor Leo. Yes, it had all begun the day after the funeral for Doctor Aron. There was like a shadow over his face and some said that he had started to talk to himself or to some other lady. Some even said they had heard him call for someone he called Eva. Maybe he should be off on a holiday?

Judith was of the same opinion. But no way would he listen, he just had to pull himself together. "Maybe we could take a couple of days off just the two of us, hire a car and have a drive around Crimea?" "Who shall be driving then Judith?" "I of course". "But do you have certificate then Judith? What is it that you have kept a secret to me?" "Well, I thought it would be smart to have this certificate in reserve in case we should ever need it. Isn't that all good then?" For sure, he couldn't drive at all unless it was automatic and even so he wasn't too confident about it.

"But are you not happy with my suggestion? In fact, it was Eugenia that came up with this idea". He gave her a smile sort of. "Yes, my dear of course I'm glad". So, the two women had cooked up this plan together for this outing. But inside himself he felt this as just another confirmation to his own misery.

"But Leo we don't need to go if you don't feel for it. Maybe you should consider take a few days up in Kiev with your darling Eugenia instead?"

No way he should bother her with his depression. "It is okey Judith, if you can do the driving". His smile was more a natural one now, she thought for herself. It was all too early for him to be an old man.

His name was Vladimir, and he was studying political science in Moscow, but right now he was a guest student with the university in Kiev. Her father was absolutely right that it was good for her to come to a new environment, not least meet with other Russian students as well. Although they belonged to other faculties, she found it inspiring to meet with them. This was especially true for Vladimir, a handsome student, although not that concerned with his studies, this Moscow boy. He was still nothing but a boy.

"We shall never agree about Stalin's deportation of close to 10 million Ukrainians to the absolute certain death during the Second World War, all to save necessary provisions for the army. A genocide by a lunatic it was Vladimir!" "Yes Eugenia, but there wasn't food enough for everyone and Stalin's man Khruschev did a good job at it, I mean with this ethnic cleansing". "So, you admit then that this was an ethnic cleansing?" They always came back to this theme she felt, Big Brother Russia against little brother Ukraine.

It was late one night and she should have been home at the students' home long ago, an important exam next morning would need her be at her best. But Vladimir was that stupid, so she couldn't just leave him with what she called erroneous ideas without correcting him there and then.

But all of a sudden, he stood up. "I can see that you are excited now Eugenia. But I shall take you home and make sure that you are in place tomorrow morning for your exam". "Silly you, and how do you think you shall get into the girls' dormitories?" "Leave that to me, come on you!" "But what if we both are expelled?" "Just you relax, I shall fix it".

The long, light summer dress covered all of Vladimir and with her hat on top and bare feet, then he could have played whatever female role in any play.

Finally, he was inside. "You shall have to lay on the floor Vladimir!" "Yes of course". "And Vladimir, we must not over-sleep and you know I simply have to sleep". "Yes of course". His smile was as always irresistible.

They had never been sleeping together, but at times it had been pretty close. But Vladimir was a nice guy, he never overstepped her limits. But this night he had been drinking, so what now? But she had been drinking, she as well.

For safety, she put on an extra wide training's shorts outside the slip she was wearing. She had a good look at herself, this shouldn't be easy if there was an attack. For sure she would wake up if he tried something, her little drunkard.

The kissing wasn't that intense, Vladimir seemed pretty tired and thank God to that. She just dived under the cover, pitied him a little as he had nothing but a very thin blanket as cover. But she could soon hear his snoring, so she had to get up and give him a kiss and then she was gone, she as well.

Maybe she shouldn't have taken that sleeping pill on top of the drinks. She rarely drank alcohol and for sure she almost never touched sleeping pills. But now she had this box of pills from previous times and she felt she had to be completely awake when facing the exams tomorrow morning.

She was up already at 06.00 hrs. and went straight for the shower, while Vladimir was sleeping like a rock. But both her slip and the white shorts were wet and sticky on the front. Had she really relieved herself while sleeping? But she was not only wet by herself, this was semen. How on earth could this have happened?

Vladimir? No. He was lying fully dressed under the blanket shivering of cold. "What is it with you Eugenia?" "Have you been intimate with me in my sleep?" "Have you been dreaming now Eugenia? Dreaming about something you have long wished for?" "Yes, look at my underwear, it is all sticky and wet!" "But my dear girl, I was loaded and fell asleep not even taking off my clothes. I was sleeping fully dressed up as you see me now". "And what about the door then? Has it been locked all the time?" She ran to the door, and it was open! Then she teared his pants off and touched his boxer and OMG. They were sticky as well and it smelled of sex, not only his.

She had been reading stories like this in books, but never should she herself fell straight into it. "I have to run for it now, you looney, imagine at long last sleep with each other, and to no pleasure, neither to you nor me". She smiled at him. "Now exams!"

Strange it was, after only five hours sleep, she felt relaxed and ready for whatever would come. And her results coming up three days later were impressing. All tops. The professor was extremely satisfied.

Five weeks later, and during this time, she and Vladimir had been inseparable, but no sex she had said. "Now, it is all about the final exams for both of us".

Her monthly period was already 10 days overdue, when she started panicking. Her last day of exams was over and they were to celebrate before he was off to Moscow and she to Odesa, overexcited for her daddy's comments.

But now she knew it, she was pregnant and that was a fact. "You have to have it removed Eugenia; I cannot marry you. At home they had come up with a young girl to be my bride. And I simply cannot get away from it, less I am done for, with no money". "But don't you worry, I am soon to be a fully licensed doctor so money wouldn't be any problem and you can get yourself a job". "Yes, but I'm supposed to join my family's business and they all consider me engaged to Raisa". "Then you have been cheating on me bloody Vladimir!" "No, I have not, we have been the best friends ever, but never did we talk about any future together for us. What happened that night none of us know anything about". "But are you in any doubt whatsoever that this child is yours?" "No of course not, the evidence is utterly clear. But what about abortion? I shall off course pay for it". "Boys always come up with this type solution, abortion and they shall pay. But I have to talk about it with my daddy". "Your Daddy?" "Yes, he is a doctor". "So, what then?"

ANOTHER GOOD-BYE

"You look a bit tense today my child". Child? 5 foot 4 and blonde with her boisterous hair write down to her shoulders, Bermuda and a top that seemed glued to her breasts. Her mother should have seen her now. "And your notes?" "See for yourself Daddy". "This calls for champagne my golden baby!"

But he could see there was something on her mind that worried her and she hardly touched the bubbles in her glass. "OK then Eugenia, spit it out!" "Daddy I'm pregnant, a sheer mishap Daddy. He is Russian and engaged into a super wealthy family and maybe he also has some love for his Raisa as well, he says. None of us know what really happened!" "So, so, just tell me all about it now, but slowly". And even her father being a doctor, she found it ever so special to talk with him about it. But Lars had problems hiding his panic. Was it to be Rebecka one more time?

So, what now then, abortion? He felt the pain to his tummy, his fear for it all was clearly that visible. The scenes with Rebecka and her pain came to him again. These terrible scenes when he lost not only Rebecka, but also little Melchior. Could he endure this one more time? "What was on your mind right now Daddy? You were gone to me, totally pale in your face!" "No, this was just something coming on to me". But it was no good lying to her. "Oh, you were thinking about mother of course. But that was an accident Daddy, I am young and well and I know how to take care of myself". "Right so. Your mother didn't do just that. But I think you shall give it some thought, but don't wait too long. And this young man, you have never been in love with one another?" "No, not for real we have". "Well, it is of course for yourself to decide and whatever decision you make I shall support you and you know that".

He had to talk with someone about all this and of course it had to be Judith. "I cannot take this one more time Judith". "But who says it will all go bad? Giving birth is usually a normal thing, not any danger to it, right so? Admittedly I don't know as I have never been pregnant myself." He was not sure if she expressed her private sorrow to it, her voice was sore and he felt he had to comfort her, so he embraced her strongly. "My dearest Judith. You know well what I think about you and us, but I simply cannot". He then went into his study and she could hear him crying through the door. Now was not the time to disturb him. She knew what was to come for that night. His cries for Rebecka and then Eva and in between his sobbing for little Melchior, her doctor Leo!

Circumstances would have it that Eugenia came to start as an intern at the same hospital where her mother had worked, but the Chief surgeon had retired by now and the seniors were new.

She thrived in her new job, and it was all well, but one month before her estimated date she started to get some strange rides of fever that lasted for maybe a day or two. This made her flaccid and uncomfortable and the fear was all over her father. But he had to take care not to show it openly to her, she wasn't to be frightened his Eugenia. But he was happy that he had her cut hard work to half a day now and then ask for leave the last 14 days. But the fever wouldn't go away, so he went to the hospital to see the gynecologist. "Do you have any idea what this stems from doctor?" And then he told him about Rebecka and little Melchior. "Do you think this might be genetic? Maybe we should all go up to Kiev to see a specialist?" "Let's leave this for tomorrow, Dr. Leo".

But the next day she was all well, fit as a lark and there were no more signs that something was the matter. She bloomed like a rose and was happy for the baby and he with her, but the fever didn't go away.

The gynecologist had no answer to this mysterious either. "But doctor, if she is delayed then you shall order cesarean, no matter what she says!" "Deal!"

Two days before her date, she didn't wake up her usual self. The gynecologist was immediately summoned and Caesarian was done, but then she was gone, she just passed away. No explanation to it

Lars did not cry anymore, there were no tears left, but Judith she cried all the time when he did not see her. He had enough to himself now so she would not bother him with her own feelings. But her crying was not as much for Eugenia, yes of course she cried for her too, but mostly it was for Lars, the man she had loved throughout all these years and what was Lars to do now with the little Theresa, they had already baptized her up at the hospital.

But could Lars take care of the baby and at the same time do his job at the surgery? No, he could never have made that. Should he consider to have her adopted? Unthinkable! So, it had to be Judith then to make the sacrifice, but was she considering it as sacrifice? She had soonest to know what Lars was thinking. But if she was to take care of little Theresa, what then would the congregation say and what would the neighbors think, she moving into the girl's room. She wanted of course have them to think that it was all about she being a servant and nothing else. Judith would never ever suggest to him that they should be married. If there ever were problems, then she would have to move down to the nursery on the floor beyond.

The Rabbi in the congregation had touched upon the subject. Would Lars have the energy for a new round with a baby and all that had to follow? And what about Judith? Shouldn't he consider for Judith to be his lawfully wedded wife? But Lars told him that they had no physical connection and that they would never have it, but that he held her dearly considering not least her sacrifice for life to him and his family.

"Maybe you want for me to ask what she thinks Dr. Leo?" "Yes, I love for you to do it, tell her I should have asked her myself but I didn't want for her to have me impose on her".

"So, no way would you consider marrying her?" "No, the two women I have lost shadows for all". "But you have had other women, haven't you?" "Yes, but that is a long time ago. But it is these two women that I have truly loved and none others may come in their place". "Your hope is then that Judith will accept to live in the shadow of the two?" "Yes, yes Rabbi, and if she cannot accept it then I shall have to talk with her myself and explain it all for her, to stay or to leave if she cannot live with it".

This was the way it had to be and he should compensate her well economically. He was suddenly struck by the thought about Eva. What if he could have taken little Theresa with him and gone back to Eva, asking her to start over again? Would she have taken him to her with the baby? Oh no, she was for certain long time married now to someone else, maybe she even was a granny now and why should she care for his little granddaughter?

But Lars, about you going home? The law for those having denounced their country for certain is still in place and how would it be for you to come home with your tail between your legs? Have you gone nutty now, and who would you think should look after Theresa all those years, you in a labor camp, or in an ordinary jail? Right so, it would most probably have been the Official Child Care she would be left to and then and she would have been adopted to someone. He felt the cold over his shoulders and down his spine.

No Norway, this sacrifices you shall never have, ever. He felt the bitterness hitting him. He had never been any Nazi, never did anything bad to anyone. You just forgot about the partisans then Lars. The shots of mercy and all that happened at the crossing of the Bug. Well then, admittedly he had things to ask forgiveness for he as well. And now you just forgot you having nursed German officers at the hospital in Odesa during the war, Norway's enemies they were.

He couldn't take any more right now so he left the surgery and went straight up to his grandchild and Judith. Beautiful she was his little Theresa. Dark brown hair but then probably her father had brown hair as well.

"Judith, the Rabbi must have been talking to you by now and to put it simple, it would have been bloody unjust of me to offer you like a fake marriage. You know well that I could never act as a true husband in such a relation, not possible after Rebecka. But if you would stay with me, then my soul shall love you for it. And should you decide to leave us, then you shall have no financial problems".

He finally had come to tell her now, tell her how it had to be. "I have decided by myself Lars, and you should know that I would never have considered to leave you or your granddaughter". "But what about people talking then, gossiping all over Odesa?" "I couldn't care the least Lars. The delight I feel by being near to you and your grandchild overshadows all that may come of evil talks".

But what about my evil talks then Judith? But he should spare her to these.

THE GRANDCHILD THERESA

She had just got 16 some days ago. Beautiful? Yes, and well-shaped for her age. For sure he had to look out for her. "Today we are going to a restaurant and talk". "What about Judith then?" "No, I have spoken to her and told her that this is going to be a private conversation between grandfather and grandchild. Only the two of us today my dear".

"Are you seriously ill grandfather?" "No, no, but we shall have a nice talk and of course we shall also talk about serious things, about your kinfolk's and what you shall have as profession once you have grown up". "You can't see I have already grown-up grandfather? I push 5.6 and I have the nicest breasts in the whole class". "One doesn't talk with one's grandfather about such things Theresa". "Dear grandfather, I'm so sorry. You have always treated me as your little kitten, haven't you? Your dearest baby to sit in your lap and I shall never grow up but always be that Golden Kitten". She laughed out loud now. And he as well.

"I don't know dear you if my lap can take you anymore, my prosthesis has gotten worse. Either I shall have to have a new one or I will take this one with me down in the ground". "Dearest Granddad, I shall not have you talk like that anymore. Come on, we shall go for the restaurant".

It did of course turn out to be a very pleasant lunch, then suddenly she said, "when are we to talk about all the serious things?" "My dearest Theresa, I don't know for how long I shall live but I have written a diary or whatever you like to call it. There you will find the most important notes from my life, not least why I could never go back to Norway". "But you have told me about all this before Grandfather. It wasn't just that you wanted to talk about today, was it?" "So, so, not that impatient little lady". "5.6 don't you forget that!" "Well, yes of course, but what I wanted to talk about today is how your grandmother died and also let you know a bit about he that should have been your uncle, our little Melchior". She shrugged now! "Do we have to talk about that right now?" "Yes, we simply have to and then we must talk about your beautiful mother, she as well died in childbirth, but you made it. They have left me, all my women. First it was Eva and I don't know if she is still alive or not and then my beloved Rebecka and finally my daughter, your mother".

"Is there a pattern to this my grandfather?" Pattern, was she already a grown up now his granddaughter?

"If you by pattern means if there are similar problems in my family in Norway, then I don't know what to answer you. But if you are thinking in religious terms, and this was to be my punishment and these women where the sacrifices, then maybe a sick brain could find something of a pattern here. But not me, educated in natural science and being a doctor.

But dearest if something similar should happen to you, then I as well would have to think about it all as a curse". "But Grandfather, the thought about me having a baby, that's far into the future!" "No, it is not. And maybe it would be to the best for me if I were to die before that. If there is a curse, then let it die with me". The next second she was onto his lap the big girl. "I don't want you to die ever, ever!" "Please I am suffocating, let go of me. If you hadn't made it during your mother's tragic death, then I would probably been placed in some old folks' home, dried up and be gone. It is you Theresa that have kept me going".

"Don't you forget about Judith, our kindest Judith!" "Judith had deserved me once I was younger and vital. She had the choice when you were born to stay with me as a hired woman or leave us and start a new life. I told her how much I was glad for her, but that this shadow from the previous women made a complete love to her impossible. So, I have been all open to her about it".

"But Grandfather she has had a lot of pain and sorrows as well, so when you were coming home from your surgery and smiled to her, then I have seen like a glory over her head, a glory of happiness. Please don't take it away from her. It is all she has to herself". "Wise words you speak my girl".

"But now", and it was the doctor's voice that talked to her now, "once you come of age, and you are going to have your monthly periods, then I shall insist on you going to regular gynecological controls. You shall tell the gynecologist about your family and what has happened with all the women".

"You were so right Grandfather; you are really getting old. I had my first period more than 18 months ago!" He got red in his face now. "All right, so Theresa I look after my patients, but haven't a clue about what's going on at home".

"But Grandfather I have something serious to talk to you about. Can we do that right now?" "Yes of course, spit it out". "My dad, do you know who he is and what's his name?" His face darkened now. "Yes, I do, sort of". "What do you mean by sort of?" "Well, yes, I have a name, hmm, and an address". "So, I shall write to him and ask him what he can do for me at the National Ballet School in Moscow and", she almost turned solemn now, "Bolshoi". "Have you just lost it Theresa?" "No, Grandfather, the leader here at the Odesa Opera House says she has nothing more to teach me here".

"So, you are not to study medicine then?" He tried in vain to hide his disappointment. "No, Grandfather, let go of it please". "Ballet and opera, that's what I want to concentrate on and they say here I have the talent to it, lots of talent.

You told me once that he had married into a rich and powerful family, did you not?" "Well maybe so. Let's go home now and I shall see what I have of papers concerning your dad. But do swear to me now that you will be utterly serious about what I said about seeing the gynecologist!" "Yes, Grandfather, I swear to that".

Just think about it he said to himself, this is the third woman that have had influence on my life here in Odesa. But then there was another voice whispering to him, don't you forget about Judith.

"Oh, what a handsome boy! I mean man, this is Vladimir's address?" "No, but it shouldn't be that difficult to find it". "May I take it from here? Yes, I shall do just that and then write to him and tell him all about myself, not you Grandfather. I didn't upset you now did I?" "No, only if you leave me, leave Odesa". "But Grandfather, when I'm playing in Moscow or in Kiev, then you shall come too and of course when we have guest performances here in Odesa!" "Oh, my girl, my dream girl!" "And you know what?" "No?" He looked wondering at her. "If you don't get angry with me, then I shall tell you". "Yes, go on then. She hesitated a while and then the she burst it out. "I have been thinking about this for a long time. I want to go to Norway and see the land where you grew up. May I go and will you come with me?" "I cannot do that Theresa", and then he started to cry, the real sorrow cry and Judith came running. "What has happened Theresa and with you Leo?" She almost never called him Lars.

"Come with me and lay down, you shall not go back to the surgery today. I shall call the new young doctor and tell him that you might not come back tomorrow either". "No! For sure I am going to the surgery tomorrow!" "Ok then, so it will only be today that you are not at the surgery".

Theresa was sitting quietly in the corner of the room her head in her hands. Now this fine day and of course she had to ruin it. "Don't you be sorry Theresa my child, of course you shall go, but will you please wait some years till you are grown up".

She should never mention it to him again as long as he lived. And he on his part hoped that she wouldn't go there until Eva was dead. But he didn't say that.

Later Judith came to her and she asked her what it was all about this Eva name. "I know and I don't know. But his nightmares have been many, he then has asked her for forgiveness when he woke and cried, and cried. We have to leave that for now. Someday he shall tell you about it all, don't you think?"

MOSCOW

"I hope for your sake that you have stopped growing taller now dear. Yes, and I am thinking about ballet and height!" These were his first remarks when he met her at the station, she coming from Odesa.

"Welcome to Big Brother, well yes, I mean the country of course". But the man was amiable. But what had happened to the lean handsome guy she had seen on his picture? She would never have recognized him. He was a grown man now, but he had only grown much larger. But his eyes, were they not still beautiful? No, they were not. It came on to her, yes, she wanted to ask him straight, are you happy now my father?

But the question would have been uncalled for. It was obvious that his life had been more about money and power than about happiness. And the uniform of the driver in the limo just strengthened the impression oh precisely that, money and power.

"Welcome to Moscow, Theresa. We cannot be our real selves; I mean father and daughter here as my wife spy on me all over the place and maybe she has her reasons to that. I have always missed your mother albeit we never came to love one another for a real. Here in Moscow, I shall discreetly give you all the help you will need. Officially you are the daughter of a fellow student of mine there in Kiev and that's as close to the truth as well. Now lunch and we shall put you up where you're going to live".

"Well thanks, but obviously you don't know much about this. I shall be a roomy with a fellow Russian student right by the school and thanks for helping me into this school." "No matter Theresa, but when you switch over to Bolshoi, then I shall provide for you a nice place to live if you will let me". She had to laugh, "Vladimir", she wanted to call him dad, only she didn't quite get the ring of it, "one doesn't just switch over to Bolshoi. One might get nominated if one is lucky and then comes audition and furthermore the committee discusses if one is at all suited to pass the needle's eye".

"Well then, you don't seem to have gotten some of your mother's super optimism I gather. To her nothing was difficult, all but challenges". "Yes, I understand. But in this trade optimism alone doesn't pull you through. Here it is question of super intense work over years. If you fail at one small detail then you're out. There are hundreds, not to say thousands ready to take your place. That's the way it is, as simple or as hard as that".

"Have you many children?" He sorts of sank together in his chair there at the lunch. "No, I have none". "So, what is your work then?" "I have my degree in social economy and I give some lectures. For the rest I'm a house slave to my wife, whenever she is at home and yes, I am a counselor to my father-in-law". "So, your wife has her own business then?" "She is on the board of some companies, but for the rest I don't know. Theresa, we live in the same house and in the same dacha and we meet at meals. Anything further?" "No", she had tears now for this man who after all had been that close to her mother.

"Now don't you cry. I chose this life all by myself and it happened to be the wrong choice. But I cannot live my life over and again. Unfortunately, we cannot meet in public and maybe it shall be difficult in private as well. No worries to me personally, but she could make difficulties to you and your career. Jealousy, it's her most prominent character".

"How extremely terrible you," she said. "But Theresa my child, I can contact the school and leave messages to you!" Then a kiss and he was gone, her daddy.

It should be three hard working years at the Russian National School of ballet and with very short leaves home to her grandfather in Odesa. During this time, she was invited for two guest performances, simple roles at the Odesa Opera House and she now was all excited, would she make it to the Bolshoi merely on her own efforts, or would she have to count on Vladimir? Not that much she had seen of him.

But she was never to know. One day she was summoned to an audition and the very same evening she could read on the net that her daddy had passed. Was it only her grandfather and possibly Eva that were to live in this family?

One day she was back in Odesa for an audition. She was to play Mimi in La Boheme. A dream role to anyone. She asked the chief of the ensemble if her old grandfather could be present at some of the rehearsals as he might not live to the premiere in the fall.

She stayed home with Lars as she has come to call him now, nothing had changed and Judith was quietly around helping us before. Her grandfather was no longer attending the surgery, he was totally focusing on his diary now.

One Saturday when she had her leave, he wanted for her to come with him to the cemetery to her mother's grave. But not to the grave for Rebecka and little Melchior. No, he didn't want to see that double grave this day.

So, they went onto Eugenia's grave. "The most beautiful woman in all Odesa she was your mother, Theresa. Even today when the Odesa girls do their careful makeup, none of them would ever be near her outer beauty and above all her radiation. Today there are many beautiful plastic girls to see, but no radiation, no warmth".

"My dearest Mother, I shall think about you, sing for you, only to you. Sing Mimi to you". And inside herself she was humming the well-known phrases. But when she came to the tenors," why does your little hand shake?" Then came the greatest outcry. And she kept on crying and Lars cried as well, but finally they had to move on.

"Why did you not want for us to come to this grave Grandfather?" "Well, as you can see it is a kind of a strange grave is it not?" "Yes, I can see that it's much larger than the others, kind of double as wide is it not?" "Your grandmother Rebecka and little Melchior are lying to the one side. I shall have the other part my dear, although I'm still alive now, am I not?" "What shall be the inscription on your tombstone then Grandfather?" "I don't really know, maybe there should be only one stone to us all, a new one. If not, I want the inscription to read Dr. Leo, Lars, Rebecka's husband, father and grandfather. But this will be your decisions to make now". The color of his face changed from red to white and back to red again. "Grandfather, I think it is time for you to go home now and rest yourself". Was he about to die on her, here at the cemetery?

"Yes, my dearest but we had to make this trip together". She waved at the cab outside of the gate and then the driver came right onto the grave where Lars had sat down and helped him out into the car. There was dirt on his clothes in several places, but he didn't seem to care and the driver brushed them off, put a cover on the seat and helped her grandfather to lay down. "I think, my dearest Grandfather that I shall need help to get you up the stairs". She nodded to the driver. "I shall of course pay you extra for that".

"No way, it shall cost you nothing. My grandparents, they were regulars to Dr. Leo whenever there was something the matter, all the time until they passed. I think they were some of the poorest in all Odesa, and he didn't charge them a cent in fee. Not even once!"

She looked at him. "Are you a Jew as well?" "Yes, my old ones survived the massacre".

"Did you tip him this boy?" "No, he didn't want any pay at all". "There was something well known about him was there not?" For sure Grandfather, his grandparents were patients in your surgery throughout their lives". "Well, yes, they didn't have much to keep them going did they!" "Come on now." Judith was at the stairs. "Maybe we shall make you some soup?" "Yes, I would like that, and then I want to talk with Theresa alone and later with the both of you".

Was it time now? Time for the Great farewell?

THE DIARY

"As of tomorrow, Theresa, you are free to do whatever you like. Plan for visiting Norway, meet your kinfolks if that's what you want". "But why, and why just tomorrow?" "I shall bid you farewell today; I can feel that it's soon time now". "No, it cannot be that soon Grandfather. You shall come to the Opera for our rehearsals and yes of course you will come for the premier as well and you will live for many years still".

"My child, I am totally exhausted, worn out. I have endured almost unthinkable sorrows over my dear lost women, and yes possibly some physical pain to my missing leg as well. But twice I have seen new life, first with your mother until she passed at the age of 22, and now with you all these years, although you have been away in Kiev and Moscow. But I have talked with you all through the weeks and kissed you goodnight every single evening". He pointed at the photo of her at the mantlepiece.

"But this is my voyage and at some time she'll come to an end and here in the beginning of my diary I have written some about my childhood, my growing up and my first big love to Eva whom I might have betrayed". This was the very first time he spoke the name of this woman without the slightest fever in his voice. So maybe he was at peace with her now?

"If she is still alive, do you think she is an old bitter woman now?" "I don't know Theresa; I know nothing more".

"Shall we not continue with this tomorrow, Grandfather; I can see you are tired after this trip to the cemetery". "Not tomorrow my dearest child. All has to be done today!"

She had to go to the bathroom to wipe off tears. "Is it going downhill now?" A soft question from Judith. "Yes, it seems like he has decided to die tonight or early tomorrow morning".

It was for Judith to fall apart now and Theresa had to console her. "You have sacrificed your whole life here Judith". "No sacrifice dearest Theresa, no sacrifice whatsoever. It is I who have gotten this life with you here as a gift, totally invaluable".

"You shall please ask Eva about forgiveness for me If you can muster it and maybe she will forgive and then you can come to the cemetery, to my grave and tell me all about it. Will you do just that?" She was back at his sofa now, didn't know what to do, what to say anymore. But he helped her on. "I shall also ask you to buy the most beautiful wreath to my mother's and father's joint grave there in the county of Hedemark. But maybe you had rather talk to the church clerk to have him plant something everlasting there at their grave and then you secure it for some 100 years. There are rules to that in Norway. So, pay him well and make sure to get a receipt". "Will you be in need of that grandfather?" "No, not I, but you, so you are certain that they won't let you down". "Grandfather this is a church and the cemetery to the church is it not?" Well, one couldn't be too certain about the attitude prevailing in the county following his own participation in the war. But come what may!

"And maybe you could sing a song from a Jewish burial there at your great grandmother's grave". "What, was she Jewish?" "Yes of course she was. But she is lying there in a public graveyard as all her grown life she had to deny her faith. I'm referring to some leaves from the Torah of the father of your great grandmother, leaves that she took with her from her dearest Karelen. And this must have been a very, very old Torah. All kinfolks from the Karelen where my mother came from where exterminated and they plowed up the cemetery to grow potatoes". "Are you not tired now Grandfather?" No, he was not, there was a fire inside him pushing him to getting all this done with.

"You must then of course talk with the county Sheriff and the county Judge about your heritage. If Eva didn't get married and have children, then there are no other heirs to two farms. So, make sure that you bring with you your birth certificate and then you shall find out if you will make claims based on Odel before it will be too late". "What is Odel then?" "Don't you think about it right now, but it is a kind of right to inheritance. All the rest you will find in my diary, the full story about why I left and why I did not go back. But now I have to talk with Judith and I want for you to listen in and take care of all the economics".

There was a lot of tears now in that dire moment. "I have written all about it in my will, but I want for you both to hear it straight from me that Judith shall be taken care of as was she my own".

They went through all and every detail now, and Judith said No, all the time she said No, but he was adamant.

"Theresa, time has come when Judith and I shall say goodbye to one another!"

She left quietly, but all the time she heard Judith, the always calm one, crying and crying.

THE FIFTH BOOK,

THE GREAT REUNION

THE LAST VOYAGE OF LARS

They had bid their farewells, her grandfather and Theresa. Now all he wanted was that she should sit with him, keep his hand in hers and have him float as he put it. Maybe he would get lucky and leap from here on a sky of happiness in the end.

Theresa had no more tears and Lars was floating away. "I am so glad that I should be able to come home to you and explain to you all, before I thank you for being just you. I am old now, no longer the tall blonde guy who left you for that damned war. I'm on the bus now, there I can see the road-crossing and the sign on the door, Surgery. Yes, it has been like that all through 100 years, although I think my father Trygve has brightened it up at times. I can see it looks brand new, maybe in plastic, times are changing as you know.

Yes driver, I am to be off here. If I know where I am? What a question! My crouches, thanks I was about to forget about them. But I am well now and maybe you can have them if you want to? You won't have them? Well then just throw them away then.

No, I have not any baggage except for this small rucksack. Cheerio driver, but no one heard him. If I can make it? Of course, I can, I am from here you know!

The mosquitoes are nastier now than when I grew up. Again no one heard him, but I shall soon be through the little forest and over to the open glen. Maybe I shall go see Trygve first and my own home from childhood? No, I don't think I shall bother them now. I only want to go up to the little stream and drink fresh water and look into the pond where I was fishing all through my childhood. Maybe Eva will see me as I walk up the fields? No, maybe she would not recognize who is sitting there by the pond? Maybe she thinks I'm just a stray man, so she best locks her doors. For her to keep worrying about that, still I guess she shall be surprised. I shall have a sandwich now, yes what's left of it from what they served me on the plane. Then I shall fill water into my hat and drink from it just like another gypsy.

My oh my, it tasted heavenly this fresh water and how nice with a cool hat now to my top. Maybe I've got some sunburn or could it be the fever coming back? I wonder what she will say once she sees my leg or rather the one missing. My prothesis isn't that bad, but I cannot run and I cannot do much farm work. But we still have our hired hand here, Ivar. We shall see now if she has managed to wait for me. Well, I have met with a couple of women that became dear to me, but they all will be just shadows in comparison to you, my Eva.

But look, there is someone coming out on the porch up there. I can see that it is a tall blonde one, in a beautiful summer's dress and a wide brimmed hat to protect against the sun. Still, it isn't that much sun now is there?

Maybe she is just protecting her skin to make her look young and fresh to her boy, now finally coming home to her. I think you are more than beautiful enough to me Eva; I can see that you still have your long blonde hair there under your sun hat. Should I wave? She doesn't know does she, that it was today I was supposed to come home. I chanced at it. Hello there Eva, I waved to her with my wet hat and for sure she knows that it is I.

"Lars my boy!" she shouts from far away. And I managed to answer even if I'm thick in my throat, best let the tears flow before she comes to me. "Just you sit there Lars, I'm coming to you!" she waved to him and in seconds she was close to him sitting on his lap touching him and she said "oh it's you Lars, my boy". And there was suddenly a lot of light around us, and she takes off her hat and my whole girl becomes golden and light is flowing all over. "My dearest, Eva, I knew you would wait for me, can you forgive me being away so many years?" "Yes, my Lars, as long as you say my girl, my girl, my girl!"

Is this a dream? Then I don't want to wake up from this dream. "Kiss me Eva, kiss me and now close the door to the others. Eva!" he cried out, "I am so happy!"

His hands folded over his flattening chest, my grandfather my dearest grandfather. "My God, you look that happy!"

And now, what kind of life will be there after? Now she was alone, the last of the kinfolks. But maybe there were still some up in Norway?

THE 9TH OF AUGUST

So, this was her farm now, her heritage from grandfather, still, not officially. His enlisting to the SS had put a stop to that. She went to talk with the county Judge as Lars had instructed her. She could see that he was puzzled this relatively young Judge. A young, foreign, beautiful woman coming here onto the rural Norway asking for documents. But for sure she had evidence to see the official documents about Lars' farm.

When the old lady up at Øvre Elvegard was to buy the big farm Nedre, following instructions from a great, great grandfather, then the old county Judge, now retired, came up with this old declaration making it possible to life heirs down to the 4th level to take back the farm for only 1 Ncr.

There must have been strong reasons to this. But the declaration gave no explanation further and the county Judge wouldn't say no more. "And if you are to talk about your Odel and your rights, then you have to make a regular appointment". "I haven't come here to crave for anything, least not now and maybe never".

"Then you are not interested in your rights then?" All can't be measured in money Judge. We shall talk some other time. Thanks for the information you have given me". "Well, yes, your name was Theresa, wasn't it? Please remember that things may be obsolete". So, it was all about her possible heritage that was in his head.

On her way out of his office he had a final remark. "You should know that the old Judge is still alive. You may find him at his home. It is of course totally up to you how you choose to introduce yourself to him. But think twice before you decide to meet him. My predecessor was an ardent man of the resistance. The Nazis had him under observation all through the war, but he was clever in covering up, that Judge. And once the war was over, no one ever questioned his integrity, so he kept his job until he finally retired at 92. Best of luck to you".

Following the conversation with the new Judge it seemed evident that it might not be very popular to have a visit from the grandchild of an SS man, a so-called Front Fighter. She shuddered a bit by the thought of what the family of Lars had been through, not least his fiancée at the time.

The older Judge was a hard nail to most people, that much she had seen from newspapers in Hamar, the nearby city. She had looked into the archives from 1945 and onwards and seen the picture of the old Judge in connection with several trials for betraying one's country. Many of the general public wanted death penalties also for the Front Fighters. But the Judge had taken a clear stand against this, according to the newspaper. Who was to sentence a 16-year-old to death or even an 18-year-old, that in the turmoil of the war in 1940 chose Germany, to fight the Bolsheviks? More than half of these youngsters never came back, but ended in mass graves on the East front. Who were to know at the time, that it was England and Stalin going together and 5 years later, craving victory over Germany? Stalin's mass deportations and murdering was totally in line with Hitler's, at least when it came to body counts.

But the Holocaust, the extermination and harassment before that, clearly that was only Hitler's doing. The newspaper did not question the old Judge on this issue. But the deportation to Siberia, more than 10 million dying of famine in Ukraine alone, all Stalin's doing. Why didn't the newspapers write anything about that? And the Genocide? Yes, there should be no other name to it, the killing in Ukraine all arranged to save food for the Russian army.

But this was like it always was, the victorious decided what was coming on print, whether it was in newspapers or in history books. It was always like that.

It had turned out to be a very heavy day for her in Hamar so, she wasn't quite sure if she was up to the confrontation with the Judge, the old-one as they called him now, least not this evening. She would of course have to give him the long story about Lars's enlistment to the SS and all that followed. About the war as such, grandfather later joining up as medic for the Russians and the partisans, and finally as a medic to the Jews in Odesa. All this being the back cover to the very dramatic decision of not going home and have his sentence, nor judgement.

Fair judgment, here it was again. One issue was how this was looked upon from a judicial point, but the cry for justice from the people at large, unconditional loss of statesmanship, loss of all holdings, farms and land to himself or to his heirs, and finally 10 years of hard labor in camps. Did one ever consider the possibility for someone to stand up thereafter? No, and probably it was not intended either. The punishment should be for life and through several generations as well, when having picked the wrong side. It came to her an article in an old newspaper, a sort of conversation between so-called good Norwegians, from 1947. Only two years after the war at that time: "There he goes, well you know his uncle was a Front Fighter. A shame it was to the county that his nephew later succeeded to take over his uncle's farm. That family should altogether have been run out of this county". "You mean deported no doubt?" "Yes, deported to Finnmark to help rebuild the land, all of them. And now, as soon as he has done time this Front Fighter, then he will come home and take care of the farm as before. No shame seen on him while I shall have to live in the annex. And you know his daughter Sigrid, she should have married this Ragnar at Nes, she now lives in Sweden, waiting". "Forever faithful to this jailbird? "Yes, I mean the traitor to his country, he shall soon be 23 now and was only a boy of 18 when he left for war".

Yes, that was how the county people down at the café talked with one another according to the newspaper. But this could have been her grandfather and Eva as well.

The stately shape of the old Judges' houses was to be seen on top of the steep hill. The long main house had a clock tower, not at the stabbur as was customary. Now, it was like the main building had gotten an extra lift to it and the cover of the tower was in copper. These stately houses were in fact government property in the older days, but the Judge had been able to buy it from the state when he retired. Now it would forever be called the Judges' Farm by the public, that much she had read from the newspaper this morning.

Where was she to park the car? On the gray white shingle in front of the main entrance? Wouldn't be very popular by that. She parked the gray-blue Golf right in the driveway and then she went behind the main house to see if there were other cars parked there. But the welcome from a big race hound scared her back to her car. It was a Doberman, heritage probably from the Germans when they had left? She heard shouts of command and the dog abided to this and she could safely leave the car. She would just have to leave it 50 meters from the main entrance. But suddenly there was an old lady there, ever so skinny with a white apron and white bonnet on her head coming running over the shingle and pointed to the backside of the house where other cars were parked. She was onto the window of the car, her hand looking more like a claw and wanted to know if she had an appointment. "No, I just have to see the old Judge, me coming straight from Ukraine". Seemingly the lady didn't understand nothing even though Theresa spoke distinct in English, she disappeared ever so fast. She heard her mumbling something about Ukraine whatever it was and then suddenly there he was on the porch the Judge retired, now in his robe only.

His rest after lunch was probably over, if it wasn't Theresa's visit that had disturbed him, the old man. The dog now was resting quietly at his side.

"Who are you?" His voice carried a long way, but she had thought long about this encounter. Should she mention grandfather, Lars, right from the beginning? No, it was probably best to start with her great grandfather Trygve, the county Doctor and resistance man, who had served as field-medic as well for the Finns in Karelen in their fight against the Bolsheviks.

The maid had gone now, but she could still see her bonnet in the window on the second floor. Even if his voice carried long, no doubt it was an old man standing there. He had been a mere 25 years, April 9th. 1940, she knew, some apprentice at the time, but his boss had fallen 3 days later in a fight with the Germans up at Stange.

The leader of the local Nazi-movement had told him about it the day after. "I shall make you our next county Judge. We need new blood you know. If you join our Nazi Party now, then the job as county Judge for sure will be yours".

But the 25-year-old apprentice did not bend. "If I am appointed, then I shall serve all the Norwegian people, not one single community like the NS and should you happen to have other candidates then you just pick one of them". But the Nazi leader responded; "don't you make the same mistakes as your predecessor. Then I shall promise to come and see to you ever so often. But best you join us and I can surely guarantee the job will be yours. Our new Secretary of Justice will come visiting as well and inform you about your duties".

"What do you mean by that? Our new Secretary of Justice?" "Germany and Norway shall join together in a large European Association and then we shall have a new government with Vidkun Quisling as our leader and secretaries with the right attitudes. You shall receive a letter appointing you to temporary county Judge within days".

This was the citation from the interview with the old judge from 1945. A hard nail he was already at the time and now she faced him only 10 feet away. For sure she had done her homework Theresa, but would it would it be of any help at all?

THE OLD JUDGE

She kept her car keys in her left hand now, feeling that her right hand was extremely sweaty. He was not to recognize that she was nervous so she grabbed the hanky she had in her purse and at the same time put her keys in there. Luck to her, her hand was now dry again. "Had she not heard his question?" He addressed her in third person. She responded in English; "I am the Great Grandchild of Trygve at Nedre".

"Trygve is dead!" "Yes of course I know that". "So where do you come from? For certain I did not know that he had any great grandchildren". But she knew well that he was lying. She was convinced that he had received a phone call from the young Judge's office. He knew for certain that the girl standing there in his courtyard came from Ukraine, from Odesa, the so-called Orange city by the Black Sea. She wondered if he knew that she knew, or at least had her suspicions. He should be close to 95 by now, but according to people in the county he still had his sharp tongue and his superb memory.

She wanted for him to avoid any further lies, so she put it right to him. "Did not your new Judge down in the village tell you where I come from, I presume he has called you?" She chose to help him into the safe net. "No, he just said you were coming from the Black Sea". "Kind of unprecise don't you think?" Now the ice was broken. No doubt the two judges had talked about the sensation by this Theresa showing up. This young woman that had won the role as Mimi in La Boheme with sharp international competition. The opening was set for October and maybe this was the edge to be received at all.

She approached the old man, his back was not the straight one of a younger judge anymore, like in his old days. But he could still have tricked many with his age. The powerful eyebrows and the marked nose together with his steel gray eyes signalized power and authority, even now several years after his retirement. He still had his hair and maybe he gained from it now being silver gray. But for sure there had to be something appealing to him, in spite of his appearance, making him well thought of and when she got close to him, she saw it. His lips were tight but he couldn't hide the smile to his cheeks and she laughed. Now she was at a mere 5 feet distance to him. Even the dog winked with his tail as to mark that he was no danger to her.

"I am Theresa, I'm 24 and I'm here to meet with my unknown kinfolks. My Norwegian is not that good but I can manage if you speak slowly".

Her hand was already out and the older looked a bit confused for a moment. Overwhelmed by her picturesque charm and openness. Who was to dismiss a beautiful young woman coming towards him with her hand out.

Apart from odd visits to the library in Hamar and such, his only contact with the female sex was with his Jensine, quite elderly his maid. Well and then the family of course, but their visits had become rare.

They didn't come for Sunday dinners anymore; in the old days it was more or less a rule. But since his dear Ragna passed close to 30 years ago, then he had to realize that it didn't go without saying that his children and grandchildren should come to the Sunday dinner. Oh yes, he was of course invited to them, but when he had retired then he was considered of less and less interest. Both his sons had their careers in brokerage, ever so distant from judicial and local quarrels.

He felt intuitively that this woman coming from the great unknown could be his way back to focus. He bowed to his dog to gain time, patted him behind the ears and then he straightened up with a big smile and a welcome to the Judges house. "I beg you excuse me for the rather unpleasant reception, the barking of the dog etc., and not least for my tenue".

Well, she was standing there in jeans and a three quarter long red coat, no makeup, she wasn't in need for it, only used a touch of lipstick and she had a cross of silver hanging to her neckless, open white blouse. No heels to the Italian shoes, no socks to her ankles. Quite fitting to young people's style, they might even call her cool. She had this magic and at the same time elegant posture that even women in Paris envied the women from Odesa.

Her hair was in braids as had once Yulia Timoshenko, Ukraine's earlier prime minister and this strengthened the impression of a young, but independent person. Now in Norway hunting for facts and they both knew that she was to get them right here.

"We don't have young artists coming visit us here that often. The more you are very, very welcome. And I take it for granted that you will stay for dinner, maybe even for breakfast? But first we have to see how the evening develops, right? For sure I know almost everything you will like to know and I have most answers to your questions, maybe all. Let's go into my study where tea is being served. Yes, you were indeed expected to come". He laughed quite bouldering.

So, she had hit it with her presentation, by starting off with Trygve, her great grandfather and she had hit jackpot not least with her choice of tenue. Now, it was time for all the questions and for all the answers.

THE JUDGE'S FARMHOUSE

"I have turned my library into being my study now" He begged her excuse the flow of papers onto his desk. "You still do process?" "No but I have taken special interest in old, not resolved cases, not only from the county but from all over Norway".

She was tempted to ask if this activity had contributed to resolving cases, but decided instantly to change theme. "I drove by the new opera house when coming up from Oslo. I hope I shall have time to visit it, but clearly, I didn't come to Norway to do just that". "No for sure you did not". He looked at her with compassion. "Sugar or suzettes? Of course, the young ones are worried about their waistline, but no way you have such worries", he smiled.

"No, ballet has been my main interest and of course my main engagement at the Odesa Opera, before that I spent several years at the Russian National School of Ballet in Moscow, and finally one year at the Bolshoi". "Did you not stay there for 1 ½ years?" Suddenly he came aware of his slip of the tongue, but she saved him from what could have been an awkward situation by not commenting on his question. It was clear to her now that he had been quite thorough in his research about her. "Yes, I almost forgot that they lent me out to some guest parts at the Kiev ballet".

"I'm sorry, I should not have started on this art train, as you know well, I came here to know more about my family, and of course the connection between the Elvegårds, not to forget Eva, for sure I'm going to visit her".

He looked at her, more like examining her this time and was much more concentrated now, obviously he didn't want to have more slips of his tongue. "Can we not start with you? Is Lars still alive?" My grandfather died three months ago and showed me clearly that he was never a Nazi. At the end of the war, he worked as a doctor and a surgeon for the Russians and later also for the partisans. After the war he had a large group of patients to whom he worked for free. Well, they were his own so to speak".

"What do you mean by that Theresa?" "Lars was half Jewish and he married a Jewish girl and they had a child together. She was my grandmother. In his later years he worked only for the Jewish people and following Hitler's definition it is clear that if mother or grandmother was Jewish then Lars in this case was considered 100% Jewish as well".

The old Judge was seemingly confused at this point. "Do you mean that your great grandfather, he was a Jew? Unthinkable, I knew him all his life and I knew his kinfolks as well". "No, but my great grandmother, Lars' mother, the wife of Trygve, she was a Finnish Jew from what once was known as Karelen".

He had become ever so quiet now. Maybe it had occurred to the old man that labeling Lars as a betrayer to his country no way was justifiable, least not totally. Could he the old Judge, when he was in office have misjudged the situation totally taking it out on his old friend Trygve, the county medic? He had to sit down the old man. Evidently this was tough to him. "But your grandfather was reported killed in action following the great battle at Vinnitsa.

I remember his old mate coming home here with his Death Mark. Trygve received it from this Loke before the latter reported himself to the Council for traitors to Norway, ready to take his punishment. Well, yes, both of them had enlisted together to the SS. And remember Theresa, it would have been impossible for the courts to free Lars without freeing a great number of others. To be pardoned for lack of consciousness, spur of the moment might have gone well for those of 16, 18 or 20 enlisting to the regular German army, but not for anyone enlisting to the SS.

And Theresa, don't you forget his contract was for one year and no way he had needed to renew it".

"What you are saying now is plainly bull, big excuse for the expression Judge. I'm sure Trygve told you exactly what happened, now you listen up!

They were all to spend the first six months at Sennheim. But Lars stayed only three months there as he was asked to join the Cadet school in southern Germany. From there he left as soon as possible to fulfill his Medical in Berlin, prime subject Field-medicine, specializing in surgery.

Even with this extreme tempo, all this had to take time and finally he was allocated to the Odesa Oblast for practicing. What do you think would have happened if he had cut it short after one year, gone home and started to fulfill his education at Ullevål Hospital? No way he would have his degree till the war was well over considered that the medical institutions here in Norway never approved of education done elsewhere.

And how do you think his fellow students and the exam board would have looked at a man coming straight from the front, first as an SS soldier, later an SS officer?"

"But Theresa, he wanted to go to Finland to fight the Bolsheviks, defend his mother's land, right so?" "But he didn't make it, the war was long gone when finally, he got three months leave to serve as a field-medic and surgeon there in Karelen.

No doubt about it, he would never have made doctor in this country, not in many, many years and on top of it all with a judgment from the courts, as being a traitor to his country. Such a judgment could probably have stopped him from final medical exams and his right to practice medicine at all. Not to forget that he might have lost his Norwegian citizenship and would have been judged to lose all his belongings and of course his right as an heir".

"You seem to have studied this very closely Theresa". "Not doing it would have been an offence to you, my counterpart, I shall have to call you just that. And what more, I have read my grandfather's diary; it is for you to read it provided you swear to me not to destroy it but you shall hand it back to me first thing in the morning, undamaged. And I want this in writing!" "You are not in Ukraine now Theresa. Here in this country a man stands to his words, but you shall have it as you want it even if I for my part don't deem it at all necessary.

I shall spend the night reading it but now let's go and have dinner and during the meal you can tell me all about your life in Ukraine, I hope you will do that Theresa?"

His maid, yes, she was a cook as well, she had really put her mind to this meal. The table was beautifully laid with special roses from the garden, damask and high glasses. The silver cutlery was from old ages, the same were the plates in pewter. The old Judge was at his best now introducing here to the meal: "Mushrooms from the forest picked by the maid and rolled in Norwegian camembert from goat and flamed with the best French liquor. Flambé but not burnt, restaurants always maltreat the food due to shortness of time. Port right through, an alternative being the world's best Cremant, even the French mistake this one for being Champagne, the latter is three times as costly in Norway. Pity with the Cremant, we could have had that one right through the meal. But my own Cockburn Port shall be with us again to the desert".

The trout from a mountain spring came on the table followed by a young Chablis. "By the way, do you know how many types of Chablis there is?" But she cut him short. "Your maid told me that you have your own well up here, right so?" "Meaning what?" "To this mountain trout I would have preferred fresh Norwegian water from the mountains, please!" She let him no choice the old gentleman.

Then the goat cheese was back, this time accompanied by homegrown raspberries and the renowned Cockburn.

She put to her mind that he willingly spoke about food and drink, in fact all that had nothing to do with the postwar trials and settlements for those having betrayed the country, nor did he talk about anything related to the kinfolks of Lars. Did he save himself until he was to read the diary, or was he on his tiptoes to avoid any possible mistakes on his part, that he would next morning have to apologize for once he had read the diary? Yes, it had to be that way. And she decided to let him have it as he wanted. She wasn't at all here to cultivate animosity.

"I would like it to have an early evening Theresa, you understand why and the night isn't that long up here in the north". Night, it was like full daylight even now at 9 o'clock in the evening and the maid had said that with this weather they were likely to have now, then the night wouldn't be dark except for the very few hours between midnight and 3 o'clock and possibly not even in that short period of time.

"Good luck with your reading then Judge!" "That formal now Theresa?" "Well, it is in your capacity as county Judge that you are to read the diary, is it not?"

But he didn't seem to grasp her comments and there was only a faint goodnight when she thanked him for the excellent meal. Maybe he was already back there, back in 1945?

THE NIGHT AT THE JUDGE'S

The Judge's library was quite extensive. A poem of Nordahl Grieg was framed there on the wall. "To the Youth", to all those that sacrificed all to their country, like her grandfather meant he had just done for his mother's Karelen.

Among all the books about the young heroes she picked two, one by Max Manus and the other one by Shetlands Larsen. Both books were about young heroes having chosen the right side as viewed by the public at large. But to these guys there had been no choice apparently. It was the Germans that were the attackers and per definition it then was the Germans they were to fight. But none of these heroes had a mother from the Bolshevik occupied Karelen as had her grandfather. It wasn't the Germans that had made her kinfolks over in Finland suffer, but the Bolsheviks. They had removed the tombstones at great grandmother's cemetery east in Karelen and then plowed the graves to be fields for potatoes. The ground was of course perfect to that.

She shredded by the thought of the disgraceful treatment of the graves of her great grandmothers' relatives. Maybe there even popped up some relative when they were doing the plowing, these Bolsheviks, or maybe even an arm or even a skull with a bullet hole in. They have burned the churches and now it was all Russian and there were no traits from the Karelian Finns, all gone forever. This was all happening at the time when her beloved Ukraine had become the Bolsheviks closest allied, still only "the little brother" as the Russians called her home country.

Her mind was back to the question of right or wrong side, so what was all this about? Well, Norway was occupied, but as she had read about it, it might as well have been England and France taking the land like they attempted to do in the Jøssing Fjord and later Narvik. Churchill, the prime minister of the Uk had set his mind to it, but didn't get the House supporting him.

And what about the Norwegian merchant navy? 2nd largest at the time. They were handsomely paid, sailing for England and the Allies, but they didn't have a choice, did they? In fact, they were more like a prize, were they not?

There wasn't much to be found in the books of the two heroes except for their last four adventures and the courage they had shown in their battles. But then, then she came to the chapters about Telavaag and the massacre in the West Country.

The SS and the Gestapo that she read about, they did not act like soldiers, but like the worst animals, quite like the soldiers her grandfather had encountered among the Bolsheviks on the East front.

She thought of the horrors she had read about in diary, the horrors imposed by the Russians, especially their Siberian units; pregnant women were split up and they even grilled the babies they took from their mothers' wombs. And he had written about others cutting of the genitals of German soldiers, then showed them into their mouths while they were still alive these soldiers, finally to be strung up by their ankles in trees close by. Other German soldiers where hog tied, then thrown into some vessel filled with water and left to freeze to death, 40 degrees below, totally naked and with their private parts cut off.

When her grandfather first had told her about these atrocities, she had begged him to stop telling such lies. But they were not lies. He had shown her pictures from precisely such atrocities. Pictures he had saved for the international courts, but no one seemed to have been interested and later grandfather had realized how dangerous it was to show these pictures to anyone.

Hungry Schäfer dogs on the German side were free to tear their masters in pieces and eat precisely their masters, to great pleasure for the Russian soldiers watching it all.

A partisan said that they later skinned the dogs and barbecued them. Food was in great need.

It was now close to 2 o'clock in the night and she had no sleep. She had seen one carafe with Cognac down in the library and she sneaked herself quietly down the stairs with only her red coat around her. She was standing there barefoot like a thief caught in the night. "You as well, I mean you couldn't sleep either?" No accusation to the Cognac. "No", she said somewhat ashamed, being a thief in someone's house. "The history came close to me, well let me have a double", he cut through.

"Norway, it's beautiful, this my kinfolks' homeland". She was standing by the window. "I was traveling through parts of the Karelen on my way to Norway. Her throat went thick now, she had to compose herself, change theme. "Did you know my Great Grandfather Trygve that well?" The Judge was already on his way to his room, but stopped by the door. "Your great grandfather became one of my closest friends, disregarded of our age difference. We were both to become old lonely men". "But you still did not know that his wife was Jewish and that my grandfather, the SS-doctor was a Jew?"

BREAKFAST AND ADMISSIONS

"For how long have you had this so-called diary, Theresa?" "I am not sure I like this allegation, so-called, Judge. You better take this back, or rephrase the question as the judge in court would have said". His breath went heavy now. "Yes, your Honor, and how long have you had access to this diary from your grandfather?" "Since his death, barely three months back". "Did you know that he wrote a diary?" "No, not until he told me about it just before he died". "Do you think that your mother, or even your grandmother knew about it at all?" "I don't know why you ask these questions, but I imagine that you would like to know if they may have influenced on the content of the diary. I on my part don't think so. I imagine that he had planned to send it to Eva if she was still alive. Thus, she would have gotten first-hand knowledge about the life of her fiancée and why it turned out as it did".

"Well then Theresa, what's on your mind now?" I have by coincidence run into this young Trygve or Junior as you call him. You have this saying in Norwegian haven't you, 'he was like squeezed out of the nose' of his grandfather Lars". "Are you telling me that Junior might be your grandfather's grandchild and that the two of you then should be 2. nd cousins?" "Yes, but I haven't met with Eva as yet, but for all that it is worth this can easily be established by DNA".

"No one has ever mentioned this to me, but for sure Eva may have thought it to be like that and then I guess my good friend Trygve would have done the same".

"But Judge, my grandfather Lars he was never to know about the baby, that he had a son and an heir to both farms. Why did no one wright to my grandfather about the baby? Nor Eva and not even his parents?"

"I cannot answer to them, now they are both dead. But for sure they might have had their reasons, not least when Lars was declared fallen at the front halfway through the war and Eva, she would have feared the worst even when Lars was still officially alive. Feared that he would just be rid of her, following the rape".

"The rape? And by whom? I haven't heard about that until now, is there something I should know about?"

"Maybe Eva herself would come to tell you all about it, but as long as I was not to know about it, then I reckon she was keen on having it all concealed". He had stood up now. Enough was enough. But she wasn't done, by far she was not. "What now then, and why do you cut it short here?"

"Eva's dad, Tore came to me with an envelope short before he passed. 'What is this to me then Tore?' 'Well, one never knows Karstein, when a case gets outdated'. 'Thinking about what then Tore?' 'I often think about if Lars is really dead, or maybe he is in a Russian concentration camp or whatever. The same thoughts are harbored by Eva.

Someday he or his descendants, if he ever has any, they might come to Norway, being interested in what happened here on the farm during the years of war'. 'Tore, I don't know what is in your envelope, but why don't you go see Trygve, I presume the content in the envelope has something to do with Eva and Lars and who is then nearer to know about it than our good friend Trygve?' 'Eva would never have forgiven me if I did so. That's why I say that this envelope must not be opened till both Trygve and I have passed'. 'But could not Eva have kept this envelope to herself?' 'No, she doesn't even know that there is an envelope. She wants all to be forgotten so that she may carry on with her life quietly, mend her pain, mend her sorrow both two Lars as well as to the dreadful event'.

'She lost her boy Roald very early and we shall think as she does, that Lars is his father. Even if the vicar wrote 'father unknown' in the church registry?' 'Yes, I know, quite so'. 'And it remained that way until Trygve insisted and claimed the fatherhood to Lars on his behalf. Then the church annual was corrected. Lars was officially dead at the time and there were no protests to this amendment, neither were their demands for a DNA.

Fate had it as you know that Roald was not to live for very long, neither did his wife, Ingrid. Well, you do remember about the car accident in Sweden and that only the baby or Junior as we now call him was brought home alive'.

'But what does Junior know about his grandfather, yes it has to be Lars has it not?' 'Yes, that's what he thinks and that is painful enough as Lars would have been labeled a Nazi, if he had survived and later come home.

People are not likely to forget about such things here in the rural county. Even when Junior came home after seven years study to be a doctor, he noted that people around wouldn't have any talks about his grandfather. And some stayed away from both Junior and old Trygve, on the ground that Lars had enlisted to the SS. But no one of course asked for his reasons. He going to Karelen in Finland to fight for his mother's land against the Bolsheviks. And this Karelen, what was that? Just a small piece of Finland that the Russians just enacted, although after many years of bloody fighting and now it was gone, no one ever to talk about it'.

'But Tore, you have to come to the very point; what is it with this envelope and its content?' 'I must insist that Trygve shall never know about its content, nor shall Junior. And Eva of course must not know that there is an envelope at all. But I came across Eva's diary and I must admit that I feel like a crook now, when I tell you that I copied the part that is from wartime. But believe me, I did it solely to the end that future relatives shall know what happened if they ever were to ask'. 'But why can I not ask Eva directly?' 'That's precisely what I am trying to tell you; she would never ever dwell with that time again'.

'And now you mean that I shall?' 'Well, yes if you are asked about it'. 'Why not just take the envelope with you to the grave without having it opened at all. And then there will forever be a lid on this tragic story?'

"And what then Judge? Did you stick to your promise? Obviously not!" Theresa face carried anger now. But seemingly he didn't care for her look, nor the accusing tone of her voice.

"Eva stayed unmarried and then her father Tore died, and later then Trygve died as well, so finally there were only two back; Eva at the upper farm and the grandchild Junior at the lower one, a rightful heir to both farms. Nedre was for him to inherit, even if it was Eva that now owned it, according to the documents". The Judge looked at her as he wanted to say that this is a close to the story. But they both knew that it was here it was to start. "And you then Judge, you are still here even though you have retired and there is a young man running your former office?" "Yeah, that's correct". "Then there are three of you living and still having your parts in the drama. Because it is a drama Karstein?" They were coming onto first names now. Something had happened to him as he evolved the story, or was it the meeting as such with Theresa and above all the impressions from the diary that finally had gotten to him? No way he looked as strong and vital as he presented himself only late yesterday afternoon.

"Yes of course", he mustered after some time. "Yes of course it is a drama. You haven't asked me straight or maybe you did ask me? But when the two of them, Tore and Trygve had passed and no one came and asked about anything and Eva, I hadn't seen her in 10 years, then I had to break my promise. That's the way it was and I don't know if I am to ask the dead ones for forgiveness. If you hadn't shown up, this envelope would have gone with me into the grave".

"So, you did open the envelope then Karstein? When you did that, did you feel that Tore looked at you from the grave or from the Heavens? Or was it maybe your best friend Trygve who questioned you if your judgment would be as harsh now over the boy that never came home? So, tell me now please, what were the feelings of having read not only once, but twice, the letter from the grave?" "Do you know what's in this document Theresa?" "No, but I have read one diary full of despair, and I can imagine from what you have told me, or what you have not told me about the rape, that the text copied from Eva's diary is just as gruesome, possibly much worse". "Should we burn it together then, let no one get access to the content?"

"I don't know Karstein. I suggest we skip lunch, least as far as I am concerned. I think I shall have myself a long walk and do some thinking. Think through if I really want to know about all this, or if I shall content myself with what Eva will tell me".

"Very sensible Theresa, utterly sensible. But thank you for coming to me so we were able to bring things out in the open before I pass. You have been a great helper to me, much more than you can imagine".

She gave him a faint smile. "Karstein, yes, I call you Karstein now, like you call me Theresa. Two grim fates we are facing here. One dead and what about the other? I wonder if Eva has really led a life, once she got the message of the death of her fiancée? Maybe she has just existed sort of?

But now I shall go up to Hamar and see if they can get me a proper dictionary, Norwegian to Russian, Russian to English or something like that. I feel there are a lot of shades in our conversations". "You do that Theresa and give my best to Halvorsen, the man at the bookstore".

"But Karstein, before I leave, did it never strike you that Eva's father, the leader of the resistance group, him never saying anything negative about this son in a law to be, having enlisted to the much-hated SS? It seems clear to me at least, that Tore no doubt had realized that Lars's enlisting was all connected to him standing up for Karelen and that it had nothing to do whatsoever with Hitler!"

But the old judge didn't comment to that and she left, wondering if she ever would have an answer to this crucial question.

FAREWELL TO KARSTEIN

She wasn't back till late evening as she got problems with her rented car and no one at the Judge's home answered when she tried to phone.

When she finally reached back, it was already late and she contemplated the weak sunrays, probably the last of this day and there was no dog barking this time. But there was light from the windows in several rooms and when she parked her car at the backside there was already three cars there. Gosh, had he got guests? She should have been prepared to that and have reserved hotel for the night.

The maid Jensine, was even more pale in her face than usual, still she was wearing the same uniform when showing her into the living room. There he sat the old Judge in his usual, special chair holding un envelope in his right hand like in cramp, his head slightly bowed to one side. Two younger men were standing at his side, a little boy was holding hand to one of them. They all looked up when Theresa came in. "My grandfather is dead", said the little boy, "he just sat there dead, right so Jensine?" "Yes", she nodded. But the boy went on, "who are you then?" "Hush Ola", said the man, for sure his father. "No, no it's OK", Theresa said. "I am the Great Grandchild to Trygve at Nedre Elvegård. I stayed here last night. But what has happened? Has Karstein just died on me? Are you his two sons?" "Yes", they introduced themselves. "And I am Ola," said the little boy.

The younger of the two looked at Jensine. "Should we not move him to the sofa until the doctor come? And for sure you have called the doctor?" Yes of course she had.

His two sons then lifted him over to the sofa. The envelope fell out of his hand and Little Ola was quick to pick it up. "To Theresa", he had written on the front of it. "Are you the one?" "Yes," she said and she was handed the envelope.

"Do you know what's the content of it?" The younger one was eager to know. "Yes, I know much of it, but he wanted for us to look through it and talk about it today". "So, then you know what it is all about then?" "Yes, I know that it is about my family and it was to be burned at his death, well if I hadn't come here now to learn what happened in a very sad part of the lives of my dear ones". "Then it looks like you made it then Theresa. That is your name?" "Yes, and right so, I just made it. We had a lovely time together last night, yes even this morning".

So where do you come from and what kind of work are you doing?" "I come from Odesa by the Black Sea and my work is in opera and ballet". "That young?" "Yes, I've just got lucky so I shall go home now to my Puccini and my Mimi". She burst out with it just like that. "But first I shall go visit Eva up at Øvre". "Oh yes, the daughter of Tore". Obviously the older one knew of the farmers around. "You did say Puccini did you not?" "La Boheme", said the younger one. "Yes", she said affirmingly. So, they weren't quite lost here out in the rural country these boys. It seemed clearly like an obligation to ask her to stay the night. "You have the guest room from yesterday so?"

The two brothers were clearly done with their father, not much compassion to see there and if she wanted to stay, then it would have been to stand at the side of the one who really cared, Jensine. But this meeting with the two of them, seemingly cold and impersonal was definitely not to her liking. She gave each one of them a visiting card with mobile number and of course they handed her theirs as well. "I do thank you, but I shall go to the hotel now". "For how long are you staying here in Norway? By the way you speak quite good Norwegian, even so it seems better for us to continue in English". "I don't really know, but I shall let you know later on, maybe I should come to the funeral?" Well, yes, they were to tell her.

Even though Lars had passed away without his beloved Eva at his side, for sure they still loved one another. Eva was the last word he cried out before he was gone and yes, his grandchild had been there with him to the end with her love for him. The contrast to the goodbye from the two sons to their dad Karsten was ever so striking she felt.

Karstein was never to experience his sons being close anymore, if ever. Well, what was it to her and what did she really know about it. But at the end of his days the only one being close to him was his Jensine. She had been there as a faithful employee for more than 50 years; while no one of his own folks seemed to care for him any longer. To them he was of little interest. A great man he was, and now he should be off to the grave.

"How long will you stay with us?" It was the receptionist at the Radisson Blue Hotel asking. Hamar was too close, so she had chosen Lillehammer.

But Theresa didn't catch his question. She was still with the old Judge, her Karstein. "Excuse me miss", he tried once more, this time in English. "Excuse me miss, but?" She turned to him. "Oh, you are asking for my credit card". She had to come back to reality now. How long she was going to stay? How was she to answer that question. "Let's say two nights then and could I please have the menu for room service, thanks".

CRYING AND MORE CRYING

"My dearest Theresa. Do prepare yourself for crying and sorrows. I don't feel at all well and maybe I have passed before you come back. I have come to value you a lot and maybe I shouldn't have left you alone with the envelope, as I count on that you will not burn it until you have read the content.

You best prepare yourself to a lot of crying. But being the grandchild even to Eva, sort of, then you are for certain a strong one and no doubt you have the strength from your great grandfather Trygve as well. He was a good man". The old Judge said nothing about Lars, but then he had never met him.

Now it was only Eva back there and Junior of course. Did he look after Eva? He was after all her grandchild. The old sad story from Eva's Diary read as follows:

"The Nazi Jens had during all the years had a crush on me, ever since school days. And I have always turned him down. Short after the breakout of the war, dad got a central position in a resistance group. So, now when this Nazi leader was coming on to me stronger and stronger, my dad asked me to treat him politely and correct. Sort of assurance to my dad's activities, never to be questioned I guessed.

He came to visit up on the farm several times even after Lars and I was engaged, but he knew nothing of our engagement this Nazi Jens.

When Lars left to defend his mother's land and in an SS uniform, then the road apparently was open to the Nazi leader. I then had to ask my future father-in-law Trygve, to talk to my dad and have him stop using me like a shield. Old friendship was set to test and when my dad Tore demanded that I should continue entertaining the Nazi to safeguard my dad's resistance group, then finally it got too much to Trygve.

"If Eva consents to it Tore, then she can move in with us, even today for that matter".

They never talked to each other again on the matter the two neighbors. I knew nothing about this before long, so I stayed on with my daddy.

Then came the night when dad was away on a secret meeting, about a month after Lars had left. Jens the Nazi came to the farm after the milking was done and the hired hands had gone home this Saturday night. So, I was alone at home sitting there by myself writing a letter to Lars, my fiancée.

It was then that a car with the Nazi standard drove into the courtyard at full speed. Jens was driving himself that night. My dear Diary, no driver and you probably anticipate what's coming now. I shut down the lights and bolted the door, but Jens knew quite well what there might be for him and a locked door was nothing to him being tall and strong.

So, I just sat there in my nighty and felt this man's greedy eyes on me. "I shall not touch you Eva, but you know what will come if you don't bend, you know I shall have you whatsoever."

My body was trembling by his words. I tried to divert him by offering him more coffee and got myself into a gown. "Should you not take your coat off in case father is soon to return?" He just laughed at me. "No, your father will not be back in a long time. Do you know where he is tonight?" "Well of course I know, he is at a meeting in the County Council". Jens had himself a big laugh. "Just you go on believing that. No, he is not at the County Council. He is at a meeting in the resistance group, officially a group for shooting training, but we know it's a real resistance camp. I shall have you Eva, but voluntarily", he gave himself another laugh. Yes, I did say voluntarily or, by your free will, if you would rather have it that way.

Now here I have something for you to think about. First if it wasn't for my protection, then your father would have gone straight to the camp at Grini and then further on to Auswitch. I have enough proof on him and the resistance group he is the leader of. This group has liquidated a number of my colleagues at Lillehammer. Very smart of him that to carry out operations outside of his own district. I have had your dad under surveillance for a long time. I can of course spare him, but his group has to go! Be sure of that.

But that's not all my dear. Your fiancée, yes, I do know about that as well, he is soon in training at Sennheim Germany. He shall later be allocated to our elite division, Gross Deutschland".

"And how do you know about all this then?" "Your Lars haven't got the clue about all this but I, I have arranged this with his superiors to make sure that he shall stay away from here for a long time, he might even be killed there at the East front, or the Russians may capture him and he will rot in their camps".

"He is not going to the East front; he shall go to Finland and fight the Bolsheviks there!"

Big laugh again. "Believe whatever you like Eva, but I know the better of it. But if you don't come with me by your free will, then I shall make sure that he is sent directly to the East front and be placed in a so-called Punishment company. One out of ten officers' lives more than a month in that place, privates maybe a day or two.

So, then it is all up to you, my friend. It is for you to decide whether this will be empty words or not. I shall give you one week to consider it all and if you don't bend by then, I shall start with your father. He will subsequently be moved from here next Friday. If you tell them about all this and he escapes to Sweden or wherever, then he is finished in this community, never to return and you, you shall be transported to my mother's, while you are preparing for our wedding. And if you don't agree to this, then I shall have this letter sent to Division to whom your fiancée is to report, once the training session is over!"

He then showed me a letter from the High Command of Norway, of course it was fake and in German. He knew I couldn't understand a word of it, but I could see the name of Lars several places in the letter.

"I shall leave you for now Eva. Do think about your closest!" Did he plan to kiss me? Oh, I shuddered on the spot looking at the big body least 120 kilos, a greasy hair and open buttons, his uniform too small to hold him in.

Then he was gone and I could cry my heart out. I should have been proud for my cool in this encounter, but my desperation overpowered everything. Then I heard my daddy at the door downstairs. "Are you still up my girl? And what has happened to the front door?" Jens was here and he sort of collided with the door frame, he is that big as you know". "Well, then I shall have to repair it tomorrow then".

"But how was your meeting, Dad? Did you come to make any decisions?" I had to pull myself strongly together now to keep my face. But on my inside, there was only room for sorrows and tears. "Well, we most certainly did, at long last, but all the separate interests at times makes it difficult to reach common grounds". "So, what was your most interesting topic then?" "I presume you would not be interested in all the details this late in the evening". "Yes please, you tell me". And he started to talk about buying up grounds in connection with a new road project. "Just you stop it, Daddy! You can't go on lying for long, can you?" He got red now, all the way down to his chest. "What do you mean child? Lying? How can you ever speak to your dad that way?" Now, should I just jump into it? Tell him all, tell him that yes, the Nazi had it all figured out now. And that her daddy was on top of the list to be detained. Tell him about the consequences to him and not least to Lars! And to myself then!

"I am no longer a child Dad and stay calm now. Don't be silly and start calling someone until you have heard me through!"

Then she gave him a full account of Nazi Jens's threats. "And Daddy if you go on the run, then Lars would be deported to a punishment company at the East front and I shall be forced down to Jens's mother".

"No, I shall not run away, but I shall be gone for three days as from tomorrow. I have to make a trip to Sweden. No risk for that one at all my girl". Thank heavens, no more my baby now.

"We shall have to do some serious thinking now. Jens said he would be back in a week, not so?" "Yes, and then he wanted to have a firm answer from me. The answer being that I say yes to his proposal so he then can go to the vicar and have him prepare for the announcement in the church".

"I don't need ask you what you think about all this, but there has to be a solution. I shall be back on Thursday, give me time till then. He is not to come back till Sunday as you told me?" "Yes, it is on Sunday that he will be back for dinner. Invited himself sort of".

My dad was already gone when I came down to breakfast. Our hired hand said Tore had left by 6 o'clock. He was picked up by a car down at the road-crossing.

I went down to Nedre and wanted to know if there were news about Lars. But there was no one at home. Trygve was of course in Finland, but there was no answer from the annex either.

The Swastika was flying at the flagpole and two soldiers were on guard by the main house. The door was opened and the colonel came out, looking his best in his uniform as always.

"The servants are up at the hill farm and madame has gone to Hamar", he said in broken Norwegian. "Would you care for a cup of coffee miss?" I bowed to him, shook my head and uttered a "no thanks". He pretended not to understand, so I squeezed out a "Danke Nein" and made a run for it around the corner.

The days went by and I tried to dislodge the upcoming visit from Jens Nazi. I wished for Lars to be here, or Trygve for that matter. My dad was due home Wednesday night and then it would all be better.

But on Tuesday night there was a Mercedes car coming at high speed and braked so the shingle was thrown in all directions. A soldier with helmet and a rifle immediately came out. He then changed seats with a big man emerging from the driver's seat. Oh my God, it was Nazi Jens coming towards my front door in not so steady a pace.

It was obvious that he had been drinking. This could turn out to become really dangerous. In split seconds he was banging at the door. Now it was too late for me to run away.

I opened my window from the 2nd floor. "You are waking up the entire house Jens. You were not to come back until Sunday and we are all asleep here!"

"Since when did the hired hands start to sleep in the main house? And I know that your dad is not at home, so you might as well open the front door or I shall smash the lock".

"I shall be down in 10 minutes, need to put some clothes on". "No, you shall come down right now. Just you put on a nighty if you think it's too cold to you!" He started to bang on the door and I no longer had any choice. "How do you know that my father is not sleeping in his room?" "Your dad is in Sweden; we have surveilled him all the time. Not me of course, but my men and the Swedish border police as well. We work closely together, see. The Swedes want to have this illegal crossing of their border by so-called good Norwegians come to a halt". He took a flask from his inner pocket and had himself a large drink. The belts that came afterwards were ghastly and smelled ever so sewer. I twisted myself by the thought me having to share bed with him, unless my daddy came up with a viable solution.

But what now if he got really hammered? I was already feeling quite unsecure. "What about coffee Jens?" Maybe I could have him sobered up with the coffee. But I was no way fast enough and as I tried to squeeze away from his long arms, my nighty hitched to the edge of the table and even worse, it was pulled off by my movement all the way.

I was totally lamed by this terrifying situation and in seconds I saw that all I was covered by slowly dumped to the floor and I was standing there stark naked.

Even at the distance of close to two meters I could hear the sound of his breath and I then knew that trying to escape from him, that would only make him even more excited. My thoughts were with Lars but he was of course far away.

I carefully bowed to pick up my nighty. Did it ever so slowly so my breasts wouldn't look even larger, but it was too late, the bump on his trousers was enormous and I knew quite well what was to come next.

His grunt was like the one from a pig. "You are mine now Eva!" He then came to me, lifted me as I weighed nothing at all. The door to my room he kicked up and then he just threw me onto the bed. I was lying there all naked, terrified for a moment, until I managed to pull the cover over me.

"This is rape Jens and I shall have you reported to the police!" "Yes, just you do that and then both Lars and your father will go down the drain, remember I told you about that last time, but now Eva I'm just going to have you". He got his clothes off in a hurry and the enormous dick was out, pointing halfway upwards.

Now, I was to be taken like another whore, but would it do me any good to fight? No one could hear me if I cried out, none except for the driver, but he was working for Jens and for sure he knew well why Jens had come here.

His dick was that big that I was truly afraid to get hurt, so maybe I should just receive it and then I should live? Hopefully he would not try for my bottom, then I certainly would have been seriously damaged by his enormous tool.

"Wait, I need something to oil myself with, you are that big". But he would not let go of me so he just carried me to where I knew there would be some Vaseline. And then I was carried back to the bed.

I put on a lot of cream, thought of my darling Lars and then it was only to open up, have him come to me with this enormous tool. I hoped for him to be satisfied with only one run. Maybe he would come faster if I touched these balls, and yeah, I could now feel the pain when he came all the way in and his pulse was going faster and the smell from him was worse than from the pigs.

My darling Lars, please help me to stay strong! Maybe it is our child that is now growing inside me. I closed my eyes and after him having 4 maybe 5 takes right to the bottom of my vagina, then came the cry as from an ox. I was familiar with it when my dad had borrowed the great oxen at Nedre to have the cows copulated.

In spite of all the Vaseline I felt sore down there, very sore!"

Theresa couldn't take it no more. She switched off the telephones. Had long ago given up the thought of room service. Now she was just crying and crying. What a strong woman and what a strong love to her grandfather Lars. And how unjust wasn't the world? Just think about it how gruesome that the two would not be together in the end.

When Theresa woke up at 4 o'clock in the night, she found herself dressed like the evening before. She got herself something to drink. Looked out of the window and the sun was already coming up. She had a glance at the menu card. Yes, she was in Lillehammer and slowly her memory came back to her. Now where was the envelope and the letter? And why was she wet, down there?

She felt with a finger and it was stained with blood. She had to calculate. Yes, she had obviously got her monthly. One week early. This story from Eva had come on her too strong no doubt.

Her underwear and all, just blood-stained and the bed linen as well. First shower and then sort it out thereafter.

This hotel was well equipped and Theresa found tampons and subsequently was able to remove all and then called for the house made, still being asleep? But another one showed up and they both said sorry, most Theresa and no thanks, she should make the bed by herself. An hour later she was ready for coffee and started to read the final pages of the letter.

I then heard a banging on the door; it was the driver calling out for Nazi Jens. "Is it all OK Jens, you know they are waiting for us down at the captains?" "Be damned he cried back. Give me another 10 minutes".

His dick had gone soft now and he had fallen out, but he tried to kiss me with his piggy mouth, but I squeezed away. He then started to have a go at himself to have its stiffened again, but there was semen and Vaseline all over, so it didn't work.

"Damn, damn, next time I shall fuck you harder than ever, no one to disturb us then. You are good in bed my girl". I shrugged, my girl, that was for Lars to say, not this horrible Nazi.

He had now got dressed and was on his way out. "Come Saturday Eva, I shall be here to pick you up. Get your things in a bag and make sure not to forget the Vaseline. We shall definitely be needing it". He was finally gone and I could let myself cry out. Oh Lars, how is this to end now? Now that I am impure? Could it ever be the two of us again? And what about our baby?

I didn't know how long I was just lying there. But I knew that I was soon to throw up and then had to take off the bed linen, get it washed and not least wash myself. Oh, I was that rigid. It felt like I had been shattered down there when I tried to get on to my feet.

But I did not get far when I heard someone at the door. OMG is he back again? But now it was my dad! "Don't you dare come in here Daddy!" But it was too late, he saw me laying there totally naked and dirty. So, he turned halfway so he should avoid seeing me naked. "Don't come further into the room Daddy and don't look at me, Nazi Jens just left. I have been raped!"

Some hours later: Dear Diary, it is already late at night, but neither I nor my dad will be able to put this horrible event behind us and go to bed. For sure we know that none of us would catch any sleep at all.

I had washed myself, scrubbed myself and my thoughts were all with my Lars. But maybe he wasn't mine any longer? What was he to say, would I lose him now and what about the baby I knew I was carrying? Was he to grow up like a changeling? And what about Nazi Jens who would come to pick me up come Saturday? Was he to think that it was his baby and would I at all be capable of being his wife?

But Eva you are already his, I heard my inner voice. You have been taken as his own have you not? But could I live with this or should I venture take my own life? Would my daddy be capable to live with that? Having already lost his wife, my dearest mother?

Lars might not even come back from the war once it was over. OMG, what horrible thoughts I had to myself.

"Eva this dreadful happening it's for no one to know about and you shall never move down to Nazi Jens!"

"But dear you, how am I to avoid that? You know that I cannot sacrifice you, nor Lars and for sure it was no empty threats that came from Nazi Jens".

"No, I know that my child, but please never talk to anyone about what happened. Jens as well as his driver shall be gone by tomorrow". "But what about his mother?" "Well, she is already a loony so no one cares to what she is saying". "And what about his father then?" "They never talk to each other. His father is part of my resistance group. Don't ask me how all this is going to happen, but I leave now and please keep the door bolted in the evening".

"Oh Dad, you must be extra careful now. When do you think you will be back?" "I don't really know, but I didn't like to hear what Jens told you about the Swedish border-police. So, we shall have to take a different road over the border to Sweden this time". I clinched to my daddy, clearly knowing that the risk he was taking now was all for me. Maybe this will be the last time for me to see him alive? Suddenly he was gone.

Lars's father, Trygve, came up to me early afternoon. He asked for my daddy, but I had nothing to tell him except that he was on travel till Saturday. Trygve had intuitively understood that something was wrong up here. "I heard noises from a fast-driving car up here last night. Did something happen?"

Now, I had to put myself extra together. "No, it was only this Nazi Jens from down at Nes, he wanted to have a talk with dad. I gave him a cup of coffee and then he was off". "You shall be careful with him Eva". I felt I blushed. "Yes Trygve, but my dad says I shall be friendly, friendly so he doesn't turn into an enemy of my dad." "Don't be befriended either Eva". "Trygve, you know that it is your son and I who shall share the future together. Are there any news by the way?"

She was happy to change theme and now talk about Lars. "No, nothing new except that he hopes to soon get to Finland. That was the reason why he left from here in the first place. But I shall have to go now, patients are waiting". And he was off.

But I knew that Trygve knew something was wrong, but luckily, he had no clue to what had really happened. Totally ignorant that his son's fiancée had been raped the night before. Nor did he know about the threat about me being moved down to Nazi Jens come Saturday, and that this was a real threat. My poor Trygve, how would he react to all this?

Theresa wasn't able to put away the copy of Eva's Diary now, she was all too curious about the continuation of the drama up at Øvre.

In the afternoon a "Kubel Wagen" came on to the courtyard in full speed. Could it be Jens that was back that soon? But no, it was an SS- man and a Norwegian translator she knew from the grocery store.

"Where is your father?" "On travel somewhere, I don't know more about it". "And the hired hands, get them over here! On the double!" Soon the hired hand Ivar and the two maids came running.

"We have seen Jens traveling this way last night. Since then, there has been no sign of him nor his driver and the Mercedes has disappeared as well".

"Yes, he was here last night on a kind of a courtesy visit. As you know he has come visiting here many times before". "Was there something special about him?" "No, he was quite good humored had brought with him a flask in his inner pocket". "And the driver?" "I did not see him, but I heard he called for Jens after some time, saying they had to leave here, they were expected somewhere else, at some captains, yes that was it". "And you others, you were not here last night?" The servants looked terrified at each other and nodded; no, they did not stay here at night. "But was it that late?" "Yes", I said, "I had almost gone to bed". "But did Jens say anything special?" "No, nothing except that he would be back on Saturday to have a chat with my father". "They seemed to get on quite well Jens and your dad?" "Yes, as I said, he has been here a number of times over the last months, but is something the matter, has something happened?" He came close up to me now, whispering. "The Mercedes has been found in a lake by the Swedish border. Half the car was down in the water". "Jesus and what about poor Jens?" But it was dad and Lars I thought about right now. What would happen to them following this accident, if it was really an accident?

The SS- soldier was clearly irritated over the whispering from the translator. "Nothing here, nothing to be found, nobody knows nothing", the translator shouted to him. "We might just as well leave".

This was my dad's doing. But would he stay clear in an interrogation, would he keep his life and where was Jens and his driver? If they were found dead, then for sure there would be a reprisal.

I decided to go down to Trygve, wondering if he had any news. "No, all I know is that the car had been driving into the water at a bend of the road and that they were dredging in the water for the two missing. But do come back tonight, I'm certain my patients will have more to tell later in the day".

But my daddy was the first to come home already at 6 o'clock in the afternoon. He knew nothing about it all and I had to believe him. We were going together down to Trygve, but we had hardly come out from the porch, when a Mercedes with a motorbike escort run into the courtyard.

I recognized the SS-soldier and the translator from earlier in the day. But now there was a captain with the scull mark on is bonnet as well as on his jacket. No doubt he was the boss.

The servants were called out again but the questioning with them was quickly done with. A mere repetition of what had been told earlier in the day. No, they knew nothing. No, they had not seen Nazi Jens. No, Eva had been home, all day except for a short walk down to Nedre round midday. But when had Tore come home then? They didn't know as they had been out in the fields, but for sure it was less than one hour ago.

Now it was my turn. I had to repeat all that I had said earlier in the day. Yes, my father came home about an hour ago and that was all she knew about him. Were they able to see that I was lying and that I knew about my dad's visit from last night? For sure I could say nothing about it.

But did she know that her father was part of the resistance group? No, she hadn't the faintest idea and no way she believed it as dad and Jens seemed to have a good understanding and met quite frequently.

The questioning of me was translated. But the man with the scull mark did not look like it mattered to him at all. But then suddenly he came on to me and teared open my blouse. The top of the bitemark was clearly visible over the top and now he could see the marks from Jens's bite. "Is your fiancée not in the SS in our fatherland?" For sure I was quite pale in my face now. "Yes, he is Captain". "But in spite of that you mingle with other men and have bite marks, or should I be polite and call them kissing marks?" I knew that I should be very careful now. If I told the truth then there would have been an obvious revenge motive for my father. If I was characterized as a whore now, then the road would be ever so short to an officers' brothel in Oslo, rumors from the waiting room down at the surgery of Trygve.

I looked in despair at Ivar, the hired hand. At first, he flushed, then suddenly he got totally white to his face. "I was excessively drunk and had a go at her". "What a swine you are!" The whip took a blow over his face and left a line, fresh blood pumping.

"Imagine using violence at this girl whose fiancée is fighting at the front!" Oh, dear God, don't let this captain destroy Ivar. "Yes, yes, but he was very drunk and I got rid of him. He has served us faithfully for more than five years now".

My dad had kept quiet all the time, but when the captain pulled his pistol, he had to interfere and pray for the hired hand.

"The Germans, our allied are dependent on the food we can produce here at this farm. Without our hired hand it will be impossible to fill the quota set by the colonel, Captain. I have given the colonel down at Nedre a forecast to our expected production".

The captain called for the two SS-soldiers. They laid Ivar over a saw buck, and then the captain flogged him first and his whip drew blood. But when he got a stain of blood onto his polished riding boots, he gave the whip to the translator. "Better to have Norwegians whip Norwegians, but with real force, no less than 20!" Poor Ivar! Dad looked at me and there was reproach in his face, was there not?

The two maids, they saw what was done to Ivar, and they were questioning if the poor guy really had assaulted Miss. But Ivar, he took the blows without a sound. Blood was running from his body and down to the ground.

Now it was my dad's turn. "Why are you so often out on travel, you should have worked more on your farm instead!"

Obviously, they did not know that he was insurance agent as well. I was sent into the kitchen to pick up his travel-bag and I was super nervous as to what would come next.

"You understand German well?" "Yes, some at least Herr Hauptsturmführer". "So, you are well acquainted with Jens? Dad nodded again. "Answer yes or no!" "Yes, Herr Hauptsturmführer".

"OK then, but where were you last night between 23.00 hrs. and 1600 hrs. today?" This was obviously going to be awkward. The captain addressed the translator. "Put this question to him totally clear in Norwegian!" And the translator repeated it in Norwegian to my dad.

He seemed completely calm now my dad. Still, was this to be the crucial moment? The captain had pulled out his pistol again tapping at its stock. "I was in Gjøvik". "From when until when? And how did you travel?" "I arrived in Gjøvik last night at 20.00 hrs. by bus and train on the regular Gjøvik line". "Do you have documents, tickets to prove all this?" "For sure I have the ticket", he wanted to look for it in his pocket but then the captain had the pistol aimed at his chest. "Hans, he pointed to the translator, search it for the ticket". And it was found instantly. "Is this correct Hans?" "Yes, this ticket is stamped and it's all OK". "Who is to know if he came back by car, it is after all only question of a two hours' drive, so?"

"If the captain so wishes, then he can see copies of contracts I signed last night and this morning". "And where did you spend the night?" He was quick to answer. "At the farm of Rolf Nielsen out at Kapp". Do they have telephone on that farm?" "No, but his neighbor has telephone and Rolf may be summoned". The captain nodded to Hans the translator who immediately was at it. 20 minutes later it was all in the clear. My dad had spent the night at Rolfs farm.

The poor Ivar was still laying over the saw buck and the blood had started to coagulate. I knew that it would hurt when I was to wash it off and put on bandages. Maybe he wouldn't even let me do that? But why had he sacrificed himself? He must have known that Nazi Jens was here? The question was how would he have known about that? Was my secret not that secret after all?

"If we don't find the two missing alive Tore, then we shall be back for you!" They were ready to leave, when a sergeant and to SS- soldiers came speeding into the yard, saluting the captain.

The car has been brought out of the water now and they have found the Nazi leader and the driver, their colleague, the SS soldier Jacob. They both were drowned. No signs of outer wounds to neither of them, no, except for some shrub wounds and a possible broken collarbone. "It seems like it has been an accident due to high speed and a puncture", concluded the sergeant.

The words of the captain were ice cutting like a blow from the whip. "That is for the Accidents Commission to decide. Now start up full investigation and hand me a list on the possible reprisaliens, five to each of them and you, he looked at Tore, you shall be topping that list". He nodded to the sergeant. "Make sure of that!"

It was evident to the captain that this was all very fishy.

No, I was not allowed to wash poor Ivar. The housemaids got that privilege, but I had to talk to him. But my father was the first one to address it. "You owe Ivar big time Eva! Our Ivar had his mind to the situation and immediately knew that it would have resulted in serious problems if the captain were to know that Jens had visited you, had been forward and no doubt he would have claimed that you invited him to it. The codex of the SS would have made it impossible with an assault at you". "Yes, but Father", I tried to cut him short. "Nazi Jens was not a member of the SS". "No, but according to the captain, when Jens was visiting together with this SS- soldier, then he should be bound by the same rules as for the SS: "We don't take food from people, we don't rape and we don't shoot women and children".

"But tell me Dad, how was Ivar to know about the rape?" "He was back to see to things in the barn and then he had heard what was going on. But the presence of the SS-driver stopped him from intervention".

"So, what now then Dad? You think you are in the clear?" "No, from what you told me about their knowledge of my trips to Sweden, then I don't think so. First, I shall go to Trygve and then further on to Sweden on a different route over Finnskog. You will hear from me via reliable contacts in Stockholm. I should try to get to England from there". "But what if you are caught then Dad?" "No, that won't happen and listen now, the caretaker down at Trygve's he can handle the two farms together with you and Trygve".

Theresa wondered if Eva, when they met, would she be telling about all this? And should she, Theresa keeps quiet about her knowledge about the rape? Ok, but Theresa felt there was one thing she had to know, know if it was Lars who really was Junior's granddad.

"You wouldn't have a couple of sneakers to lend me?" "Yes of course", the receptionist who was back at work was more than service minded.

"But what about breakfast then? And you didn't order any dinner last night, did you? I shall have to see about that. I beg you excuse me, but has something happened?" "Do I look that awful?" She tried to squeeze out a small laughter after all. "Only problems with sleeping."

Finally, she was out and onto the woods. But there was one thought that wouldn't let go. Would she be up to a meeting with Eva after all this?

TO EVA, OR HOME?

It was beautiful up there at Maihaugen, but she hadn't recognized anything, not even a mother with a little girl at her hand. She almost ran them down.

But when she had come across them on her way back, she had smiled and said sorry and they had smiled back to her, to the pretty lady with clay and dirt all over her. "But she was still pretty, not so Mammy?" "Well, yes, my dear, but terribly mucky. She cannot have looked where she's put her feet, just run straight out into the mud". "Not so with us, we don't do that do we?" And she adjusted her nice skirt, the curly blonde, only four years with braids.

No way Theresa wanted to be dirty all over by clay and mud, but she didn't sense anything until she was back at the museum seeing the frightened faces of the tourists. She could of course not ask to use the toilet there; better wait till she would be back in the hotel.

Her brain was coming to her now and she pressed on to get all the horrible with Eva out of her mind. Then suddenly she was struck by joy right in the midst of this misery with clay and everything. Her joy and the tears that followed, simply came to her because she was that happy that the old Judge would not once more be confronted with this gruesome past and the endurance of Eva. Maybe he even wouldn't have been up to it and simply died in her hands? Better so now sitting in his armchair waiting for the beautiful young girl from Ukraine, the great grandchild of this best friend Trygve. So, he just died there Karstein, looking all that peaceful.

But what now? Home to the hotel and a good clean up and suddenly she felt hungry more than ever. When did she last have a meal? The dinner and the breakfast by the Judge's? But that she felt like ages ago, more like half an eternity sort of.

The sun made her really hot now and it was great to be by herself and just feel her hunger. Now, what would she possibly be facing when meeting with Eva? Should she really have her confronted with all this past and now finally meeting with her fiancée's unknown grandchild from Odesa?

Unfortunate that she had earlier ran into Junior and for sure he must have told his grandmother about this lady, this foreign lady that had driven right into the courtyard as it was her own.

Not to forget about the young Judge and the sons of Karstein? Wouldn't it be quite likely that at least one of these contacts would lead to Eva, and then she would know that someone from Odesa had been visiting? Asking for kinfolks and relatives? Most probable. But now she felt she wanted to go home, home to Odesa, and tell her grandfather about all she had experienced and what she now knew about the folks in Norway. She pictured herself standing there, facing the tiny inscription on his gravestone, Lars the Jewish doctor. He hadn't wanted for his family name. The letters were in Hebrew.

'My dearest grandfather, I have been there where you played as a kid, run about for more than 70 years ago'. 'Is Eva still alive though?' He talked back from the grave.

Then the tears were pressing on again, she couldn't hold back, overwhelmed by her thoughts about her grandfather, so she had to stand up and get into the woods, so no one could disturb her, nor she them.

"Thanks for the loan of the sneakers, I shall have them washed and could you please send a couple of sandwiches to my room?" "What would you like then?" "I should go for shrimps and salmon, yes being a good tourist, I shall". They smiled to each other. "And listen", "Yes?" He was back with her. "I shall pay for both nights now, but I will leave in the afternoon". "No way, it shall only be for one night and room service". "Well thanks then, I shall remember you!"

What was this about? Some cliché? Or was it her subconscious telling her that yes, she should be back in Norway come time?

EVA, LARS'S FIANCÉE

Nervousness grew on her as at each mile she was getting closer and closer, till she finally was at this beautiful house up at Øvre Elvegård. All seemingly in the best of orders, all very neat. The rosebud flanked the main entrance. And a bit further in the courtyard she could see the place where Ivar had been flogged and blood then was running and further down, she could see the lower farm, her great grandfathers house. There was no swastika on the flagpole now. But they did fly the Norwegian flag. But why at half-mast?

Maybe someone had passed in the county? But there was no flag here on the mast up at Eva's. She parked the car, composed herself went to the front door and knocked.

Knocked again and even one more time. But no answer. Then off to the barn and the servants' quarters. No, no sign of anyone around but there was an old car there, a Volkswagen. Must at least be 20 years old by the look of the model. Shiny dark blue. Although with some rust at the front. Inside it was all tidy. A small, well-worn ladies' handbag was left there on the front seat.

She sighed a little. I didn't stand up to it grandfather. Sorry to disappoint you. Too bad there was no one at home, but maybe some other time. She sat down on the porch and wrote a note to Eva, her grandfather's fiancée, whom she never was to meet.

"I am Theresa, Lars's Grandchild, and you would have been like my grandmother dear you, if you and your Lars had ever come together again? Unfortunately, you were not at home, but if you like you can then write to me at this address. Your Lars is dead now, but your name was the last he cried out before passing. He wanted so for you to read this Diary, but Eva I want to have it back sometime. Maybe we shall meet later on. Dearest wishes to you, yours Theresa.

She picked up the Diary and put it in a big envelope together with the small letter, wrote private to Eva on the front and put it in the mailbox at the door. But then she got panicky. Perhaps the envelope from Karstein had gone into the big envelope as well? This was not to happen and she ran back and thank heavens, it was not there.

But before putting the envelope back one more time, should she have another go at the front door? Maybe Eva was just having a nap or something? She knocked again, still no answer. But her conscience got to her again, I shall give her another 5 minutes and then back to Oslo and home.

She felt this force inside her to look down to her great grandfather Trygve's house one more time. This was the beautiful place that Lars should never come home to, he her most wonderful grandfather.

But there was something going on down there. The flag was hoisted at top mast and there was an old woman saying her goodbyes at the house. The woman started to make her way uphill but it didn't go that fast with her. But finally, she was by the creek separating the two farms exactly like her grandfather had told her.

Then suddenly emotions took over completely and Theresa started downhill, laughing and crying in-between. "Hey Eva, it's me Theresa!" But no way Eva would know of any Theresa? "I am the Grandchild of Lars", she cried out. But she then saw the old lady falling and further down she saw Junior, yes it had to be him coming running with his medical bag.

They both reached Eva at the same time. "Thank heavens she is alive! What did you cry out to her, she must have gotten some sort of a shock? But she is a strong person so we shall just let her rest right here. Now you must be the lady that came here two days ago? Are you not?" He listened on Eva with his stethoscope. "Yes, thank God, she is ok".

Theresa teared off her blouse, now she was standing there in jeans and her bra, and she ran off to the stream, dipped the blouse into the cold water, then back and started to cool down Eva's hot front and face and soon the most beautiful blue gray eyes were looking at her. "Who are you, you said something about you being Lars's grandchild, did you not?" "Yes Eva, I shouldn't have come here giving you this shock. But I suddenly felt this overwhelming happiness when I saw you down there. In my heart I knew it had to be you".

"Yes Theresa, it was a shock in more than one way, because today we flagged at half-mast on this the very birthday of Lars. I mean it was the first time we flagged at half-mast to him, because only now I was certain he had passed. But then you come to me, you beautiful flower and I have to believe you when you say that you are his grandchild. Everyone around here said that Lars had fallen in the midst of the war. But I on my part always refused to believe just that. No, I never have believed that!

She must have been beautiful your grandmother, yes and of course your mother as well, not to forget that Lars was a handsome man".

"But we cannot stay just here Theresa, you said Theresa did you not?" Junior was cutting in. "We have to get her up to her house. I shall get hold of a stretcher and then we shall carry her down to the car. We can make it together, right so?"

And even if Eva had weighed 100 kilos she thought, still there wouldn't have been any greater happiness than being allowed to carry her, just the two of them together.

THE FIRST NIGHT WITH EVA

The shock was more or less over now, Eva having met with her beloved Lars's grandchild and Theresa now being that afraid to lose her, even before she was to meet her properly.

And then there was Junior of course, the grandchild of the two, Eva and Lars. But he was a man and Theresa hadn't known any man for real. Of course, there were men in the ballet and in the opera, but apart from that, there was only Lars.

But Eva soon reckoned what was going on. In spite her age she immediately took command, seemingly she was used to just that. "Junior, I think we girls shall have this afternoon to ourselves, alone. Yes, I can see that you are disappointed, but you shall better understand it all tomorrow". It was obvious to Theresa that Junior would have liked to know her opinion, but she just looked away to make it clear that this was not her home, and that it was not for her to make any decisions.

"But Eva, what if you shall need a doctor then?" Junior tried to loosen up, wouldn't be that easily rejected. And the somewhat stern atmosphere was broken. "Junior, I promise you I shall stay one extra day for us". So, he had to leave, although in a better mood now, following the promise from this beautiful girl.

Second cousins they were. She, already a star from the big city. Junior, know your place, remember we are far out in a county in rural Norway. At a place where probably no one had ever heard about Opera. Well, he was ready to move if only he was allowed to do so by his grandmother.

Next minute she was onto him from her mobile. "Theresa has gone upstairs to change so I may have a few words with you my boy". So now they were to come, her words of admonish. "Her boy?"

"Junior, you have chosen isolation sort of her out in the county and I am of course glad for that in most ways. But and there is a big but to it. You have guarded yourself from beautiful, young women and I could see that you are easily influenced by Theresa. But don't you forget what kind of life she is leading back in her country, plus she being your relative!"

"My dear Grandmother, have we covered most of it now? I shall call you and say goodnight later", and he hang up.

"Who was that, Eva? Shall I call you Grandmother, I guess I cannot do just that? After all I am not your Grandchild, even being Lars's". "Please don't say grandmother, it makes me always be an old lady. Just you say Eva". "Now don't you talk this away Eva, it was Junior was it not, he had left only a while ago?" "And you, what is it to you then Theresa? The boy just phoned to know if everything was OK here!" "Eva you are not a very good liar!" And then she laughed it all away.

"Maybe we should sit down now, have a bite and talk about my fiancée?" But then suddenly she sank together in her chair. "Oh Theresa, I don't know if I'm up to this. You talked about a Diary did you not? Maybe you can read a bit from it?" "Are you really up to hearing from it, also the parts about other women?" "Just you get going, come with it all Theresa". "Now when do you think he started writing this Diary?" "It isn't that difficult. Boys don't have a habit to writing diaries, but Lars was probably different". "But just answer me, Eva!" "Well, this Diary probably starts when he was writing about the war, if there was to be a war and when it would come to us". "Yes, that's precisely how it is Eva, but those are just headlines. The real poetic part starts the night neither of you could sleep". She blushed now the old lady. "You want me to skip that part then Eva?" "No, just you dim the light a bit and start reading, but not too fast please".

She had come to this section where Lars goes down on his knees and asks, "will you marry me, Eva?" She looked at Eva, tears were running and running. Could such an old person have that many tears? And she continued reading. "I wanted to penetrate her, but Eva said wait, wait and then we were just lying there, our sexes playing with each other, till suddenly I was deep inside her, my beloved Eva".

Theresa now stopped reading and Eva just cried and cried, but then they were both saved by the mobile. "Just you take it Theresa", she cried and sobbed. "Yes, it is Junior, I just wanted to tell you that I shall not be a night raven tonight, so I just say goodnight to both of you right now. My best to my grandmother and good night to you". "Goodnight Junior. Nice to finally have met you".

"Thanks Theresa. I couldn't possibly have talked with him on the mobile right now". "But shall we make it an early night now Eva?" "Yes, let's do just that and then Junior may join us on the further voyage tomorrow".

THE VOYAGE WITH LARS

"But why did he have to go Eva? Why did he have to set himself checkmate, come Germany's defeat? Did none of you, not even your father see that this could turn terribly bad? Or did the question about Karelen overshadow everything?"

"Most likely it did, and in 1939 or 1940 very few of us had any thoughts about how our country would look like, come 1945. Lars wood hardly ever talk about it when we were by ourselves. He just wanted to talk about this war and joining up".

"But Eva, no one up here was friendly to Germany? Your Father was even the leader of a resistance group, saved himself to Sweden and then England, following several liquidations of Nazis and Germans". "But it was more present to us what the Russians were doing to Sarah's kinfolks in her beautiful Karelen, assaults and butchering at large". "You are referring to Lars's mother, my great grandmother I take it?" "Yes of course".

"I don't want to talk about the Jews", she said to herself. That part better come from the Diary once we are together the three of us. But Eva was holding on to her own memory. "Yes, and then England declared war on Finland". "Making it no way easier you mean? But could he not have stayed at home then, or be gone with his father to Finland as an assistant medic or something?" "No, he had it in him that he had to learn how to fight, and then Germany was the only road forward in his mind.

And then we have Loke, an ardent antagonist to England. He was driven by his will to defend Norway against the Russians and especially protect Finnmark, that's what he claimed was his ground for enlisting".

"But that was all lies, not so Eva? Even Lars figured that much, although very late". "Yes, I know and I tried a number of times to convince Lars that his best friend was gay and had a super crush on Lars and that he never could let go. This was his reason for enlisting, going fighting with

Germany, but only if he could go together with Lars." "But do you blame it all on Loke then, being his fault that Lars enlisted?"

"No, but maybe it hadn't been that easy to sign on, if he was to go alone. But I don't know". "So Loke was gay and an ardent hater of Jews as well? And how has he been faring once he got home?" "I really don't know Theresa, but rumors have it that he only got two years of imprisonment, although the state of Israel was adamant that he had taken part in mass-murdering of Jews, amongst other places in Lviv, in northeastern Ukraine. Subsequently he should have been punished for that, not only for treason to his country". Theresa could see that she had great difficulties with this very word. To Eva this was the very word, treason, that denied her to unite again with Lars, her fiancée for life.

"Jews yes, what do you mean Theresa, will there be much about Jews in Lars's Diary? I cannot at all imagine that he took part in any massacres! Never in life!" "Me neither Eva, and this we shall learn more about when Junior joins us and I shall continue the reading". "Do you think I shall be up to this Theresa, learning about these other women?" "Well, you must, must you not? You know I'm just not coming out of thin air, am I? I had a mother and a grandmother and she was a Jew".

But it wasn't for her to talk about it all, it was for Lars.

THE SS-HAUPTSTURMFÜHRER LARS

"Here you have a picture of your fiancée Eva, and here you have another one of father and son in the surgery tent in Karelen. Strange it was that Trygve said nothing about your child, not so?" "Yes indeed, and as I understood from Lars, he knew nothing about any child.

But I wrote to him once Trygve was back home and there I told him everything". "Well, he talked sometime about a letter, a last one from you and that he had noticed it disappearing in the boiler of a Finish girl, Marija Lisa, there at the front in Finland". Eva was all ears now. "What does it mean disappeared then Theresa?" "According to him he had just managed to read "My dearest Lars" or something, and then immediately he had to do surgery on the skull of some Finnish hero".

"But do you think he would have come home if he knew he had a son? Come home and take his punishment and asked for forgiveness, seeing his imprisonment like a relief? Maybe they would just have sent him on special duty to Finnmark or whatever as a medic? Please say yes then Theresa, say yes!"

It was for her to cry now. "I truly don't know Eva, and how am I to know, but at the time he was almost finished with his plight service in Karelen, so maybe, just maybe? Once done in Finland there was nothing tying him to the war anymore, so maybe if he had known about his son, then he possibly might have come home to you".

"Oh, so you have started without waiting for me?" Junior was at the door. "Sorry Junior we were just looking at some pictures and then we just could not let go". "Not quite true that Theresa, we had come to this point in the Diary were Lars got my letter up in Finland, the letter where I told him about a Roald and that this letter disappeared in a boiler there at the front. That was the crucial point, Lars not knowing about his son, a fact that could have tipped the balance and made him come home, already in 1943".

"Junior it was like that. Lars he concluded two himself that Germany was to lose the war and that he, as a result of this could have no future in Norway, being sentenced for treason to his country and possibly looking forward to 10 years in jail or camps.

If he had known that he had a son there back home, a son that waited to meet his father, together with the love of his life, then the turn of the tide might have been totally different. But you seem to forget about the other women Eva, and we shall learn about them later, but I feel we are going a bit too fast. Right now, I want for you to hear about Loke and Sennheim, Loke in Lars's bed".

Eva's face was twisted in pain now. "I knew it all the time. He just wanted Lars he. Did they sleep with each other then?" "No, please stop it Eva, don't jump to conclusions until we have read it all together!" "Agree", Junior cut in and then she started to read about Sennheim.

"There were talks about Jews and harassment of Jews at all times and arguing about how to take the lives of millions of them. I lost 10 kilos during these three months and what about my brain? If my brain was to shrink then for sure it had done that as well. While these talks about extermination of the Jews were going on, my thoughts were all the time with my little, delicate mother, the most beautiful flower of Karelen, the Jewish girl who you chose my father and Norway and who was never to meet her relatives over in Finland again".

Now it was all that silent that she could hear tears dropping to the floor. At first Eva's, then those of Junior and finally her own.

So, they never knew, never had known that Sarah at the lower farm was 100% Jewish. And think about the Germans, yeah Germans that had lived in her house until she passed in 1943.

As the reading proceeded, it finally came to them that Lars himself was a Jew, and then Junior, he just as well. "And then you Theresa, what about you?" "My grandmother was Jewish, she being a daughter of a Rabbi in Odesa, and I for my part for sure am ¼ Jewish".

"What happened to your great grandfather the Rabbi?" They then were to hear about the gruesome story about the hanging and the burning at the Parade square in Odesa and not least about her grandmother's courageous, still dangerous march to the mountains.

But Eva was more concerned about Lars's mother, beautiful little Sarah, she would have been sent directly to Auswitch and the crematories.

But the two of them came to wonder how Lars could have been holding out these three months with all the time this degrading education about how to exterminate all the Jews and possibly having to endure more of the same at the cadet school.

"I can see you have pictures from that school Theresa". "Yes, Junior, and what I do know from there is that this Lisa showed up and Lars told me that he was the only one she wanted, and one night he fell for her, his longing for Eva was unbearable. I think he was considering to take his own life following this unforgivable sin, as he called it. But sheer luck to him, he was sent to Berlin to the med-school. Almost round the clock he worked, studies during daytime and training in surgery in the evenings. It took him only half a year with this extraordinary engagement to get his degree as a field-medic, surgery his specialty.

And from now on his focus was only on getting done with his plight service and then off to Finland and Karelen".

"But Theresa, you skipped the part about Loke in Sennheim?" "Yes, Loke was tops now with the persecution of the Jews. But the last night for Lars in Sennheim, he woke by Loke lying on top of him with an enormous erection". She flashed a bit. "I don't know what else to call it". But the one getting super red in her face was Eva. They looked at her the two. "What is the matter, Eva?" "No, nothing really, my thoughts were just wandering". Wandering to the terrible with Jens the oxen, but she kept the latter to herself.

"But what about Lars? How did he react?" "Lars told him to fuck off. But he had to thread carefully, considering that he once had been talking to himself about his mother, she being a Jew and all that, and maybe Loke had come to hear part of this. He was of course extremely glad to be off, come morning".

"Do you have a picture from Berlin then Theresa?" "Yes, here is a picture of granddad as a fresh lieutenant and with all exams finished". Once again it became too much to Eva. "Yes Eva, and right then he knew that he would never come to forgive himself and go home to you.

Sometime later he ran into Loke in Lviv. Loke had been promoted to staff sergeant, having been in charge of a number of exterminations of Jews. They were not to meet again until Lars lost his leg at the battle of Vinnitsa".

"Now, who is the girl on this picture then Theresa, and who are all those officers, all with lots of medals?" Eva had found a magnifying glass.

Theresa then told them about General Steiner and how Lars happened to get in contact with these officers. "But you skipped the girl", Eva was on to her again. "Oh yeah, her name was Birgitta and Lars sat next to her on the night train from Berlin to Warszawa, and he came to put his head in her lap, slept all night and called her Eva". I wonder if grandfather ever said just that. Well, he might have done so and it was good for Eva to hear just that.

"This one is from the hospital in Odesa, here he stands together with the Chief Surgeon, they had become very good colleagues". "But who is this girl next to them, I mean this beautiful one? She does have Jewish traits doesn't she Junior?" "Maybe so Eva. Was she Jewish?" "Yes, and she worked as a nurse at the surgery". Theresa was about to go on. But then suddenly she said: "This girl, this woman was Rebecka, she was to be my grandmother. She come to be Lars's only true love besides you Eva, you that for certain he should never see again".

"I'm soon to have patients", Junior stood up. It was getting hot in the room now, more than hot. And they could all feel it, the pressure. "And I shall need to lay down a bit", Eva raised from the chair as well. "And maybe I should go for a walk", Theresa joined in.

"Tonight, when we are having dinner together, then we may talk a bit about Karelen, when Lars finally got there". Theresa lightened up. "Let's do just that then". But Rebecka was after all her grandmother and no way could she deny her, just to make pleasure to an old lady up here in Norway.

"But we were not quite through with his feelings when leaving the cadet school. It was all about his terrible longing for you and then came the first great sin, which he was never to forgive himself for. He was so strongly taken by this that already the next morning he asked for transfer to Berlin and then to the East front. He felt he could not live with this terrible sin against you. And he was convinced that even if you should come to forgive him, then he would never be able to forgive himself. His conscious was totally black".

"Now how was she this woman?" "Her name was Lisa and she worked as a house maid there at the school. Grandfather said she was very beautiful. Reminded him of you and that she was very forward, wanted him and did not conceal that. But in his eyes that was no excuse for cheating on you and he came back to this ever so often".

Theresa observed that now it was almost getting too much to Eva, excused herself and said she wanted to have a short run, telling Eva not to wait too long for her. Maybe this whole business with the Diary was getting to them all.

When she got outside, she could see Junior was waiting for her down the road. "Hi Theresa, is it okey by you if I make you company down the road?" "What about your patients then?" "I have deferred them.

Theresa, you are all the time coming back to the point that Lars could not forgive himself, having betrayed his Eva and that he felt for sure that she would not forgive him. That was why he could not return to Norway, not even on a short leave. This is part one of my question, so please don't interrupt me. But there shall be a second part where he had started to think about Germany as the losing side and that he then could not go home. So now my question is: when does he start to be conscious about all this?"

"He had of course met other Norwegians who had heard the rumors about 10 years prison for betraying their country and further losing their rights as citizens. But he was incredibly slow on this matter or he just put it aside. And the others did not talk serious about it as they were going to the East front to fight Russians and partisans and their chance for survival was 50% or less. And if they should happen to be taken prisoners, then for sure they would be sent to Russian camps, many there dying of starvation and sickness. I would imagine that betrayal to Norway might well be of minor interest in such a context".

She was quick now to add that since Lars weren't to die at the front, then he had to prepare himself for what would be the realities in Norway, once the war was over. "But this never came clear to his mind Junior, until after that night with Birgitta". "The girl from the train?" "Yes, the girl from the train.

But let's stop right there, Junior. It would be unfair to the old lady if we go on just the two of us". "The old lady is my grandmother Theresa, so of course I agree with you. I shall soon have to go to my farmhouse, but please tell me a bit about your Odesa before we split, please will you do just that?" "Yes, let's sit down a while just here".

Time passed quickly and they stood up first when Theresa felt that it started to get chilly, maybe she wasn't dressed for the cool evening or was Junior getting a bit forward?

JUNIOR'S WORLD

He came back at six, on the dot. "Talk about being on time!" Theresa laughed at him. She had just managed to have a shower and change after their walk. But where was Eva? "Go up and look for her Junior, after all the two of you are the closest". But then suddenly Eva called on both of them.

"Children, I don't think that I shall be with you tonight. This has become quite too much for me. I have prepared the dinner but now I have put it back in the fridge, so we may have it for lunch tomorrow if neither of you we'll eat here tonight".

When the first concern was over for Junior, he put up a serious face and said: "No don't you fuss about and strain yourself Eva. I shall invite Theresa to a simple dinner down at Hamar. Well of course it's up to her, she may of course say no thanks". "Yes, I think I shall do just that, say no thanks".

She could see his face darkened. "No thanks, because I'm totally fed up with restaurant food, no thanks because I would rather invite myself home to you Junior to see the house were Lars grew up. Where he played and where he stayed until he was of age and then I also want to see pictures of his parents, my great grandparents.".

"Now you almost frightened me Theresa, I was frightened but now I am glad. But please bear in mind that I am a bachelor and that my Toril comes to me to do house chores only once a week, and now she isn't due until tomorrow and it does of course look awful, especially in the kitchen and I have no food either. But for sure we can have some bread from our Eva, so don't you beg to be excused". He laughed at her; "at least I have a bottle of red". "But I don't drink", she said, "except on occasions, when I say yes to tiny drops of Champagne".

"Can you manage by yourself tonight then Eva, or shall I call for Toril to come up here and stay with you?" "Don't you worry about me now Junior, but behave yourself and off with the two of you".

'This is no good to you Junior! The voice from his inner self taking him back to reality was hard to him. Yes, I am tough to you. Right now, you were on the way over the cliff. Theresa is nothing to you. You shall find yourself a Norwegian nurse and maybe it was the visit from Theresa that awakened you're lust to a woman. That is good for you Junior, but please let this opera star go back to her Odesa without you kissing her'.

Junior had not exaggerated about the mess in the big house. Three rooms were in impeccable order, both bathrooms as well as the surgery itself. The rest was as he had put it, a total mess and disorder. "But you said something about this Toril coming here once a week to help you, did you not?" "Yes?" "But when she comes here, what does she actually do? No way you could make such a mess in only one week? And I wonder how your room looked like when you studied for medicine?" He laughed sort of embarrassed now. "Pretty much like here, total mess, but I was in control and my exams were ever so good. But Theresa, my life is not about chores, but about my patients and taking care of the two farms together with the senior hired hand. Then I simply must find time to follow up as closely as possible all the improvements in the medical field, new and adequate treatments that would apply to patients here in the county, in particular what I can do better to increase their life quality.

And not to forget about Eva, our dearest Eva. Do you really think that there would be time over to do other things once this list is done with?" No, she did not think that, unless he organized himself differently. "Yes please, just tell me how and I am all ears". "But Junior one other question first; when did you last go away on holiday and did it last for one week, two weeks, or three weeks?" He laughed at her. "I attended a medical conference in Trondheim last spring. But I had to cut it short after two days and go home, one of my patients needed me".

It was for her to laugh now. "How many times did you and Eva talk on the phone on this trip? I presume you traveled by car?" He really flushed now. "Shall we say 30 times then Junior?" "Not that many times". "But more than 20 then Junior?" But he wanted out of the trap. "What about going to Hamar and having something to eat there. I can put the sandwiches in the fridge until tomorrow?"

She laughed at him, he clearly relieved. "I am glad to that decision, if not, someone would have to arrange for table and chairs here.

But your house itself looks well maintained, after all superbly maintained". "Yes, and thank heavens for that, the caretaker looks after it all". "But Junior, before we leave from here, what keeps you going, I mean you have to live from something, is it the surgery that gives you necessary funds or is it the farm?" "I don't think that there is any great surplus from the farm, of course there are the wages for the caretaker and the other hired hand, and then I have to pay for the maid up at Eva's, and then Toril down here with me". "So, what are you saying? Are you saying that without the funds from the surgery, then you couldn't have lived from the revenues of the farm alone?" "Have you been studying economics Theresa?" "No, and you know quite well what's my profession and where my income comes from. But for sure I wonder if you shouldn't start thinking totally new about this farm adventure of yours? But let it be for the moment, I'm starving".

"Ok, I agree, now we go to Hamar and stop talking more about chores and economics and I promise you that it shall all look tops when we shall have that special day together". "Promise?" She twinkled to him. "I hear what you are saying, but can we get off now!"

Restaurants in hotels, always the same with few exceptions she thought. Even here in Norway. Boring single men, standard menu on filthy menu cards. Yes, she recognized it all and she wouldn't have dinner here. "Isn't there a tiny little restaurant here in Hamar then Junior?" "I don't know as I always come here, but I shall ask the receptionist". "No, we shall ask a taxi driver, just wait a second and I shall find out". And yes, the taxi driver had a good answer to what she was looking for, and some 15 minutes later they had themselves a table with checked red-and-white tablecloth and dimmed lightning, shabby candle on their table.

"Satisfied now Theresa?" "Yes, splendid this is". They ordered and both had wine to the lasagna, even she felt an urge for keeping him company with the carafe of red.

"Now, I want to talk about Eva, Junior. How much can she take hearing all this from the Diary? I am not going to leave it behind, because then I fear that she would bury herself into details about what is written, but maybe more what is not written. But whatever, I must read to her and discuss with her the very night when Lars finally realized that the train had left, and no more Norway. His very hope was to die in the war. I must tell her more about my mother and grandmother as well, and how my grandmother and Lars got together again after that he was officially declared dead. I think you shall be present then and Junior, bring your medical bag, but do it discreetly".

"But can't we just go through this part of the Diary without dwelling too much with details. I am worried for her medical condition". "But you said go quick as a hare, can you please explain to me?" He laughed at her. "Theresa, it's about a clever one, like the hare, just jumping away at high speed. Not worrying about details". "I completely understand that, but sometimes I guess, even the hare may come to jump over the parts that might be the most important ones. Don't you think so Junior?" She looked at him now with a roguishness. Almost flirting he felt to himself. But he cut it short with cheers to her.

"But Junior, I won't accept to leave my mother's family in a misty vale so to speak. My great grandfather there in Odesa, he was one of the city's most important Rabbis and even his brother was a Rabbi. They were responsible for one synagogue and one community each of them.

My great grandmother, she was a highly professional nurse and my grandmother happened to become the same, not to forget that she was ever so clever with Kalashnikov and bayonet.

It was not evident for a Jewish girl to survive at the time. My mother she was born in a horses' stable and a German field-medic was responsible for her birth. Just think about it, a military man, a doctor helping a Jewish woman giving birth to the little, very beautiful Eugenia. She in her turn died in labor when I was born. She couldn't have a Jewish name till after the war and then she was named Sarah after Lars's mother, your great grandmother. But we might stop now. Not going any further without Eva being present.

What is important to me now, is to make it clear that Lars, following that night, said no to Norway, but later yes, to Rebecka, my grandmother and her family.

And now, Junior, please tell me more about yourself, how you grew up and you did lose your parents while you were still a kid? How was it to grow up with only old people around you? And how do you visualize your future? I heard nothing about any women when you told me about all your challenges. Would there at all be room for a woman at your side? Or a man for that matter?"

Deep, red color came to his face. I am not gay Theresa, nor have I any girlfriend. I happen to meet some women at medical conferences, but there are less and less single women. Although some are divorced as they never had time for their husbands". A good laughter followed.

"I don't think any of these hard-working women would suit you, Junior. Quite possibly you would have become responsible for a number of their kids, because they do have children these women?" "Yes, you are so right and they would never be my children as they would have to be made from the bottom and up". "What does 'from the bottom and up' mean Junior? Is it another connotation as with the hare?" "Difficult subject that is", he flushed again. "But Junior how were you to explain to your patients that their children must be made from the bottom and up? And please tell me Junior, tell me how it is done".

He was saved by the Diary. "Theresa, I haven't come to read that part from the Diary as yet, but I figure that Eva and Lars created my father Ragnvald from the bottom and up".

He was that cute that she shed a tear, no two tears and she had to kiss him straight on the mouth. "Where is the ladies room?" she asked the waitress.

Then she was gone and what was all this about? Junior was just sitting there by himself and felt ever so left out, all alone. Did Theresa feel something for him after this short visit and what about he himself? What had Eva said about all this? Two totally different worlds. She, a renowned star, studied at Bolshoi and guest performances in Kiev, maybe at the Metropolitan New York, the world playing at her feet so to speak. Then what about him? A bachelor from a rural county in Hedemark with two worn down farms, quite sizable though and an old General-practice inherited from his great grandfather Trygve. And with a duty for life, one that he never could leave behind: Take good care of his old grandmother. But still, he should allow himself to spend a nice evening with a recently discovered relative, should he not? Yes, it must be OK. But not since he was a student had he felt his heart beating that fast through his sweater. He thought about that girl from western Oslo, her father was a doctor, her brother as well. Her uncle was a professor in judicial medicine, her grandfather was a lawyer at the High Court, now retired and Martha she was the single child and no way she could live east of Theatercafeen. Only Oslo West, and no more than two kms further west neither. And he on his part could he ever move and leave Eva behind? Now, he felt a tickling for the first time since Martha.

And then she was back, this star from Odesa, his beautiful relative. "What are you thinking about Junior, you look like you were far away on a long, long travel? Were you not?"

"So, we are the last ones then Theresa, I mean on both families side?" It was she that turned serious now. "Yes Junior, with the exception of Chaim, my grandmother's first cousin, he saved her from the Germans on several occasions and for a period they were thought to be lovers. Chaim was the strong leader who would not just lay down and ask to be killed by the

Germans. He left my grandmother's auntie Esther to Ben Gurion's land, Israel and became a colonel in the Israeli army only two years thereafter. He was said to have fallen in the Yom Kippur battle, but it has never been proven and they never found a grave. There were rumors that he was taken to an Egyptian hospital and then further on to USA, blinded on both eyes.

There were also talks about him being the father of my grandmother's baby and Chaim let them think it was like that, but the tall blond girl with almost white curls, she was like you put it here and what was that again?" "I can imagine", Junior laughed, "you mean like twisted out of her nose, no doubt to her being Lars's child?" More laughter. "But can you please explain to me Junior, how a child might be twisted out of one's nose?" Now even more laughter and it was a long time since she had enjoyed herself out at a restaurant or at home for that matter. 'Hm', she said to herself, what's actually going on with me?

"Shouldn't we be phoning Eva by now?" "OMG, and our little resto is also soon to close now, and we are the only two guests".

"You are enjoying yourself then?" It was Eva. "Yes, I feared you would do just that". "But we shall soon be with you, no worries!"

"What did she say Junior, are we wanted or something?" "No, she had just feared that we were enjoying ourselves". Feared? Well, she was not the only one.

He waved to the waiter for the bill. "No, no this dinner is on my account and you know why?" "No, do tell me?" "Because the farewell dinner, we shall have back at your place and it will be all your responsibility, not to forget that we shall have it in a tidy house".

After a short good night from him to Eva, then they were just the two of them, Junior having left. "And now it is all about the two of us Theresa". "I don't know what you are hinting at, I just came to say good night" "So, tell me please what happened?" "Yes of course". "So, please take two minutes with me before you go to bed. I am certain you can't sleep anyway". "What? You are kidding me now, is there really something wrong here now? And why shouldn't I get to sleep?"

"And what does Junior think about you, were you to talk man to woman or vice versa as it is called nowadays?" "But Eva, for certain that is very private!" "But you didn't stop at that? Ok then, where you to talk about private things? More so, do you like him?" "Yes, he is a nice man, but a terrible mess of a man, I mean in private". "So, you got that close then? This was all I wanted to know; I mean if you had a boring evening".

So, what did she fear Eva? That Theresa should turn Junior's head and that his grandmother should be there alone one more time, be the loser again, sort of? That would have been a heavy assumption, would it not?

Next day was Saturday and Junior who regularly had patients on Saturday, quite a few even, he had finally succeeded in having them deferred to the next week. Already at 7 o'clock he observed the caretaker in the driveway so he was quick out and invited him to a cup of coffee. "You might have come earlier for that matter; my night was a pretty restless one". "Now, how can I be of assistance this morning Junior?" "Well, you have your education from the agricultural college down at Ås". He could see the caretaker was totally at array here. Junior never interfered in the running of the farms.

"If I gave you the possibility to run the farms as you pleased, do you think then that you possibly could have increased the return let's say by 40%?" "That was an extremely tough call Junior, and it would require a total change here, maybe from cattle to grain, yes totally". "Would you be ready to that?" "Well, keep a couple of horses and I shall be open to whatever suggestion. When do you think you can come up with a plan that we can examine together?" "I think in a week's time." "Splendid, we agree on just that then".

Now it was time for Toril. "You are very early at it this morning Junior, is something the matter?" "Well, it is a beautiful morning, isn't it?" She laughed to him, "let's meet in another half hour then Junior".

She ran into the caretaker out in the courtyard. "He is at his sharpest this morning Toril, so you better be prepared". And yes, she was ready.

"Toril, I shall need your help". "Help with what Junior?" "It doesn't look too good here, I mean it certainly needs a cleanup". "No problem, Junior, it shall take me only half an hour to have it all spick and span if I may say so".

"But Toril, there has to be a change to all this. Could you possibly start with coming twice a week and in addition to the surgery, the waiting room and the two bathrooms, I should ask you to have an extra go at the hall, the living room, the library and the kitchen".

She started to laugh and he joined in, even not knowing why he was laughing. "So, you mean a cleanup of the entire house then Junior?" "Yes, and for sure I forgot about the bedrooms upstairs".

"Two days a week then and full days if necessary?" "Yes, and could you get started today?" "Well of course Junior, I am here right now. This is your day.

But Junior, don't you think it would have been better if we could cooperate on all this, I mean especially the private rooms? And if I could go to the stores for you once a week, I mean for milk and bread, some dinners etc., and of course detergents. And I am also quite adamant that you should skip your old dishwasher and even get you a washing machine with a dryer". But she wasn't done with just that.

"Not least it would be an advantage if you would buy a new board for ironing and a damp iron. All these things you have now are more than 30 years old. I have one more point"; "yes, go ahead". "I think you should have a visit from a kitchen supplier and ask for a sketch to a totally new kitchen, with fridge and stove and not least a microwave oven". She wondered to herself if she hadn't gone too far with her absent-minded doctor? But there had been no changes since the time of his grandparents. But Junior was open to all. "Just have this kitchen man come next Sunday". "On a Sunday?" "Yes, I would have no time for him until then Toril".

"You know Junior that this will cost you?" But he seemed like he wasn't hearing. "And please Toril, make a list to me of the things I should look after here in the house at all times". "To you?" "Yes, evidently I'm not up to it myself without a list." Toril laughed again. "Are you planning for a lady to move in here?" "I sure would wish to that too, really, but sadly it shall only be the two of us". "As you know well Junior, I both have children and a husband, so sorry". Another laugh and once again he had to laugh, he as well. Now, if we can have all these changes done, then for sure it will take a while till next time we embark on a similar operation". "Yes, and I strongly believe you to that Junior".

"Do you think this kitchen delivery man, or woman could show up tomorrow morning at 08:00 hrs.?" "Tomorrow, that's Sunday Junior, but I shall for sure try". "But no later than 8 o'clock then Toril. My oh my, I have to go to Eva now, it's almost 9 o'clock".

ON WITH THE DIARY

"Are you that early every day Junior?" Theresa had just returned from her morning jog, walked through the shower and had just got her lipstick on when Junior was at the door.

"I have noted that there have been people coming and going down at your house since early morning Junior". "You keep track then, don't you? I had to have an early meeting with the caretaker and then I sorted out some things with Toril. But for sure keep an eye on me, there will be people coming and going tomorrow morning as well". "Oh, so there will be patients even on Sunday?" "No, but I expect visit from a deliverer of kitchens and for sure I need to get rid of some electric appliances and get new ones in place. You know, washing machine without a dryer". "It is called a tumbler Junior". "Ok, then a tumbler". "But it seems like someone has put a rocket in your back". Eva wanted to be part of this as well. "Maybe Theresa should take you to some shops and have you bought some modern clothes as well". "Please stop it now Eva, I don't use suits and jackets and such, I only change my doctor-coats when they are out-washed". "Yes, precisely and I shall talk with Theresa about this, once we are just the two of us".

"So, we shall be off to Hamar then?" "No way, it will have to be Oslo and then you could have lunch at Theatercafeen". "But are you up to that trip then Eva?" "I shall have to think about it, but now we shall have breakfast and I suppose we can talk about the Diary while we are eating. We still have a lot to go through, right so Theresa?" "Yes", she said ever so quietly. Was she the one that had put a rocket to Junior? And what would happen when they just were to be the two of them, a whole day and an evening? Did she feel something for him? And he for her? Not only one coming by, helping him to put things orderly? But could she at all have left Odesa and moved in here with Junior, living his life? Never ever! She was a city girl and was totally dependent of a ballet-and opera environment to live her life. And what about New York? They were waiting for her final breakthrough there. Many would come to the opera in Odesa and the premier of la Boheme. With success there, then the Metropolitan in New York would be the next step, right so? Maybe, she had said to herself. For sure, they had said over there. No, there was no room for Junior, nor any other for that matter, whispered her inner voice firmly.

"You are looking a bit lost right now Theresa, please stay with us, I shall be glad if you can serve the tea and bring the Diary with you". "Yes Eva". She was her charm smile now and she bubbled even in herself. OMG it was lovely here with Eva. How on earth had Lars come up with this totally stupid idea of his, going to war, leave this wonderful girl and never come back. But then you wouldn't be sitting here you either, would you?

They had now come to Finland, Karelen, his ultimate goal for enlisting with the Germans. 'I am finally free', he wrote, 'free from the duty I have felt so intense, the duty to fight for my mother's land. But have you been fighting you, Lars? No, but I have been a life-line to fighting Finnish heroes. Many of them would not have survived without me carrying out my duty here. But enough is enough. Now I want to go back to the hospital in Odesa. Go back to what? To be a medic to German officers? Yes, I know and I know as well that I have to think about what there will be for me once the war is over, what about my life then? But now Warszawa, farewell Finland'.

"You think you can take this Eva? Now, there shall be another woman in his life". "If it is your grandmother once more, then it's ok to me". "No, this is the woman he met on the train from Berlin. She is the one he sat next to on the train, fell asleep and she had his head in her lap throughout all the night, and he called her Eva in his sleep".

"Yes, it seems to me that I have been with him wherever he has been traveling".

'I had planned for myself for a real lavish evening of goodbye to Finland with all the luxury I could muster as compensation to my poor life up there in Karelen. So, I went back to hotel Leopold and for sure got royal treatment. A big, suite, a large bath-tub and Champagne, that was exactly what I visualized. But I was just as much preoccupied with my thoughts about what life there would be to me once this war was over. I definitely needed someone to talk this through with. And there was no one better but Birgitta, if she was to be found and was off duty. Most likely she was not. That's the way things are.

But having my second glass of bubbles there in the bath tub, she calls and says that she shall manage to come, but that she is not in for any shower, changing out of uniform and all that. But would he be okey with her coming straight from work in her uniform and then possibly have a quick shower at his place? 'Yes, please do come', and I run a bath for her and served her bubbles, ordered room service for dinner, but the food should be cold before we got to eat. Her task now was to listen and give her best advice.

I told her about my gruesome breaking of my woes to Eva and which forever would make it impossible for me to return to her'.

But now Eva had started crying once more.

"And do you know if your Eva isn't waiting for you and that you might have a child together?" "Then she would have told me about it, or my dad would have told me back in Finland". "But Lars, maybe he thought it was for Eva to tell you about your child?" "Yes, it had to be like that.

Whatever Birgitta". She had come out of the bath tub now and we were both sitting there in our bathrobes. "What am I to do?" "You mean if Germany should lose this war?" Next second he was over me, "don't talk, the walls have ears here". "Yes of course!" 'But what was he to do? Go home to Eva, for certain she wouldn't wait for him to be free after 10 years imprisonment? And what about the farm, it might already have been confiscated and no way could he work as a surgeon at a later stage, nor would patients come to him, the Nazi Doctor, would they?

And would Eva care for having a child with a Nazi? A child that would be scolded down the road? Patients that wouldn't come to the surgery and poor daddy who would suffer from all this.

Better to reestablish myself in Switzerland maybe, or in Spain with General Franco, or maybe the best issue would be to go to the East front and suffer a heroic death. All done with then. And Eva would subsequently receive a message that I had fallen on the very East front, fighting the hatred Bolsheviks and now she was free to live her own life'.

"Get to the point Theresa; did they sleep together?" "Yes, for two minutes or less and then it was over; and they were never to meet again. But at times he thought about her, that she could have been the one saving him to a new life, somewhere in Europe".

"Will there be more women now, or are we done?" Junior saw that it was already getting too much to Eva. "Yes, we are done, there will be no more new women". "Then we shall take the tea with us out on the terrace Eva".

"But I want to hear more Theresa". "Yes, then it shall be from the hospital in Odesa, the one he came back to from Finland. He then learned already the first day that the very clever nurse Svetlana, whose name was Rebecka, my grandmother, she had been living at the hospital under false name and that now she had escaped once they knew who she was, not least that she was a Jew". "But what were his feelings then Theresa?" "He hasn't written anything about that, nor about Svetlana called Rebecka, the woman of his own tribe, the pursued Jews".

But there wasn't much time for thinking, the hospital was to be shut down and patients to be sent north to Poland, some to go to the field lazarette further north, while waiting for the Great Russian offensive. "Maybe he hoped for a heroic death here?" It was Eva again.

"No, he writes nothing to that matter. He only writes about the horrible battle taking place, where night turned into day by the continuous bombardment; a true Armageddon". Then he wanted to save a Russian soldier that had been hit by splinters, ignoring the colonel crying to him, "idiot he is an enemy, idiot leave him be!" Yes, for sure he was dead that soldier and when Lars then tried to stand up, then he had no left foot. His knee was just standing there. Right out in the air and then he was gone.

Lars keeps on writing. 'I woke up in a muck cellar and recognized two people talking to one another and then I seem to know the voice of the girl. She said something about me, not going to make it. That they have found papers with text in Yiddish, most likely from the Torah and that I have all the time cried out for this Eva'. "Must be his mother, the man said?" "No, I don't know, I simply heard him crying Eva, Eva, my Eva".

It had been too much now for the old lady. "I shall have to lay down now Junior; can you please help me to up my room". Theresa was deeply moved, but luckily the worst part was over for now. She felt she had done what her grandfather had wanted from her and she could leave the Diary behind and go home, possible already tonight.

She knew it would be terrible to Junior, him "taking over it all" now, but she could promise him to come back next summer could she not? Oh, what a tempting thought this was! Just stand up and leave and maybe it would have been like a relief to the two of them, the old lady and Junior as well. No further interruptions for the old one, nor for Junior. Junior could cancel the supplier for a new kitchen and all would be just like it was before she came to disturb them.

But what about herself then, her roots? Maybe she would meet this Chaim in New York, by pure coincidence if he was still alive, but there was only a maybe to it. And apart from Chaim there was no one left now of her family, not out in the big world either. They were here, here at Hedemark, the two remaining ones. All else that were dear to her, now with her grandfather gone, except for her career and the success she should have at it. But could the better parts be combined? And how certain was she that there could be a joint future to her and Junior?

BITTERNESS OR FORGIVENESS

"Theresa, can we skip this rest of the dreadful war-scene Lars is picturing, this so-called decisive battle?" "Yes of course, but shouldn't we take into account his reunion with my grandmother?" "Of course, we shall". But Eva was not good at hiding her aversion. This was after all Theresa's family-chronicle as well and either she accepted Theresa and her grandmother or she didn't. So, there was no choice to it and besides there was no question to Junior's interest about her Odesa-family.

"Still, I think we should have a break, take the rest of the day off, there have been too many impressions in a short time".

The two young ones were equally disappointed, but from a different stand. Junior because he had looked forward to another day with Theresa. And she? Not really disappointed, but somewhat surprised maybe; she had wanted badly to get done with the Diary, wake up to the present, leaving all the bad and evil behind.

It wasn't only Eva that had suffered much. Her family in Odesa had no way lived only a glorious life and she thought about her mother and grandmother both having this gruesome final to their lives. Not to speak about Lars himself, having paid his price for misery and death. But God's punishment to him was much harder than any judgment from a court passing judgements on those having betrayed their country. But then not to forget the pleasures. Not least the pleasures from his grandchild Theresa and how often had he not expressed just that and then died in happiness at last.

Yes, for sure it was ok with the break, maybe some of Eva's bitterness would vanish? She herself was going to work on Mimi, another repetition, more and more repetitions. Could one ever be certain that all lyrics would be in place?

Eva for certain needed this break, get a distance to it all. Even if she found a lot of sorrow, anger and bitterness in Lars's Diary this far, so for sure he had lived a life with women he had loved, children and grandchildren that he had rejoiced with. And not least, he had been permitted to execute his dear medical profession, use his education at the fullest.

Well for sure there had been moments of sorrow and despair in his life, but there had been great peaks as well. And she then? "Yes, what about me", Eva thought. Some scarce moment of the greatest happiness on earth with her beloved Lars, the few times when he had managed to leave all the thoughts about war. But from there on and to the final there had been nothing but waiting, sorrow, and then a death message that she was certain was fake. Her Lars was not dead. She knew that, whatever was said by others, even when this Loke had showed up with the Death Mark. And Theresa now had come and confirmed that he was alive until three months ago. That he had lived happily over in Ukraine, while she, she had just hoped and waited for him.

For more than 60 years she had waited, in vain. "But you got your son Roald, did you not and there was never a doubt to you that this was yours and Lars' son. Not an offspring from this terrible Nazi Jens". No, for sure it was not, even if her father was doubtful to it during her pregnancy. But she, she knew for certain that it could only be Lars being the father of her child. And what a joy when the boy first time was laying at her breast sucking. It was like seeing Lars, the very same blue gray eyes, the same mouth and nose and above all the high tempo.

Oh yes, she had gotten Lars back. Now he was only hers and she almost loved him to death. Did she have an anticipation that this happiness was not to last? It was all fantastic even with this girl that Roald came home with, she from the West Country. And she became Eva's daughter as well and then came the godsend child, Trygve Junior.

Her grief was endless and enormous when she heard about the car accident in Sweden. Both parents had died and no one knew about the child. But one week later she could see Trygve coming up to her. He was carrying a seemingly heavy rucksack. She wanted to freshen up before he came, but too late, he was already at the door. "Just you come in Trygve, no doubt you have come to talk about the funeral, talk with him", she nodded to her father. "I on my part don't know if I can make it today". She was off to the bathroom and stayed there.

But then she heard his voice through the door of the bathroom and there was a voice of a child. Now what what's this? Had she turned blunt, maybe compression of her blood vessels as Trygve the doctor would have said? But she could hear it once more, so she ran into the living room letting her clips fly in the air on her way into the kitchen. "Hold on to me

Dad, please hold on to me", she felt like she was fainting. My God it was Junior and she ran over to kiss him and next she was down to her knees thanking God to this miracle.

"So where did he come from?" Trygve, he was composed; "They had heard cries from behind some bushes and there he was right at the riverbank. He had not disappeared into the river as claimed by the police. He had simply been blown out of the car and that was it".

"For how long have you known about this then Trygve?" "Since this morning, then I had a visit from a Swedish ambulance with a nurse and then came the county Sheriff of course". "But is he damaged at all?" "No, thank heavens, no damages, all is totally normal".

So, then she was not to lose them all then? "But what about the matter of foster parents? Could she be entitled? And what about the mother's family in the West Country?" "I don't know Eva, but this boy shall be ours, so help me God".

And destiny would have it that that the grandmother in the West had recently divorced and the county Judge was clear in his verdict. "The best for the boy would be to continue growing up in the familiar environment here at Elvegård". "The upper or the lower farm then?" She was wondering. "You did not hear me Eva, I said Elvegård, no upper, no lower".

Big smiles from the three of them, Trygve, Tore and the keyperson himself, only one enormous belch, having sucked the bottle empty for milk.

In her heart she called the boy Lars, and she felt like she had gotten a new life. But now she had come this young woman from Ukraine and she might steal her Junior from her. Brief moments of happiness and then at some time just dump him for her career, but for sure gone from her here at Elvegård.

Who was to console and comfort her at the end of her life? Are you not super egoistic now Eva? No, but she felt that Lars had gotten the best part of life and she was now just sitting here alone, bitter and waiting. So, what should it be this time, sorrow or happiness?

Happiness, if they were to find one another the two and possibly have an heir together, an heir that one day would return to Hedemark and take over both farms, as old Rasmus had wanted for it in 1633. But would she be to live that long and how was she supposed to cater on her own? She alone? No, Junior would never let that happen, he would never betray her. And Theresa, Lars's grandchild, could you ever come to love her? But then you have to be rid of your bitterness, you old lady! Was there someone talking to her, or was it not the voice of Lars she had heard?

THE DAY WITH JUNIOR

"Today is our day Junior", they were having breakfast together. "But what about the Diary?" Did he try to sneak away? "I think Eva now may have it alone by herself until tomorrow". Eva nodded. "And you will be off to Oslo then after breakfast, not so Theresa?" "Yes, we shall see the opera house and get some new clothes for Junior and I shall have to confirm my departure for tomorrow night, Odesa via Moscow.

The premiere back in Odesa is in exactly 4 weeks and for sure time is getting short now". They found that they got on quite well now the three of them once the Diary and the women-tales were not in focus. Or maybe it was that simple as that she had announced her departure? Shame on you Theresa!

No, there was a certain calmness over Eva. For sure she had more pronounced bags under her eyes this morning and she mentioned that maybe she would need new glasses. Could it be that she had been reading the Diary all by herself, and in particularly the last part where Lars is dreaming of his homecoming before he passes? And maybe that was the reason to her being that calm now? In some way it seemed like here at the end they had come together, the two of them, in spite of all the difficulties life had brought to the both of them?

Theresa didn't dare to ask, but her intuition said that this had now come to an end, just like it should. Lars had finally come home.

"May I keep the Diary with me here Theresa?" "Yes of course, If you promise to take good care of it. It is the most sacred item I have from my grandfather, not to forget all the memories. But many of them came alive to me now, when I read once more his own tales. But Eva don't be surprised if I come back here next summer or maybe even for Christmas". Eva looked expectingly at her, although with mixed feelings. This had only gone too fast, much too fast. "You know I'm getting old I as well Theresa, but if you promise to come back, then I shall wait for you. So off you go now and come back with a new Junior". "Yes, we shall. Theresa smiled back to her. "He doesn't know what he has promised, said yes to". And quite possibly, neither have you, Theresa.

But none of them heard these last words, and her reflections came only half an hour after they had left.

Junior had looked into his father's wardrobe and have found himself a loose hanging, really smart leather jacket. And he did not stop at that; a matching pair of corduroy trousers and matching boots he produced as well. His father had been concerned with fashion and they were about the same size now, his father being 27 when he died in the car accident.

Junior had never opened that closet. Even today he felt it was like a sacrilege, but he could not go to Oslo in his doctor's gown only, and no way he would wear costume. He didn't change till after breakfast and the applaud from Theresa told him that his father's fashion was still up to it. But she said nothing more about it and Junior sticked to the driving all the way down to Minnesund.

One of them had to break the ice at last, but Theresa looked like she contemplated the stillness and the landscape. "She is really a beauty this lake Mjøsa. Is that the name of the lake Junior?" She patted him over his neck. She was wondering from where he had found these clothes. Fashion from years back, but still up to date, almost retro. Maybe he had clothes hidden away, clothes that Theresa wasn't to know about? "You are very handsome in this outfit Junior. Why on earth should we go shopping. Your tenue is super". He started to flush, first at his neck. "Does Eva know about your fashion clothes, because that is precisely what they are?" No, he had never used them in her presence, for sure she wouldn't have liked that.

Then he unfolded the whole story. "Poor you Junior, this must have been painful to you". Once again, she felt this lust for patting his neck. Make sure you don't burn you, she said to herself.

"Yes, I mean losing your parents, they being that young". Well, I didn't know much about all that, I was only a little kid at the time". And a big one now she thought, not wearing the doctor's gown.

Unplowed field, farmers would have said. One of the expressions she had noted from her stay, not to forget this about the hare and the one about someone being twisted out of one's nose. For sure if the two of them were to be together she would have to learn Norwegian. Junior with his single mind to medicine, certainly it would have taken him years to learn Russian.

"My mother's family came from a tiny village on the west coast of Norway. She was the only child, and studied to be a nurse. I'm sure her parents were divorced. Eva just got a letter of condolescence from them. They started separate families". "Then for certain you have a flock of cousins there, Junior?" "Not so according to Eva". "And you have never heard from anyone of them?" "No, not a single word, again according to Eva". "But Junior, is it Eva that check your mail?" "No, not any longer, but when we were living together, then it was practical with only one mail address, as with the Post".

She felt that she was on really thin ice now, had to stop it before it was too late, but clearly, she wondered if Eva at all had a clean conscience to what she had done. Theresa was quite certain that the grandparents to Junior had both written and telephoned to hear about the progress of the little child. Subsequently they must have been rejected, and this had made it possible to Eva to secure for her parental-right for the little child, then 18 months old.

So, for sure she was not a Saint this Eva. Not so, she had only wanted to be the world's kindest grandmother, having taken care of her grandchild to avoid adoption or differing to an institution for homeless children, the poor one! And what would have been Lars's reaction to this if he had ever known about it? No doubt the glory of the Saint would have faded then?

Well, she decided there and then to put a lid on it all, but not quite. "When the time come and you get to marry Junior, then you must make contact with the other part of your family out in the West Country. Would you promise me that?" He looked questionably at her. Why did she start digging into that part of the family? He himself had long ago dislodged his disappointment to them, all quiet they were.

"Do you have plans for getting me married? And how soon is that going to be?" Clearly, he had in mind to add to the question, is there anyone you have your eyes upon? But no, that would have been to forward to him. It was for her to flush now, but she was soon on the offensive again. "For sure you have to procure for an heir Junior. There must be someone to care for the two farms comes time, right so?"

"Complicated this is Theresa. You are the lawful heir from Lars down at Nedre, I after Lars and Eva up at Øvre, and then after Lars as well down at Nedre". But you are a man Junior, and what's the name for this heritage business? Right, by Odel, Allodial privilege or something like that?"

"What do you know about all this Theresa?" Did she sense some disquietness? "Nothing at all, except that the county Judge through some words up in the air. Yes, that young fellow, he was putting it straight to me, "have you come here to Norway to crave you're Allodial privilege or something?" "And what did you answer to that Theresa?" "Judge, I have come here to look for my kinfolks, nothing more to it". "And as you know Junior, girls don't have this Allodial Privilege, maybe no Odel at all. After all this is a man's business and to make it utterly clear, I am not going to be a farmer".

"Please don't let this come between us Theresa, but the legislation in Norway has been changed, so now girls and boys have equal rights in these matters". "Can we just leave it be Junior, please?" "It was you starting this Theresa, you that started to talk about succession". "Okey then, I was merely thinking about you getting married so that you could secure the succession".

"Fair enough, but no way it shall be today, or would you be free on the market to accept a proposal?" "Now you stop it Junior, but this expression, on the market, is that another of your hare expressions?"

She felt that the danger was over for now, they had come to the center of Oslo without even knowing it. Theresa had seen photos of the new opera house and she was super excited about the building and the design, wanting to know more about Snøhetta and the architects. It was so different from the traditional, classic opera houses.

They were handed some leaflets once inside, but the whole theatre and the scene were closed for the public as there were rehearsals going on.

"Too bad, but I am just here for today and tomorrow, then I'm off". "Sorry for that young lady, "said the man at the information kiosk. "Junior would you be kind enough to buy two coffees?" He looked questionably at her. "Yes of course and what about you?" There was a queue behind them now. "I have to talk a bit more with this man at the information". A large German speaking lady tried to force her way, but Theresa wasn't done yet. She picked up a visiting card from her purse. Never did she take advantage of her position, but here there was no other way. She addressed the man at the information saying: "if you would be good enough to give this to the director of the ballet, then maybe she would find time to show me the scene". The clerk was just gaping, "Bolshoi?" "Yes, this is my card, do you need some more identifications?" She was speaking English to him now. "No, no, no and then he was gone. The German lady almost exploded: "Uncivilized English or maybe you are even American?" "Please don't be angry, he shall be back in no time". And two minutes later he came running. The director of the opera ballet followed calmly behind.

"What an honor, please come with me". And Junior then, he had to greet her as well. "Unfortunately, I shall have to leave tomorrow, but maybe some other time and perhaps you might come East sometime? Maybe we can exchange emails to one another?" The director was totally overwhelmed. "Yes, and maybe I shall come here for Christmas as well, apparently I am in part an heir to one or more large farms up at Hedemark", she gave Junior a warm smile now.

They were taken for a quick tour and on the way out, Theresa whispered to her; we were to make a round to different shops to get Junior, well it is not his real name, but they stick to it, to get him some new clothes. Where do you think we should go, bear in mind that we are short of time?" The director just laughed; "we have as you know quite a large stock of costumes here, but I guess that was not what you had in mind". They were both laughing out loud now, so Junior wondered what would come next. "For sure you will find something at Steen og Strøm".

"We shall only spend half an hour at this Junior, merely to the satisfaction of Eva. I think you are looking great as you are and I'm sure you will find more suitable clothes to wear in the closet back home".

A bit later, and they had been really quick at it, she had pointed to things she found suitable and Junior had paid. "I think we should skip this Theatercafeen now Theresa. I have a strong desire to show you this city from the rooftop". "Rooftop?" "Well, I mean from where you can have the most magnificent view of all Oslo". "But what about the lunch then?" As you are to see, we can eat and have the view at the same time". "And when can we go for a walk then?" Always at high speed this lady.

"First we go up to Frognerseteren!" And she was over herself looking at this beautiful city. "Only millionaires living here Junior?" She looked at all the well-kept villas down towards Riis. But Junior didn't want to talk about money. "These people are stockbrokers etc., Theresa, they are nothing to me, but soon we shall be at the Frognerparken for our walk".

Once inside the park, a new world opened to him as well as to her. Rain started to come down and they had only one tiny umbrella. And when the rain stopped, she wanted to do like other young ones, holding hands. And when a young couple in front of them stopped and kissed, then she wanted to do exactly the same.

And Junior felt he was filled up by a large number of butterflies, so he fell totally silent, just pressed her hand even stronger and she fell silent too, until they came to the Monolite statue. "Who was this incredible artist, Vigeland?" Thick her voice now.

Later, on the way to the parking, she spotted one of the few record shops still in business. "I want to buy you a present Junior, just you wait here". "When can I have it then?" "Now you wait, child!"

Back in the car she took the present out of the box, handed the box to him. "Am I not to unpack my own present at least?" "You shall have to wait come Christmas Junior". Did he sense a kind of promise in the air? But then the air was filled by Rachmaninov's Isle of the Dead, and she started stroking him again.

Did she have a crush on him? For real? Yes, she was definitely in love. But was this a sort of love that would soon pass? She had to see if it would endure, and what now, she was to leave tomorrow and Junior had no doubt asked Toril to secure the groceries for the dinner and Theresa had promised that she couldn't just leave him now, early in the afternoon.

Toril had arranged for everything. The mountain trout was cleaned and dried and so were beautiful summer vegetables ready for the salad. She had even been to the wine- and spirit monopoly, bought a bottle of bubbles. So clever of Junior, having caught that she drank but Champagne, if at all, nothing else.

They made dinner together and then she asked Junior to be kind and phone Eva, tell her that she would come up to her later. Now she just wanted to know if she was all well.

No, she didn't want to go up to the old lady now, she wanted to go out in the summer night, look at the fields, hear birds singing, and for sure she realized that this was all wrong. Totally wrong considered her career. But when was she ever in love in the past? She hadn't been, not for real. She hadn't even slept with anyone, no. "Quite horrible", said her closest girlfriend's. "You shall end up like an old spinster". But then she didn't quite know why she always was holding back. Could it be her fear for being pregnant and die during birth, like her mother and grandmother? Her granddad Lars had talked a lot about that, calling it a possible family curse. But what about tonight, if Junior wanted to have her? Could she, and did she want to?

It took some time before Junior came out to her. "Something the matter dear?" "No, but our Eva just couldn't get to sleep". They could see there was still light in her windows.

"I think she feels a bit sorry that she might lose control Junior, don't you think so?" "And what about us then, are we on the edge of losing control?" "I cannot Junior, even if I feel that I'm ready. Don't you get sorry, Christmas is only five months away. May I come to you then? And then

I want to stay down here Junior". "Maybe in the annex then?" He gave her a laugh.

"I shall count the days, Theresa. For sure I shall have a maxi calendar up at the wall and make a cross for every day".

It was nearly three in the morning and the dew was all heavenly. Junior accompanied her up to Øvre. "May I count on you later this morning or shall I have to take the bus? Breakfast will be at 6, not many hours to go".

Eva played sleeping and Theresa sneaked quietly to her bed.

Not later than 5 o'clock, she heard Eva preparing coffee and she knew that she had to get up as well. Junior was already at the door in his worn-out doctor's gown. She had to laugh, looking at her little boy.

"You may keep the Diary from Lars for some months Eva, and then I can have it back in December sometime". "December?" "Yes, Junior has invited me for Christmas at Nedre and I count for all the three of us to be together. I take it a solemn promise Junior?" His smile was a boyish one. "We shall have to go now to catch the plane".

12 MONTHS LATER

The young intern looked at him. "You are to stay away for 12 months then Junior?" "Yes, and should I come home sooner, then it shall only be to run the farm. No way shall I try to go into your way, it is for you to handle the surgery. A word is a word Johan!"

"Excellent Junior, and I shall keep my word, look after Eva every day, come sun come rain". "I guess you meant come shine come rain!"

"But Junior, what if you were to stay longer?" "No, not this time, but who is to know what might happen in five or ten years from now? But then it won't be in New York, but in other parts of the world I shall commute to, to be with my beloved Theresa".

EPILOGUE, CLOSING REMARKS

She was past 90 years of age, my Maria, when I interviewed her years back. I have given her a different name to not reveal her true identity. For sure she wouldn't have liked that.

So, I call her Maria, the very name the Bible has given to the woman being the closest to Jesus. Maria was one of the few survivors from the icy day of horror, October 23. 1941. Not from the Parade square, where the hanging and burning of numerous Jews took place, done by Romanian soldiers as butchers, but with powerful assistance from the German SS.

She was a witness to the long death-march North, not as a participant, but as a despaired and crying spectator, and one of the many witnesses to truth that day.

And the long march North, one of the many with one end, extermination by famine and /or cold.

This is a novel and I have taken the liberty as author to set this march to October 1941, although this particular one was planned for the winter 1942

SOURCES

I have examined many of the books and newspaper-articles on the Front-Soldiers, Front Fighters, Front Soldater, Frontkjempere in Norwegian. I have done my best to find out about the motivation for the choices made by these young boys.

I have equally examined the Internet and libraries as well. I have paid special attention to three books, the first one being, Shetlands Larsen by Ragnar Ulstein. What is so particular about this book is that it was totally unthinkable for young boys to join others than England, yes it would in fact have been an absurdity, least to us living in the West Country or having family there, all close to the North Sea.

The next book by Odd Helge Brugrand, 16 years and a soldier of Hitler. This is the book about the 16-year-old Ivar Skarlo and his reflections about enlisting with the Germans, barely passed confirmation age. What was it that drew him and others in his environment to enlist on the opposite side? To Germany? He as well grew up close to the North Sea. So, there were exceptions!

The third book is Guy Sajer's, The forgotten soldier. This book I feel shows more than others the total, blind violence of war, with destruction of body as well as soul. The realistic picturing from the battlefields where Norwegian Front Fighters fell by the hundreds as well. Young Norwegian boys, many from 16 to 20 years of age, with their brains popped full of propaganda by Quisling and his followers. "Go and enlist yourself, and you shall later be the core of the new Norwegian army".

But even the fact that Sajer's mother was German, still this wasn't his war? No, he had barely reached 16, and adventure looked tempting. Join, be a soldier, be part of a unique fellowship, that was the picture he painted to himself. Hitler, Der Führer, he was never to be seen. By the way, who was this, Hitler?

But not least have I talked to people out there in Odesa, Ukraine and also to people in the border city Lviv, previously Lvov. I have also met with some survivors on the Rumanian side of the Carpathians, in villages like Satu Mare.

But now, there are almost none still living from that war, no more witnesses, all dead, one of the few exceptions was my Maria that I have mentioned especially in the epilog.

I have sometimes come to wonder in retro perspective, if it was at all necessary to write about all the atrocities. Yes, I think so because the narratives from the generals, they are more like reading commentaries to a game of Cheques, however exciting that might be. But the tales from the generals were miles away from describing what actually happened on the ground to the ordinary soldier, day in and day out. And partisans, long dead now, claimed that maltreatments often could be much more gruesome than what I have pictured, based on their stories. But could any atrocity be more gruesome then?

It may at first glance look like the SS has come relatively well off from my war. This compared to tales of Russians and partisans. And for sure there was no reason for me writing about atrocities carried out by the so-called Einsatzkommandoes, Himmler's dirty workers. But Lars was never part of those forces.

Why are Jews all the times in focus in this book, not so Gypsies, nor other Slavic nationalities? The simple answer is that almost all of the lead persons in the novel were Jews or married into Jewish families.

Above all, this is a novel about one that didn't come home after the war. A man that happened to choose the wrong side although for a sacred motive: Save his mother's land, Karelen, Finland!

I take it as granted, having read this much background-material from novels or newspaper articles, that some of this may have inflicted upon my writing. Not deliberately, of course. In all some hundred books and articles from Scandinavia and beyond have given me insight into this gruesome part of our history. But please note that World War II is just a back-carpet to the central element in my novel, the epic love story and the fatal choice of a young man.

SOME KEY- WORDS

Front Fighters, common denomination to Norwegians enlisting to fight on the German side

Odesa, 2nd largest city in Ukraine, bordered by the Black Sea

SS, paramilitary organization, said to be Hitler's special guards

Eastern front, towards Russia

The star of David, yellow badge, compulsory to wear for Jewish people

Rabbi, leader of Jewish congregation

Dalkin, village north of Odesa

Der Führer, Adolf Hitler

Jahve, God to the Jews

Synagogue, Jewish temple

Yiddish, Jews' language

Torah, first part of the Jewish Bible

The second temple, year 515 BC

Karelen, south in Finland, occupied, later annexed by the Soviet Union

Nygårdsvold, Norway's prime minister during World War II

Government of the broken rifle, nickname to the Nygårdsvold government, because of its refusal to rearm

Swastika, 1000 years' old symbol, in the 30s taken by Hitler to be used in the Nazi flag

The Hippodrome, riding venue in Oslo

Jøssingfjord, known from the start of the war in Norway

Little Norway, Norwegian training camp for pilots in Canada

Golden Cock, locally produced gin in Norway

Stalin, dictator in the Soviet Union from 1925 to 1953

Herman Gøring, Reich marshal, 2nd in rank after Hitler. His responsibility that Germany lost the fight over London. Also, to "blame" for the delay in Germany's production of the nuclear bomb

Heinrich Himmler, chief of the SS, the responsible for the death camps, Holocaust, and the Einsatzkommandoes, with extermination of the Jews and Slavic people as their prime task.

Bolsheviks, organization of the masses in the Soviet Union, founded by Lenin, the father of the Russian Revolution and the first chief of government in the Soviet Union. Died mysteriously in 1924

Waffen SS, the military part of the SS

Sennheim, recruit school for the Waffen SS, primarily focusing on ideology, extermination of the Jews

Das Reich, the Greater German Empire

Die Wehrmacht, the regular German military forces

Debes, later Lieutenant General in the SS

Berlin bleibt immer Berlin, well known saying in the 30s and onwards

Unter den Linden, The parade Street of Berlin

Gestapo, German security police, directly under Hitler

Mein Kampf, Hitler's ideological document, also published as a book 1925 to 1927

Felix Steiner, SS- General, founded and led Division Gross Deutschland, the elite division in Germany

Ghetto Warszawa, enclosure for the Jews

Terboven, highest ranking leader for Germany in Norway

The Geneva Convention, international rules for protecting POWs'

Kalashnikov, 7.62 automatic weapon, Soviet Union

Depeche bag, name on wartime military message bag

The Iron Cross, German military medal, two classes, widely used under the Second World War

Masada, Jewish fortress where the last of the defenders took collectively suicide, when they had to give up against the Roman forces in 72 AC

David Ben Gurion, freedom fighter in the Odesa oblast, saved himself to Palestine and became Israel's very first prime minister in 1948

Popov, nickname for a Russian soldier, pejorative

Karl Marx, German philosophers and economist, founder of the socialism

Vladimir Lenin, planned and carried out the revolution in Russia. Was strongly in opposition to Stalin's craving for superpower. Died of damages? January 1924

Maria Waleska, polish Duchess, was said to be Napoleons mistress. Visited him even at the Elba.

Wagner, Hitler's favorite composer, particularly infatuated by his work, the Niebelungenring, The Ring Pearl Harbor, Hawaii, where the Japanese Empire sank most of the American Pacific fleet, December 7th 1941

Aida, opera by Giuseppe Verdi

Madame Butterfly, opera by Giacomo Puccini.

Stalin Organ, rocket launch named after Josef Stalin

Tupolev, Russian bomber plane

Haubitzer, a light movable canon

Mauser, German standard rifle

Borsj, Eastern European soup

Khruschev, Nikita, secretary General in the Communist Party, born in Ukraine, was president till 1964

Bolshoi, Moscow, world's most renowned ensemble, ballet and opera

Telavaag, Fisher village on the Norwegian west coast, totally destroyed by the SS, revenge

The Met, Metropolitan Opera, New York

Bjørvika, Oslo. The site of the Norwegian Opera House

Steen og Strøm, department store Oslo

Alea iacta est: No going back. Julius Cæsars famous statement when crossing the small river Rubicon, in 49BC

SOME SS- GRADES, REFERRED TO IN THIS NOVEL

SS-Sturmmann	Vice corporal
SS-Rottenführer	Corporal
SS-Oberscharführer	Sergeant
SS-Untersturmführer	Leftenant
SS-Hauptsturmführer	Captain
SS-Sturmbannführer	Major
SS-Obersturmbannführer	Leftenant Colonel
SS-Standartenführer	Full Colonel
SS-Oberführer	Brigader
SS-Gruppenführer	Major General
SS-Obergruppenführer	General

Sketch East front

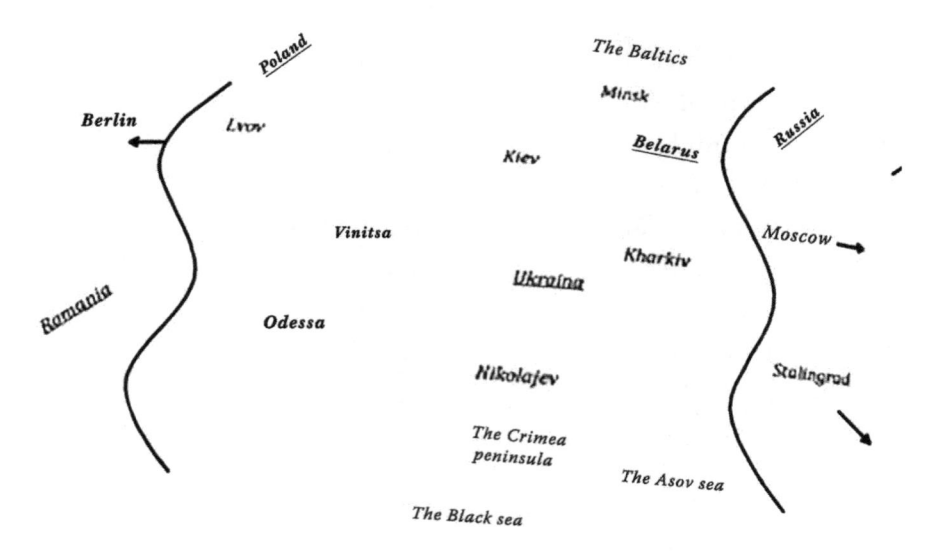

Poland

The Baltics

Minsk

Berlin Lvov

Russia

Kiev Belarus

Vinitsa Moscow

Kharkiv

Ukraina

Romania Odessa

Nikolajev Stalingrad

The Crimea
peninsula

The Asov sea

The Black sea

Sketch Odesa center

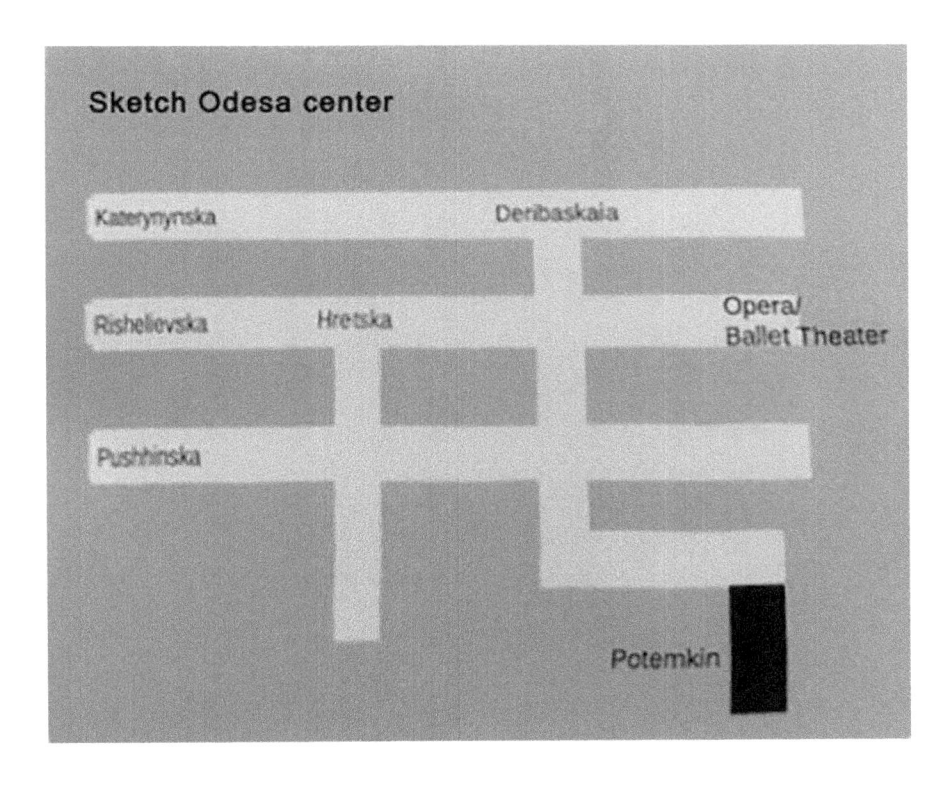

Kateryrynska   Deribaskaia

Rishelievska   Hretska   Opera/
                                       Ballet Theater

Pushhinska

                                       Potemkin

Milton Keynes UK
Ingram Content Group UK Ltd.
UKHW010730160124
436122UK00001B/66

9 781962 313773